I0563491

Pitre

David Pyle

This book is a work of fiction. References to real people, events, establishments, organizations, or locales are intended only to provide a sense of authenticity, and are used fictitiously. All other characters, and all incidents and dialogue, are drawn from the author's imagination and are not to be construed as real.

Pitre. Copyright © 2012, 2013 by David Pyle. All rights reserved. Printed in the Unites States of America. No part of this book may be used or reproduced in any manner whatsoever or stored in a database or retrieval system, without written permission except in the case of brief quotations embodied in critical articles and reviews.

FIRST EDITION

Library of Congress Cataloging-in-Publication Data has been applied for.

ISBN-10: 0615877958
ISBN-13: 978-0-615-87795-2

To all those who believe in things unseen.

Pitre

PROLOGUE

The heavens broke open as if the sky below had torn in half, there was thunderous noise..., deafening.

I'd never imagined this many of my brothers in conflict, never known the pain of confusion. The noise..., suddenly I understood that I played a role in this massive drama unfolding.

I hurried to find safety..., but there was no safety.

All was war before my freshly opened eyes as brother after brother I'd served with fell and disappeared into the abyss below.

I was hit hard from behind and immediately hurled into the vast throng of violence. Then a hand grasped my ankle and no matter how hard I thrust, I could not free myself from its grip.

Down..., together..., down I plummeted into darkness.

When I awoke, my tongue was glued to the roof of my mouth. My back felt torn and broken. I could barely breathe through my sand caked nostrils.

Once again, my world blinked dark and just as quickly revived to raw dim light.

CHAPTER ONE

The remainder of our current assets were finally released by the South African government making our egress to the United States complete. As my small family stood together for the first time on American soil, I pondered the many connotations to the word *Asylum*.

My verbal English was tainted only by the lingering British accent of my childhood and where my sweet wife Elizabeth Ellen Schumacher and I had lived for the last eighteen years.

Funny how something that you never think of, the way you speak, can be the only indication that you're not American born and raised. Strangely enough, our quaint dialect was our open door to several possibilities where we relocated in the United States.

Our pasty white skin, despite the lingering effects of the scorching South African sun, became our blatant malady while we lived among so much diversity of cultures in Zambia, South Africa. My wife and I were so desperate to make a difference in the lives of needy children that we volunteered to a twenty-year stint as a diplomatic token of good will.

We'd lived through the ending of the illicit regime of Apartheid, which had made our lives all the more at peril. Finally the world took note and new leaders emerged; along with them, hopes of sanity to a torn country.

As with all unwelcome change, bitter differences still existed where we lived. It came in the form of racial violence, not only against my family, but also between the competing populace.

Elizabeth and I were never accepted by some, despite the daily efforts of medical relief at our clinic. As a result, the ataxia between the leaders of the indigenous tribes and their so-called witchdoctors were the only constant; the one collective commonality among all the varied tribes.

The first few visitors to our medical clinic in the light of day were drastically overshadowed by the steady stream of knocks on our door during the cover of darkness. As our reputation in the region grew, so did our clientele. Soon it became expected to find a fever-burdened child cradled for miles in the arms of a desperate parent, brought at night for fear of repercussions from their leaders and peers.

Daily attempts at some medieval curse, mutilated animals, or feces on the doorsteps of the clinic we operated became our opposition's calling card. Consequently, we were always coming down with some stomach ailment from having ingested a nasty root or native caustic flower clandestinely inserted into our food and medical shipments.

After eighteen years of sacrifice we finally gave up, tired of the violent opposition and continual political upheavals, but those events weren't the reason we decided to leave.

Even stranger, as fate often is, after all the trials and bitter struggles were over and we were received into our new country, Elizabeth became ill and quickly passed away.

The American physician, a purported specialist, believed it was some rare malady, possibly contracted while living among the several different indigenous tribes, quite possibly some poison that they had never seen before.

The evil continent's tentacles wouldn't let her go even after we were separated from its soil.

My Elizabeth was an exceptionally skilled surgeon and physician; the best I'd ever known. I considered it an honor to work alongside her with my common pediatric skills. While I was always immersed in treating a wide foray of parasitic infestations, or childhood diseases; Elizabeth was tirelessly mending broken bones, gunshot wounds, or vicious cuts and contusions from the blade of homemade weaponries. Angolan rebels regularly frequented our facility, sparing us for our services rendered.

She was always relieved to be away from the violent aspect of her profession, such as when assisting the birth of a child. The bright innocent eyes of a new generation gave us hope.

God I miss her.

I think…, I know, that it was my efforts at helping our daughter Chaste understand the loss of her mother that helped me maintain my own sanity.

Chaste has become my one reason to go on.

Elizabeth and I never intended to start a family while we worked through our twenty-year commitment at this primitive location. Please understand, our commitment wasn't some legal contract. No one was forcing us to stay, we were mostly self-funded; it was our own mutual dedication to what we felt was a worthy cause. The only assistance we received was from the European Medical Association in the form of medical supplies and the gift of diplomatic status for our medical practice.

When was it?

I believe it was…, well Chaste Ellen Schumacher was born on December first, eight years ago, …do the math.

The first threat to her life was when Elizabeth and I went straight to the American Consulate in Johannesburg and applied for citizenship in the United States. It seemed that one of the feather-headed aborigines decided our presence was responsible for some intertribal confusion and we were bound to repay for our meddling.

After personally saving the life of a young tribesman named Owasu Satiiri intended for assassination; a young fellow with dangerous ties challenging a local tribal leadership, then all eyes focused on our little girl.

Our unintended enemy demanded recompense in the respect that Chaste Ellen would become his personal *cochon de lait*.

The evident barbarism in third-world areas of the globe still repulses me.

Putting our lives at risk on a daily basis was our decision, but our innocent child, the baby girl that I helped birth with my own two hands certainly did not.

Chaste did not ask for the peril, and well…, I don't feel the need to explain further. If you are a parent, or for that matter a rational human being, you understand our reasoning.

After Elizabeth's passing and as soon as the last of our South African resources reached our bank in Phoenix Arizona, Chaste and I began looking for a place to put down permanent roots.

We found just such a place between Scottsdale and Fountain Hills; a radically modern designed home with various angles, lots of glass and plenty of scenery. It was far from being some ostentatious show of wealth, but considerably more than the tiny habitation we'd just left; certainly more than the two of us needed. Our real-estate agent said it was a wise investment considering it cost less than half its market value; something about a buyers market.

It seemed a nice quiet community with its own small park and a decent nature trail just a few hundred yards away. We were also a short drive away from the Tonto National Forest. Both of our outdoor attractions were without the dangers of hungry predatory animals at every turn. It was much needed bliss.

Chaste loved the fact that she could ride the bus to school into Scottsdale without fear.

Fear of what you might ask?

Of being mobbed, blown up, shot, poisoned, rotten food hurled at her and constant vile name-calling, not to mention the final threat of some sort of ritualistic human sacrifice.

When you're a child, especially puttering through the formative years, how could you possibly comprehend the reasons? At forty-four years of age, I don't understand them.

But that's quite enough about the past.

The peace of living in a protected society was so much a relief that we didn't know where to begin…, now only the two of us. I knew that she needed a mother's nurture, but I confess I had denied myself the idea of finding a mate. I've tried to put it off on Chaste, devoting my time helping her cope with the empty space left by her mother's passing, but I just wasn't and I guess I'm still not ready.

The first school year passed quickly. Chaste seemed to be enjoying life, coping well, enough so that we had discontinued the counseling sessions. At least her nightmares had ceased.

We both still had those moments…, you know the ones, the ones with memories attached, but they were getting farther apart.

It was the last week of fourth grade, right before the summer break that our lives changed yet again.

CHAPTER TWO

Today was the culmination of a month's planning.

"What are you doing today, Dad?"

Chaste stared at me, patiently baiting me for an answer.

"Finish loading a few things, do some shopping."

Then I remembered one last item I'd forgotten.

"Oh..., blast. I forgot to cancel the rubbish collections for the next eight weeks."

"Garbage pickup, Dad. They call it garbage here, remember?"

She frowned, pursing her lips at my linguistics error as if it were some foul taste in her mouth.

"Young lady, careful with your impertinence or you'll wind up across my knee."

Chaste laughed at my faked threat, nearly choking on her last bite of breakfast, "As if...."

I swallowed my piece of French toast watching her expressions as I made another note in my planner. Chaste was trying unsuccessfully to hide her excitement.

"It's obvious you need me here. Why can't I stay and help?"

"Because...," I said with a shrug.

She rolled her eyes just as I expected, then tried another slant.

"Did you decide where our first stop is yet?"

"I thought we'd head northeast, spend the night in Pueblo Colorado."

She crinkled her freckled nose, "Sounds boring already. What's in Pueblo Colorado?"

Her iPhone buzzed and she smiled, snatching it from the kitchen counter, saving me from having to give a snap answer. My hands pressed out an angrily-crisp map of the United States onto the countertop, covered with lines, notes and circles.

I took the chance to turn and pour a cup of tea, "I'm sure some of the scenery will be redundant, but I hardly think it will be boring."

"Will we see mountains?"

Her piercing blue eyes made me smile, "Most definitely. See here."

I pointed my finger at the shaded elevations on the map of Colorado, "Denver will be our second stop. I promise."

She giggled and upended her silly looking backpack dumping out everything except a thin folder and threw most of the rest in the wastebasket.

"I want to see the Statue of Liberty and the Smithsonian. Will we see snow?"

"That I can't promise until next winter. Why don't we pick one of our favorite stops for another trip this Christmas?"

"That sounds glorious!" she gasped.

"Any other requests?"

"No, I guess not. The rest is up to you."

Chaste zipped her backpack and slid it over her shoulder, ready for her last day of school.

"I still don't see why I have to go to school today," she whined. "Can I please, please stay home? We could get an early start."

She wrapped her arms around my waist, begging with her eyes, batting them furiously.

"It's only one more day…, a few hours actually. It will spoil your record of perfect attendance."

Her arms slid away in a huff, but she was instantly staring back into the face of her cell phone.

She'd been home schooled by Elizabeth and I since she was three years old and placed ahead to the fourth grade when she entered the local educational system. Public school was a difficult decision but I wanted my daughter immersed in the culture of her new surroundings. I wanted her to have friends she'd never had and to feel herself a part of this new society.

Our bags were packed and stuffed in the back of our vehicle, the postage delivery stopped, and only the electric and telephone left on to enable the security system. My last call would be to the local authority to alert them of our intended absence.

I had gone over the checklist in my head at least a dozen times.

We were going to tour the United States by auto during the summer; A walk-about on wheels. Both of us wanted to see the new homeland that we had chosen for our futures. A holiday..., I believe the term is vacation here.

I dropped Chaste off at school instead of the usual bus ride since it was her last day. Our trip to school was uneventful, our minds revolving around the day. During our drive, I glanced over several times to watch her fingers dance across the face of her new cell phone; I suppose she thought it was a pretty brilliant status symbol. I saw it as an added security feature for the upcoming travels.

At least until that afternoon....

Her long cornsilk hair bounced off toward the school doors and finally merged with the stream of students pressing in.

I could still hear her voice begging to stay home that day. Today was only a play-day; attendance was a mere formality. I told her to enjoy herself and get the names and numbers of those she liked so that she could have someone to share the progress of her travel experiences.

It all seemed to help reassure me that the choice for public school had been the right one.

The day rushed by as I checked the final items off my list.

My lists...

Elizabeth teased me incessantly about my need to plan everything down to the last minute detail. She warned me that I was taking away the surprise and mystery that life had in store, that I should allow life to pull us along at its own leisurely pace.

Of course I told her my lists were for my own benefit, just in case life hit one of its usual snags and I needed something to fill the void.

In retrospect, I never dreamed that the snag life would offer would be the loss of my life partner, the plus to my minus and the equalizing buffer which I relied upon.

After recognizing my usual foray of memories encroaching my day, I turned to my list once again, to keep me busy, to fill this gaping void life had tossed in my path.

I prayed that this time spent together with my daughter would instill new memories, new places, new dreams; just the thought of our impending travels caused a swell of relief to spill over and siphon away the daily ebbing grief of loss.

As the afternoon drew do a close, I stopped to pick up the last few items to fill an ice chest at a nearby grocer. After all, this was the *American Way* according to my research on holidays.

I was standing in line waiting to pay for my last minute items when the power fluctuated, shutting down the lights and registers.

With a nervous glance, my wristwatch said that I had only fifteen minutes to checkout and travel the six blocks to my daughter's elementary school. It was eighteen minutes later when I walked out the front door of the grocer.

The urgency had me jogging to our forest green Range Rover in the parking lot, pushing a rebellious metal cart. The perishables all went into the heavy ice chest, bags and all; I could rearrange them before we left town.

Oddly, the usual route to the school was diverted for some unseen road construction, men in hardhats waving flags and all that.

Twenty minutes later, I was in the exceptionally long pickup line of parents, with the air conditioner cooling off the pre-summer heat.

The bright idea of my daughter's cell phone unfolded a crease in my mind and I reached to call Chaste, to let her know I was there; make her feel important, special.

When I slid it out of my jacket, I noticed that I had three missed calls, all from Chaste.

How did I miss her calls? Somehow, my phone was set to Silent.

I hit dial, her cell phone rang…, several times, "Hello, This is *Chase*, talk or text me."

She sounded so grown with her Ameri-Brit accent. Even the nickname her friends had given her seemed refreshing.

I ended the call with a smile, just as the car in front of me moved about four feet, then decided to check my messages.

"Hey Dad. Where are you? The power went off, we're out early. Come get me and let's go vacation! Love you."

- Beep.

"Hey Dad? Are you coming? It's been fifteen minutes. I'm out front."

- Beep.

"Dad? Oh, there he is…."

- There are no more messages.

Ignoring the phone, I looked around frantically, expecting Chaste

13

to pop against the passenger door at full speed, but the school grounds were nearly empty now, the line slowly dwindled to myself and two other cars.

The teacher on traffic duty leaned into my window, "Hello Dr. Schumacher. Can I help you?"

What did she honestly think I was doing there in the last of the gruelingly long line?

"I'm here to pick up Chaste of course; she just called a few minutes ago."

"I…, saw her get in your Rover about ten or twelve minutes ago. Across the street. She seemed so happy at the time."

She pointed to a vacant curb across the street and looked at me questioningly.

"I doubt that it was Chaste, I was caught at the grocer on Culver St."

She tried to smile, "We only have one Chaste Schumacher…."

"Did she return inside the school maybe?" I asked.

"I'm afraid not, all the entrances lock automatically after the third bell."

That was when the first tinge of panic twisted my stomach into a cinch knot.

I snatched the steering wheel to the right and parked askew against the curb.

She jingled some keys as the last car in line drove away.

"Don't worry, we can go inside and look. I'm sure everything is fine."

She must have seen my transformation into a wild-eyed parent.

After jogging the halls to the two nearest girls' restrooms - they were locked - we hurried to the main office.

The complacency irked me at once.

"Your daughter probably forgot and rode the bus."

Not bloody likely.

The principal smiled stupidly from behind his desk, I'm sure to try and calm the situation. The effect was just the reverse and I felt no inclination to waste my time explaining my daughters' messages on my phone.

"I'll call the dispatch and see if the bus is back yet."

This is America I reminded myself, but after eighteen years of daily threats, I was a little skeptical. Excusing myself, I headed back out to the front of the school in hopes of seeing my little blond headed wonder standing, pouting, against the fender of my dark green Range Rover.

Not a car in sight, the quiet had me shaking. It suddenly thrust me into memories of nights in the African bush, west of Zambia, when the night birds quit singing and the crickets hushed. Those nights that something horrid was being proffered on our front door steps. When the memory of that awful ebony face surrounded by colorful feathers and his grinning threats against my family drifted into my mind; true panic tore at my soul.

I grabbed at my cell phone and called Chaste once more.

"Hello, This is Chase, talk or text me."

"Please call me...."

My whisper was all I could manage but I'd already rang off.

I walked across the street to where the teacher said I had already retrieved Chaste. A hundred cars could have been parked there that day for all I could tell.

I dialed once again...

There was a muffled chirping behind me.

"Hello, this is Chase...." I hung up and dialed again.

On the ground about ten feet from the curb was the silly pink and white rabbit phone cover of her brand new cell phone.

CHAPTER THREE

A female police officer handed me back my cell phone with the picture of Chaste still glowing on the front screen.

"We've issued the Amber Alert. They'll be broadcasting it in the next few minutes."

She turned and walked away, but I saw her concern. Her eyes were worried, cast down at the ground and into the hedges, searching the evenly cut grass where I had found Chaste's cell phone.

"Mr..., Dr. Schumacher. When did you see your daughter Chaste last?"

This was the third time, the third officer I had told that I had dropped her off at school that morning. I didn't care, I would repeat it again a thousand times to a thousand more faces if it would help find my child.

"Now..., the teacher that was on pick-up duty said she saw you parked over there earlier and your daughter ran across the street and got inside your vehicle."

"I can't explain that. There must be other people with green Range Rovers. She could have mistaken it for ours."

I was trying hard not to show how upset my emotions were running.

"Officer Pritchert?"

Yet another chap, clad in an ill-fitted black suit, walked up and addressed my latest interrogator.

"I'm Special Agent Lily with the FBI, ...missing children."

This one flashed his badge and the Police Official seemed overtly relieved to do a hand off.

"Dr. Schumacher, I need to ask you some questions."

I took a deep breath, trying to contain my desire to run to my Rover and scour the streets looking for another one like my own, one that had my little girl sitting....

Oh God..., the thought hit me, another kick in the belly; was she sitting? Was she safe..., alive?

That was when I watched the tunnel grow dark and the face of my newest interrogator disappear.

"Dr. Schumacher? Dr. Schumacher?"

I snorted and my vision slowly returned. Whoever discovered the effects of ammonium carbonate, smelling salts, should be shot...; my nose burned and I wanted to gag. I snorted again, sitting up, dizzy and nauseous.

"He's back."

I desperately wanted to hear, *"She's back."*

Another officer approached quickly and presented a scuffed and scarred backpack. It was that silly pink and white rabbit again, the twin of my daughter's cell phone cover. The officer had on the same blue nitrile gloves I had used so many times to dispense medicine and antibiotics to the daily line of children in our clinic.

This different purpose made them look vulgar on his hands.

I nodded, before he could ask me the obvious. I saw the sewn-on patches; it belonged to Chaste.

He unzipped it in my presence and carefully pulled a few items out. It was her clothes. The ones she wouldn't let me help her pick out to wear that morning; I nodded again, just before he pulled her knickers from the bottom.

I suppose I did the most unmanly thing I can think of.

"God..., no," I cried.

Of course, my tears were only the precursor to the anger and frustration I was suppressing with all my ability.

Someone in the distance shouted that the backpack had been found two blocks away at the corner of the intersection.

Then I realized where they were referring to - it was where we always hopped on the jaunt leading to Interstate 10; where there was a flood of east-west traffic hurling along at 80 miles per hour.

Mr. FBI, escorted me to his vehicle. I assumed it was to join the search for my daughter.

Officer Pritchert hurried over, "We have a chopper in route."

"I don't think we'll need air support Officer."

I almost didn't see the clandestine nod. I instantly panicked that the silent information which passed between them was something worse than I already knew.

"State Troopers are in route to setup checkpoints around the area," Pritchert said and hurriedly walked away.

The FBI Agent barked toward him as he departed, "South and West of Scottsdale and Phoenix?"

Pritchert jerked around and nodded, choking out orders on a microphone anchored to his shoulder.

What would Elizabeth think of me? After everything we struggled through to get here, to get someplace safe. I had let our little angel get snatched right from under our..., from under my nose.

Why didn't I simply walk out of the grocery store and come back to it later? Why did I put my phone on silent? Why couldn't I remember? Why wouldn't this oaf hurry up?

I felt my stomach try to heave.

CHAPTER FOUR

The grotty room stank of bodily odors and vomit and I couldn't fathom touching the tepid bottle of water on the table, much less opening it, even though I was parched.

As I looked around, the stains on the floor reminded me of the ones bleach couldn't extract from the concrete floor at our clinic. Probably blood or fecal matter.

I'd spent the last thirty minutes squirming in a horrid excuse of a chair staring at a wall-sized mirror and watching the red light on a ceiling camera blink on and off; thirty minutes I could have spent looking for my child. I felt as if I were going to explode at any moment if someone didn't present themselves and explain what I was doing here.

I stabbed at the screen of my cell phone and listened to my daughter's voice once again.

- Beep.

"Hey Dad? Are you coming? It's been fifteen minutes. I'm out front."

- Beep.

"Dad? Oh, there he is…."

If it had only been me that was parked there at that curb.

Tired of waiting, I ended the call and stood to leave when the door to the room suddenly snapped open.

"Please have a seat Dr. Schumacher."

"I've been seated here for a half hour already. What else could you possibly need from me? I've already told you everything I can remember about the entire day."

"Please…."

He motioned me back to the uncomfortably filthy chair and shoved the bottle of water my direction.

He dropped a thin folder on the table and took a seat.

"I just need to clear up a few more facts that will help us."

Something intangibly disturbing about him made me nervous and I fought the repeated urge to stand up and leave.

"I have the information about your recent emigration to the United States. I understand that there were some mitigating circumstances that brought you and your family here; threats against your family?"

I nodded.

"Have you received any threats since you settled in…, Scottsdale?"

His eyes continued to skip across whatever he was reading and back up to my own.

"No, none. We've been very happy."

"What about enemies? Have you made any more enemies since arriving here?"

"What? No. No, of course not. We didn't make enemies where we came from. The locals felt threatened by our medical services. They initiated the attacks, not us. You should have that information in our records."

"Yes, it's here."

He began giving me the patented stare. The one intended to make someone uncomfortable and shy. To watch which way your eyes twitched or pupils dilated. Then I saw something else that I'd seen countless times before, something fixed in his eyes. Those eyes said that he'd not only killed before, …but that he'd enjoyed it.

When he saw me looking back inside him, he quickly lowered his gaze back to the folder on the table.

"Why exactly did you choose to move your family to this country? Is there a reason neither of you wanted to move back to Great Britain?"

Bloody hell…, is he wanting to deport us?

"Neither of us have…, neither of us had… any living family where we came from. We wanted our daughter to have more opportunities."

"Can you tell me briefly the circumstances around your wife…, Elizabeth's death?"

My stomach clenched.

"What does this have to do with finding my daughter?"

"Your wife…, Dr. Schumacher?"

I was sincerely starting to despise his droopy red hair and blotchy melanotic freckles.

"You have the information there in front of you."

Despite the fact that I had come to terms with my wife's passing, even the fact that we'd lived with the threat of losing one another for eighteen years, I didn't want to relive this again.

I finally relented, if only to speed whatever this was along.

"The doctor's here couldn't find what caused Elizabeth's death. They thought it might be some type of poison in her bloodstream, something native to where we moved from. Every vital organ in her body shut down at once. It was a horrible death."

He scratched nonchalantly through the folder.

"How would you classify your marriage?"

I stared bitterly at him. Maybe I should have stayed in the therapy sessions a little longer.

I held up my empty ring finger. Both our simple gold bands were together in Elizabeth's grave.

"I'm no longer married."

Bloody idiot.

I saw from his dullard's face that it wasn't what he wanted to hear. This was taking forever. I felt bile rising and stared at the clear unopened bottle of water that had stopped sweating on the table between us.

"Could you check to see if there's been any word from those searching for my daughter?"

"They're doing everything that they can."

"Surely someone can tell me something."

He continued that demonic wretched stare without blinking.

"Your marriage, Mr. Schumacher?"

He was like a dog with a bone, which at the moment was my ankle.

"We were best friends and partners…, in everything."

"With her estate and yours combined, you're exceptionally wealthy, …now that your wife is gone, wouldn't you say?"

"Why? Has there been a ransom demand?" I asked quickly.

He didn't answer at first but kept that retched stare.

"Not yet. Is that what you're expecting?"

It was like looking directly in the eyes of the devil himself. I'd had the misfortune to see them many times in my forty-four years.

"You were about to tell me about your estate?"

"I was exceptionally wealthy *before* I met my wife."

My heart began thumping in my chest. There was no reason whatsoever to delve into the history of my family estate or my inheritance. I returned his dead glaze with equal intensity.

"Why didn't your wife combine her estate with yours when you first arrived here?"

"That's bloody well none of your business."

I heard, rather than felt, my chair slide away behind me as I stood. I refused his attempt at motioning me to reseat myself.

"How long have you been in this country, Dr. Schumacher?"

It was beginning to feel I'd been here far too long. He was enjoying my uncomfortable plight. The bastard was enjoying my being pissed at him.

I turned from the camera and mirrored window and took a breath.

I'd been questioned by better than him in South Africa while staring at the open barrel of an AK-47, when wounded rebel soldiers frequented through the clinic.

"Fourteen months, give or take a week."

I turned and sat back down forcing the frown from my face.

"I couldn't help but notice, your Range Rover was packed with quite a bit of food and clothing; were you in a hurry to get somewhere?"

"My daughter and I intended on leaving today straight from Scottsdale to go on holiday."

I could hear Chaste correcting me.

"V… vacation…," I sputtered.

"Where were you going?"

He slid back in his chair as if settling in to do this all night. How I wished for South Africa. At least the local authorities would be pointing guns in vehicles searching for my daughter. My long-standing reputation within the medical community had afforded me that much.

"We were going to drive to the east coast, up to New York, then follow the northern border to Washington and back here…, a summer tour. Probably a couple hundred food and restroom stops also."

He ignored my sad attempt at sarcasm.

"That's why your house looked like you had prepared to abandon it?"

"Abandon it?"

I almost gave in to his tactics again, when my voice rose two octaves.

"Am I to understand that you suspect me in my daughter's disappearance?"

"We have to look at all possibilities, mister Schumacher. Your daughter…, she goes by Chase or Chaste? Where were you when she went missing?"

"At the grocer six blocks away, standing in line."

"Can you prove you were there? I assume you have your receipt?"

"Of course."

Then I remembered the power outage.

"No, I didn't get a regular receipt, there was a power failure. We all paid in cash. It was why I was late to pick up my daughter."

He made several notes and looked back up. He had more tricks up his sleeve.

"Is there anyone that can verify that?"

I sat there wondering if we had chosen the wrong country to find sanctuary. Peaceful hell.

My wife is dead, my daughter is missing, and I'm sitting in a filthy room with a slouchy excuse of a man accusing me of participating in her abduction.

I did the one thing I knew would piss him off.

I looked at my wristwatch at the time; it was almost nine p.m., roughly six hours since Chaste disappeared.

I got up and walked to the door without a warning…, to leave.

"As much as I'd love to sit here in this filth and chitchat, I'm going to look for my daughter. If you have any more questions, feel free to read the information in that folder."

I heard him yell my name and order me to stay just as the door closed shut behind me.

CHAPTER FIVE

The FBI agent had actually helped me without knowing it. How might you ask? He reminded me that I was not without resources. Living a simple life for the past eighteen years, where any show of wealth built unseen walls or frankly could get you killed, had addled my reasoning.

I immediately called the American Consulate that helped my family emigrate and asked for the list of the top three private investigative services in the country and called the one closest - U. S. Marshal Investigations, located in Dallas Texas.

According to my one reliable resource, I needed someone with multi-jurisdictional reach, ensconced in bypassing the usual bureaucracy and red tape that could hamper a timely investigation.

It was well after midnight when I heard a knock on my Phoenix hotel room door. The private jet would cost me dearly, but money was no object and time was of the essence.

Two quite sizable gentlemen in suits, one with a weather-tanned face, the other ebony black, greeted me as pleasantly as they could. Instead of grilling me with questions about my past and personal motives, they instantly took out a worn map of the area with plotted times and possible destinations the abduction may have taken. They'd obviously put their time aloft to good use.

Brent Rand, the tanned, weather faced gent slapped his hand down and swore offhandedly.

"There can't be many forest-green Range Rovers in this area."

Carl Smith, the black fellow, nodded his head in agreement.

"I'll have Collette access the DMV database."

It was a little awkward looking up at Carl, tall fellow. Brent was my eyelevel, six feet or so, but Carl was a bit intimidating.

Carl opened his mobile phone and in ten minutes had the information.

"There's only four Range Rovers with that year and body registered in Arizona with that specific body color. Dr. Schumacher's is one. Two are sitting on dealership parking lots. One belongs to a rental agency up in Prescott. Collette called them; the rental was reported stolen only about five hours ago. That was after they did their end of day inventory of the lot and found it missing."

I wanted to rant over spilled milk and ask why the FBI couldn't have done that. He must have seen my angst.

"The rental vehicle has a remote locater system. The rental agency is looking for it now."

We spoke hurriedly of what I remembered from my talks with the crossing guard at the school and what I could garner from the chatter around me minutes after I discovered Chaste was missing.

"Who has your daughter's phone now?"

I told him I didn't have a clue, the police, the FBI, the school janitor for all I knew. It was the first time I saw the bright white teeth of Carl's smile.

"I do have her last voice messages to me."

I handed him my cell phone.

"Is this your daughter?"

He held up the large screen on my phone and I nodded.

"She's beautiful."

I saw the increased concern on both men's faces, only for an instant.

Carl quickly accessed my voicemail and put it on loudspeaker. We listened quietly to the soft assertive voice of my daughter.

"She obviously thought it was you."

Brent tapped his fingers nervously on the map.

"That narrows down the vehicle description. Let's go look at your Range Rover."

As we were about to walk to the parking lot, Carl's cell rang.

"They located it."

He listened carefully, made some notes, and thanked Collette before ringing off.

We walked outside and circled my auto for about five minutes, while Brent flicked his mini-mag flashlight over every inch of its surface.

"Is this the only identifiable decal on your Rover?"

His torch was reflecting off the huge triangular decal from the Tonto National Forest plastered on the center of my windscreen.

"You and your daughter go there often?"

"Every two or three weeks, weekend getaways."

Carl trotted out the hotel door.

"Their locater was dead on the Rover."

Another disappointment. I turned to walk away, rubbing the back of my aching neck.

"But the rental agency has a new onboard system that uploads data from their high-end vehicles every hour on the hour. It went dead just north of Roosevelt Lake over in the National Forest Area."

Brent and I caught the inference immediately.

"Tonto National Forest?"

Carl looked at his notes and nodded.

I told them that I knew exactly where the lake was, but I asked one of them to drive. I was in no shape to sit behind the steering wheel at one o'clock in the morning as tense as I was.

The closer we came to our destination the sicker I felt; the angrier I became at the local law enforcement. I kept my own council of silence, just in case the two professionals sitting in the front seat were affiliated somehow.

I almost dozed off from exhaustion and sour adrenaline when Carl got my attention and asked directions.

As we entered the Tonto National Park, I had an epiphany of sorts and leaned over the front seat.

"What if the other Range Rover has a Tonto Park sticker on the windscreen?"

The two men grinned and glanced at each other.

"Windshield..., that crossed our minds too."

Another linguistic faux pas; Chaste wasn't there to correct me and I felt the deepening loss of my child yet again.

Carl's cell phone rang causing my insides to lurch.

It was their helpful investigator with more information.

The Rental agency had sent Collette the vehicle travel data. The other Range Rover had indeed been in the vicinity of the Franklin

Elementary where my daughter attended.

I wanted to wretch at the information.

Almost three in the morning, we were turning the last bend in the narrow winding road to the north end of Roosevelt Lake and saw two black SUV's.

Phantasmal red and blue lights scorched the landscape, their strobing illumination distorting the sight of a wrecker pulling a green Range Rover from an overgrown ditch by the waterfront.

"I don't believe it," grunted Carl. "You seeing what I'm seeing?"

"The wrecker's destroyed the crime scene," said Brent, sliding to a stop.

As we jumped from our vehicle, we were met by the raised hand of none other than my evil interrogator.

"I'm sorry, but this is a crime scene. You need to move along."

Brent and Carl exposed two U.S. Marshal's badges.

I heard Carl's booming voice ask, "Where is the local law enforcement? Why wasn't the crime scene contained?"

I couldn't hear the entire conversation over the obnoxious whine of the wench on the wrecker, but apparently there was some sort of pissing contest in progress.

"…not their jurisdiction now."

Carl continued to argue while Brent scoured the area with his light, dodging the jerking motions of the cable from the wrecker.

Brent walked back to the still raging disagreement, shaking his head.

"…there are international implications!" bellowed Carl.

I watched Brent unfold a small piece of paper and thrust it towards the FBI fellow.

The agent held it up in the beam of the SUV's headlamps.

I heard Mr. FBI mutter a curse, then ask who they paid to get a writ from the Department of Homeland Security.

Apparently, I had hired the right gents to work in finding my daughter Chaste.

Suddenly the not-so-Special Agent glanced my way in recognition, followed by an unmitigated snarl before walking back to his black SUV.

Whatever the private jet cost me was worth that look on his face.

Brent hurried over to where I was standing and begged me to go back to our vehicle; reminding me that I might not want to see what they might find.

I reluctantly agreed.

Once the wrecker had won the tug-of-war and the other Range Rover was free of the ditch, I circled it from a distance, with my heart hammering in my chest.

When it reached the glaring lights and it was on the road, I saw it.

On the center of the windshield, was a large green triangle with a glowing reflective T in the center. Minus the dents and abrasions, this vehicle was almost a carbon copy of ours.

It was no wonder Chaste charged across the street at her school, anxious to begin our vacation and jump inside.

CHAPTER SIX

The Special Agent must have been angered far beyond my initial calculations. The next morning, I had been asleep in my hotel room for roughly two fitful hours, when the door splintered open. A stream of Gestapo look-alikes with automatic weapons raised to their black face masks poured inside. I was summarily arrested.

The charge was suspicion of kidnapping and murder.

A hoard of media personnel were waiting behind the arrest vehicles, flashing cameras and chattering into microphones about a British Doctor from South Africa that had done something amiss with his wife and now his own daughter.

One by one they managed to slip past the detail of officers and zoom in on my bewildered face. My body and soul was too tired to fight, which I'm sure made me look all the more guilty to the cameras and accusations.

Then, seated and handcuffed, I noticed one of the team members of the self-congratulating Mr. FBI making a statement into the frenzy.

Brent and Carl looked on wistfully, letting me know they would still be on the job and motioned for me to button my lips. The last thing I saw Carl do was stuff my cell phone inside his suit jacket. It wasn't bloody likely anyone would dare to try and remove it from him.

I was still at a loss concerning American gestures or colloquialism, but I knew I was to call a lawyer and keep my mouth shut.

It took twelve hours before I was allowed that privilege.

As soon as I was processed, inked, and photographed, I was ushered into a similar stinky wretched room as the night before.

The scorned Agent Lily was not at all happy about the previous night's folly. He blasted me about using my money to get my way and assured me that money wouldn't keep me from a life sentence in prison. Even I knew they were idle threats; it was nothing more than harassment and overstepping the boundaries of his office.

I dozed off twice, head on arms, with my interrogator barking accusations and nonsensical questions; while my precious eight and a half year old daughter was lost in the hands of some unknown filthy creature. Human nature had me transferring my deep-seated anger at her abductors toward the poor excuse of human flesh holding me captive.

A man by the name of Arthur Jernigan, my friend at the American Consulate, heard of my situation via Brent Rand and Carl Smith. Within a few hours he sent a local reputable lawyer my way, John Shoemaker; I thought the similar nomenclature befitting. His kind demeanour and American Indian dark brown eyes helped me relax as he carefully explained my plight.

After posting an exorbitant bail, despite radical protests from the arresting parties, I was finally allowed to leave and collude with my hired team of investigators.

They forced me back to my hotel room, now their center of operations, fed me and made me sleep.

Despite my weakened state, it never once crossed my mind that while I was detained, I hadn't been offered so much as a stale cracker, not since noon the previous day.

Hours later, the muffled voices of Brent and Carl stirred me awake while discussing the latest information. The last diffused bit I heard was their questioning how the FBI had arrived so quickly both at Ben Franklin Elementary and at the stolen vehicle.

Apparently, whoever performs the detailed inspection for crime scenes, could not find anything definitive about the stolen Rover the abductor or abductors used. They did however find definite proof that Chaste was in the vehicle. Two or three long strands of delicate yellow blond hair was crunched in the rear seatbelt clasp. I didn't need an expert to tell me the odds of her cornsilk hair being found in the discarded Rover.

Wearily I looked at my cell phone at the digital photo only a few days old, my last image of Chaste.

My semi-wrested mind wretched at all of it once again.

By now, Chaste and I should have been full of lunch and on the road from Pueblo Colorado, headed to wherever the wind pushed our sails. Our cheerful new beginning in a new land.

I rolled out of bed and felt myself walking to the restroom, then heaved stenchy bile before I got the chance to take a morning piss.

A knock at the restroom door reminded me I had to hold myself together and hurry out.

It was Brent.

As I opened the door, he handed me an overnight bag he had retrieved from my vacation ready auto. How convenient.

That day proved fruitless.

And the next.

And the ones that followed, even with the help of another half dozen highly skilled investigators from their team.

There were no ransom demands, no phone calls, no indications of monetary motives whatsoever and absolutely no cooperation from the FBI or other local agencies.

The only blurbs on the news concerning my daughter's disappearance smeared a lurid repetitious image of my face all over the screen, walking handcuffed and scruffy to the back seat of an official vehicle.

Brent and Carl ushered me aside in my home almost a week to the day that Chaste had vanished.

"Dr. Schumacher, we need to talk. We've found that in cases similar to this that if we don't find…."

I could tell he was having as hard a time saying it as I was receiving it.

"That is…, we have a window of opportunity of more or less 24 hours, maybe 36 hours, before there is foul play; especially where there are no ransom demands."

Twenty-four hours.

My first twenty-four hours after Chaste disappeared was spent in an interrogation room. I felt undirected rage flood my face.

"We did manage to get this."

Carl frowned at Brent as he handed me my daughter's cell phone.

My hand must have been shaking because he placed it on the table between us.

I finally picked it up and touched a few images on the screen.

"All of her personal information, contacts, voice mail, pictures, text messages..., they were all erased when we got it."

"Who would do that? Why would anyone do that?"

"We don't know, Dr. Schumacher."

I slid the useless phone away. I didn't ask where they found it and they didn't offer. They probably knew it would only sicken and anger me further.

Carl brought us back on topic.

"The State Troopers managed to interview about 46 local registered sex offenders, but all had concrete alibis for their whereabouts that time of day."

His list of investigations went on for over half an hour, most I'd been in collaboration with, yet all had been unfruitful.

He finally spoke what was on his mind, "Kress, if there were ransom demands or any witnesses, anything...."

The Phoenix Police had interviewed many of the parents and teachers and some of the children from the school that day. It was the last day of school however and minds were rampant on their two months of freedom, not on which auto picked up the little blond Brit girl. The few that did get a glimpse said that she got in her dad's green 'blazer'.

"Is there any hope at all?"

"There is always hope, but we need something, some thread to follow and this was obviously planned well in advance, in great detail."

He looked at his partner and ducked his head.

"I have some things I need to explain...."

"First of all, your cell phone was tampered with. The technicians at our lab in Texas found a piece of spyware installed. Someone was monitoring you remotely, possibly why the ringer was off, if you remember. The identical vehicle that was used..., we believe the road crew that diverted you was probably involved.

"They were the ones that cut the underground power junction to the school's neighborhood and they packed up and disappeared without a trace."

"That's ludicrous, how could anyone know where I would be to time all those events?"

"It wouldn't have mattered where you were. Think about it Kress.

If your daughter had taken the bus, the children assemble on the other side of the street from where the other Rover was parked. Chaste would have seen it and done the same thing. The electricity was cut to accelerate the timing. Half the kids were already gone before you got in line to pick her up. Even if you were in the long pick up line, Chaste would have seen the green Rover out front far before noticing yours down the street. Same result."

All hope began to sift away, "I can't believe this. Who would do such a thing?"

"Kress, the only candidates you've given us with a motive live on another continent.

"We've called and made written inquiries to the embassy in Johannesburg, but the only thing they would tell us is that the clinic you and your wife operated burned down."

CHAPTER SEVEN

A hearing was held in the Phoenix courthouse and thanks to my astute lawyer, Mr. John Shoemaker, the case against me was thrown out. The precious lady that was at the checkout counter of the grocery store remembered me in line that day, placing me inside the gloomily lit grocery store instead of abducting my own daughter.

Yet it wasn't fully her testimony that freed me from the clutches of my accusers; it was a battery powered video recording of my Rover parked just outside the grocer and unmoving for the entire time in question.

I assumed that the evidence of the stolen identical Rover would have been sufficient, but I can't remember if it was even presented to the judge.

Mr. FBI and his ilk left the courtroom in cool silence, much to my astonishment.

The judge brought me into his chambers and offered his sincerest condolences at my loss, wishing me the best for my daughter's safe return. Behind his desk were multiple framed pictures of a family strewn with young ladies.

A clot of media was just outside the courthouse doors, cameras ablaze. All their questions seemed to mutate into a glob. I do remember hearing '...murderer free to walk the streets' and '...his own child' several times.

With the charges against me obliterated, you would think that Mr. FBI would have buggered off, back to his own sphincter. It was not to be so.

I spent the next week having copies of flyers printed up, offering a substantial reward, with the likeness of Chaste in the center.

Visits into Scottsdale and Phoenix were riddled with stares and whispered accusations, thanks to the rampant media attention. It was agony.

My new friend and lawyer John Shoemaker obtained permission for me to distribute my flyers within the Tonto National Forest grounds and they were stapled to the front office and every campsite and cabin in the park. The local Boyscout troops were instrumental in helping with this enormous task, refusing any offer of payment.

In the span of those next eight days, I received no less than twelve traffic citations for everything from one mile per hour over the speed limit, to driving too slow in downtown Phoenix.

I was being hounded by those scorned through their own justice system. I was at a complete loss as to why.

Finally, two weeks later, my lawyer and I went before the judge that had overseen my hearing. Mr. Shoemaker handed the now twenty traffic violations to him and explained the circumstances.

All the tickets were dismissed and the judge told me to bring any new ones to him directly and he would take care of them.

I didn't get any more traffic citations, but that was only the beginning of my woes.

Twice, my electric service was disconnected at my home; both times the termination order looked as if it was given by me.

Finally, I visited the electric company's main office and paid an estimated four months in advance with assurances that I had no intention of disconnecting.

My telephone service was next, but proved not so easy to remedy. The landlines were cut somewhere between the telephone company's junction box and my house, underground. Three times, the telephone servicemen found the break; each time by the edge of a long bladed spade. I finally discontinued the service when I was informed that they could not afford to keep a working line to my residence.

Now, due to the lack of a working phone line, my security system was useless. So although someone had taken to pelting rocks into the profusion of glass on every side of my home, the alarm only served to wake me up in the middle of the night, at least twice a week.

One morning at six a.m., I awoke to the sound of breaking glass and the alarm, to realize that I was back in South Africa. The tribesmen were my neighbors, or wore uniforms and carried badges.

I hired a bloody security guard, installed an eight-foot iron fence around the perimeter of my property, complete with electric gates, and purchased a watchdog with a pissy demeanor.

The dog was the only one that earned his feed. I fired the guard two days later for sleeping while the dog was barking its lungs out at two men crashing stones into my living room.

Through all of this, I was never deterred from my quest for finding Chaste.

I looked at her face on my phone every morning and said a prayer for her. I had to find a balance between turning off the crushing heartbreak of her absence and the building hatred of the obsessive trials from the miffed law agencies, neighbors, and some unknown horde of malcontents.

Even the spectacular view of the distant canyon from my back deck seemed a curse.

Regular trips to the Tonto National Park as well as various outlying townships were my new life. I watched mile after mile accrue on my vehicle as I daily frequented every highway in the state.

Brent and Carl called every week or so, asking if I had heard anything else, offering their services at no expense to help me.

Wonderful chaps, just wonderful.

I wandered inside coffee shops from time to time just to have a friendly face to talk to. These stops also reminded me of my missing child and her love of a frozen caramel coffee.

The third week of August, I received a pre-enrollment form to the fifth grade for Chaste along with her fourth year grades.

I was numb.

After looking at her grades a dozen times; all perfect scores, I didn't know what else to do.

I filled out the form.

I had to.

If I hadn't it would have been admitting to myself she wouldn't return. Then a flood of rage overtook me and I tore the form into giblets and stomped them against the floor. There was no way on earth I would ever send my daughter back to the same place she was taken from me.

I prayed that someone would call as I drifted into a fog.

CHAPTER EIGHT

The days turned into weeks. With morbid regret, I cancelled my continuing education classes at Arizona University; too absorbed with my daily obsession, looking for my daughter.

I was approached by multiple medical associations asking me to lecture, to share my lifetime of experiences in actual fieldwork.

After rifling through a box of photographs and copies of articles my wife and I had written over the years, I tried to leverage myself into some externally related agendas, then found excuses to abort every one.

I was becoming the textbook example of clinical depression.

Everyday I hoped for some sign that Chaste was still alive; that was as asinine as watching a stone skipping across the top of a dark pond and expecting it to float.

The weeks turned into months and soon it was December first.

I made a small cake and put a single candle in its center, then propped one of the flyers of Chaste beside it. With the candle lit, I prayed for her safe return and begged Elizabeth for her forgiveness.

I was crushed beyond repair and were it not for some morbidly slim hope that my daughter was still alive somewhere, I would have considered self-extermination to end my misery. I quickly learned that suicide was not for the squeamish or for cowards.

The nameless guard dog was now my only friend on our lonely hill and we celebrated Chaste's ninth birthday together.

I found that my mongrel liked the taste of a beer that day, almost as much as I.

I slept the first few days of December. My dreams tormented me in relentless recall, the most vivid, one of a planned second honeymoon with my wife.

Elizabeth and I had planned a trip to Paris, our tenth wedding anniversary. On the eve before our departure, a large truck rumbled to a stop at the clinic. One fellow gripping a rifle, bloody and wounded and obviously in shock himself began wordlessly lifting one wounded child after another, bringing them inside. When he was finished, there were twenty-two of them between the ages of four and eleven, bruised, broken, shot, and hacked by blades. One tribe tried to exterminate its neighbors over the available food and water rights.

Elizabeth and I worked side by side close to seventy straight hours in one surgery after another, managing to save all but one.

It was when Elizabeth fainted from exhaustion that we both realized we'd missed our trip.

The eleventh of December, I received a cryptic telephone call from someone that wanted to meet me in Sedona, far northwest of Scottsdale.

It was a man's voice, he made no demands, offered no information about Chaste, desired no reward; he wanted to talk.

As I recall, my insanity was peaking somewhat that day, along with a blustery cold norther.

I made my way up Interstate 17, watching my rearview the entire way, expecting it to be yet another trick to earn another traffic citation outside the safety zone of my county; or something worse. How I was learning to hate living here in this God forsaken land.

Sedona looked nothing like I remembered from my earlier months of trespassing. The road that led into the town looked as if it would dead end against a huge backdrop of red mesa. The towering red wall rose up proudly, conspiring to touch the sky. It was both inspiring and majestic.

I found the coffee shop described to me in the telephone call and the small deserted park across the street as well. It was a strange place to arrange a meeting, but anything was better than the previous weeks of silence and seclusion.

I purchased two hot coffees and walked to the closest bench in the freezing wind and sat waiting. There was a steady stream of people milling across the extraordinarily wide street. Shop owners busy with hordes of colorful lights and decorations for some up-coming Christmas to-do.

My coffee had cooled enough to drink without blistering my tongue and was about half-empty when a derelict in filthy clothes ambled up.

His cane bent precariously, barely supporting the weight of a game left leg and he grunted as he collapsed on the bench beside me.

I tried to brush him off, but he ignored my demands. Finally, I explained that I was waiting for someone.

"Did you get my coffee?" he asked.

I could not discern his accent, not English, not German, possibly something local.

"Are you the person that called?" I asked bitterly.

I wanted to kick myself for believing anything at this point. I had been duped by some homeless person that saw the reward poster and wanted a free coffee out of the bargain.

I handed him the coffee. It was just as well.

My anger dissipated when I realized that he was probably just as lost as I.

I got up to leave.

"Aren't you interested in what I have to say?" he asked.

"Not particularly, unless you have some information about my missing child."

He turned caustically, sipping at the cup of coffee and stared blankly across the street.

I sat back down.

"I'll give you five minutes."

In five minutes, I'd be almost frozen, yet he was willing to sit here in the cold wind and chat like it was a warm summer day.

He sat hugging his cup of coffee and sipping it for a good two minutes before speaking.

"Any trace of your little girl?" he asked.

"Would I be here if there was?" I asked, somewhat sarcastically.

Okay, it was very sarcastically. I was ready to be done with him.

I too sipped on my now lukewarm coffee, then remembered the emptiness awaiting me at home when I returned.

"Look, if you want to talk, let's go inside the coffee shop where it's warm."

"Can't, I'm not allowed."

He looked nervously from side to side up and down the street.

His eyes had that look of dead zone I'd seen recently in my own dappled reflection.

"For goodness sakes, why not?"

"I was like you once. I had a family, a wife, and a son."

Wonderful..., his introduction had all the familiar beginnings of a support group session.

"I had a business, made good money. My wife loved me. I went to all the school functions, played baseball with our son."

I didn't want to be harsh.

"Sir, I feel for your losses, but if you don't have any information concerning my daughter...."

He turned to look at me as if he might have actually heard me.

"Steven..., that was my son's name, how he loved to play catch. Had an arm on him too."

Okay, he wasn't listening.

I got up to leave once again.

"Please..., hear me out...."

Despite my reservations, I caved.

"Only if we go indoors; someplace that's warm."

He grunted and took another sip of coffee. It had to be ice cold by now. I know I was.

"Is there anyplace nearby that will let you inside?"

"The shelter down the street, maybe."

I cursed myself for being a bleeding heart.

"Right..., Come on then."

I grabbed him by the arm and lifted. He was skin and bone, no more than ninety pounds, disguised in layers of raggedy clothes.

"My God man, what have you done to yourself?"

It took me a while to help him and his cane down the sidewalk. Surprisingly enough, he didn't have the usual sewer smell of the homeless, not that he was spring flowers by any stretch.

I pulled him into one of the local franchise burger shops and ordered us both a large meal.

As soon as we were seated, a roguish man with a homemade nametag on his chest that read Manager walked over and made an inappropriate comment in his native Mexican language. He seemed to recognize my face but seemed more flustered by my choice of companions and walked away, staring. It appeared that neither of us would win a local popularity contest.

I leaned forward and whispered to keep away more stares.

"Fine, go ahead and talk then."

"My son Steven was twelve when he disappeared. We were hiking, you know, in the high country. Beautiful up there.

"Rocks look like they're on fire in the evenings.

"One night just after dark, he went to take a leak, never came back. Couldn't have been more than fifty feet from me. Not a sound."

I went and got our food from the counter and sat back down. He was still talking as if I had never left.

"My wife blamed me. I guess she had a right to. I blame me too. We went through the process, you know. I'm sure you know by now. They questioned me for weeks. My wife even began to doubt me and believed the accusations."

I knew this part of the story well, as I listened between bites of gritty overly salted French fries.

"One day she up and left. I took off so much time from my business to look for him it finally folded. Soon the money was gone, the house was gone. Everything gone. Everything."

His voice trailed off to not much more than a whisper.

He opened his burger and tossed the meat aside, a strange sickly expression on his face.

I couldn't listen to much more of his despair; it was rallying my own grief to chew another hole in my mind. What's the saying? Misery loves company?

"What do you want from me?"

"Not a thing. I want to help you."

I was exasperated.

"If you can't find your son, how do you expect to help me find my daughter?"

It was a reasonable question. Harsh maybe, but reasonable.

"I had a chance to find my son. I failed."

"What do you mean you had a chance?"

Foolishness overcame me as I took his bait.

"What would you say if I told you there was a way to find your daughter?"

I'd had enough. My pity was quickly turning into anger.

"And I ask you again, if there was a way, why didn't you find your son?"

"I failed. I failed the test."

He lifted his game leg out from under the table.

"Cost me my leg, almost my life. Now I wish it had."

"What cost you?"

He crouched closer across the table, brushing his food aside to get near me.

"I was too old, too weak."

He gripped my arm with fleshless cold fingers and shook me.

"Too weak for what?"

"Pitre."

His voice was barely above a whisper.

"What?"

"A creature that can give you the power to see into places no one else sees."

I looked up at the dingy tiled ceiling in despair. I had heard rumors of Sedona being a center for spiritual awakenings, shamanism, and all sorts of New Age babble. My short-term companion had obviously fallen victim to his grief, to outlandish claims by a local soothsayer, or some sort of hallucinogenic in the local water supply.

I pulled out a twenty-dollar bill and dropped it on the table.

"Sir, I wish you well. I pray you find peace over your loss."

Hurriedly, I stood up to leave and he grabbed my arm again with gnarly brown fingers, much tighter than I thought he was capable.

"Sir, let me go," I whispered, not wanting to make a scene.

This was obviously why he was not welcome inside any of the merchants in town.

"When you get desperate enough, come back and see me. I can help you. But don't wait too long."

He let go of my arm. There were big drops of tears in his eyes, hanging, not turning loose. Such sadness to look upon. Somewhere in his dark eyes, I saw my future. Somewhere past the hard retched shiver screaming down my spine, I looked away.

"And where would I find you?"

I couldn't believe I was asking. I was only giving substance to his warped delusion.

"When you come back, look for me on one of the park benches. I always stop by the park around noon."

"When I come back?"

He sounded so certain.

His thin lips tried to smile, but didn't quite make the transition.

I took my half-eaten meal and hurriedly dropped it in the trash bin beside the door and looked back to get one last look at his weathered, bearded face.

He was gone.

I looked around the dining area where two other couples were seated.

How could a specious cripple old man move so quickly?

There were only two doors and I was standing next to one of them.

It was then I remembered I had a few more flyers offering a reward that I could disperse in the cheerful little town of Sedona.

CHAPTER NINE

I arrived home just in time to see the backs of two silhouettes scampering off through the darkness.

I engaged the electric gate and there lay my guard dog, gutted, spoiled and dead.

It was pathetic. A demented child's prank.

A bed-wetter's compunction. It made me sick.

I won't attempt to describe what happened to a young native girl that happened to come to us for help against her tribe leaders wishes. Her precious body was nearly ruined at the hands of their jealous superstitions.

This was nothing compared to what we had lived through.

I picked up the freshly gutted remains and hurled it angrily in the street in front of my driveway.

I screamed into the darkness.

"You'll have to do better than that!"

Not the tasty retort I wanted, but I was spent for the day.

Apparently my arrival had thwarted whatever else the intruders had intended. The house was still intact, no new broken windows or dents against my front door.

The next morning when I woke from a dreary nightmare, barely daybreak, I rolled over on my side with my left arm aching. I didn't pay it much attention until later, when I made my morning trip to the restroom. It was then I saw that my wrist was bruised.

Supposedly, it happened when I was throwing the remains of my late beer-drinking companion into the street.

Then curiously, I noticed that my fresh capillary discoloration, already turning from strawberry red to hues of blue and green, looked like a handprint and remembered the old crank from Sedona, land of the strange and mysterious. After pondering his sudden burst of strength for a few moments, I got on with my day.

I found two larger meaner dogs that morning and set them loose within the gates, like sharks into a tank.

I tried to hire a local contractor to install an electrical wire atop my eight-foot fence; the kind used to keep sheep or cattle at bay. I found out that it was against the landowners guidelines.

My reasoning was skewed with anger. It was just dandy for my neighbors to destroy my home, kill my beer-drinking canine, repeatedly cut my telephone lines, among a dozen other scuttlebutt acts of hatred, but I wasn't allowed to protect my investment with a deterrent the strength of a taser on the top of my fence?

They could bloody well sue me.

So I hired two young men walking by in need of Christmas money and it was done, that very day.

It was satisfying to hear the dry frigid air crackle around the high-voltage electrical wire, but I was beginning to lose sight of my goal.

I was making my own prison, inch by inch, day by day.

What was the name of that person, mitre…, spider, pitre?

I nabbed a cold Heineken from the fridge and sat down with my cell phone, the twin of my daughter's phone. The internet wasn't something new to me by any means but it was exasperating to try and use the little screen to search for anything. Chaste used her nimble little fingers and mind to trolley through page after page, buying her favorite songs and such.

It was currently my only resource. I'd learn if it took all night.

It took more ale than hours.

I found no references to any such folklore or mythology no matter what search criteria I entered.

Suddenly I found myself standing at the open back door, ready to hurl the phone far away into the canyon behind our house. Instead, I reverted back to using it only for its primary function, a telephone.

I fell asleep hunched over the dining table, listening to the recorded voice of Chaste; 'Oh, there he is….'

The beer wasn't helping any longer and I found myself considering much stronger painkillers. In fact, I was actually getting a bit of a pudge, something that had never happened before.

Christmas Eve came and I threw the rest of my alcohol away. It was a present to myself.

There's nothing worse than a sad, depressed drunk.

I sat down at the kitchen's little breakfast nook by the back deck, the tall glass panes thick with condensation…, and saw the small residual handprint of my daughter. It was as if we'd just finished breakfast together and she had stepped away; as if I could call her name and she'd come trotting down the stairs from her room in a riot.

My heart crumpled and I looked out on the landscape at the placid scenic view. It had snowed during the night. Chaste and I had planned to be somewhere together for a white Christmas.

I cried.

I hadn't even put up a Christmas Tree.

How could I? I couldn't find a reason to.

I cried all the more, my self-esteem guttering.

I put on my foul weather gear, hopped in my infamous green Range Rover and drove to Sedona Arizona.

CHAPTER TEN

Snow blurred the entire trip and although it wasn't sticking to the highway, it was making it difficult for me to see.

After missing a few turns, I found my way back to the coffee shop and parked across the street. The particular shopping district was gaily lit with what might have been a million colorful lights that all seemed gray to the coating over my eyes.

Still early and gloom skied due to the weather; the trip had taken much longer than my last.

I hurried into the coffee shop, tuned out the happy Christmas music, some strolling carolers, and purchased the requisite coffee that was my calling card for the strange old man.

When I breached the sidewalk, the snow was falling in delicate swirls. Nevertheless, I walked to the bench across the street and stood, feeling like a complete fool, in the snow, freezing, and holding two paper cups of coffee.

My Rover was only a few feet away and was looking pretty darn good as opposed to the inch of snow sticking to the wooden slats of the park bench.

Just how desperate was I?

If I went back home alone, it would be my last trip anywhere.

I scanned the three hundred and sixty degree space around me, not seeing a soul. No one propped on a cane or limping along on the ice was anywhere to be noted. Looking at my wristwatch, it was a quarter past noon. Maybe I'd missed him. Maybe it was a wasted trip. Maybe it would have been a wasted trip even if I did talk to..., whatever his name was.

The heater in the Rover began to call my name and I scooted carefully down the sidewalk to get inside.

"That my coffee?"

The voice was familiar.

Turning around, there was the old withered man from my first meeting.

"You move pretty fast for an old cripple."

"You move pretty slow for a young one."

He stuffed his bent cane under an arm and took the coffee from my hand, shivering in the cold.

"Let's get in my auto."

He nodded and began weaving to the passenger side door.

I had the engine running and the heater on full by the time he succeeded in crawling into the seat.

"I never did get your name."

It was a blatant hint.

"Nope. You didn't."

I sat waiting while he sipped the warm coffee.

"Do you want to tell me your story?"

"Nope. I don't."

"You told me to come back when I was desperate enough. Well, here I am."

"I see that."

I was becoming frustrated with the guessing games.

"I don't understand what you want from me."

"I want you to find your little girl."

"How do you intend to help me? What did you mean when you mentioned…, mitre, spider was it?"

"Pitre."

I saw myself circling the drain, just for asking my next question.

"Just who is this…, Pitre?"

"Not really a who…, more of a what."

I was mentally forming the long list of dead ends I had encountered trying to research this person or creature, when he finally decided to talk.

"Pitre is a silent legend, you won't find anybody that'll admit he exists. Even in circles that know about him, his name is forbidden."

I wondered instantly if that was because he didn't exist.

"How did you find out about this…, forbidden creature?"

"Old Indian. Lives about twenty miles from here, on the top of a mesa. He's older than dirt, don't speak much English."

"And I suppose you want me to believe that he told you about this Pitre."

"I was out looking for my son."

He tried hard not to choke on his swallow of coffee.

"Every trail I followed was a dead end. I must have walked every canyon for twenty square miles. Days…, weeks? I don't know how long. One night I was hacking at some sage to build a fire and a snake bit me. It was too far to walk back to anything in any direction, but I have to tell you…, I wanted to die. I didn't want to come back without my boy. I finished building my fire and lay down beside it.

"I don't know how long I was there watching the flames until I passed out.

"When I woke up, a wrinkle faced old piece of leather was sitting over me, blowing smoke in my face and waving a bunch of feathers over my head. Never figured out what tribe he was from. Wouldn't matter if I did; still couldn't speak his language. It was a good thing he knew mine."

"Is that what happened to your leg, the snakebite?"

"No. Snake didn't do this. I'll get to that."

My guest shifted uncomfortably in his seat and continued, "Took a couple of weeks before I was able to get up. The old guy took care of me, fed me, the whole nine yards. He never asked me why I was out there wandering around. Like it was to be expected. He said I was on some spirit quest.

"I started asking him about my missing boy, but he said I'd already told him the story. Several times as a matter of fact."

"And then he told you about Pitre?"

"Yep, he's the one. He said there was a way to find 'that which is lost', that's how he put it."

I was getting impatient at the storyteller and wanted him to cut to the more pertinent facts. I felt as if he were trying to sell me on the idea of Pitre, rather than help me understand. I was in fact waiting for him to tell me how much he would charge me to take me to the mesa and meet this Indian chap, most likely his partner in some sort of elaborate ruse.

"I ended up staying with him for several weeks while he explained what this creature was. If you won't get in too durn big of a hurry, I'll tell you."

Then I did something exceptionally stupid.

"Why don't you come back to my place? Stay awhile and tell me all about it."

The silence became annoying while he churned my offer around inside his withered head.

"Only if you don't make me sleep on a bed."

What a strange request.

"What would you prefer to sleep on?"

This was going to be good, I had to hear this.

"The floor, someplace warm."

That was a letdown.

"I think I can manage that."

"And I can't eat meat."

I put my Rover in gear and we headed back toward Scottsdale.

CHAPTER ELEVEN

It was the verge of darkness when we arrived at my home and my two vicious mongrels behind the fence were whining like three year olds begging to be fed.

The fence was still making that wonderful crackling noise as snowflakes drifted past the tiny insulated wire on top.

All was normal in my world for the moment.

My passenger slept the entire trip, but was spry enough to instantly claim a corner near my living room fireplace as soon as we hurried inside my home.

I had so many warning sirens going off inside my head, telling me this was a bad idea, I thought my head would explode.

"Since you don't eat meat, what should I feed you? Just so I don't have to play more guessing games."

"Salads, grains, ...no wine or alcohol either."

He must have seen the dozen empty beer bottles in the bin by the garage door. I guess my guilt made me explain.

"I gave that up too."

He didn't look as if he quite believed me and stared around the living room and grunted, "Merry Christmas."

I ignored the blatant contempt in his voice, nevertheless I felt like Scrooge and parried his personal affront.

"Shower is in there."

I pointed to the closest guest bathroom.

It was more than a hint, but he didn't seem as offended as I'd hoped.

"I'll see if I can find you some sweats to wear."

Honestly, I didn't know if I had anything that was near small enough, but I found a set of sweats that had shrank too small for me to wear and hoped for the best.

"Got a garbage sack?"

I must have looked puzzled, because he grinned and explained.

"For my clothes. You can store them in the garage if you want to."

I wanted to burn them.

I threw an armload of split piñon into the hearth, lit a starter and took his enormous plastic bag full of clothes to the garage.

When his thin frame re-emerged, he looked almost human. The gnarly beard was gone and his mottled gray hair was tied in a stringy tail behind his head; high cheekbones revealed some local native heritage.

The sweats swallowed him, even with the legs rolled up in cuffs, but he seemed almost childishly beside himself at something clean to wear. I had a stack of blankets ready for his 'bed' on the floor and he wasted no time in making a thin pallet.

He reminded me of some of the humble natives that would spend days and nights on the cold floor of our old medical clinic, waiting for their mate or child to recover.

"What do I call you?"

He stared at me for a few minutes, either deciding to make up a suitable name, or remember his real one.

"Does it matter?"

We stared at each other until he conceded.

"How about Charles, Chuck, Hey You? Any of those will work."

"Okay..., Charles Chuck it is."

"Well?" he asked.

He backed up to the heat of the now burning fireplace and stared at me.

"Oh, I'm Dr. Kress Schumacher, Kress is fine."

"A doctor..., you don't say."

"Of pediatrics, actually. Would you like something to eat?"

He shook his head no.

"I'd rather get on with it if you don't mind. I have a lot to explain to you. You go ahead and do whatever it is you need to do. I don't like to start and stop. I lose my train of thought sometimes and it wouldn't be good if I left anything out."

What a strange, strange man. I hurried about with my usual, feed the dogs, feed myself routine and made him a bowl of salad to ease my conscience.

I grabbed a blanket, threw more wood in the hearth, and fixed myself on the couch across from 'Charles Chuck'.

"Pitre is horrible little creature," he began.

He rubbed his leg as if reliving some torture.

"He sees into a world that's all around us, things that we can't even imagine. Critter's about the size of my fist; looks like a bald rabbit at first sight. But it can change its looks to match wherever it's living. He mostly lives in one area, but I'll get to that when the time comes.

"Almost impossible to catch sight of it; it lives in a hole in the ground. That's the only way you'll be able to find him. That hole...."

I couldn't help noticing his flip-flopping between calling Pitre a he and an it. He turned uncomfortably, shifting his weight in another direction as he lay on his bed.

"I have a cot, if you prefer."

I didn't know what else to offer him, he seemed so determined to camp on the floor.

"I guess there's no getting around it. You'll never understand any other way."

He struggled to stand and slowly slid the pants leg of the sweats up his game leg.

In the medical profession, I've seen most every malady known to man, but this was indeed strange.

His exposed leg was not much more than twisted bones with strands of sinewy muscle attached and draped with skin. It looked painful. I am surprised that he could walk on it at all.

"This is minor to what can happen to you if you don't listen to every word I say."

"Pitre did that to you?"

"And more...."

"Why in God's name would you knowingly let a creature do that to you?"

"If you don't know, then you aren't ready."

"Letting some large spider have at you was supposed to help you find your son? That's absurd!"

I'd seen some aborigines in my clinic from time to time that had suffered emaciated limbs caused by strange venoms in their trek across the Kalahari Desert regions.

This particular poison must have damaged the very marrow of the bones. He angrily yanked the cloth back down over his withered leg and lay sideways on his blankets.

"I don't know if I can help you, Doc."

My curiosity was at its peak, if only as a professional.

"Please, continue. Actually, I have a question. How is letting a spiders poison that potent supposed to help you?"

"Ah, didn't say it was a spider, but now we're getting to the important part of my story.

"If it was only some spider that did this, I'd be nothing but a fool."

He ducked his head, I suppose wondering if he wasn't a fool indeed.

"That place you keep thinking about, where all the natives are, is that where you used to live?"

He must have seen some of the pictures on the wall in the hallway.

"For eighteen years."

"That dark fellow with the peacock feathers around his head…, said he was going to take your little girl, bake her over open coals."

I didn't know his game, but I'd had all I wanted.

"That's quite enough."

I stood up off the sofa and glared down at him. Someone had filled him in on my family's personal information. This was probably a hateful prank from the charming FBI stooge.

"Who paid you to come here and do this to me?"

"You're wife Elizabeth called you Dr. K in private."

I could feel the steam from my head as he continued his attack.

"That's it, get your things, I'll take you back where I found you."

"Matches the K birthmark on your hip."

No one, only my wife knew of the correlation. My parents had named me Kress due to the birthmark.

I sat back down, dumbfounded, "How?"

"The other part of me that was poisoned. Another side effect of Pitre."

CHAPTER TWELVE

Our conversation, my horrid Christmas Eve tale, ended for the night. I needed time to contemplate the fuzzy white rabbit my guest had pulled out of his magic hat.

That night I dreamed the... most... awful... vivid dreams of my last moments with Elizabeth. I listened to myself rehearse solemn words of promise to my dying wife to keep our daughter Chaste safe. I relived the moment's right up to when I picked up our daughter's cell phone by the curb and knew that the unimaginable had happened.

I awoke in a sweat, just before first light, wondering what spell my vile houseguest had forced upon me. Had I run from one group of curses to invite another into my very sanctuary?

"Merry Christmas Kress Schumacher," I spat out at my mirror.

My voice sounded hollow in my bedroom, angry that sarcasm was becoming my new vernacular.

I heard a scuffling downstairs in the den and threw on my robe. I was in no mood for any more surprises.

Chuck was seated on the floor, facing the small remnant of a fire, staring into the flames as if he was trying to find something hidden in the dance.

"I see you're awake, Doc. Bad dreams?"

His voice was weak.

"How did you know?"

"I have that effect on people. It's why I'm not welcome anywhere, even the mission in Sedona. The old priest said I had a

55

devil."

He turned and looked up at the banister I was leaning on.

"I failed. Don't you see? Pitre left me mutilated. Sometimes, I can see things I shouldn't, I see in smoke and mirrors. Nothing I can do about it. I can't find my son, even though I know he's out there somewhere."

His one-track mind was grating my last nerve and I didn't think I could abide another session similar to the previous night.

"No more fortune telling, agreed?"

"If you say so," he nodded, although somewhat begrudgingly.

I fixed us cold cereal with fruit and he asked for more.

My phone remained silent as always. There had been no messages during the night and I knew it would be same that day.

"Of course not," I groaned, it was Christmas Day.

Pain of my lost child deepened further than I ever imagined possible.

I fed the mongrels that were huddled together in their warm garage haven away from the foot of snow on the ground outside and brought in another trolley of firewood, swapping it for ashes.

The fire seemed to be the only thing that warmed my guest even though the house was a cozy seventy-two degrees.

The firewood popped loudly from time to time and filled the house with its resin-tinged flavor. Chaste loved the smell of it and that made me love it as well.

Charles Chuck seemed to realize he had left off with his ridiculous tale of demons and began following me around with his well-rehearsed and theatrical non-stop chatter.

"Pitre's hard to see, but even harder to find. The burrow can only be seen with eyes full of despair. He has an alarm string in front of his burrow like a trip wire that lets him know when food wanders near.

"It plays like a guitar string when the ground vibrates and he can tell if it's something he can eat, or some danger…, like us. I'll teach you how to trick him into coming out of his hole in the ground."

There was something very wrong with this scenario.

"What makes you think I can make out any better than you did?"

"You're younger, stronger, faster than I was when I tried. I was about fifty-six when I met Pitre. That was over two years ago."

"Why not place a net or trap over the hole?"

Charles, Chuck, *Hey You*, laughed, then coughed dryly at the effort.

"Haven't you been listening?"

My eyes rolled upwards, "How could I not listen? You haven't stopped prattling on since you arrived."

Apparently, insults were meaningless to this walking talking Pitre theologian.

"He's not of this world; he's nothing short of a devil. You can't catch him. It's not possible; never been done according to my Indian friend."

He took a raspy breath and continued.

"If you do manage to find Pitre's lair, that's when the work begins. We'll have to find you some gold foil. Doesn't have to be real gold, just gold colored and heavy. You have to shape it just smaller than the hole where he's hiding, then pluck the string in front of his door and roll the foil down inside.

"As soon as he comes out he's gonna be real ticked off. This is your only opportunity to seal off the hole. You have to seal the hole so he can't run back inside or he won't come back out."

It didn't sound like such an ordeal to me. Thump a gold marble down the gopher hole and stomp it when the little bugger comes out.

He must have known what I was thinking again, but wanted to keep his promise of no more mind reading.

"The burrow is a little smaller than a hardball and he's quick and mean. When he first comes out and sees that you're too big to eat, oh boy, he's gonna be some kind of mad. You can't let him bite you. If you let him get that close, it's all over. End of story.

"Nobody will ever know what happened to you. His pincers won't leave so much as a trace on your dead body. He's not afraid of anything or anybody, no matter how big or how mean."

I had that confused look, I'm certain I did. What was the purpose of knocking on the devils door?

"He's fast, deadly, looks like a puff of dust when he's running around, almost the size of the hole he comes out of. But..., that is his deception.

"To get what you need from him, you gotta put him off, make him madder and madder.

"Here's another thing you aren't going to want to accept.

"He can understand what you're saying. Pitre understands all languages. You could speak your Afrikaans to him and he would understand. Even your British accent won't throw him off."

There he went again; he couldn't know that I spoke bits and pieces of three African dialects. Afrikaans was around us on a daily basis, but it was a necessity to know the basics of Se Tswana and Sesotho.

"The way to make him really mad is to spit on him in a spray, and insult him. Call him stupid, call him small and disgusting, dance around him just out of his way when he jumps.

"I'll help you practice staying out of his way. That's almost as important as what comes next."

I saw tears well up in his eyes, as he seemed to be remembering his own confrontation with this monster, Chuck's imaginary monster.

"If you are cunning enough to bring him to a perfect rage, he'll puff up even bigger than his original size. Then the real fun begins. He'll show you his stinger up over his back, like a scorpion.

"While Pitre is in this state, you have to force him, make him mad enough to sting..., not bite you..., sting you seven times. Seven perfect times."

I couldn't take any more of his ludicrous tale.

"That's absolute madness. If the bite of this Pitre can kill you, what would a stinger do to you?"

Charles Chuck was on a roll however and ignored my question.

"The first sting is nothing less than blinding pain.

"No words can prepare you for this, it has to be experienced. You can't quit though..., spit on him, call him names, insult him, so that he stings you six more times. A total of seven. Remember that..., seven times.

"That is where I failed..., I only made it to the second or third sting. I fell to the ground, paralyzed for hours, dry and thirsty; I heard him coming, scratching and running toward me that last time. All I remember is the pain and then unconsciousness."

My insane storyteller stared into space and gathered his breath before he continued. There was no use stopping or interrupting his discourse. He was blithering mad.

"Ah, but that seventh perfect sting, my friend.

"Pitre will realize that you tricked him. This will be worse than the first time you felt his pain because the seventh and final sting carries the seed of his power.

"Despite the pain, despite everything inside you telling you to run, you have to let him, force him to sting you all seven times. If you succeed, that final sting will place the seed of his power within you.

"Then he'll deflate and bury up in his old burrow where you found him. You'll nearly be dead, but you won't die; you will wish you were dead. That last sting will cause you to fall where you are like a dead man for several days.

"You will dream wondrous dreams of things and places you have never heard of or seen."

My storyteller's eyes were large, round, glazed into some quasi euphoria of his tale, waving his arms in emphasis.

Charles Chuck was a bloody..., raving..., lunatic.

"When you revive, you're life will be changed forever. That's the price you'll pay for finding your daughter. You'll be able to see into another world. Other people, places and things will be visible to you that you didn't know existed.

"You will be able to ask for their help in finding her. You will know who is lying and who is telling you the truth."

Chuck railed on in a stupor. This had to be the incarnation of insanity's folly, and my last hope of ever finding Chaste was built on this madness?

I shook my head before glancing at the lone flyer propped on my dining table. Chaste's smiling face was staring back at me from somewhere unknown.

If any of this was true, it was suicide; actually after seeing the man before me, worse than suicide.

He believed so completely, his delusion so authentic; I feared that it was possible he would crack at any moment.

My decision was made; my mentally deranged visitor was going back to the small town of Sedona as soon as possible.

CHAPTER THIRTEEN

That next morning I had a new voice message on my cell phone.

I'd already placed the sack containing my guests filthy clothes in my Rover, looking for a peaceful way to let him know his vacation was over. The last thing I wanted was for him to fly into some delusional rage and harm himself.

I chose to listen to the message before breaking the news to Charles.

It was a moderately pleasant female voice from the FBI, requesting a call to a number in their Missing Children's Unit.

Almost seven months had passed since Chaste had disappeared without so much as a peep from any of the responsible agencies.

I swallowed hard. If it was good news they surely would have rolled up to my gate outside, announcing that they had found Chaste Ellen Schumacher, my daughter.

I switched on the television to a local news channel.

There was only the usual political unrest accompanied by the forlorn scorning brow of the newscaster, but not the rolling announcement of a child's recovery.

Of course not. Only bad news and bloodshed gets notoriety; something Chaste and I learned quickly before vowing never to watch it.

As soon as the television went silent, I was left with my hanging decision.

I wanted to call immediately; I didn't want to call at all.

The voice of fear screamed into my mind; they had found a young girl's body to be identified with directions to the morgue.

My fingers fumbled at the touchpad and dialed the number before I changed my mind again.

After several rings, a gentleman answered and I announced that I was returning their call.

Several clicks later, a familiar voice picked up.

It was Mr. FBI. I gritted my teeth, put on a pleasant voice.

"Dr. Schumacher, I was going through old case files and thought I'd give you a call. Have you had any more information about your daughter?"

Old case files indeed.

"Nothing…," was all I could force out from between my clenched teeth.

"I'm sorry to hear that. After we were pulled off the case, we had a few calls but they led nowhere."

"Pulled off the case? I don't understand."

My heart sank further.

"After forty-eight hours, only about three percent of all abduction cases end well. When there aren't any ransom demands, there's pretty much nothing we can do. Someone must have explained that to you."

I fully believed that someone, somewhere, was looking for my daughter. I felt the phone slide from my face, then pressed 'end call'.

Seven Months….

Was I a fool to believe Chaste Ellen Schumacher was still alive?

I walked downstairs, where Chuck was and slumped into a chair. Something inside me I can't quite place snapped like a dry twig. No tears fell, no pain…, only emptiness so black it engulfed my mind.

"Are you ready to start?" he asked.

"Yes, I'm ready."

I was in a fog for days before I realized that I had changed my mind and that 'Chuck' was running every ounce of fat off my body. Somehow I always managed to stay in good physical condition; boxed a little before I began pre-med, then gave up that silly notion. After all, what does a children's doctor need with the skills to pummel off someone's head? Then there was a little time on the rugby field when I was at University, but nothing like this.

Who, *whom*, was I kidding?

In the last six months, I'd graduated into a slug.

Chuck had me running before breakfast, running in the evening, then holding a ten-pound weight in each hand and jumping. Up and down, side to side like a madman on a pogo stick, to exhaustion. It was like training for an odd Olympic event.

Around fifteen days later, he announced that I was ready to begin the next phase of my training.

He had me purchase a tall cane pole and attach a long string with a ball tethered to the end.

Chuck found ways to make that ball hit me no matter how I moved aside, dodged, shifted, jumped, or ran.

For days we played this game until he became tired or slow and wasn't able to hit me as regular. It never occurred to me that my reflexes may be getting faster.

"You're ready for the next step."

I assured him I wasn't, but that didn't keep him from exchanging the ball for a heavy prickled pinecone.

"Watch it close and never take your eyes off it. Anticipate its move."

He whipped the cane and the spiny projectile hit me, stinging like hell.

"Again!"

My two Rottweiler guards were lying near the house watching with fixed anticipation, unabated by my torture.

Yet another swath nicked the side of my head and scraped my ear.

"That could have been my eye!"

What was this fool doing?

"If it was Pitre, it could have been your life."

The brevity of the situation unnerved me and my mind seemed to clear.

What if I was doing this for naught?

I heard the whip of the cane and ducked as the needled cone whizzed past my nose.

"You're not paying attention! Concentrate."

Again, the cane whipped and reversed, as the cone implanted its thorns on my posterior. That would leave a mark.

"Eyes on!"

CHAPTER FOURTEEN

Nearing the end of January, the weather was clear, crisp and cold. I was still a dog in training.

I didn't know which of us was more insane; Chuck for training me to pit my wits against a mythical creature, or me for believing his folly. I suppose grief will do strange things to the soul, because I no longer cared one way or the other. The strenuous activity seemed to anesthetize the pain lurking in my deadened heart.

"We go scouting today."

I didn't feel ready. My body may have been ready, but not my mind.

"I thought you said this creature only lives one place."

He smiled at me.

"We're going to practice with something else."

Bloody hell. He never smiled.

"Trap door spiders have a similar nest. We're going to go scouting for one and get your eyes trained on what to look for."

"Spiders? In the middle of winter?" I laughed. "Not likely."

"Trust me."

It seemed innocuous enough, looking for a spiders nest. I should have known better. It was a final test of my patience with my guest.

The day was sunny and warm near the southern border of the state and the shallow gullies soon became treacherous arroyos with various familiar trails of wild predators dipping in and out at irregular stations.

We struggled half the day getting Chuck down the rugged terrain to a place that he was happy with. Admittedly I'd swatted past a few brush-to-brush stringy webs and observed a few buzzing insects hovering around our heads; I was still doubtful.

We settled in a relatively warm sunny little hollow, profuse with scrubby conifers and cedars.

He sat down, winded, but that creepy smile was back.

"You only have one advantage over Pitre. He can only jump in a straight line. Wherever he's aimed, that's where he's going. You can't catch him with gloves, traps, mirrors, or any type of weapon. Remember that; he's half in and half out of this world. He can slip right through solid objects. So don't hide behind a tree, it won't protect you. You can't let him touch you."

We each picked a weathered boulder to sit on and Chuck began scanning the area. I saw nothing but stubble, sand and rocks. Although it was unusually warm where we were seated in the glaring southwest sun, I was still skeptical.

After only a few minutes, he pointed.

"There."

About twenty feet to my left was where he pointed his bony tanned finger. I saw absolutely nothing but leaves and pine needles.

"Fix your eyes on one spot at the edge of that shadow and don't blink."

My eyes began to burn immediately due to the dry air of the climate. I had to blink, once, twice.

"There, you see it?"

It could have been my imagination. A leaf and a few scraps of debris twitched. If I had blinked when it happened I would have missed it. It was lightning fast.

I nodded and he urged us closer.

We stopped and watched as once again, the ground twitched and settled.

Finally, we were only about four feet away.

A little leaf sized flap popped up and slapped back shut. Fast as the blinking of my eyelid.

Chuck was obviously elated at our good fortune.

"Good. These little guys will play with us all day."

He reached in his pocket and pulled out a handful of acorns.

"When he opens the door, you throw one of these inside the hole."

I laughed. I did it quietly.

"You think this is funny? You'd better get this down right or you're as good as dead already."

"It's not possible to get this in the hole. Did you notice how fast it opened and closed?"

"You're not paying attention."

I sat patiently watching as two more times the lid popped open and closed, catching yet another unwary something trespassing over its doorstep.

Then I saw it. Just an instant before the door sprang open; it twitched, ever so slightly, with the spider peeking out.

"Does Pitre do that?"

"Their habits are almost identical."

He took a long thin twig and scratched at the ground where an almost invisible string of web began to vibrate.

I took careful aim and watched for the spider to peek out the door. As soon as it twitched, I threw my acorn.

The door popped open, in went the acorn, and the door popped back shut.

"Beginners luck."

Chuck scoffed angrily at my successful first attempt.

A few moments later, I understood what Chuck meant when he said that these little spiders would play all day. The door popped open and out rolled the acorn, easy as that.

I laughed, despite myself.

Twice more I dropped the acorn in the hole and the spider returned it.

I don't know if it was overconfidence or just my luck changing, but it took another dozen tries to get my timing back down and get on the mark.

A couple of hours of this and I was fairly consistent and getting consistently bored, when Chuck grunted at me.

"Help me up."

He looked as if he was in pain.

"Our children are alive."

I could barely whisper as I stared at his trancelike state.

"Tell me where they are."

"I..., don't know. I can hear them calling, but that's all."

Was he delusional? Hearing wistful voices?

"When did this start happening?"

I wanted to shake him until his bones rattled, force him to speak to me.

"When I first called you. It's the reason I haven't given up. For both of us."

Could this be nothing more than a hallucination? A psychotic break? Schizophrenia caused by his multiple losses?

If so, then I was not far behind him.

I had to almost carry him back to my Range Rover in silence. He offered no more conversation, as if he wished to retract his voluntary burst of information.

CHAPTER FIFTEEN

The first part of our drive back home was silent.

I began to consider my final destination. I saw the results of this old man's journey with Pitre. Yes, I had resolved to myself that Pitre was a real creature of some sort, yet hardly the supernatural beast Chuck portrayed.

If the vile poison could manifest the voice of my child through some strange metaphysical aberration, then I was willing to succumb to its torture. If it would only lead me to her location.

"Tell me. What should I expect if I succeed?"

I thought he had fallen asleep, his eyes drooped and closed.

"You'll have every resource you need to find your daughter."

I was terrified, yet hopeful, then terrified again.

"Will..., that happen to me?"

I pointed at his withered leg.

"Only if you don't succeed, but you're young, strong."

Why didn't I feel young and strong? It wasn't a physical thing.

"You'll be able to see into the spirit world. Other people, places, and things will be visible to you that you didn't know existed."

He was starting to repeat himself almost verbatim and my internal warning lights went ablaze once again.

Then it hit me. I understood plainly, clearly.

"That's the reason you called me. It wasn't to find my daughter; it was so I could find your son, Steven."

He looked as if I'd slapped him.

"Yes. But that's not entirely true. Somehow, they're linked

together. If you find one, you'll find the other."

"Tell me, tell me the truth. Are they okay?"

The torture of not knowing was crushing. Even a delusion of her life, of her existence, was better than the void I'd endured.

"I only know that they are both alive and that they are not terribly far away. Their voice is faint, but there. You wonder about my sanity. So do I. What if every day when you woke up, you heard your daughter's voice calling you, asking for your help? I hear my son's voice..., but not every day like I used to. He's giving up hope of ever being found.

"Then last June, as Steven's voice was fading, I began to hear another faint voice, a girl. She was repeating the same verse over and over in her head.

"My name is Chaste Schumacher, I live at Number 9 Deer Run, and I'm eight years old."

There was more he wasn't telling me. I didn't need to have a mythical creatures poison in my blood to tell that. I wanted him to take me to this undocumented creature, to begin the process, right that instant.

"Someone's trying to brainwash my daughter into believing she's someone else?"

We pulled in my drive, past my gate and he grabbed my arm.

"The important thing is..., they are alive."

There was something in his voice betraying him, I could feel it, but not tell what it was.

If my anxiety level had tapered off, it was now running at full power. If subconsciously I had begun to accept that I might never see Chaste again, it was quelled. I was sold, led to the abyss, and ready to jump into the darkness below.

I found gold foil, Christmas wrapping that was on sale, and rolled it to the size I would need to drop into the home of this creature. It was a complete leap of faith that Pitre even existed. I was taking the word of a homeless person with some strange insight beyond my comprehension.

I believe that the expression is 'putting all of ones eggs into a single basket'.

We practiced another day, going over every detail in endless repetition.

"I'll go with you to where I had my encounter with Pitre; but I can't walk the distances you'll have to go. I will be waiting for you to come back. I'll know if you succeeded."

I was thankful that he didn't add '…or failed' to the end of his promise.

Once again, I loaded up the Rover for a week's journey, with supplies for a camp in the wilderness. The weather had turned foul, but Chuck reassured me where we were going would be a different climate.

We headed east on Interstate 10, and drove for an eternity in desolation until he urged me to exit somewhere in southern New Mexico. Our journey turned due north through Silver City.

I assumed that the next road was under construction, but there were no signs indicating so. Near sunset, we crawled into a little town named Piños Altos, if town is what you would call it. Community was better; ghost town was more precise.

We drove past a weathered old mission with its foundation built high on native stone, and bricks for sides that were missing half their plaster. A sign indicated it was erected in 1898.

I suppose it was a miracle it was there at all.

The sparse houses were dark, crudely fenced, and looked unoccupied. Strangely, the streets were empty, not a soul walking from origin to destination, and why would they? The town spoke of abandonment.

I wondered what oddities the log cabin trading post had hidden in behind its shadowed plank porch or the tales it could tell.

The town looked as barren as Hannah. That was befitting; it was no place for children.

Glad to be rid of that curse, we forged on northward, up narrow dirt and rock trails, past old silver mining hovels with chunks of pink granite in large stacks of abandonment.

Chuck seemed to know little tidbits of information about the area and as an afterthought would blurt a would-be tour guide comment.

I, however, barely noticed the scenery had improved before Chuck announced that we were now between the Mogollon and Black mountain ranges. Signs started to appear announcing the Gila National Forest and some notable cliff dwellings.

Instead, we took a steep unmarked road, I daresay was off limits to anyone except the National Forestry Service, when finally my guest motioned to stop.

He pointed westward toward the silhouette of a hill in the not too far distance.

"That's where you'll be headed, sunrise tomorrow."

I assumed that meant we would be camping out here in the middle of nowhere, on the face of a heavily forested canyon. At least we were well equipped.

The doctor still residing in me was glad that I had packed along some medicinal bare necessities. I wondered if I would be capable of the rational thought necessary to apply them, should the event arise. My deeper fear was that I would somehow fair worse than my ninety pound, twisted and maimed companion.

Once again, glimpses of sanity yanked at me, begging me to reconsider my folly. That was before night fell and I drifted into an almost catatonic sleep.

That night my dreams forced me awake on several occasions, as if someone or something knew I was there and was either trying to frighten me away, or size up its enemy.

An hour or so before daylight when I had endured the last hallucinations my mind could suffer, I dug out of my sleeping bag. The coals of the campfire were still glowing red, pulsing with a chill night wind across our fire pit. I threw on a few more sap-caked sticks, enjoying the heady resinous fragrance as they popped and began to burn.

"He's here you know."

Something, some unspeakable presence was here, without any doubt.

"Yes, and I'm already exhausted from my dreams."

My waking friend lay still, buried in his cover.

"Try and sleep a little more. You're going to need every ounce of your strength."

I put a water pot beside the coals for tea and began to listen to the morning noises around us. It was then I began to understand more about my adversary; for the creature Pitre was not my enemy - It was a means to an end.

Terror settled into my bones; the entity I had been training to joust was suddenly real; real beyond my illustrious trainer's repetitious commentary. Somehow, I'd postponed that reality to a future date and ignored my self-administered blindfold in hopes of seeing Chaste once again.

I had no desire to remain affixed to this life with our..., with my..., only child missing and in the hands of some unknown deviant mind. Without Chaste, I had no desire or reason to remain in this realm.

Pitre seemed to know this, to know my resolve, to know my determination and was already weakening me; turning my adrenaline against me and burning me out.

I sat staring at the leaping flames in the quiet twilight until the water boiled over and hissed.

Already I had fallen into some kind of trance and that hissing was some unknown creature jumping at my face.

My new instincts latched onto my body and threw me into a roll on the stony ground, leaving me kneeling and wild-eyed, searching for movement.

Chuck was now sitting up, looking like a bent pretzel in his mummy bag.

"Fix your tea. It's almost time for you to get started. You're going to need all the daylight you can get."

I opted for the American alternative of strong black coffee, which seemed to please my companion.

The sun was only a quarter hour away from poking its face over the hill to the east when Chuck handed me a bag of mixed nuts and dried fruits with some maternal unction that I eat them along the way.

"Don't lose sight of that tallest pine with the scars at the top and you won't get lost. He'll be surrounded by some type of thicket and most likely the burrow will be at the edge of a clearing."

I nodded and shifted my backpack up a little higher.

"Remember everything I've told you. Both our kids are depending on you."

CHAPTER SIXTEEN

Despite the cold air down in the valley, my forehead was beading with perspiration as the shadowy trail decidedly took an upward turn. From where I stood, there was no tallest pine; there were clusters of tall pines in every direction.

There were no immediate signs of wildlife, no trails, only the incessant chirping of several species of native birds. With the morning sun over the eastern ridge and climbing higher in the sky, I couldn't seem to get my bearings. There was only the steep incline to guide me.

I could tell in an instant why my sleep had been so important to disrupt. Two minutes of sharp uphill trek and my legs were already turning to rubber. I sat humbly on the ground and dug out the bag of fodder Chuck had shoved into my hands, along with a cold bottle of water.

How I desperately wanted to lie back and take a quick nap.

There was a rustling near the bottom of a draw and I watched a stocky whitetail buck busy scrubbing at a tree with this season's antler rack. He would have made any hunter proud if only to claim sighting such a perfect specimen.

A bird screeched some unknown terror far up the hill over my shoulder and the deer jerked his head erect, then bolted off into the shadows and brush. I suppose his wary nature was the reason he was still alive and in good health.

It made me wonder if I was lacking that same good sense of self-preservation as I focused my attention back to the top of the same hill.

Chuck was right, the odd mix of food and water had rejuvenated me as I began my ascent once again.

The hour it took to catch sight of the tallest scarred pine came with mixed blessings. It not only told me I was close to my destination, but held that foreboding of something unknown and evil awaiting me.

This Pitre, this creature, wasn't one to be easily trifled with. I had seen the evidence in the body of the one that had done his best to train me and describe what was to come, what was to be endured. His own twisted and dried leg, his diminished body, was more conclusive evidence that whatever awaited me was real and that he had drastically underestimated it.

Or had he? What if he had been taught the same way, with his Indian friend, and his bitter outcome was not hinged on that training, but on...?

I instantly stopped that convention of thought. Was I defeating myself before meeting the creature, already assuring myself of defeat? What if this demonic mythical creature was manipulating my thoughts outside of the dreamscape I had experienced last night? I wanted no more of that!

I started counting my cadence up the loose rock and debris, zigzagging up the steep incline, forcing my mind on the taste of the crunchy food and the raucous chirps of the birds in this area; surely a birdwatchers paradise.

The bramble of fallen limbs ahead was most likely the evidence of some storm and it took a few minutes to see a possible way around. That new route quickly proved an impasse and I moved in a lateral direction looking for another passage upwards, until I remembered what Chuck had told me.

Was this Pitre's outer wall of defense?

Totally absurd! The tiny creature described to me wasn't capable of the strength necessary to move and stack limbs larger than my thigh. The fallen wall of limbs was only about six feet high and I decided to climb over the top of it to prove my theory and press on.

At the top of the dam of limbs, I was rewarded with a heavy layer of thorny vines. I was thankful that the local snakes were in a state of hibernation. The last thing I wanted was a timber rattler flashing its square jaw up out of the tangle to latch onto one of my limbs. My only retreat would be a clumsy backwards dash through treacherous dried limbs and thorns.

If there was any chance at stealth before reaching my vantage point, it was now long gone. This was surely my destination.

I have to admit that my reason for perching atop this hillock of brush wasn't just to rest or try and see my quarry's den. I was petrified.

The fallen tree limbs and brush formed a circular pseudo coliseum with a bare earth center wide enough to allow the sun to remove the gloom of the surrounding tall pines. It looked as if a bulldozer had worked hours to design the smooth thirty foot clearing.

My appetite for trail fodder was gone and my mouth already dry as I slipped out of my backpack.

Moments later I heard another rampant bird shrill an alarm, chattering away at the edge of the clearing not fifty feet in the distance. I had already grown tired of the incessant noise from this nuisance and quickly chose a stick to throw at it so I could hear more clearly. That would have been a huge mistake, my last mistake, a death knell and end of my journey. Fate shrugged for only a moment and before I could swing my projectile in the bird's direction, there was a deafening snap of the air and the bird disappeared before my eyes. Then there was a god-awful silence.

My ears ringing, I remained frozen in my squatted perch, looking for evidence that I had missed the birds retreating flight.

I did not.

The stick slowly slid from my fingers back into the mass thicket below me and I listened, barely breathing.

Moments later, I suppose as an afterthought, the birds head ejected from some spot on the ground a few feet from where it had disappeared. The head spat out, arching through the air a good ten or fifteen feet and rolled to a stop next to at least another half dozen others like it.

I sucked in a breath and froze, staring at the birds head and its predecessors, their eyes gazing blindly at the late winter sun.

It appeared that my noble adversary was carnivorous with a distinct liking for the local birds.

Bloody hell.

That would have been nice to know, even as an afterthought.

What else hadn't I been told?

Then I saw it. It was the flicker of needles and debris on the ground. The trap door was as big as an old mans toupee. The hole was much larger than I expected; larger than I had been led to believe.

While contemplating my next steps, the flap quivered and out popped a few bluish gray feathers with a puff.

I was about to move closer to get a better look when another bird, most likely the previous one's mate flittered to the ground at least four feet away from the hole. It began dancing in a circle on the bare earth, chirping, as if protesting the death of its missing partner.

I assumed that it would eventually get brave enough to dance just in front of the trap door and it too would become brunch for Pitre.

That fallacy was momentarily dispensed as well. This rather dully colored bird, I assume the female of the species, was five to seven feet from the lair of Pitre when the air cracked like a fine leather whip and this bird too disappeared into an invisible throat in the ground.

I had spent the last several days comfortably two feet away from the hole of a trapdoor spider, confidently dropping acorns into a marble sized hole; playing catch with a sub-miniature version of this freak of nature.

Charles, Chuck, or whoever he was, was a liar. Of that much I was certain.

The backpack was full of golf ball and tennis ball sized rolls of golden foil. I would have to resize them to just larger than a small melon and be as experienced and accurate as a knife throwing Carney.

There I sat, most uncomfortably, for another hour waiting for the next sacrificial bird to come and dance for Pitre and become an afternoon meal, when I realized that I still hadn't glimpsed my adversary.

If I'd had accurate reconnaissance I would have better prepared myself, maybe brought a metal shield for this bastard to bounce off of as it lunged for my vitals. If I believed my trainer, a shield wouldn't work. Still, it would be better than nothing, which is what I had.

Then my anger began building as I understood the truth. If I had been told the truth, I wouldn't have walked up this hill.

It was obvious that I had been wearing my grief-goggles, missing my precious daughter Chaste, and my deceased wife.

Acting on the only knowledge I had, I crept around behind the trap door, assuming the door opened only one way, which was into the clearing. This assumption would be the first one to save my life.

As soon as I had perched myself some ten feet behind this little monster, the door jostled slightly, similar to the trapdoor spider. Pitre knew I was there, without a doubt.

If it had met me in my dreams last night, trying to ward me off, it must have fears also. What could something so fast and fierce possibly be afraid of concerning me?

This would take some thought, but as soon as the flap opened fully, I knew it would have to be an afterthought; if I survived Pitre.

Up and out popped a little bugger about the size of a guinea pig that looked like a fat hairless rat. It was pale pink with mottled gray stripes; a perfect camouflage for its surroundings. Six legs, the front four small and bisected similar to an arachnid, the back two legs were large and muscular. My observations were interrupted just as I got a perfect up close view of two wide pincers, inches from my neck and the resounding sound of air crackling in my ears. I fell flat of my rear in an unmanly backwards shuffle.

At once, the terrible beauty of its amethyst colored eyes focused on nothing but me.

One thing Chuck said was factual. Pitre could only jump in a straight line, but he neglected to tell me that Pitre had a leash. This wasn't some apparent physical attachment, but rather some invisible length it could reach before snapping into reverse. Pitre had an invisible bungee cord attached to the rear of his fat little butt. I forced back a laugh of relief.

This could be propitious in my attempts to avoid feeling the crunch of those snapping pincers into my jugular.

Then I remembered the whole of the matter; why I was here and what I had to do.

I laughed, I sat where I had fallen and guffawed at the thought of how ridiculous this little killer was with an elastic hook anchored in his arse.

At once, I realized that another item of instruction was correct. Pitre did not like laughter, or to be laughed at.

Maybe Pitre wasn't as learned as Chuck or his Native American

Indian teacher believed. The birds which I'd witnessed, came and chattered and met an untimely end. Maybe their noise was perceived as that same cackling of laughter that annoyed Pitre.

Maybe I was stupid. My laughter was obviously perceived as a direct challenge and Pitre squared off at me, digging his back feet into the stony ground. I was about to see the wrath of Pitre once again.

I jumped up from the ground as quickly as I could and picked my right side to jump toward when he lunged at me.

The air cracked and the side of my neck stung in a hazed instant. There was Pitre parked smugly on the ground, wiping his face with his front legs.

Immediately, he crouched for his next lunge.

Holy hell. There was no warning, there was no time to jump and roll to the left or right; he was barely a blur in my vision just before he retracted. This little monster was avoidable only by his invisible leash.

My training was spit.

It was a hazy reflection that had me feel my neck to find that I was bleeding, just a tinge, but bleeding nevertheless.

He must have really been pissed to stretch his leash and graze my neck. I instantly felt my neck again to test a theory. The little scratch was the skin just over that precious blood carrying vessel in my neck at the least protected point above my jugular. If nothing else, Pitre was a skilled perfectionist.

I backed up about twelve more inches and laughed once more, taunting my foe.

Surprisingly, Pitre relaxed his back legs and squatted.

Maybe it wasn't the laugh after all?

I would at least try a taunt, but admittedly felt a little foolish at first.

"You stupid little…, fat hairless pig!"

Instantly, the muscles tensed and launched with a hiss, his pincers missing me by mere inches, further stretching the invisible harness.

I laughed and he ignored it again.

Another imbecilic idea crossed through my peanut sized cranium.

I backed up yet another six inches.

"Stupid little bird eater!"

Just as soon as I finished my phrase I spat into the air.

Rabid, visible anger and snapping fury flew at my face.

Missing me once again by a thin film of air, Pitre landed back where he began, hissing, murmuring, chattering, and wiggling in a futile attempt to remove my spittle.

He shuffled dust on his body and readied another attack.

I forced and worked up spit in the side of my mouth, thinking of my next volley.

"Filthy rodent!"

I spat for all I was worth just as I heard the loud snap of air and his pincers click in front of me.

Words cannot express the violence as the little bird-murderer rolled, hissed, and made more chattering, murmuring sounds in the dirt.

My next thought was actually rational. Was I insane?

I didn't have time to continue that train of nonsense, before Pitre straightened up, dirt sticking to his slick little body where my spittle and dust mixed.

In an awkward attempt at catching me off guard, he dug in and shot toward me, catching another mostly dry spray of my spittle. I was quickly running out of spit ammunition.

Pitre turned and crawled straight back into his lair making the same loud hissing, guttural noises.

Had I failed? Was this the end of our confrontation?

I waited and finally there was silence.

I was angry at myself for not doing more to provoke my nemesis. Now would I have to start all over again?

One careful step forward gave me very little vantage and the disappointment hit me. After all the time spent with my delirious trainer, could I have thrown away my one chance. Would I have to retreat in defeat or risk death by digging into the burrow with my bare hands. It was then I remembered that there was a folding spade in my belongings.

I turned to go back to my backpack when the trapdoor flew open from my direction and I barely missed yet another bursting attack.

Then feeling a sudden draft of air, realized that my flannel shirt was torn and my shoulder was bleeding. He had extended his attack almost two more feet.

What if I'd hesitated for another moment and I'd been those two steps closer to my enemy?

"Fat little spider!"

I was truly angry with my threat; ready to swing a fist at his next blinding attack.

He did not pursue, did not launch, but retreated backwards out of the shadows into the clearing, into the sunlight.

He began to shuffle in the dust. It reminded me of the hens kept by some of the African natives, taking a dust bath.

"Lice bag!"

I screamed it. It did little good to assuage the strange commotion or dance the oddity was performing.

At least I knew my volley with the creature Pitre was not over.

CHAPTER SEVENTEEN

Something peculiar was happening. The creature before me was obscured by a sudden cloud of dust. Chuck had forewarned me of this but my immediate competition with Pitre had dampened my memory. It was almost my immediate undoing.

Pitre continued to shuffle in the dirt, throwing dust in the air, making it almost impossible to see his fat hairless little body.

The dust ball became larger and larger and I looked for some way to retreat, but there was an immovable coliseum of timber fencing us in. My foolishness had placed me inside a larger trap, much bigger than the little hole in the ground. I was taken off guard as I considered that this could possibly be the main event.

Dust filled the air and then it became quiet; I could see nothing through the cloud. The slow mountain breeze finally cleared the air and I beheld the real Pitre.

I felt my bowels loosen and I clenched with fear.

No longer was I confronted by the small freakish guinea spider hybrid with its bright amethyst eyes.

A hairless brindle colored creature as big as a wolf was now glaring at me with huge eyes the color of blood rubies.

A totally different foe from what I expected.

The two front legs had scaled human-like hands, the back four were muscular armored protrusions, in fact he was an oddly collected contraption of mobility that made no sense whatsoever.

But that wasn't what I was focused on when he looked up at me with relished hatred in his eyes.

Pitre hissed loudly, twisted behind himself with a pincer-like motion and with a loud clip, loosed himself from his invisible tether. The outline of his body was like a wisp of smoke; something not entirely of this world; half here and half in hell.

I wanted to run in terror but couldn't convince my feet to move.

From behind him lifted a fat segmented scorpion like appendage with a single three-inch long black thorn hovering toward its intended target…, Kress Schumacher.

I knew what I had to do, what I was supposed to do, but my mind had lost all coherence. My eyes refused to look away from this atrocity to plot a route of escape. Oh how I wanted to run.

The little monster was gone and a full-fledged demon had set himself against me.

I did the only thing I knew to do, I prayed.

Prayed that I was doing the right thing, prayed that I could endure what was to come, then as reality seeped in I prayed that death would be quick.

Pitre hissed at me.

"Stupid Englishman."

It began to circle me like an amused spectator.

"You…, you…, can talk?" I stammered.

It took a few cautious steps to my side and I understood that it wanted to force me into the center of his choice battleground.

"What did you expect Englishman?"

The hissing speech was clear and concise, nothing I could have expected from a mindless predator.

I was dumbfounded and remained silent.

This was surely a demon from the pits of hell.

Pitre continued to force me into the clearing as I backed away, looking for a stick or rock, anything to hurl in defense.

The creature shook all over as it chuckled and backed up, mocking me. The huge ruby eyes squinted knowingly at me, as if looking at his next meal. It was going to let me go; not something it said, but something I knew.

It was then I remembered once again why I was standing here in the middle of this clearing. I remembered my daughter Chaste, remembered my vow to my deceased wife to protect our daughter with my life.

"Vile creature!"

It came out before I could stop it from my lips.

Instead of being offended, Pitre bowed and nodded his rounded head in a garish display of megalomania, showing a row of sharp jagged teeth in a mock smile. I thought I heard a slight noxious chuckle.

"How sad. A creature such as yourself reduced to hiding in a hole and eating birds."

Pitre laughed at my satire, hissing through his knotted teeth, then exchanged an equitable curse at me.

"A creature such as yourself coming to beg of me is even lower. Just imagine if Elizabeth could see you now."

It was a slap in the face and I lurched forward, causing Pitre to raise that black spike in a high quivering arch over his back.

"You know nothing of Elizabeth," I spat.

My obvious lie was still hanging in the air when he laughed again, lowering his tail. He obviously knew my wife's name.

"I know everything. I know you failed her, failed your daughter, that you are a failure, like all the others living on this miserable ball of dirt. Go home Englishman. Live out your pitiful useless life."

I was the one supposed to be infuriating him, but he was the one berating me! Then I thought I understood something. Maybe it was a cursing contest. I tested my theory....

"And look what you do with all that knowledge; you hide in the ground like a groveling worm."

His evil thorned lusus arched again slowly and his blood red eyes blinked once, twice, thinking.

"You thought that you would come to me and I would simply tell you where your pathetic child is? Ha! What could she possibly mean to me?"

Somehow without my seeing, he was inches closer to me now. He hadn't been contemplating his retort; he'd been listening to my heart's quest. His execration couldn't have hurt any worse if his stinger had plunged into my heart.

I couldn't find immediate fuel to retaliate.

"And you have no children, you have nothing but yourself, all alone, a pathetic excuse for an existence. What is a stupid Pitre anyway?"

I spat on the ground.

There was no way to have expected it, no way to have prevented it. I didn't know how much this demon revered his own name.

I fell to the ground just as the stinger extracted itself from my right thigh in a blur of motion. I never saw him move towards me. My breath evaporated in a whisper, there was no time for a scream of pain. My diaphragm wilted.

I imagined death as a friend come to take me away as shimmering wisps of images surrounded us, fading in and out.

Pitre chuckled, glowering in his victory.

"Hmm, interesting. So you thought you would come and torment me? Useless... arrogant... human."

I stood back up on my left leg, my right leg was useless, a limp dead thing; I hid it as best I could.

I laughed; it was weak, but better than nothing, then dusted myself as casually as possible.

"Now I see why you live your life in a hole, Oh powerful Pitre!"

I spat nastily on the ground.

I nearly lost consciousness when I saw the black thorn blaze in and out of my left thigh.

Once again, dark silhouette's danced before my vision, blotches in my failing mind.

I couldn't fight this creature, then I remembered I wasn't supposed to. I was to cajole it, force it to attack me. It was ludicrous, frightful insanity. It was also my last and only hope.

I can't explain what held me up. As a physician, I would have to guess a constriction of muscles or even a strange rigor mortis in my legs as a result of powerful venom.

By whatever miracle, it worked to agitate my opponent without my uttering another word.

A third advance and flash of his hideous stinger impaled my right arm near the shoulder and he circled me, inching around, looking to fell his adversary, yet somehow by the grace of God, I stood.

I was speechless, my spirit to continue gone, ready to end my protracted confrontation.

My heart palpitated suddenly, beating heavily, thrusting slowly, laboring in my chest.

Whatever poison was in Pitre's appendage was beginning to do its work, causing my voice to slur. It was then I knew I had only seconds before all would be lost and my journey would end where I stood.

"Oh great and mighty Pitre. Why would I come to you for anything but to pity you?"

I spat dry spittle. It was only a noise in my mind.

My left arm burned with the blinding fire of hell and also went limp, mimicking my right as he impaled it with a fourth sting. I bit my tongue from the force of the impact and it began to bleed.

'Four..., four', I repeated in my mind.

Pitre finished his survey and now crouched in front of me, watching what was left of me drift in and out of consciousness. It was as if I was in the past and present at the same time, reliving old events, some exotic dream world.

Then I heard it..., a faint whisper in my mind.

"My name is Chaste Schumacher, I live at Number 9 Deer Run, I'm nine years old."

Not eight years old..., but nine years old.

I smiled and my heart heaved in revival. I laughed in ecstasy until tears forged a muddy trail down to my chin. Blood drooled down the side of my open mouth. I'm sure I was hideous to behold. I had heard my precious daughter's voice from somewhere not inside me.

"Thank you, oh gracious Pitre, King of earthworms! Hail to the kingdom of dirt!"

I spat hard as I could. Blood and saliva splattered his direction in a spray.

Five and Six came so well aimed and quick into both my hips, the force alone finally pummeled me to the ground.

My scream was choked away with bilious fluid and I gasped to breathe. The rest is so much a blur I cannot vouch as to the authenticity. I remember talking to Elizabeth, reliving our vows, her tender touch. Then the voice of our daughter laughing at some undeserving joke told around our dinner table.

One vision faded away and the other became clear again.

When I saw Pitre next, he was glaring at me, inches from my face, with a tooth-filled grin.

He hissed at me as his voice roiled the air with hubris.

"You failed..., again. Go join your Elizabeth, stupid human."

I was flat on my chest with my face turned toward his, my cheek in the dirt, failed, undeniably dying.

"Pitre...."

It was barely a whisper that blew dust in the air.

I spat what must have been a mixture of blood, bile, and dust in his sparkling red eyes.

I saw the rage in those eyes; I saw things too terrible to write in their glare, as he lifted his quivering thorn for the last and seventh perfect time.

It fell into my head with the thrust of a sledgehammer....

I heard insane laughter echoing around me. I heard what sounded like the hissing and clicking that Pitre might have made, scrambling around me in a circle.

I believed he was rejoicing over my demise, my death, my obliteration.

My limbs twisted and constricted, contorted in pain. I knew it was too late to pray for death before the pain that was to come; I was bound to pass through this portal and it was a one way ticket.

I faded into the realm of the dead.

As I spilled from the world of pain and mortality, I seemed to be standing above my limp and dying body, above what was happening. Then I drifted even higher, watching from another floating perspective. There was a host of tall dark creatures standing in a massive circle around us, all laughing and jeering, not at me, not at the pathetic human as I'd supposed, but at Pitre.

"Pitre the mighty has fallen," they chanted as one in a repetitious chorus.

My blurred visage of Pitre saw him flitting from one spectre to the next, flashing his useless, deflated stinger at each one.

Each one was pointing, each one debasing him.

"Pitre has fallen, he's failed; fly away Pitre."

Finally, he shrank into the little creature I first met and crawled feebly, as if wounded, back to his burrow in the ground.

Too many things transpired for me to recall them all, but I remember seeing other worlds, some heavenly, some hellish, some peacefully rejoicing, some violently screaming. I was warned never to speak of them, yet..., how could I?

How do you explain something there is no vocabulary for? With no common frame of reference, could an amoeba understand the culmination of universe around it? Of course not, even something as simple as an emotion would be an impossibility to explain.

Finally, I swam back to this earthly plane of existence, the present, viewing other places or times. Creatures of a multitude in diversity, hidden in shadow, were walking among the living. Some followed and huddled around people whispering in their ears, turning them like a horse at the bit. Other grinning creatures impossibly too large to bear in life were riding upon the shoulders of many people, weighing them down.

Dark winged creatures stood motionless observing, pointing and directing those lesser.

I recall one other notable spectacle; some people were glowing with white, these people or beings, all the other malcontents avoided with a wide berth.

It was as if Dante's revelation of Hell was turned upside down and sifted upon the living.

I wished not to witness any more of the vile and corrupt interactions and immediately I was in a different place.

It was quiet and I floated, slept, healed, and finally passed through a magnificent open gate, after which, I awakened.

CHAPTER EIGHTEEN

When my dried and dirt caked eyes scratched open, I was still lying face down in Pitre's mock arena. There was no dark host of creatures lining up to inspect me, no hairless piggish Pitre to torment me. Only a faint cool breeze twitched a sprig of my hair in my eye as I tried to blink it away.

I felt as if I had awakened from a long journey and began to remember most of what had transpired. I also remembered that there was someone still waiting for me back through the distant valley and up the next rise.

How long had I been here? Days? Weeks? It was impossible to tell. The sun was up, it was early, and the ground was crisply cold.

I sat slowly with a shiver, my body aching and stiff. The thought of inspecting my body terrified me. After the last thing I had felt, I pictured all my limbs in grotesque contortions, mangled, and unusable.

There was no use in putting off the inevitable as I rose to a seated position on the ground. My arms and legs seemed to have strength to them, although I was a bit wobbly.

I closed my eyes and inspected each arm slowly, carefully, and felt strong firm meat on their bones. My legs were next, one at a time, from thigh to ankle, with nothing out of the ordinary to report other than large swollen mounds the size of teacups where I had been impaled with that enormous black demonic thorn.

I cautiously stood, testing every movement, every feeling, everything.

Was my confrontation a dream? Had some strange and exotic drug induced me into the nightmarish dream of what transpired? It would have been a simple thing for Chuck to put something in the bag of fruits and nuts.

The painful bruises on my body were definitely not a dream.

Chuck, Charles..., that wasn't his name.

I heard it first in a whisper, then louder, clearer..., Thomas.

How could I know that?

I wondered aloud, "Is this death? Am I dead?"

I heard a noise behind me and turned.

A tall slim faceless creature of a man in wispy white clothing stood motionless, as if waiting.

Before I could speak it whispered, "There is time, you must go."

Instead of asking the obvious, who and what are you, I had to ask, "Go where?"

It extended a pale-skinned hand toward me.

Too terrified to run, I resigned my fate and took it.

I was instantly standing beside my green Range Rover, looking at a sleeping Chuck..., no..., Thomas.

I looked for my helper to utter a thank you, but the creature was gone.

Instead, a vision of Chaste flooded my mind, overtaking my senses. I was seeing through her eyes. She was rubbing her wrist.... I knew where she was. My breath left me.

It was as if I had been there a dozen times. Happy water spouted from my eyes like a fountain.

I rushed to Thomas and shook him awake, ready to decamp.

"Get up. We have to go..., now."

He sat groggily as if from a deep trancelike sleep.

"What are you doing here? You were supposed to go face Pitre! The whole day is wasted."

He was delusional and I was tired of his nonsense.

"What are you talking about?"

"I just watched you disappear through the brush, so I lay back down. Now you won't have time to get to the top of the hill before late afternoon."

"I don't have time to argue with you. I've already been there, Thomas."

He sputtered and stared at me.

"Who gave you that name?"

I ignored his question and hurried for my cell phone in the front seat of my auto. My fingers tapped furiously at the touch screen. It was the same morning that I had trudged down the hillside, while begrudging my nightmare riddled sleep. The same day I had climbed over the barrier and confronted Pitre. But the time was only ten a.m., about the time I stopped and watched the buck scraping at his antlers.

It was…, not possible.

Even my time had been given back to me and in an instant, I knew that gift was for a dire reason.

Fueled with an inner fire, I hurriedly began stowing and repacking our campsite, thrusting it askew into the back cargo area of the Rover with exigent need.

Thomas seemed too dumbfounded to do anything more than stare at my frantic attempts to load everything at once.

"You met Pitre?"

I felt it was a rhetorical question and only glanced his direction as my sore arms and legs heaved the ice chest into place and closed the rear cargo door. Despite the pain I was surprised at what little effort it took.

"Do you need me to help you get in the Rover?" I murmured, as I kicked dirt over the smoldering ash of our fire pit.

"Not until you tell me what happened…."

I couldn't explain, there wasn't time. I shook my head and walked to the driver side door and got in, then slapped the key into the ignition.

It wasn't until I cranked the vehicle and backed it up that he began his feeble trek to get inside. I guess he finally understood that I was going to leave him on top of that deserted hill if he didn't put forth some effort.

My experience was life altering, mind altering, a glimpse into a reality never meant for humans to envision. With my obsessive recollections of a secret world around us, there was the constant reminder that there was something I wasn't supposed to speak of, even though it was a fog.

My companion and I barely said more than a few sentences to each other until we reached Interstate 10 and headed due east. That was when Thomas began some sort of ill-fated rant.

"Why are we leaving? Why did you give up your only chance?"

His very words, his voice grated on me. I wanted desperately to tell him about the grey mist attached to his body, which might be the cause of his emaciated condition. I could not. I only knew it was something evil, possibly one of the evils fading from my memory. How could I tell him without offering some type of solution?

Thomas was twisting uncomfortably in his seat, waiting impatiently for my reply to his inane questions.

"I met Pitre. He was nothing like what you prepared me for. You lied to me."

He actually seemed stunned.

"I told you what you needed to hear to get you up there."

I waited for yet another lie in the sudden hushed silence....

"You met him? You faced him? Why didn't you do what I told you? You need to go back."

I heard the desperation in his voice, but I also heard something else I couldn't place my finger on.

"Thomas, I did. It's over."

"You're a liar! You ran away didn't you? You coward."

What happened to his smug self-assured mind reading? Why couldn't he tell I was being truthful?

I forced the Range Rover to the shoulder of the Interstate and parked as a drove of traffic blurred past us. After a half-second argument with myself whether or not to oust him onto the side of the road, I ripped open my already torn shirt and showed him the enormous distended whelp on my right arm near my shoulder where a three-inch thorny stinger had slammed mercilessly into my flesh.

"All seven."

"It's not possible...."

His voice was barely a whisper, diminished, and it sounded angry.

"Now who's the liar, Thomas?"

I put the vehicle in gear and merged back into the stream of traffic on the Interstate, while fixing my tattered shirtsleeve. I dragged a cloth from under my seat and wiped the crusting blood from my chin and neck.

Then I understood a little more about the mysterious Thomas.

He was actually angry that I had survived the encounter, jealous was a better word. He expected me to drag back to camp eight or nine days later, half-dead, and a wisp of my former self.

That was only if I had survived.

Thomas was bitter......at me, and himself.

I heard an angelic beacon again, louder, stronger. My daughter Chaste was mourning the loss of some tiny trinket. Something she had been hiding that helped her focus on home and her life from almost eight months ago. Her despair was sickening. I prayed to God to send her hope and let her know I was on my way.

Steven, Thomas' son, was either silent or I wasn't able to hear his voice. I couldn't tell this to Thomas, but I considered that he already knew something was wrong. Maybe it was part of what he was trying to hide from me. I couldn't bear to feel his despair deepen any further.

My mind may have been exhausted, but I was somehow running on pure adrenaline. I had to make several stops along the way, to get out of the Rover, walk away from the highway to listen and build my hope. My daughter's voice was strong now; my baby was alive.

I danced like a fool in the desert for the passing cars. Chaste Ellen Schumacher is alive!

It was near dark when we reached El Paso, Texas and the sea of amber lights was unforgettable.

There were no decent hotels available and we settled into one that had me on edge for most of the night.

The dreams came and went, but were more viscous, thick with emotions and colors I could both smell and taste.

I heard gunshots at one point near daybreak, rolled out of bed, and got dressed.

Thomas was still snoring softly in his bed; the floor was too filthy even for his raw tastes.

Restless, I walked across the street in the predawn to get breakfast from the internationally recognized golden arches. The sounds of traffic on the nearby Interstate and side streets were already an incessant roaring behemoth.

A group of locals in hooded sweatshirts were huddled just outside the restaurant in the chill air, watching every move of every patron coming and going through the front entrance.

Suddenly, I saw it.

Hovering behind the malingerers was something from my visions, but I forced myself to keep walking. The grey creature was at least eight feet tall and slim as a utility pole; steady, stolid, watching me. It seemed unaware that I could see it and so I tried not to stare.

Nervously, I hurried inside and bought us two large meals just before I remembered Thomas couldn't eat meat. He could eat the fried potato cakes.

The group of malcontents were still milling out by the front entrance, so I tried to use the side entrance. That door was locked until 6 a.m., forcing me back out the front exit.

As I passed through the door, I glanced over my shoulder and saw the set of vacant eyes following me. The tall grey suddenly lifted an arm and pointed my direction and the gang of local hoodlums followed suit. Their hungry motives were for violence and quick money. I was their intended 'happy meal'.

The young men scattered like a trained pack of predators, already spread apart and moving my direction as I crossed the dark street. I could see that I was not going to get to my hotel room door before they intersected my path. By no means did I feel cowardice, but the odds of my fending off an entire group, possibly carrying weapons, were not worth projecting.

"Help."

I whispered it, but it was only to myself and not a plea I expected an answer to.

I was suddenly in an easy sprint, listening to the scuffle of their footsteps perhaps a dozen feet away and closing quickly, when Thomas turned on the outside light above the hotel door. It was blazing white.

The pack of predators seemed momentarily confused and stopped as I hurried the remaining few feet and rushed inside. My heart thumped as I lay my back against the inside of the door, clutching our bags of food.

Thomas however was not standing just inside to greet me but was still curled and immobile under his covers.

I looked out and saw the pack jogging, merging as one, back across the street, back where I had seen their phantom leader.

The light. Who had switched on the light?

I peeked out the door into the blackness. Above the door where I had seen the blindingly brilliant white light was a bare dirty brick wall.

"Thank you."

Somewhere I had an unseen helper.

I woke Thomas. He was grumpier than usual, most likely because of the soft bed.

"Damn dreams."

He railed on as he threw back his tangled covers.

I switched on the pitiful excuse for a television hoping to catch any local information or weather. Early monsoons were the main focus of discussion and something called El Niño that I didn't quite follow. Rain was forecast in a few days and could last a few weeks, all out of season. Not good for what I knew was coming.

As soon as there was daylight, I dug my cell phone out of the Rover and was surprised to see a full signal. We were lucky to get one bar on the tiny meter at home.

"Can I speak to Brent or Carl?"

I couldn't remember their last names, but I was sure that anyone inside their group knew the pair well.

"Brent, can I help you?"

I hurried through the cordial formalities and quickly explained that I had information concerning Chaste. I didn't know the local customs and restrictions for crossing this country's southern border into Mexico.

"Where are you?"

He sounded very concerned when I told him I had spent the night in El Paso and planned to cross into Juarez, into the neighboring country from there.

"Kress, I don't recommend you do that. It's way too dangerous."

It was the first time anyone I considered a friend had called me Kress in ages. It sounded foreign, distant.

"But if you're serious, let us come and meet you there."

I explained that time was of the essence; that I had to cross as soon as possible, today or tomorrow. If I waited, whoever had Chaste might move her again.

Brent was silent for a moment, thinking.

"You plan on driving across or walking?"

He was fishing for information.

"Driving."

"So you're not just going to Juarez. Then walk across, rent a car and insure it to the max or kiss the Rover goodbye. Got your passport?"

For some reason, I still had it stuffed with all my pertinent papers in the glove compartment like a good little U.S. Citizen.

"How deep are you going?"

I hesitated. I didn't want to involve him in something that might compromise the integrity of his position.

"A place called, Laguna de Patos."

"Jesus, no. Kress you'd need an armed escort to go that far from the border."

"It's Chaste, Brent, my daughter. I have to go."

This was followed by a moment of thoughtful silence before he answered, "You're right. Okay, well…, don't take anything with you that you don't want stolen."

I could hear the frustration and raw fear in his voice.

"For all they know, I'm a tourist."

"Not there. That's lawless territory. There are bandits that scour that region for people like you."

At least I'd have stories to tell my grandchildren and at least I'd have grandchildren to tell them to.

"We can be on a plane out there…."

I heard Brent swear into the void.

"…tomorrow evening at the latest."

"If everything goes well, I'll be back across the border by tomorrow night."

"Sounds like you have a plan, Sir."

"I might need some help getting Chaste back across the border."

"I'll get copies of both your passports from the Consulate's Office and bring them with me, just in case. And Kress? Don't make me come looking for you."

CHAPTER NINETEEN

Thomas didn't have a passport and was livid at being left behind. I didn't want to explain to him that where I was going would involve running, possibly through unlovely territory. It was nearly impossible for him to walk on pavement with his cane, much less forge through unknown circumstances. He would be responsible for guarding our things and meeting Brent and Carl when they arrived.

I took care of the hotel fee for another night, brought in some food, and slept as much as I could, which ended up being a succession of cat naps. I needed as much rest as I could get to be fully functional the following morning.

All that afternoon and that night, I lay listening to the thoughts of my daughter, chatting away, imagining herself home. I prayed that night that she would be safe just one more day. If I succeeded, she wouldn't have to imagine herself at home.

Early the next morning, I crossed the border with fresh clothes on my back, a few hundred American dollars, some Mexican currency, VISA, drivers license, passport and cell phone.

I managed to paste a smile on my face and say fiesta a few times, hoping to make myself more believable. My Brit accent brought instant smiles and helped me once again.

Getting a rental was a little more difficult.

I felt drawn to a particular rental company; Rojas Rentals with a rundown office and rusted awnings over their available vehicles.

The first car the agency tried to pawn off on me was barely roadworthy and refused to start. When I started to walk out the door and look for another rental agency, the proprietor rushed to the door smiling. He said that if I could possibly wait a half hour, he would bring me a nice car.

Bueno, I waited.

The car that pulled in under the awning was a cherry red Volvo. Clean as a whistle with brand new tires.

"Insurance?"

Suddenly his English was remarkably clear as he waved and made a gestured smirk, "You won't need insurance."

When I insisted, he seemed extremely disappointed.

I filled up with petrol, bought some sealed bottles of water and sealed food, and a few locally made colorful blankets, then headed due south out of Juarez.

The only road sign on Highway 45 was Chihuahua, 212 miles, but it was the right direction and my daughter's voice was clear in my head.

I was determined to purchase fuel at every available stop along the way after seeing the bleak country I was headed into, but there were no stops.

Cactus, white winged vultures, and carrion crows were the only signs of life for the first fifty miles.

The road became worse; potholes, ruts, and sand drift all the way into the center of the lane. The one thing I forgot to make sure of was a spare tire, just in case.

A persistent odor, something sweet and sickly wafted from the back seat and I realized that the rental company hadn't had time to clean out the car before passing it on to me.

I waited until there wasn't a car on the road in either direction for miles before I pulled over. The scent was becoming unbearable and I hurried to open the back door. A white cloth was stuffed underneath the back of the driver seat so I cautiously pinched a corner and pulled it free. It was covered in stale dried blood, definitely the source of stench. My best estimate told me that it had been curing underneath there for at least six to eight weeks inside the sealed vehicle. I threw it out on the ground and surveyed the car for more ill fated gore. I could just envision a body in the trunk and scurried to open it.

It was clean and empty, except for a spare..., a real tire.

I got back on the road and my efforts had managed to clean the inside air, but I began to wonder more and more about the blood stained cloth. I reached to the glove compartment and it was stuffed with personal belongings. Items that shouldn't have been in a rental spilled out.

One at a time, I pulled items out and placed them in the passenger seat beside me: an expensive looking makeup case, lipstick, a few tampons, cell phone, and…, a small pistol.

I had the strangest revelation that this car was most likely stolen. I had to rid myself of these things; should I be stopped by the local authorities, I could easily be mistaken as the car thief…, or much worse. Should I keep the pistol? The thought did cross my mind.

I quickly wiped each item free of my fingerprints and threw them one at a time off into the desert along the highway.

That would prove itself a mistake.

The scenery was bleak, cold, and distracting. A range of cloud-mottled mountains followed me on my left and every twenty or thirty miles there appeared a dirt road leading to a little one-room shack, surrounded by nothing; no electric whatsoever. I tried to envision the type of existence of the residents to distract my mind.

It was just after I noticed an encroaching bank of dark clouds on the western horizon that the voice of my Chaste boomed in my ear, nearly causing me to swerve off the road. It was so real and loud she could have easily been seated next to me, then something new and unexpected happened, leading me off the road bouncing into the desert sand.

The road before me disappeared and I was looking through someone else's eyes, not my Chaste. After practically standing on the brakes, I sat listening to the idling Volvo as well as the sights and sounds of some stranger. There were muffled voices, I recognized the language instantly as Spanish, and that wasn't all, I understood beyond my meager education of the language. Whoever this mystery person was, this portal, understood the words and was acting as a translator to me.

I heard the words 'move immediately' and 'airplane tonight' very clearly. It was easy to fill in the blanks and finally understand why I had been forced into immediate motion. Several things crossed my mind, but the most prevalent worried me; had my encounter with the mysterious tall creature triggered this urgent event? I was sure of it.

After witnessing the previous mornings events with the strange grey spectre, there was no doubt in my mind that dark forces were rallying against me.

"I'm going to need more than a little help," I whispered. "I'm going to need a miracle."

How could I, one man, rescue my daughter? I suppose I had as much mettle as the next fellow, but never pictured myself as the courageous type.

Obviously I hadn't thought my plans all the way through.

How could I not try? Only hours ago I had faced a supernatural killer and survived. Had I assumed the rest would be easy?

My own sight faded back to me and I was parked just inches away from a hideous cactus, tall as a tree.

I was learning to trust, not an easy thing for me.

It seemed that the closer I got to my destination, the more of what I needed to know was being handed to me, piece by piece.

Minutes seemed to drag by down the next few empty miles.

I saw the road sign standing askew and faded pointing toward Laguna de Patos as an afterthought, forcing me to slam on the brakes and turn around. The highway was pitiful, but the rutted dirt road was much worse and when I looked in my rearview mirror, my heart sank like a stone. My rental was leaving a dust plume high in the air behind me that could be seen for miles away. I had to slow down to a grueling fifteen miles an hour to keep from announcing my arrival to the inhabitants near the Laguna.

Sooner than I expected, the scenery started to seem familiar, part of my original vision I believe. It was time to park the Volvo and hide it. There was only one rock formation tall enough to park beside to offer any type of cover.

It was then I regretted my decision to take the glistening red auto. I used what was available. The heavy, stony sand had already caked the sides of the car. I grabbed one of the water bottles and applied a liberal spray of moisture on every surface, quickly followed by handfuls of sand. When I was through, I stood back, proud of my ingenuity and handiwork; it looked as if it had been abandoned there for at least a year.

Time was inching forward and the dying sun had crouched behind an ever-advancing bank of dark clouds rolling my direction. I was wasting precious time. I carefully climbed atop one of the boulders beside the Volvo to get a better look.

In the distance, I could see a string of single room adobe shacks standing like dominos about to fall. Vivid memories of a place I'd never set foot became a strange dizzy sensation in my head. About a hundred feet away from the huts was one larger unit that was dark and silent.

I set out, following rain-washed gullies, staying low behind the sparse shrubs and weeds; circling far away from the buildings, stopping every few minutes to watch for activity.

There was only one person, possibly a sentry, walking lazily from hut to hut. Behind the line of buildings was the lake in the distance, pristine and blue reflecting the darkening clear eastern sky.

Then I caught the scent of something horrid and saw the source. A dilapidated loo, and not twenty feet away was a rusted pump handle to a water-well. So much for hygiene.

I was quickly reminded of the urgent timing; first I heard distant thunder over my shoulder, but then something else made my heart sink. The hum of an airplane. A twin-engine aircraft had topped the ridge of mountains, heading my way, only a dot in the sky.

My new question was which hut? Or was I even at the right place? It looked like what I had seen.

Learn to trust, I told myself.

The cloud darkened sun and the mottled terrain had created an early twilight effect, giving me a bit of natural camouflage. I timed my entrance to ensure the sentry was opposite my position as I crawled to the first cabin in the group. It had one tiny glassless window. I popped up, looked, and dropped back down, hoping there wasn't a group of bandoleros sitting quietly waiting to put a bullet in my head. There was nothing but a cot, chair, and a length of rusted chains on a dirt floor.

The hair rose on the nap of my neck and I flattened myself to the ground. Apparently, I had miscalculated the timing of the guard. I hugged the wall of the shack, flat of my stomach, not daring to breathe. His scratchy footsteps turned around and slowly faded into silence, not noticing my light tan shirt and khaki pants.

I quickly proceeded to the next in the line of adobe shacks. This too had a cot and a chair, along with a scruffy child in a filthy t-shirt, manacled to a metal ring dangling in the wall.

At first, I thought it was a boy, but after a second look, the dirty brown hair was crudely cut just above the ears of a little girl and very deceptively done.

This was not my Chaste, even as my heart sank for her captivity.

I patiently waited for the sentry to advance and recede once again to afford me more time at the next, the middle shack.

As I neared, I felt something hit me on the head. I feared the worst and looked upward to see if it was about to rain.

Again, I felt a tap and heard a click on the ground beside me.

At the window of the middle shack were a pair of eyes and the outline of just the top of the head of yet another child. This one was carefully throwing bits of gravel my direction to get my attention.

I lay my finger to my lips and made my way to the open window.

I didn't need to hear the voice of Chaste in my head any longer; she was here.

Eight months of separation crushed me. It was all I could do to compose my emotions and not fling myself through the window to grasp her. Her hair was also clipped short, stained a dour reddish hue, but when I saw her frail body, her sallow skin and sunken eyes, I couldn't help but cry.

Chaste dropped the one blanket wrapped tightly around her body. She too was adorned with an extra long filthy t-shirt and horridly stained boys jockey underwear.

She silently held up her hands to show me a pair of rusted manacles, which were connected to shackles on her bare ankles. It would be nearly impossible to get her through the window without making a huge commotion.

She moved the chair to the window and climbed aboard, extending her frail hands out as far as her fetters would allow, to greet me. I kissed each dirty finger and saw the light come back into her mothers blue eyes. She looked at me as if I were an apparition or a dream.

She was bitterly cold and silent. What had they done to her?

How was I supposed to get her out of here? I had followed all the clues, all the new messages, but I was missing something.

Once again, I whispered for help.

Help I received in the form of a bright white form inside the shack with Chaste. Instantly I remembered the vision or dream of all the creatures I had seen and the sparse few in white, avoided by all the others.

The chains slid off my daughters' wrists and ankles in a silent thud on the dirt floor and as I watched, she began scrambling through the adobe shack window.

Then..., she was in my arms, grasping me with the desperation of a vice. She weighed nothing.

We had not uttered a word to each other. Silence had become our second most precious ally.

When the sentry moved a safe distance away, I put her on my back and scrambled quietly into the distance and would have left, but our path was blocked by that same being in white.

Its arm was raised pointing.

I immediately knew what I had to do.

I eased Chaste from my back and dug a shallow trench in the loose sand behind a huge sage and had her to lie down in it. I quickly covered all but her face and motioned her to be still.

It was the single hardest thing I believe I had ever done, leaving my child to go back to the row of adobe shacks.

The hum of the airplane droned nearer, but that wasn't what brought all my senses to full alert. In the distance, blasting across the barren landscape up the road, was a pickup truck, heading straight for us. I hoped that the Volvo had gone unnoticed.

The sentry was immediately distracted and began to walk to meet the oncoming vehicle in the distance.

I peered into the last two shacks on the opposite end and found one more child in each of them. My helper in white did not make this part quite as easy and neither did the young lady in the last shack. Both the other two younger children had the natural good sense to keep all noise below the breathing level, but the young girl felt she needed to rattle and chirp loud enough to call down an army. I finally convinced her to shut her bloody mouth by threatening to leave her. I was not about to place the life of my child in further peril for her petulant tomfoolery. Thankfully, these two were not in chains, but the first child was still bound.

The plane was now circling to land, apparently on the other side of the lake, a good distance away; more good news.

I lunged through the window into the shack where I found the first child. The little one hugged my leg in silent desperation when she realized I was there to help her.

I placed one foot on the wall and gave a quick yank on the chain, pulling the rusted anchor out of the adobe brick with surprising ease. I pushed her out the window, handing her the clinking rusted links in a quick scoop.

The young girl carried the least of the captives, a tiny boy, while I crouched, carrying the girl with rusted chains still attached, back to where my daughter was hiding. They were a sorry lot, all barefoot and starved to scarecrow weakness.

As I pulled Chaste from her earthen hiding place, I realized that there was no teenage boy named Steven among the group.

As if awakening from some distant dream, I felt the gravity of all that had happened this day. It would be a phenomenal miracle if we all escaped with our lives.

CHAPTER TWENTY

Huge slow drops of rain began to fall, accompanied by violent sand filled gusts of wind. With Chaste clutching my back and the manacled child in my arms we followed my original path of ingress.

Maneuvering in a low wide arc, we were already well on the way back to the Volvo, when we heard shouts and gunfire; all of us dropping like stones to the ground. In the distance, I saw the outline of the sentry fall face forward, one fellow standing holding a gun and three others running in circles around the adobe shacks like a pack of wild dingoes.

We hurriedly set off once again and never looking back as cold drops of rain began to pelt us like pebbles from the sky.

When we neared the Volvo it was bright red once again, rinsed clean by a now drenching cold rain. Lightning creased the blackened western sky, followed by an instant report of violence all around us.

Needing no other urging, we stuffed in the vehicle, Chaste only a breath away from my side as we shot toward the crude highway.

One by one, the children began to tell their names and what little they could remember of their capture. One was from Texas, another from New York; the eldest girl was from northern California, all victims of abduction, all from ridiculously wealthy families, all glad to be free.

The quiet engine of the Volvo was a Godsend. The rain dampened our dirt trail from immediately giving us away and instead of coming our direction, the four men sped off in the direction of the landing field around the lake.

If we were fortunate, foul weather and darkness would be our fierce allies. If the plane could not fly in the turbulence and the darkness hid us, we just might actually make it back to the border. I might have my miracle.

I found that the Volvo was capable of a healthy 100 miles per hour on the good sections of highway. Something that I was certain the tattered old truck of their captors could not do.

Chaste was the least vocal of the group and after consuming all the food and water I brought with me, all were asleep under a small blanket, except for the youngest. The tiny boy was silently glaring out the back window of the car, expecting lights or some monster to come chasing us down the highway I suppose. The fact that I was continually glancing back made me wonder if I didn't expect the same thing as well.

I did find out that Chaste had been captive the longest of the group and that the chains were only for the ones that fought captivity and had tried to escape. Each of the children had been moved at least a dozen times while captive and after crossing the border, they were stuffed inside vegetable crates from one staging place to the next, until they were sold. Chaste had only been moved to the cabins at Laguna de Patos in the past few days. Just prior to that they were all kept together, yet separate, in wire dog kennels.

Also, the men who were watching them were not the culprits of their abductions, but were only guards holding them there for transport to some airstrip at the tip of Baja California.

I was staring into the dark rain pelted highway, trying my best to understand..., why Chaste? A sudden wind-burst almost forced us across the shoulder-less two-lane highway and rain descended with a fury, forcing me to slow our pace.

With the carload of children asleep, I had time to ponder the changes in my own self and what I was going to tell Thomas upon my return.

Lightening constantly fractured the dark sky, illuminating the ever-present mountain range in the distance. The haunted slopes of the mountainsides forced me to focus on the highway in fear just as another blinding flash washed the terrain with eerie light again. Another flash gouged at my eyes and I saw a tall grey figure in the middle of the road directly ahead of us, a carbon copy of the one I'd seen across the street from our hotel in El Paso. I fought my basic instinct to swerve and drove straight for it. We passed it in a blur, but it was looking right at us.

It was a warning. I had disrupted the order of things hidden.

A voice whispered into my mind and I leapt inside.

It was a woman's voice, subtle and quiet; trying to understand where she was and what had happened to her. It was compelling and sad in a way I'd never felt before. Then as quickly as it started, it drifted away like a leaf in the wind leaving me with a sick feeling in the pit of my stomach.

I whispered to myself, glaring at my reflection from the instrument panel lights, "How do I make the voices stop?"

Instantly, I envisioned the blood crusty cloth I had flung from the auto, the personal items I had cleaned and scattered along the highway. The voice was from the owner of the Volvo we were traveling in.

"I don't want to be the world's lost and found."

I didn't mean to say it aloud, but it was done and none of the children awoke from my indiscretion.

The auto began to sputter and slow down. I glanced at the fuel gauge, over half-full, plenty to get us to the U.S. Border crossing. Oil pressure, temperature, all fine. Of course.

"Okay, I get it."

I slammed my palm against the steering wheel in angst.

The engine smoothed out and began to pick up speed.

"That's not fair."

I had endured the pain; I had paid the price to find my daughter. How long would I have to pay? I felt a surge of selfishness that lingered far too long.

Finally, I realized it didn't matter. It was a fair trade, my life for the life of my daughter, my Chaste; I didn't care. I had been willing to trade my life for hers from the very beginning.

I felt the car swerve once again in the sluice of rain slick sand, serving as a reminder to focus on the remaining task ahead.

While replaying the voice of the young woman in my mind, I saw the lipstick case and cell phone, both on the side of the road where I had thrown them. I didn't see them like one might suppose, in the dark, with some sort of night vision. I saw them in my head. That doesn't make sense either, so I'll leave it at that.

I pulled over and stopped, fighting against the wind splattered rain to open my door in the pitch-blackness. I didn't have a torch to flick on, none was needed. I stumbled straight to the lipstick case and picked it up, a few feet later I found the cell phone.

The auto looked strange and deserted, idling there in the rain soaked darkness; the only lights visible…, anywhere.

Why was I forced to pick up these items? Once back inside, I flipped on the cabin light and shook off the wet sand from my treasures. Inside the case, I found initials etched in a metal plate, K R H, in intricate script. The cell phone didn't want to turn on and seemed a mystery.

I helped Chaste out of a twisted curl on the seat and saw the dark rust stains embedding the skin on her wrists.

I hurriedly turned off the light and resumed our journey to the border. There would be time for examinations later.

My daughter yawned, hugged me tight and fell back to sleep under my jacket, warm and safe. I looked around behind me at the rest of the dirt-mottled faces. I knew that their parents would equally be ecstatic to see them again.

The lowering sky over Juarez was glowing that eerie amber we had seen each night and the rain had slowed to a drizzle as we neared our destination.

How was I supposed to get all these others across the border, back into their country? Should I trust the local authorities to do the right thing?

I gawked at my phone and it was showing one bar of signal. I was close enough to reach out and touch someone.

"This is Brent, is this you Dr. Schumacher?"

"That it is."

He must have heard the relief in my voice.

"Did you bring the passports with you?"

"Yes, did you find your daughter?"

"Under my arm asleep."

"Thank God."

I heard excited mumbling away from his phone.

"Is it just you and Chaste?"

I knew who was asking for the information, but I didn't have the answer he would want.

"I didn't find Steven. He wasn't with the others."

"Others? Are there more with you?"

"Three more children. All abducted from the U.S. and looking forward to going home."

"You are one amazing man. How far out are you?"

"Minutes. I'll be in Juarez in less than fifteen. I'm on Highway 45."

Suddenly I saw, I knew I had to make a detour.

"Make that half an hour, the weather is pretty foul here."

It was a small lie. The rain was actually slacking up.

"What are you driving?"

"A rental; a red Volvo."

"I'll alert our representatives and arrange an escort across the border. Never mind that, Carl is on his way to meet you himself. Look for a Silver SUV at the port of entry with a U.S. Marshal emblem on the side. Stick to the far right hand lane."

"What about the rental?"

"We'll let the locals return it for you."

I should have known that nothing in life is that simple.

When I entered the outskirts of Juarez, I felt the car pull me where I was supposed to go. I veered to the right into an exit, into a ghastly run down neighborhood; an endless row of small housing. The alley was barely large enough for two small cars to squeeze past each other. I reached up and took out the bulb from the interior light and dropped it on the floor mat.

In the distance, beside one of the hundreds of amber lights on poles, was a scrawny local gent. The car began slowing down to a full stop beside where he was standing in the light drizzle.

The words that came from my mouth were not what I heard in my head, but neither was his reply.

His toothy grin explained how much dinero he needed for our transaction and I handed over a crisp one hundred dollar bill. He told me to wait, in English, so I waited.

I whispered to myself, asking if this was the right place that I had seen, the right person, and most importantly what in blazes was I thinking?

A knock on the passenger door frightened me. I opened it,

pulling my sleeping daughter closer to me as a frail young woman clad in a filthy mini-skirt and revealingly thin cotton shirt slid in the seat beside her. She leaned over to peer at me, past her shock of dyed red hair, black at the roots.

"One hour Señor. Two blocks, take a left. Leave her there when you're done."

"Si, Gracias."

He shut the door and I didn't wait for an invitation to drive away.

The young woman stared at me with drug-glazed eyes and then down at Chaste. She smelled of stale alcohol, a scorched sweet odor, and sex. Her damp clothing left nothing whatsoever to the imagination; she had to be freezing cold behind her drug-induced euphoria.

"Do you know your name?"

She smiled a freakish smile, "Rosetta."

I heard her name whisper into my mind and felt some relief.

"No, do you remember your real name? Are you Karen? Karen Hall?"

I snatched up the lipstick case under my feet and placed it in her hand and she stared at it vacantly, until some spark made her slide her finger across the nameplate.

"Do you remember anything? Anything at all?"

She leaned over Chaste and sluggishly whispered something very crude and suggestive in my ear; her breath was lethal.

I flipped open her cell phone and after fumbling between it and watching the turns in the alley, amazingly it came on.

I navigated to the contacts and found nothing usable, then by complete chance a picture of her. Her amazing smile and dimpled chin made me weep inside at what she'd succumbed to during her span of captivity. The girl beside me was only a remnant of her former self. The Volvo lurched forward, flying down the narrow alley. I felt that unexplainable urgency once again and looked behind us. There was a car following a few blocks away and accelerating. I'd passed the street where I'd contracted to take my hired lady of the evening and someone wasn't happy with my change of plans.

I turned sharply down another street in the direction of the main highway. Another car joined in with the one only a block behind me now and I knew it was only a matter of time before our bumpers would clash. Moments later, we hurled out onto the main road, turned to the right and headed north toward the border. The Volvo roared to life and we quickly gained some distance between our pursuers.

Half a mile before we entered the multilane chute of the border crossing, where a glut of cars and cargo trucks were crawling along, I pulled up to a viciously double-fenced gate where an armed and uniformed guard was standing.

The sign said American Embassy on the fence and the building.

I handed the young woman the gold colored lipstick case and placed her cell phone in her other hand, then instructed her to go to the man standing by the gate.

"Tell him that your name is Jane Doe."

I said it several times and made her repeat it.

"Show him your picture in the phone and tell him you need help and he'll let you inside. The people in there will take care of you and see that you get home."

"Home?" she repeated.

She obediently staggered from the Volvo up the narrow sidewalk as I drove away. Something inside told me this was not to be our intended form of exit from this country.

I whispered, "Are you happy?" as I entered the right hand lane.

Thankfully, Carl was exactly where he was supposed to be in the vehicle crowded lanes so I pulled in directly behind him and parked. I closed my eyes and let out a sigh of relief. We were only a quick step to freedom.

Moments later, there were at least a dozen guns pointed at my head and shouts to get out and hit the ground face down. I was happy Chaste was still asleep.

After the biting steel of handcuffs were crushed into my wrists, I was dragged face down along the pavement like a sack of rubbish to another waiting black SUV. I glimpsed Carl and tried to tell him to take care of Chaste as I was lifted bodily and hurled into the back of the vehicle. All I could hear was Carl's booming voice cursing and quoting some international statutes at whoever was manhandling me.

Less than ten minutes later, I was carried on tiptoes into a dirty little room with a mirrored wall and blinking camera.

Bloody Hell.

Both countries obviously took notes from one another.

I expected some blathering Mexican officials, wanting to know where I found the children. Instead, it was their Policia, a detective, crunching a mixture of English and Spanish into questions about the red Volvo I was driving.

I explained to him that it was a rental; that the papers were on the dashboard. I hoped that was the right word to call it.

He didn't seem interested in the children inside the car or the fact that they were all refugees from a child abduction ring in his country or that one of the least was still in shackles.

He assured me in his broken English, that there were no rental papers in the car, and that it was stolen.

He never mentioned the owner of the stolen red Volvo, so neither did I.

I ducked my head and sighed, not because of the current situation, but because Chaste was alive and would soon be safe. I could endure anything now that I knew she was alive; unharmed was yet to be determined.

An hour of interrogation similar to my last experience crawled past and my arms were painfully asleep behind my back, due to the steely enthusiasm of the arresting officers. When the excited police detective was tired of yelling at me with no response and his voice became hoarse, he stomped out of the room.

I lay my head on the even filthier table and dozed, awaiting round two.

I woke to the sound of yelling out in the hallway of the soundproof room. It sounded like a foghorn.

Carl burst into the room, walked straight behind me and unlocked my handcuffs. I couldn't feel my arms and he had to hold the bottle of water he had brought for me.

"Chaste is safe on the other side of the border."

I felt the surge of relief I expected as my arms began to tingle back to life and I nodded.

"Thank God," came out as a whisper as I looked up into his concerned face.

"Carl…, if I don't make it out of here, promise me you'll see to it that Chaste is protected."

"Stop talking that nonsense. You're coming back with us."

He ducked his big bald head after a swipe of his hand, "I couldn't help the others with you."

"But there were three more. A boy with dark brown hair, a little girl with her hair cropped like a boy, and a teenage girl."

Carl was obviously tired of the merry-go-round.

"All with no identification, Dr. Schumacher. What about names?"

"I'm not sure; they were all talking at once. Ask Chaste."

Carl flipped open his cell phone and moments later Brent was relaying an apparently fantastic story back to Carl.

"She can't say for sure, she only heard one name used; Steven."

I looked at him with a strange curiosity.

"Where are they?"

Carl didn't answer me, but instead stormed back out of the interrogation room.

I knew that this was much deeper and wider than I wanted to admit or understand. All I had wanted was to find my daughter and possibly Thomas' son and go back to our droll little existence. Then, melt back into the woodwork, semi-invisible to society, but it appeared that wasn't in my future.

Why in God's name didn't we move to London?

CHAPTER TWENTY-ONE

The sound of the door slamming shut jolted me awake once again, followed quickly by the ranting voice of the Policía.

I calmly asked for an interpreter. Even though he could speak broken English, he obviously couldn't understand it.

That only served to anger him more.

I had already bound and gagged my tongue never to speak of the bloody cloth or the items in the glove compartment, or the young woman. As far as I was concerned, they never existed. To admit to their existence was to put myself in the far recesses of a Mexican jail for the rest of my life.

We were at a stalemate.

So there I sat, sleepy, thirsty, and starved for several more hours.

Finally, early that afternoon, someone found the proprietor of Rojas Rentals and coerced the truth from him.

I was forcefully escorted to the border crossing and shoved through the turnstile, my small backpack pitched in my face with a warning not to return anytime soon.

Not bloody likely. Hasta la vista.

Chaste ran to meet me, gripping me around the waist so tightly I thought I would have to pry her loose.

Dropping to my knees, I had to ask as I looked into her heavily dilated blue eyes.

"Baby, what happened to the other children?"

She pulled me close and whispered, "They took them and drove away."

"Who took them?"

She didn't answer at first, but pointed, "He helped me or they would have took me too."

She was pointing at Carl.

I picked her up, but not before noticing the scabs, scars, and ringworm circles on her skin. She weighed absolutely nothing and was so emaciated it terrified me.

"What do we do now?"

Brent and Carl both looked at me with, I believe, genuine concern.

"Go home, Dr. Schumacher. You and your daughter deserve a long vacation."

"What about the other children? We can't just leave them."

"We have no jurisdiction in their country."

And that was it. The end.

I thanked both of them for their kindness and efficiency and we walked out to the Range Rover.

I didn't have the equipment necessary to perform more than a cursory examination on Chaste. I was her father, a pediatrician trained and experienced in this very element for eighteen years, but I was too emotional and scared of what I might find to consider it; so we were off to Phoenix.

There sat Thomas in the back seat, still and quiet, contemplative. Chaste crushed up against me as we buckled up. I saw years of more therapy sessions in both our futures.

"It's not over, Thomas. Not by a long shot."

He didn't move or answer.

"Chaste have you met Thomas?"

She nodded, but seemed extremely timid as any child might toward a stranger, as well as one with a major deformity.

I turned and asked, "Do you still have anything that belonged to Steven?"

My daughter spoke up, "You're looking for Steven?"

Thomas looked simply petrified when she used his name.

"But..., I don't understand.... They took him away.... It's been...."

"That's enough!" Thomas broke in, as if not wanting to hear the fate of his son. As if he knew something all along.

"But Sir, they moved him a long time ago."

Thomas looked paralyzed.

"You talked to Steven? Was he okay?"

"No. They didn't allow any of us to talk to each other. I just heard them use his name. I don't know any Spanish, but one of them told him he was sold. The day he left, they said he was going to live in a big house. He tried to tell them he wanted to go home."

She got very quiet and buried her head back against my side.

"My Stevie, you talked to my Stevie...."

It seemed enough for Thomas at the moment.

We decided to drive straight through back home, no more pit stops, no hotels; home. The two Rot's were probably starving by now despite the load of food I dumped in the bin for them.

Something still had me angered and perplexed; why did the being in white send me back to get the other children if they were going to be ushered right back into the same situation? My angered thoughts served to keep me awake for the long journey back to Arizona.

Sunday consisted only of a series of strong painkillers for me, eating, sleeping, and a silent thanksgiving for my daughter's return. There were no questions, no insistent conversations. Chaste and I stayed close as you might imagine and I read her several stories throughout the day. I encouraged her to write anything down she felt important while I kept her under constant observation. That effort was mostly fruitless as she declined into abject secrecy; the horror of any parent.

Monday morning I awoke from a grueling dream and lying next to me was my daughter wrapped under a thin blanket. I didn't have the heart to force her into her own room; frankly, she was terrified of being alone there. Something we would have to work on.

Almost eight months. What happened during that vacuum of time?

Why was no one concerned about her recovery but myself and those I had employed to aid in her return?

First things first. We would get her straight into Phoenix Children's Medical facility today for a full examination. More than likely, she'd be hospitalized for days.

I covered her and eased out of the room, she looked so peaceful.

As I was making breakfast, Thomas heard me and called me into the living room. He had flipped on the television where CNN was blasting pictures across the screen of three American children that were found by the heroic efforts of Mexican authorities. Apparently, some U.S. citizen adjacent to our vehicle had made a freelance video of our incident at the U.S. Border and sent it to all the major news agencies. It was the child in rusted manacles playing over and over with endless repetition that sold the story. It was that distorted video clip that forced the Mexican authorities to produce the children from wherever they had rushed them off to with no mention of an arrest.

Thank God, they were alright; thank God my face was not the one being bandied about the media screen once again.

Thomas' face was cold and hard as he watched uniformed men brutally snatching the screaming children from the Volvo. Were those officers involved and if so, where had they moved his son?

It seemed strange that my face, my name, and subsequent arrest were not mentioned. I wasn't going to call and complain.

It went without saying that our lives would never be the same; never normal again. We sat quietly side by side in the lobby of the Phoenix Children's Medical Clinic. I had secretly apprised the staff of the details of the situation and they agreed to see us on an emergency basis.

On the way, I had rushed in one of the local electronic centers and purchased two of their best selling laptop computers as well as some internet capabilities. This was something that Chaste had been hounding me about for months before she was taken from me. I had promised her one as soon as we returned from our vacation. I would have purchased the moon for her if it would remove the memories of her past ordeal.

Oddly enough, the last thing on either of our minds now was a vacation. It saddened me that she didn't seem more than mildly interested in anything around her. She hadn't opened the box to hers yet. I knew why. I was only hoping it would provide as a distraction. My real hope was that her youth would help her rebound from whatever horrors she had witnessed.

We sat quietly pecking at the keys on mine, making small talk, looking for a private school or possibly a tutor, not that I intended to let her escape my eyesight any time in the near future. Carefully, I searched for anything that might anchor her wounded mind back into the world of her home.

Maybe there was some sort of survivors counseling available for us, something to ease us both back to the present.

I was so elated she was alive; everything was up in the air including the option of moving elsewhere; far, far elsewhere.

I knew that public school was forever out of the question and Chaste didn't argue, but once again her apathy of all things in general overshadowed our discussions.

A nurse interrupted our silent collusion and we both rose to follow her. Chaste stopped and hugged me.

"Daddy, I want to go by myself, if that's okay."

The father in me was instantly terrified by the implications. The nurse nodded and my nine year old daughter disappeared behind the doctor-patient barrier.

After eternity and a nap, I was called into the Patient Consultation room, fearing the absolute worst.

A splitting headache followed me inside the room and I fought the opportunity to be in a foul mood.

I was informed that Chaste was still undergoing some extensive blood work giving us a chance to talk.

After minor cordialities, Dr. Melva Cort asked me to be seated while she strained to explain many things to me. Chaste miraculously had not been violated physically and the doctor had taken the precaution to record the examination. One boulder fell from my shoulders as tears threatened my eyes.

She then began to list the other maladies; parasitic infections, lice, dehydration, anemia, malnutrition, possible tooth decay, muscular degeneration, and overall hygienic problems.

I did my best to explain that our entire family received a gamut of regular inoculations because of the exposure to the petri dish where we had lived. We were all exposed to a wide foray of things that would terrify the civilized world. That region of South Africa wasn't called the Cradle of Humankind without a cause.

Dr. Cort went on to explain that she wanted to keep Chaste overnight for observation and get some fluids and antibiotics into her, but Chaste had almost gone into shock at the mention.

"It took me and my nurse nearly twenty minutes and a sedative to get her calm again. Will your schedule allow you to take care of Chaste at home?"

It seemed such an inane question.

"Chaste is my only schedule. I will be by her side 24 hours a day; you can be assured of that."

Dr. Cort still had her doctor's worried brow, "Chaste didn't test positive for any type of known drugs, but...," she paused. "Have you happened to notice the extreme dilation of her pupils? It could be chloroform poisoning or even due to a bump on the head."

I nodded, waiting for the rest of her opinion.

"It's also typical with some types of stress such as the ordeal she just survived or..., sexual assault, but..., would you keep me informed if you see any change in the next few days?"

"You said she wasn't...."

"Our examination showed that she wasn't physically abused. That doesn't mean there aren't other types of trauma. You should know that. And there's also the possibility of early onset puberty. I tried to explain to your daughter that she might have certain changes, but she told me that her mother had given her the young lady talk a few days before she passed away."

"Yes, she did and I..., I do understand. It's my daughter..., this is why I brought her to you Dr. Cort. I'm too close to be objective."

Her furrowed brow smoothed out, "Okay, I would normally recommend at least a weeks stay in the hospital, but I think in this case home care would be for the best; I think you're the best choice to watch after your daughter. Now, her electrolytes are completely out of balance, she needs constant fluid intake...."

Dr. Cort picked up a pad with lengthy scribblings, "...here are her medications and a follow up schedule, and my telephone numbers.

"You make sure that you update me on any and everything. Don't hesitate to call me at home if you need to. I'll have the tox-screen back in a few hours and I'll give you a call if I see anything abnormal. She's going to need at least two or three weeks of close observation, plenty of quiet, light exercise, and make sure she eats."

She handed me a list of very strong antibiotics as well as a few ointments for the disturbing rashes.

"Make sure you keep her hydrated with these," yet another list, "...and if her urine turns dark or she loses her apatite or there's any discomfort or she doesn't respond well to the antibiotics…."

I nodded and felt my face contort, amplified by my sharpening headache.

"Bring her to the emergency room," I mumbled.

She nodded, "Bring Chaste straight to the emergency room and call me immediately. I don't care what time it is."

She seemed nervous and put away her doctor's demeanor.

"One more thing Dr. Schumacher; when your daughter went missing, why didn't you alert your GPS provider and have them locate her?"

My world and my balance fell off axis. I heard my voice from somewhere down a long dark tunnel, "I…, I'm afraid I don't understand."

"Her implant," she explained, her brow furrowing deeply.

"Chaste doesn't have a GPS locator in her," I insisted.

Dr. Cort slapped a set of x-rays on a viewer and pointed out an inch long mini-capsule imbedded just under the hairline on the back of my daughter's neck. "She certainly does…, and it's an expensive one at that."

Apparently, during her time of captivity, she had been tagged with a GPS capsule similar to the ones used to track missing canines.

"How quickly can you remove it?"

She looked baffled at my question. "If her abductors can track her, they can come back and reclaim her wherever we go."

The implications were immense. The other children in the compound were most likely tagged as well…, maybe Steven too.

Immediately, I walked into the busy hall and placed yet another call to Brent and Carl, this time for advice. I didn't like or trust the FBI office that had mishandled our case, but some competent agency needed to be alerted for those children's sake. They let me know I should place this new discovery somewhere secure until it could be examined by professionals. We left the clinic with several prescriptions, strict diet recommendations and a happier, relaxed Chaste.

I assured her that the place on the back of her neck where the capsule was removed would re-grow its hair in a few weeks. Reluctantly, the doctor had given me the extracted GPS device and within the hour, it would be locked away in a new safety deposit box at our bank in downtown Phoenix.

CHAPTER TWENTY-TWO

Chaste was extraordinarily quiet on the way home. She kept running her fingers through her reddish hued hair, aggravated at the residual smell and oily texture of the anti-parasitic one of the staff had combed through it.

I was ever so thankful that the voices inside my head were gone, not that the ghastly headache had subsided one iota. Chaste finally turned her focus and examined the colorful box containing her new laptop and subconsciously rubbed at the embedded rust stains in the skin of her wrists.

I wanted to tell her happy late birthday, or that I had already planned to put up a belated Christmas tree so that we could celebrate together; so much had happened during her absence.

I had to rebuild our relationship, somehow.

"Dad. Why is Thomas staying with us? Why is he sleeping on our living room floor?"

I wondered if I should tell her?

"I know something weird is going on, you might as well tell me."

I smiled. How do children always know?

"He helped me find you. I promised to help him find his son Steven. He's had a bit of bad luck over the last few years and needs some place to stay at the moment."

"Is he the one that told you where I was?"

She seemed ten years older. An ordeal like she went through, we both went through, changes a person. Instead of time's gradual water dripping on stone, we were both hit with hammer and chisel.

Maybe even fractured and broken.

"No sweetheart, I received an anonymous tip."

That wasn't the exact truth. How could I further warp her mind with the truth?

"Then how did he help you?"

"It's a long story Chaste. What matters is that you're home and you're safe."

I had been holding off from the hundred questions I wanted to ask, allowing her time to get her footing and she was grilling me like an expert.

"Dad. When you first found me, how did you make the chains come off my hands and feet?"

"They must have slipped off on their own."

She was going to force my hand unless I was very creative.

"I tried to get them off every day."

She rubbed her wrists again.

"There you have it, you must have loosened them...."

"No Dad, there was that bright light and they fell off on their own."

I sighed heavily.

"Do you believe in angels?"

Chaste suddenly fell very quiet and stopped her line of questions.

"Yes..., I think I do. I thought I saw one. I thought it was a dream. A couple of nights before you found me. I..., I thought it was Mama. She said to buck up, and that you were on your way."

There were tears in my eyes. I remembered my prayer.

"Buck up...?"

It was something Elizabeth would have said, exactly what she would have said.

My cell phone interrupted our family reunion. I swiped the tears from my blurred vision to see a number I didn't recognize. That didn't surprise me. My cell number was on over 20,000 posters across the state of Arizona.

"Dr. Schumacher, how can I help you?"

"Yes Mr. Schumacher, Special Agent Lily, FBI, Missing Children Division. I understand you found your daughter, Chaste Schumacher?"

His question made it sound as if I'd suddenly found a missing house key. This didn't garner my respect.

"We need you to bring your daughter by one of our offices to answer some questions as soon as it's convenient."

I could just picture Chaste sitting at that dirty table, in that dirty room, with the dirty mirror and blinking video camera, being told that she was responsible for her own abduction.

"I think not. She's not up to it. We just left the doctor's office."

"We have to close her case file and to do it, we need to interview your daughter."

A generous pounding in my head was beginning to obliterate this vile Agent's voice, "Is it absolutely necessary?"

"I'm afraid it is."

I listened while he explained the facts as he understood them. We had until the fifteenth to prepare ourselves for the meeting. My head was now a persistent rage as my teary eyes began to well and drip from ignored pain.

As soon as he rang off, I called our new lawyer, John Shoemaker, who in turn promised to talk to the judge that had befriended me.

If nothing else, I was learning the great American pastime of covering one's ass.

I'd sat through their draining interrogations, but my daughter would not, even if it meant leaving this land of opportunity and changing our citizenship once again. I knew of a certain private jet that could take us most anywhere imaginable, well before the fifteenth of the month.

As we pulled into the drive, I realized that Chaste had been listening intently to my heated conversations.

"I don't mind telling them what happened."

"I know you don't, dear. I..., would rather you not have to relive it just yet, not until you're stronger."

In all actuality, I was the one which didn't want to know the exact details of her absence. The very idea of opening up those eight months reminded me of the first time I placed a scalpel to skin in medical school, revealing the contents of the inner man. In textbook or theory, it looked so easy and clinical, but when the patient was suddenly a living breathing human being, everything changed.

"Dad?"

I was getting frustrated, not with Chaste, it was the headache.

"Can I get my hair fixed? It stinks now and I don't want it to be this nasty color."

"Absolutely. Soon…, okay?"

She hugged me and…, it…, felt…, wonderful.

It was after midnight when Thomas and I finally had a chance to talk. I told him of the GPS debacle and that I would have the best person I could hire to take a look at it. We might just have Steven back in a matter of days if they could extrapolate his marker signature from the device that was in the back of Chaste's neck.

"Have you forgotten what's inside you now?"

His blithering one-track mind was still on the creature he called Pitre.

"How could I, Thomas?"

I carefully rubbed my arms and legs, still tender and swollen from the aftereffects of that hellish three-inch nail on my body.

"Use it. You don't need those other things or people."

Undeniably, I had encountered something that no sane person would accept or understand. Nevertheless, it had happened. Not to some stranger, not to some disconnected person in some scientific journal, but to me.

"I'm not sure how, Thomas. The only thing left from my meeting with your Pitre are these whelps on my body. Please understand, I want to help you."

He tossed me a leather patch and I looked at the worn brown emblem of a stag stamped deep into it.

"You asked me for something of Steven's."

I had, but for the life of me, I couldn't remember why.

"This is something he made. It was the only thing I found that belongs to him."

Why did I suddenly sense he was lying to me? Possibly, because of all the other partial truth's he'd fed me.

I felt the texture of the leather patch and looked at the intricate detail and care of the boy's handiwork.

My headache was rebounding and increasing in intensity. It had been a long day and I knew Thomas wanted to talk after being stuck there all day long while I took care of my daughter.

"Your headache back?"

It was the king of rhetorical questions.

"All day, non-stop."

I grabbed one of the childproof pain reliever bottles from the kitchen cabinet.

"Those ain't going to help you."

There it was again, that incessant guessing game Thomas liked to play.

"Spit it out man; if you know something."

"Where did Pitre put his last sting?"

I thought back. I was in such a daze; lying face down in the dirt, knew I was dying and there were those two blood red eyes cheering me on, inches from my face. Then I remembered, saying his name and spitting in his face; my last *coups de grace*.

"He hammered my head...."

I whispered without realizing it and felt around on my skull for a tender spot or swelling of some sort.

"You won't find it. That last one didn't hit your head, it hit your soul."

He was right about there not being a wound; I hated it when he was right, especially this time.

"It's gonna hurt like the devil for the next couple of days."

"Why didn't you tell me about this beforehand?"

He ignored my sarcasm.

"The seed is planted; you'll start to change soon enough."

I didn't like the sound of that, not one bit.

"What kind of changes? I don't want any more changes; I want everything to get back to normal."

I thought I caught the hint of a hellish grin on his face.

"Normal went on a permanent vacation, Doc. You better understand that right now."

I felt the pain in my head tighten and hurried over to where he was seated next to the blazing hearth.

"Thomas, I have a daughter that is depending on me. Either you tell me what's going to happen to me or our arrangement is terminated. I'll drive you back to Sedona where I found you..., along with your bag of filth. I'll do it tonight."

He didn't answer quite fast enough to please me and I stalked to the garage door and snatched up his black plastic sack of ragged clothes.

"I don't know everything that's going to change, Doc. The old

Indian told me he didn't know. Only that one leg would be standing on normal ground and the other in the spirit world. It was how each of the Shaman of his tribe led their people. Some of them went crazy."

"You blithering idiot!" I whined.

I dropped his sack of filth on the floor and felt the entire room quiver under my legs.

I sat down on the sofa and stared into the hearth as the flames swayed and jumped in an exotic dance.

"What have I done?"

Who would take care of my daughter if I went off the deep end? Suddenly, I had multiple arrangements to take care of, a Trust to set up for Chaste, a guardian to watch over her. How long did I have? Weeks? Days? Hours?

The threat of the upcoming meeting with the FBI seemed miniscule in comparison.

I felt the pain in my head enunciate and my eyes dripped like broken faucets. Somewhere, Pitre the demonic was curled up in his burrow laughing at the fool that came to dance with him.

I recalled the circle of dark figures pointing and laughing at Pitre, mocking him after I had tricked him into stinging me those seven times. Whatever I had stolen from Pitre in our altercation was far more than peering over into the world of shadows. No, it must be something far, far more.

I stood and dragged the sack of clothes back out in the garage.

I had made a promise ... and I saw through my childish headache driven fit. I may have been tricked into my meeting with Pitre, but my daughter was back and this was not going to ruin me.

After swallowing my palliative tablets with a glass of water, I wiped away the trail of my leaking eyes and weighed my options.

I marched back to the open living area, stuffed another armload of wood in the fireplace until it was blazing and sat down in front of it, now holding the leather patch that belonged to Steven. I had sufficiently teed off Thomas to the point of ignoring me. It proved such a blessing; I was learning to despise the man.

Now, seated before the crackling fire, a primal urge I'd been fighting all afternoon, I whispered into the flames.

"Help me please."

CHAPTER TWENTY-THREE

Sometime during the night, I fell asleep while seated before the blazing fire. I dreamed of the demonic creature, slamming that final blow into my head, over and over again. I dreamed of a young boy, seated in a room not much larger than a closet with a wool blanket pulled around him. What few clothes he had were stuffed in a box in the corner behind him. Desperation showed in his eyes for a world lost to him…, then the scrim visage faded.

When I awoke sometime before daylight, my head was pounding and my body stiff. I had somehow fallen asleep sitting straight up and remained in that fashion the rest of the night.

The house was quiet, the dogs hadn't barked all night, and I made one quick trip to my daughter's room to find her curled in a ball under her thick comforter.

I managed to find my way to my bed and crawl under the covers. Thank God, Chaste hadn't tried to come find me last night. What a strange sight that would have been, me sitting frozen like a stump staring into the hearth.

I immediately drifted back to sleep.

"Dad? Daddy?"

I felt the kindness of her voice and forced my eyes open.

Chaste was standing beside me and gently shaking me awake.

I was still seated in front of the fire and daylight was creeping in through the six floor-to-ceiling glass panels in the living room.

"Did you sleep here all night?"

Thomas wasn't moving, but I sensed he was awake on his pallet, listening.

"What's Pitre?"

My head was swimming through muddy water as I tried to stand and Chaste steadied me.

"Where did you hear that name?"

I feigned ignorance.

"I heard you talking and it woke me up."

She helped me over to the sofa and curled up next to me.

"What did you hear?"

"The last thing you said was that Pitre was a gateway."

I didn't know how much to tell her. What a strange experience, having a dream within a dream. She had found me sitting in front of the fire, just as I feared. My headache was causing my vision to swim and I struggled for an answer.

"It was just a dream, dear."

"Please tell me."

I could pose the whole matter as a nightmare, it was also an opportunity for a measure of honesty.

"It was a silly dream. I saw this creature jumping at me. That's all."

"He had a big tail and he stung you."

"Wh…, what? What are you talking about?"

Where could she have heard that?

"I know it hurt you. I'm so sorry. But now you can help so many others, now that his power is growing inside you."

My daughter's voice had descended into a deep resonant tone that frightened me to my core. Dark empty eyes stared at me from her tiny innocent face as I encountered this new unknown terror.

I jumped and fell over on the floor of the living room. Daylight was just climbing into the room and the fire in the hearth was barely a lingering flicker.

Another dream?

I stood, patted my face, went to the kitchen sink and dashed cold water on my cheeks. Was I truly awake this time?

"Nightmare?"

Thomas had risen after the noise of my scuffle and was chunking a generous armload of wood into the fireplace.

"I hate you Thomas."

He grunted, "No you don't…, not yet."

Another busy day was upon us. The headache was also upon me, relentless, nagging and gnawing at me, testing my grit.

More dreams within dreams accompanied by intense pain made me fearful of a tumor on the brain. Only by sheer willpower was I able to manage this last week.

Chaste on the other hand was looking better every day, small consistent gains in weight and health as well as her vigor. The low-grade fever was finally gone and I knew the antibiotics were completing their job. She drank water and juices non-stop and was constantly nibbling at snacks.

The six visible wounds on my body were healing slowly. My last self-examination had me palpating each hard distension, testing for infection, while noting their unfriendly hue. The odious red streaks were gone and the mounds appeared to be hardening, while shrinking in size.

I didn't dare place myself under a doctor's care because of the barrage of ensuing questions and the lies I would have to tell.

It was my hips that were aching this morning as I swallowed two of my new friendly red and white pain relievers and turned back to the food on the stove.

Thomas had hefted on an old coat of mine that swallowed him and was looking out at the canyon from our multi-tiered wooden deck behind the house. I heard the thumping of his cane and saw him stuffing tinder into our Chiminea to start a fire. What was the obsession with him and fire?

Chaste slid into the kitchen as I finished crisping some bacon and flipped it onto a platter. I stacked several plates on my arm, kissed her forehead and headed to the glass wall by the deck.

"Let's have breakfast over in the nook, maybe we can watch Thomas set himself afire."

"Dad!"

I expected that rebuke. I know it wasn't something to say to your nine-year-old daughter, but after another lurid dream filled night I was lucky I could still speak in short sentences.

We poured juice and watched as our guest scratched match after match in utter futility. Finally, he found my lighter in the box of tinder and started his fire.

"Dad, what is Pitre?"

I thought I would choke on my first bite of toast. I pinched my arm to make sure this wasn't another one of my nightly encapsulated waking dreams.

"What..., what do you mean?"

I took a swallow of juice to fix my broken throat.

"You told me about him last night. In my dreams."

She said it so matter-of-factly I wasn't sure how to answer. Her eyes fastened on, waiting....

"Is he an angel?"

I couldn't help the ghastly smirk that appeared on my face.

"Not hardly. No I don't think so."

"So Pitre is real."

It made my head hurt even more.

"Pitre is real."

There..., I had confessed. No more lies.

"Let me see where he hurt you."

I let out a deep sigh and slid an arm out of the sleeve of my robe.

The evidential swelling was still receding, only fifty-cent sized bruises with a dot in the center remained.

"Seven times?"

How could Chaste know? Apparently I wasn't the only one suffering the blasted repetitious dreams.

"Yes, seven times."

"He's how you found me."

What was I thinking? It was inevitable she find out that something was wrong, if and when changes did occur.

"It's what you told me in my dream," she insisted.

"You can't tell a living soul, Chaste. They'll think the both of us mad as hatters. Do you understand?"

She nodded and took another bite of food, but that amazing mind of hers was churning. It was the same look Elizabeth had when she was about to drop the ten question list on me.

"I'm really sorry Dad."

She looked as though she were about to cry.

"I thought it was you. When I saw the Rover, I ran across the street and jumped inside. I didn't even look. I was such an idiot."

I was speechless for a moment.

"Please, please don't blame yourself. I believe it was all planned to make you think it was our Rover."

She didn't let me finish, but I was glad she was opening up. I hadn't breeched the subject the entire week.

"I didn't have a chance to yell. They threw my new phone out the window and dragged me to the back. They drove off while the woman stripped off my clothes."

"A woman?"

"I'm pretty sure. There were two of them; a man and a woman. They were both wearing silly masks. She put a cloth over my face and I…, I don't know. I think I went to sleep. I woke up inside a cardboard box. I couldn't move. I…."

My nine-year-old daughter had frozen in a stare, reminiscent of a traumatized soldier. It was time to change the subject.

"Want some more juice?"

She shook her head and strummed her fingers through her hair, yanking at it angrily.

"It's ugly," she spat. "I hate it."

Her teeth gritted out the words and then she dropped her eyes back to the table.

"We'll get it fixed today, if we get free in time."

Chaste smiled shyly at my renewed promise and shook a few strands of putrid multicolored hair from between her fingers.

We dressed and left our houseguest on the deck, eating cereal beside the crackling fire inside our Chiminea.

We were scheduled to confer with our legal advisor early this morning before our pre-arranged meeting with the FBI. It turned out John Shoemaker actually had good news. We were to meet with the judge before our meeting with the special unit of the FBI.

Dr. Cort provided a copy of the results from the independent physical examination, which Mr. Shoemaker said would allow him to prohibit the FBI's attempts at repeated physical humiliation. I remembered the many pictures of the judges' daughters on his credenza and thanked God for small miracles.

We sat down together and transcribed how I acted independently on the information of an anonymous tip, found my daughter in the secluded location I was told of and finally the particulars of her rescue. Since the Mexican authorities had alluded to their own expert work discovering the other children, I was released from disclosure of the extended events.

Again, I took it upon myself to keep the information about the young woman I deposited at the American Embassy my own and forever hidden, as I was the only witness. The children were asleep in the car the entire time.

The written transcript of the detailed events sworn to in front of the judge would serve as my full testimony.

Then there was the testimony of Chaste.

Chaste became uncomfortable about recalling the details of her eight-month ordeal in front of our lawyer or the judge; it was sketchy at best. I could imagine what damage she would sustain at the hands of an interrogator of the same debased calibre I endured. Amazingly, the judge agreed. Protection of the child was his utmost priority, not the need for a fact-finding mission.

I don't know all the legal mumbo-jumbo, but evidently the judge somehow gave our lawyer the prerogative of being with Chaste at all times during any and all questioning. If there was the slightest hint of undue distress, she would be removed from the questioning arena.

CHAPTER TWENTY-FOUR

We met that afternoon at the Phoenix Federal Building in a room set aside for what was lovingly called a *debriefing*. What a ghastly turn of word.

There were actually two rooms prepared for separate interviews; one for me and one for Chaste. That I didn't expect, neither did our lawyer.

Someone had planned to separate us.

I'll give you three guesses who had intended to be my personal host for the noon meeting. My headache, like a new companion, was present also.

Chaste was suddenly visibly nervous about the entire process. She had positioned herself between Mr. Shoemaker and myself and had a firm grip on both our free hands.

After introductions, Mr. Shoemaker issued copies of the federal judges' orders. Mr. FBI kept his stony expression while skimming through the multi-paged document, looked at the transcript of my testimony with slightly raised eyebrows.

"I don't see any reason to trouble the young lady further. She is free to go. Dr. Schumacher, I do have a couple of questions for you."

I glanced over at our lawyer and he shrugged. It was up to me. If Mr. FBI needed some last word before going away forever, so be it.

Chaste stood just outside the door, looking through the window as we took a seat.

"Mr. Schumacher, I notice that you didn't show what medium

through which you received your anonymous tip."

If he had been this thorough about looking for Chaste, he and I could have been friends.

"No, I didn't."

"Was it a phone call? Or possibly a note? Or was it in person?"

I looked over at John.

"Dr. Schumacher does not wish to reveal any information other than what was transcribed before the federal court at this time."

This was going to get ugly, but why?

"Very well. What did you do with the GPS transponder that was removed from your daughter?"

That information was nowhere in the medical report, nor in my transcript testimony.

"Dr. Schumacher does not wish to reveal...."

Mr. FBI stood and stacked the papers our lawyer presented and placed them in a folder.

"Consider the matter closed."

John and I stepped toward the door where Chaste was in a dead stare.

Mr. FBI shook our lawyer's hand, and then extended it to me. When I took it, he leaned in to whisper a final comment.

"You may have learned the system, but I can personally guarantee that you will never practice medicine in this country."

What an odd threat. He made very sure that I was the only one that heard it.

"Thank you all for coming."

We stood outside the building in the clear crisp February air. I considered not telling my lawyer what was secreted in my ear, then..., reconsidered.

As soon as I relayed my message, I had to restrain John from going back inside to rebut the oddly puerile threat from the agent. Chaste tugged at his suit coat in an attempt to help.

"I intend to relay the threat to the judge if you don't mind."

I nodded, but knew it would do little good.

"Hopefully we've heard the last from him. I'll be satisfied with that much. Thank you for all your help John."

He started to walk away but turned quickly.

"Dr. Schumacher? This GPS device..., is it in a safe place?"

Always thorough.

"Quite. In a safety deposit box at our bank."

He nodded thoughtfully, "Surrounded by metal. Good. Let me know if you need anything else. Anything at all."

The day was gone, but not wasted. As promised, we stopped by a local hair salon and Chaste walked away with a quite stylish, much shorter perky version of her original cornsilk yellow blond.

Her weeklong patience culminated in a bright smile.

We picked up several items of groceries and made a mad dash for home. Each day, I was seeing the lights coming back on in Chaste; what a welcome sight. The odd mydriasis was still hiding an unhealthy portion of her beautiful sky blue eyes and as promised, I reported it to Dr. Cort along with her other vitals.

I so desperately wanted to know more of my daughter's misadventure at the hands of her abductors, but only when she was ready.

When we arrived, I noticed that our house was completely dark, which was not entirely unusual. Thomas was such a strange brooding individual. I had apologized for my rash outbreak of threats to expel him, to which he only grunted.

When the automatic gate refused to open, I began to wonder.

Surely the power company had not succumbed to another bout of shutting off our service.

After checking the battery in my remote device, I went to the box outside and flipped the switch to the backup power with the key code and the gate slowly growled open. Kicking the gate didn't seem to help the fact that the high voltage wire at the top of my fence had stopped crackling with electricity.

Then Chaste and I noticed that the boys were not groveling for attention and more food.

Chaste was growing fond of helping me feed the two Rot's and was gradually getting the courage to pet them despite their being larger than her and much heavier. Instead of names, they had become referred to as *The Boys*.

Some underlying angst seemed to be trying to peer beyond the obvious, but my head was as usual, pounding, always getting more pronounced as the day lingered. As a precaution, I asked Chaste to stay in the vehicle and parked in front of the garage.

I pointed to her cell phone and asked her to let me make sure that all was well before we went inside.

"If I'm not back in a few minutes, you know how to call 911."

Not that it would do any good as far away as we lived from civilization. The Rover's door locks slapped noisily as I walked away, with only my daughters' eyes and nose visible above the door.

I made it to the front path just as the door flew open with a wobbly frame bobbing down the steps.

"They were here!" Thomas hissed loudly.

Thomas was fighting with that intrepid cane, twisting his way toward me at a furious pace.

"Who was here? Get a hold of yourself man."

He dropped his cane and clung to me.

"I hid inside the kitchen pantry. I didn't see their faces. They heard something, it must have been you, and they left out the back door only a minute ago."

"How many of them were there?"

I looked over at Chaste and her big round eyes were fastened on me from the driver seat window.

"At least two, maybe more. Dressed in black, swat gear."

Thomas finally caught his breath and stooped to pick up his cane.

"Where are the boys?"

Thomas just shook his head and turned ambling back inside.

I lifted the garage door and drove inside, with that feeling of violation once again.

Chaste felt it too. That feeling of insecurity.

At once, I saw the reason there were no lights.

The breaker panel was open and several of the switches were haphazardly thrown to the off position.

I had never noticed the noise they made until I turned them all back on in the total silence. Their hammering clack rewarded us with glorious light everywhere and the electric gate began to whir closed in the distance.

I heard the television begin to blare loudly and then shut off as we retrieved our sacks of perishables.

The house looked as if nothing had been touched. Either they didn't have time to look or what they were looking for wasn't here. I firmly believed the latter, but it took some time for me to put two and two together. Had we not made several detours before returning home we would have been here caught unawares. Instead, it was our arrival that caught them in their trespass. But why did they leave? Couldn't they have easily overpowered us? If not us, then what were they after?

I searched every room, every window, and every door, but there seemed to be no sign of forced entry. Then I realized that there was no reason for something as silly as that. Thomas was here. The doors were all unlocked. There was an electrified fence and two feisty dogs roaming about. But where were they?

Darkness was looming, so I flipped on every exterior light available and began my investigation. I walked out the back deck and instantly noticed that the high voltage wire had been clipped and grounded at the corner of the back fence. Whatever possessed me to poke around in the back yard without some type of weapon is beyond me, but I did it.

Behind the garage lay the boys, listless, dead.

A single bullet hole to each of their heads. Such horrid luck with guard dogs.

I admit, I'm not the best of animal lovers, however I was getting somewhat attached to the two sweet spirited mongrels. Chaste couldn't see this. My jaded insensibilities were one thing, but my daughter was barely inching toward her own recovery.

Thomas rounded the corner of the house and saw the carnage.

"Did you hear gunfire?"

He shook his head no and slowly came closer.

"I was beginning to like them."

I sighed heavily.

"Me too."

"It won't do any good to get the law out here; I guess you already know that."

I spat on the ground. Some newfound instinct I suppose.

Thomas walked away as I stood there, stunned, until I came to my senses. I had to move the dead beasts to a more inconspicuous place. I lifted the ridiculous bulk of the first animal. I'd obviously been feeding them well. I surprised myself with the ease with which I'd lifted the limp dead weight, considering the continuous ache in my body. I hate to admit dropping him somewhat less than carefully into a corner against the house about fifteen feet away after blindly steering the short distance.

After a moment's recuperation, I slid my arms underneath the twin mongrel and felt something scrape the back of my hand.

I stopped and heaved him over and found a black toyish looking pistol, soaked in blood and packed with soil.

Astonished, I wiped the side clean with the tail of my shirt.

Glock, .40 Calibre, was stamped into the metal.

Something inside told me that Thomas didn't need to know about *The Boys* illicit acquisition and quickly looked for a place to hide it until I could think through my options.

CHAPTER TWENTY-FIVE

Chaste and I scrambled around the kitchen with our food, while I pondered the reason for our clandestine visit.

My need to regain some mode of protection and security for Chaste overpowered not wanting to bother John Shoemaker. I could always call Brent or Carl and get recommendations for a body guard. There was virtually no one I could call locally that I trusted.

The garage was quiet, so I slipped out to call John and at least let him know what had happened. My first two tries received a busy signal, then my third call forwarded to an answering service. For some reason, I didn't feel right about leaving a message, but determined to pay him a visit first thing in the morning.

After our meal, Chaste sat quietly pecking away at her new laptop, which seemed to me an encouraging sign of recovery.

Thomas was still perched in front of the television quietly. Oddly, he seemed to have an endless amount of patience now, even though we knew nothing definite about his son. When I sat down on the couch, he was flipping through stations and bounced past one of the many infamous news stations. I jumped, almost choking and had him to back up a few notches. Pasted on the screen was the face of the young girl I had paid one hundred dollars for in the red-light district of Juarez.

The news anchor was spouting that the young lady had crossed our border in Southern California to do research for her masters thesis at USC; she had been missing for months.

Her father, some ultra rich business owner I had never heard of,

137

was offering an astounding two hundred fifty thousand dollar thank you reward to the mystery person that had been instrumental in her return.

There you have it. Another missing person of extreme wealth, losing a child, without so much as a nod for a ransom demand.

"You know something about that?"

I sat my plate down and picked up my cell phone, then thought twice and put it back down.

"She looks familiar."

Thomas frowned deeply and stared at me for a moment.

"Why don't you call and get the reward?"

I fully detested his poking into my thoughts and honestly didn't want to hear it tonight.

"Have you gone mad? Have you already forgotten everything we've been through?"

Thomas lowered his hackles and I apologized for raising my voice at him, blaming it on the ever-pervasive headache.

He flipped the channel past several of the usual humdrum programming and fell on the local news.

> "...so expect much needed rain for the next few weeks...,
> back to you Tess.
> In breaking news, noted local Phoenix attorney John Shoemaker was found dead in his west Phoenix home late this evening. Investigators suspect that his death was a domestic accident, but haven't ruled out foul play. Phoenix Police aren't releasing the details at present but commented that Mr. Shoemaker appeared to have sustained some type of head injury. Mr. Shoemaker's son, John Jr., found him a few minutes after 6 p.m. this evening.
> Again, local attorney John Shoemaker dead at forty-one years of age.
> The mayor's office announced today...."

I reached for my cell phone slowly, my food was churning inside me; our only local trustworthy friend was dead.

"Dad, was that our Mr. Shoemaker?"

What dreadful timing. Chaste came and sat down close beside me.

"I'm afraid so. He had an accident. Slipped and fell it seems."

"Who were you going to call?"

I quickly put the phone back down.

"Just looking at the time. Have you taken your medicines?"

She frowned and stuck out her tongue in a blah.

"Soon as I finished my food. Tastes awful. It makes my stomach hurt."

One antiparasitic was in an ugly orange liquid suspension, the taste must be horrible.

"And what of your tablets I left out for you?"

She stared at me, little wrinkles in her brow.

"My throat's sore. It hurts when I swallow."

I rose up off the sofa towing her behind me.

"Come on then, I'll help you."

A little syrup or butter coating and it would slide down easier. After my home remedy, she swallowed fitfully, making much more to do about it than was necessary.

"Can I help feed the boys?"

I had forgotten to generate some cover story about the two dead Rot's.

"They seem to have run off, but I'm sure they'll turn up. How are you liking your new laptop?"

Diversion. Diversion. Diversion.

"How did they get out of the fence?"

Blast it all.

"I don't know. Probably the same way our unwanted guests got inside."

"Can we go look for them?"

"Chaste, it's nearly your bedtime. I told your doctor that I would be responsible to keep you on your schedule. Did you drink all of your juice?"

She ignored my question. Her dogged determination was not satisfied but she was too miffed to argue any further and stalked off upstairs to her bedroom.

"Can I put out some food for them; for when they come back?"

Only her head was visible at the top of the staircase.

"Off to bed, you scallywag!"

"You have to come up and say prayers with me."

I pointed toward her room and she disappeared down the upstairs hallway.

"She's a great little girl."

Thomas had obviously been listening and watching in great detail.

"She is at that."

He flipped off the television and the house was eerily quiet.

"How's the headache?"

I thumped my head and winced past my theatrics.

"Ghastly. Some demolition crew at work inside my skull."

"What are we going to do about the dogs?" he asked.

I shrugged.

"What are we going to do about a new lawyer?" I mumbled.

My list was growing larger and more complex by the day, actually by the hour.

My conversation with Brent and Carl respectively lasted nearly an hour; far longer than I had anticipated.

We settled several items. They would use a local team to do the research and find out what happened to our lawyer and send me in the right direction for a better security system for our residence.

I mulled over where to begin to find an attorney that was close to the quality that John Shoemaker had been. I daresay we wouldn't find one that had an open audience with the judge such as he had.

I heard a clanking somewhere that sounded as if it was in the garage and jumped to investigate.

Thomas was already wide-eyed and standing in the doorway to my office in complete silence.

He formed his hand into the classic gun motion and wiggled his thumb and I frowned and shook my head no.

I didn't own a gun.

In retrospect, the immediacy of the situation made me forget about the absconded Glock killing tool now wrapped in a towel and secreted away in my utility pantry.

It's just as well, I wouldn't have produced the pistol; I'm a physician, not a murderer.

Thomas offered me his cane and I refused with a grin.

We both heard another series of bumps and clanks and I sprinted toward the short hallway leading to the garage.

Whoever it was obviously didn't care if they were discovered by the amount of racket they were generating.

Thomas shuffled up behind me and handed me the longest knife I own from my kitchen.

I threw open the door, holding the knife in front of me, to find Chaste dragging the nearly full, hundred pound sack of dog chow toward the boys empty food bin.

"What in blazes are you doing!?"

Chaste tripped and quickly picked herself up from under the fallen bag and wiped the dust off her nightgown.

"I only wanted to make sure they had some food for when they came back."

She stared at the knife as I handed it back to Thomas.

"Do you know how dangerous it is for you to be out here alone after…."

I choked. I couldn't bear the thought of losing her again.

"You get inside this house immediately young lady!"

I pointed a shaky finger toward the open door. Chaste stood her ground and placed both hands on her hips.

"I don't want to live in a bottle."

I almost fell to my knees. It was the same phrase Elizabeth always spouted at me when we argued over the violence at our clinic in South Africa.

I ran to her and hugged her to me, kissing the top of her head.

"I know. I know sweetheart. I just want to keep you safe."

How could I make either of us feel safe ever again?

I picked up her frail body, covered in the smell of dried dog food, and carried her back inside and upstairs to her room to clean her up. After offering her several stern warnings about going anywhere alone, she conceded to keep me apprised of her whereabouts until we had a working security system around the house.

We said our requisite prayers and stuffed covers around her body until she could barely move.

I trotted down the stairs and headed straight out to the garage.

My late night mission…, to get my wheelbarrow and shovel and make a quick job of burying the boys. Chaste could just as easily walked outside the back garage door and seen their stiff corpses stacked on one another in the corner. That would have been a pretty sight and another year of therapy.

The wheelbarrow was full of collected junk, which I had neither the time nor patience to sort through. I conceded to some manual labor, snatching up the shovel.

The outside lights were already on as I walked around the back and I looked for somewhere to dig a hole in the rocky soil. It would be a long night. The two Rots weighed in at least one-twenty each, possibly more.

The shovel clanked against the side of the house and my eyes watered from my headache just as I turned the corner.

They were gone.

Both the enormous canines had vanished. Who could have taken them? Their bodies were already stiffening from rigor and the cold when I'd moved them. It wasn't bloody likely they'd wandered off on their own.

The main gate was still closed and I hadn't heard any commotion, but the fact was evident before my very eyes.

I cursed my headache as I tried to force my mind to understand what might have happened to their massive bodies over the course of the last few hours.

Thomas helped me lock and check every window and door in the entire house both upper and lower floors. For the first time in my life, I was glad for the hidden weapon.

CHAPTER TWENTY-SIX

After my shower, I fell across my bed, exhausted mentally and physically. Stress will do strange things to a man, but so does having been stung seven times by a demon. Fighting self-pity is so much harder than I imagined.

Evil or not, each time I had asked for help, it came, rarely in the form I desired, but inevitably the results always fell in place like pieces to a puzzle.

How could I wish help for my friend John Shoemaker? Somehow, I knew inside that he had fallen victim to foul play.

"Help me find Steven."

There it was done, my request was spoken, out in the open.

I didn't know what to expect. Frankly, I was afraid that the strange being I'd seen would appear before me and whisk me away to some situation I was not prepared for, especially in my bathrobe.

Nothing happened. No flash of light, no spectral visitation, no vision or voice in my head. My head..., why did I have to remind myself of my head? When would it quit making my eyes water?

I felt my eyelids droop and knew sleep was closing in and rolled over onto my chest. The headache eased ever so slightly and I could hear a buzzing in the distance, coming closer. The closer it got, the more my headache dissipated. I groped until I found the edge of the comforter and flipped it over my body, not wanting to move and ruin a good thing. Instead of drifting away, the vibrations were getting strong enough to feel, setting my teeth on edge. Then they began to spread down my neck, shoulders, chest, and throughout my body. It was as if I were a hollow tube and someone was tipping it slowly end to end, allowing some smooth liquid to pour from one end and back again in a see-saw motion. I suppose it could be described most accurately as an unborn floating in the womb.

I slid from my body like a pat of butter from a hot plate and sat up. There before me was my forty-four year old body, partially covered and fast asleep. The thought crossed my mind that I was dead, that I had died. I was on the verge of panic, when I heard a voice behind me.

"I know your question. I've heard it hundreds of times before you, in almost every language. Am I dead...."

The light behind me wasn't quite white, but definitely not grey. If I could have spun around, I'm sure I would have, but the dreamlike state was something akin to being underwater. When moving slowly, there was no resistance, but try to move fast and....

"Am I?"

"No. If you get frightened, you'll fall back inside your body."

My dreamlike spectre had no distinct facial features, almost like a statue, blank without the shading.

"Who am I?"

"Yes, who are you? What are you? If you're used to all the questions, then you must know I need to know something."

"I am Pitre..., and I'm part of you now."

Not the answer I wanted and far, far, from what I expected. I didn't know what to say or what to think.

"Kress, you need to know how I regret the circumstances of our first meeting."

He must be talking about the six obscene puncture wounds that were a constant maddening itch and just now beginning to heal.

"What do you mean, you're a part of me?"

"I'm attached to the edges of your soul. You see me here, separate, but we are like ink and water now, you and I."

I was feeling a strange tugging toward my body. Must have been part of that frightened consequence he described to me.

"Pitre. I appreciate your help with retrieving Chaste, but...."

"Yes, I know. You have what you want and now you're done."

Right on the money. Couldn't have put it better myself.

"I'm afraid that's not possible."

"Do you mean to tell me that I now have to spend the rest of my life with you…, inside…, cohabitating with me?"

Splendid. So much for privacy.

I tried to shake my body and wake me up, but my hand passed through it like a wisp of smoke. At the sight of my antics, he seemed thoroughly agitated at me.

"I thought you might be different from all the others, considering…."

For some reason this got my attention.

"Different how?"

"I expected or maybe hoped you might accept our union."

This was obviously another vivid dream brought on by my continual migraine, but it seemed so real. I decided to play along.

"There were others? What about the others?"

"Yes, the others…, they wanted to use their new insight for personal gain."

Pitre went silent, staring at me, watching me again. If this was a dream, I hated it, but what if this wasn't?

"Most? What about the rest?"

"Some went into seclusion or…, lost touch with reality."

I certainly didn't want to fall into any of the above categories. I had to hold myself together for the sake of my daughter.

"What about Thomas?"

"Bitter, power hungry; he sees himself as becoming some New Age Guru, a Shaman to the world."

I could see those possibilities in Thomas. I was about to flood this dream person with questions. My dreamlike apparition was one-step ahead of me.

"How do I know? Because with each stinging blow, I extract a sample of what that person is made of. He wasn't worthy of all seven. He only received one. No matter what he told you."

Lucky me. Now I was attached at the hip…, no… soul, with some….

"Just what are you Pitre?"

"I am…."

He lowered his head in what seemed to be shame.

"I was… an angel."

"There was rebellion in heaven. I know you've read about it and heard about it. I saw it inside you with my first test; your dominant thigh records everywhere you been and your travels and all your memories.

"One third of the host of heaven deserted the Creator for..., well I won't mention names. I was one of the many caught at the wrong place at the wrong time.

"I remember it as if it happened moments ago. There were more swords flashing than I had ever seen and the noise was like continual thunder.

"I wasn't a warrior, I was..., actually I was second in line to replace the..., the music director of all heaven; the leader of the *coup d'état* you would say.

"Some of us were captured and dragged down with the rest, just as the heavens were slammed shut behind us."

My dream..., vision..., visitor..., turned his head upward as if reliving some event.

"The fall itself was painful, everyone was screaming. None of us had ever known pain. I tried to get free and fly back up.... I tried but it was useless desperation....

"When the few of us realized that the portals from earth to heaven were closed, the others joined ranks with the fallen ones. When I refused to join the rebellion, well..., there were untold millions of them and only one of me.

"Slamming me into the earth below was their idea of forcing me to join them, but I wasn't built like them and although I couldn't die, I blacked out. I was there for..., a very long time.

"When I awoke, my tongue was glued to the roof of my mouth. My back felt torn and broken. I could barely breathe through the sand caked in my nostrils. I remember snorting at a black wasp inspecting the drying orifices of my head for use as a nest.

"When the ringing in my ears became bearable, I heard a shuffling, across the ground and unbearable mocking laughter.

"After I still refused to join them, they stood on my back and ripped out my wings. I watched helplessly until the blinding pain in my back rendered me unconscious once again."

I was speechless. I realized just how prophetic it had been, asking my daughter if she believed in angels. Now her father, Dr. Kress M. Schumacher had his own personal fallen angel attached somewhere inside.

No, this couldn't be.

It was utter nonsense and I wished for the dream to end.

We both sat in silence, staring at one another for a short time. He began where he left off when he was satisfied that the first part of his story had drifted past my unbelief.

"They couldn't kill me, so they exiled me to a little pinprick of dirt in the Himalayas. Every few centuries or so they moved me to a different location and more religions emerged as a result of trying to explain myself to the limited imaginations of those they sent me. They said moving me made their game interesting; I say it was because I started getting too close to freedom. The others, the fallen, reveled at my futility in trying to go home."

So, Pitre had become their game of choice; the two-dollar bet, with impossible odds.

"That little creature you saw is the earthbound body they gave me. It usually hibernates while I'm attached to a host, you at the moment.

"There have been so many before you...."

A deep sadness filled me..., not my own. I was feeling the pull of my dream's sham of a tale.

"Time is such an ugly thing, Kress. Even though it serves its purpose as a mile marker for humans, it only ruined my plans. Just when I get a willing co-worker in tune with what I'm trying to accomplish, they wear out and die or..., go insane."

It was so real. I actually felt such great pity for the angel I was supposedly playing host to; but not more than the pity I was feeling for myself.

"Pitre, what do you need from me?"

I could tell he was trying to find a way of telling me something that I would not want to hear and make it palatable.

"Oh for heaven's sake, spit it out."

Then I realized it was a poor choice of wording on my part.

"As you probably know, there is no redemption for fallen angels."

Actually I wasn't really up on all the laws of heaven and earth at the moment, but I felt that Pitre was about to give me the abridged version.

"Only humans have a way to get back in. Deserters don't have a Savior."

Ah, now this fabrication was all making sense. He had perfected a way to attach to the human soul and intended to piggyback, as it were, back up through the pearly gates. For an instant, I marveled at my mind's ingenuity, concocting such a farce.

"You still think this is a dream?"

"Well, yes, I've had a lot of practice this week. If this isn't a dream, then what is it?"

I flirted with the idea this could be real, then quickly ran and hid from it.

"If what you say is true, then when I die you become a hitchhiker into heaven? Absurd."

The problem was and is, I wasn't ready to bid the world of the living goodbye just yet.

"Kress, you're not listening to me. I can't force you to do anything."

"Of course not, like making me go back and get the other abducted children, and almost making my rental car strand us in the middle of nowhere to force me to pick up a prostitute. I'm assuming that was you of course."

Pitre stood with an looming glare; holy hell he was tall.

The ceilings in our home are an archaic twelve feet high and he almost touched it with his head.

He began to glow bright white and his countenance became menacing.

"It was the right thing to do."

The voice boomed at me and I felt the straining tug to fling back in my body, but he grabbed my arm to steady me.

His touch – my God - waves of something inexplicable rolled through me as I willingly reconsidered departing this world for the next.

He let go of my arm and sat back down as what was left of my senses settled back to this odd reality.

"What was that?"

I couldn't speak; it was as if I had silently hurled the words at him.

"Leftovers."

CHAPTER TWENTY-SEVEN

The alarm clock jolted me awake.

I couldn't remember going back inside my body, or if there was more to our conversation. Of two things I was sure of; last night was no dream and my headache was completely gone.

I patted my head carefully; felt my smile spread from ear to ear. I wanted to dance in a circle, but didn't think it proper to press my luck and all.

I flopped back down on my bed, just as Chaste burst into my bedroom.

"They're back!"

She ran and attacked me with her silly giggles that sounded like fresh cool water.

"Who is back?"

I hefted her up off my chest and finally managed to get my question past her chattering.

"The Boys!"

I'm not normally the kind to be a party pooper, but I personally poked a finger in the cavities where the boys were executed via a shot in the skull.

"Are you sure it's them?"

"Of course, silly. Why wouldn't I be?"

Her frown was going to start a conversation I did not want to have, so I countered her as quickly as possible.

"Let's go have a look-see, shall we?"

I crammed my legs in some slacks and headed for the back door where Chaste was already busy putting out dry food into a pan.

Did I see what I thought I saw?

The two monster-sized Rot's were happily chewing and groveling at the bottom of the pan and licking Chaste's fingers in the process.

The edges of my daughters lips and chin was crusted with..., the dog's food. All my immediate concerns shifted from the unholy resurrection of the canines to Chaste.

"Chaste dear?" I heard my voice hovering again, "Are you eating the boys food?"

"I'm sorry Daddy, it smelled so good."

She carefully wiped her hands as I'd seen her do once before; then she swallowed.

This was so wrong on so many levels I didn't know where to begin.

"From now on, let's let the boys eat their food and we'll stick to human food."

She frowned and nodded darkly, her pupils almost hiding all traces of color in their pools of blue.

I held her hand as we watched the two hungry animals crunching at their food.

On each of the boys heads was a pink bald spot about the size of a copper penny, where I had placed a finger into a bullet-fractured hole.

Pitre..., what have you done?

My cell phone began to sing and crawl in a circle on the table in our living room. It was already eight a.m., two hours past my usual time of rising.

The number on the caller ID was from my bank.

The kind voice of one of the staff came on the line, informing me that I was needed at the Phoenix First National to verify the contents in one of my safety deposit boxes.

It appeared that two boxes had been forced open, one of them was mine and it was now empty.

I didn't need to fling on dress clothes and peer into the metal box to know what was taken. After verifying my box number, I told her that there was only a small envelope inside. She assured me that the box was now clean and that I should come in and fill out an insurance claim on the contents at my earliest convenience.

The GPS capsule was stolen; from inside the vault of my bank no less. One of the most secure banks in the southwest. There was no actual monetary value that could be assessed to the tiny instrument, yet it could have proven priceless in locating more missing children and apprehending the culprits.

Although my headache was now vanquished, my mind was scalded at the implications. I clenched my jaw and rifled through my mind recalling all those that knew of the instrument's existence and those I had told of its current location.

Only three..., Brent, Carl, and John Shoemaker knew the physical location.

My attorney friend and helper had died over his knowledge of a speck of electronics slightly longer than one of Chaste's medicine capsules.

I was furious and sad all in the same moment.

"Daddy? Is everything okay?"

On the verge of tears, I dialed the number to Brent and Carl. I had to tell someone of the correlating circumstances.

"Yes Chaste, all is going to be fine."

I prayed that this new life allied with an angel would not always be this painful. Why should someone good and kind such as John Shoemaker die and others live?

I ended the call before anyone answered. I had more questions of my own that needed to be answered, yet how did I request an audience with Pitre? I couldn't spend half my time asleep or in some kind of trance state. Again I was at the mercy of some unknown; not the happiest of circumstances for the analytical and logical mind of a doctor.

I looked around and finally my thoughts cleared enough to notice that the ever-present Thomas and his bed on the floor had vanished.

"Chaste, where is Thomas?"

"He was gone when I got up. I thought you knew."

I rushed to the front door and peered out to the gate at the drive and the walkway.

Both were closed and locked.

I blinked and rubbed both my sleep scaled eyes before acknowledging the tall grey figure standing in the street, peering *over* our fence; our *eight foot tall* fence.

It didn't appear to be doing anything other than observing the house. A few moments later, the boys charged up to the fence and began their patented growl and pace in the vicinity of the grey figure. I couldn't tell if they actually saw it or only sensed its presence. No matter, they were doing their job splendidly.

The house was eerily silent as Chaste walked up to my side watching our two guards creating a smooth path in the dirt along our front fence. I felt somehow cut off and alienated in that moment.

"What are they growling at?"

"Probably some stray."

Chaste knew about Pitre, but I wasn't ready to tell her more than her young mind could accept.

"The dogs where we were kept prisoner, they used to do that all the time. The mean man shot them."

"Was it where I found you?"

She was talking and now that we had some modicum of privacy, I wanted to keep the conversation moving.

"A couple of places, and in the desert where you found me."

I hadn't seen or heard any dogs before or during our escape which conjured more questions.

"Would you like to tell me about it all?"

She shook her head no.

"You know there's nothing to be ashamed of; you didn't do anything wrong."

The look in her eyes begged me to wait and let her choose the right time and place.

I kissed the warmth of her soft cheek and walked to the kitchen to start something for brunch.

"The first ones that had me, kept me in a cardboard box with holes punched in the side for three or four days at a time. It stunk so bad. I tried to hold it."

I didn't let on, but kept choosing food items from the fridge and setting them on the countertop.

"They made me change clothes again, in front of the others and I got to ride in a crate with hay inside. I could see lights everywhere that night."

It sounded like somewhere outside the city of Juarez.

I realized that I had nervously unloaded almost everything onto the counter and began to put most of it back on the refrigerator shelves, not ready to eat four dozen eggs.

"They never really talked to us; they just pointed and we had to figure it out. They gave us canned food and sometimes bread. It was always the same thing though; usually we ate something called Alpo. I think it was Mexican food of some kind, but they never cooked it for us."

I wanted to vomit. No wonder she was interested in the boy's feed. I wasn't going to tell her it was dog food, or that it was one of the avenues she received the parasitic infestations she was taking medications for; that and lying in her own feces.

I lost my apatite.

"Orange juice?"

I could hear my voice quiver. Somewhere inside I knew I had better grow a spine and hold myself together for her sake. I'd seen much worse on a daily basis working with the barbaric conditions of the locals in South Africa. I'd seen malnutrition in children brought on by eating chicken feed as a staple diet, but this wasn't South Africa, and this was my daughter.

Chaste poured her own juice and gulped it down with one of the pills she was getting better at swallowing.

"Would you like some hot oatmeal with some fruit?"

She smiled her mothers smile and nodded.

"I met some of the other kids, but we weren't allowed to talk to each other. The others came and went real fast, but a couple of us stayed together. I heard them say we were..., special."

"Did you see their faces?"

I could tell I was pushing my luck.

"Nope. Always had weird looking masks on."

The microwave dinged as I was dicing up bananas and strawberries. She remained quiet and I assumed that she was through sharing, although her eyes were still unfocused and glazed.

"There was one of them..., his hands were always dirty.... He was always trying to reach through our crates to grab at us."

I stirred some brown sugar and cinnamon into the oatmeal and topped it with a handful of fruit and a little milk. I knew that if I displayed the repulsion I was feeling, she would believe that she was somehow at fault.

Chaste plucked at the pieces of fruit, observing them, pushing them with her spoon.

"The mean one was always yelling something at him and knocking him away from us. Then one day, they pulled him outside and he never came back."

She looked up at me with her soulful eyes.

"I think they killed him. But I didn't care. I wanted him to go away. Is that wrong Daddy?"

I hugged her gently for a moment trying to think.

"You weren't responsible for his actions or what happened to him. That's all you need to remember."

Between the revelations of my daughter this morning and from Pitre last night, I was becoming an emotional wreck. I couldn't imagine what Chaste was dealing with inside.

"It's so good to be home Daddy."

That ended the first of several confessionals that were to come from Chaste.

While she was eating, I walked back to one of the front panes and looked out at the gate. The boys were still seated with butts flat on the ground staring in the direction of our new uninvited guest.

I supposed today wouldn't be a good day for a run.

Chaste felt the need to take a morning nap, which gave me opportunity to barricade myself into my office and try to communicate with Pitre. This unorthodox partnership was already in nowise fair, but it would be even more disturbing if I were not allowed to initiate some type of conversation.

"Pitre, do I need to break out a crystal ball?"

The giant oaf appeared seated on my floor. Even seated he was still nearly my height of six feet tall; all white and majestic.

"I have some more questions for you."

"The first answer is…, he is a watcher. They've posted a sentry to watch your activities. You're just able to see them now."

Blast it all, I didn't get to pose my question.

"Well I don't like it one bit, neither do the boys. Speaking of the boys, are you responsible for repairing the holes in their heads and reanimating them?"

"Your daughter Chaste cares for them, so yes, I repaired them."

My list of questions was so long and jumbled I didn't know which to ask next.

"What happened to John Shoemaker?"

"He is dead."

I wanted to throw something at him.

"Yes, yes, I know he's dead. Who killed him and why?"

"Our enemies and you already know why."

"I don't suppose you can do something to fix *that* can you?"

His silence was my answer.

"No, I suppose not."

The clock on the wall was ticking away and time was robbing my session.

"Pitre, why me? Why my daughter Chaste? Did I commit some unspeakable evil that caused us to be chosen?"

He sat quietly and I wondered if he had the unfair prerogative of not answering.

"I did not choose you. The ones you call grey are the ones that normally choose. They have always chosen. Except for this one occasion, you were an exception.

"Please understand…, down through time, the prospects that were chosen to face me, the ones that possessed moral scruples but had no resources, would try and use my powers to get wealth.

"The ones with resources, but no scruples, sought power and control.

"The ones with neither…, you would have described them as hideous.

"I complained constantly to the grey ones that I needed someone with no need of money as well as no desire to rule the world. Of course they only laughed at my request."

I was an exception? Why didn't I feel exceptional?

"What about Thomas?"

"Yes…, Thomas. He served his purpose. He won't be back."

He was dead right about that; Thomas would not be setting foot back in my house.

I was beginning to learn that if I allowed every shaded and inconclusive answer that Pitre offered upset me I would get distracted and learn nothing.

"I've already told you that Thomas was an undesirable…. Your curiosity is unsettling, Kress. The creature you met, the one I used to test you; it was my only avenue to peer into your motives. For each of my tests, if the person is tainted with wickedness, such as Thomas, where they are stung sometimes withers. It was unfortunate.

"I formed an arrangement with Thomas. If he would help me find a more suitable subject, instead of what I was being given by the grey ones time after time, I would repair his damage."

Thomas was repaired like the two Rottweiler mutts and had taken off for parts unknown. Well good riddance.

"His son Steven wasn't even real? But I saw him...."

"You saw a boy named Steven, but not the son of Thomas. He did lose his son Steven; it was a matter of time before you knew the two were not the same.

"Thomas heard rumors from the local Indian tribes of a spirit quest that could make a person special, like the Shaman of their tribe, a healer or seer. Thomas sought me out on his own, by way of a very old native living a life of solitude in the high desert."

So part of the Indian story had skirted the truth. Just another deception. The entire debacle was a circle of lies.

"Yes, Thomas was an accomplished liar."

"How many did he bring to you before me?"

"Four."

"Other wealthy children like my daughter?"

I already knew the answer to that question and didn't wait for an answer. My next question could either make or break our relationship.

"Did Thomas have anything to do with my daughter's disappearance?"

"He was instrumental in arranging the choice."

I wanted to kill Thomas. To bludgeon him with that stupid cane until....

"I hate you Pitre. You and your self-righteous talk of getting someone worthy! Well in my opinion, you aren't worthy of getting back through...."

The pain that flooded my body and mind was unbearable. I couldn't so much as squeak a plea for help. It was as if a giant hand were crushing my entire body.

Finally..., just short of unconsciousness, I was allowed to breathe.

Pitre's voice rattled the walls of my office.

"You should not speak of things you know nothing of!"

CHAPTER TWENTY-EIGHT

The room had been dark for almost an hour before I decided to venture back and check on Chaste. Thankfully, the wrath of Pitre was only temporary or I would have been rendered useless. Even his profuse apologies couldn't stop the ringing in my ears or the frustration for my unwilling servitude.

I hated the fact that even my thoughts weren't hidden from this internal parasite called Pitre. Even if I plotted to rid myself of him, he would be lurking somewhere inside me listening to my every step and possibly do harm to me or to Chaste. I was now his prisoner.

There was no need to pursue the aspect of who had taken the GPS device, no reason to call Brent or Carl.

Then devious thoughts of self-preservation hit my mind and I hurried to my cell phone. I had no idea how far I would be allowed to roam with my plans before my demonic parasite rendered me permanently useless in another fit of rage.

After an eternity, Brent answered with his customary greeting. Some urging inside me told me I could trust these two friends.

"Yes, Brent. How are you today?"

"You sound strange Kress. Is everything alright?"

I wanted to cause immediate havoc, but kept my thoughts silent.

"We're still looking into the death of Mr. Shoemaker. We've run into one dead end after another."

"His death took me by such a surprise, my suspicions were probably an act of my own grief."

Obviously, I lied; I knew different. I started to tell him of the stolen GPS device and how John's death was connected but knew that too would be a 'dead end'.

"I have a job for you and Carl if your schedule is open for a few days."

"Anything for you and Chaste. What do you need?"

After I explained what I needed, I heard Carl cursing in the background; I must have been on speakerphone.

"We'll be happy to help you."

My next phone call was to my friend Judge Harrison. I didn't ask for anything, only offered my condolences at our mutual loss of John Shoemaker; just a bit of chitchat. I was shoring up my few friends.

Next on my list was my contact with the law office where John had partnered. I needed a new attorney with some of the qualities of my late friend and made an appointment to see them right away.

The cell phone was getting hot in my hand, when I realized that I had been talking on it for over an hour. I placed it back in its charger and went to prepare some lunch. Chaste was steadily filling back out since she had come home and her complexion was finally losing that sour pallor that gave her a haunted look.

She was still resting peacefully when I entered the room and I woke her as cheerfully as I could muster.

"Do you feel up to a trip into Phoenix tomorrow?"

Her eyes brightened at the thought of getting out of the confines of the house. I saw more blue in them than I had in days.

"If we can stop by the bookstore."

She scrambled to her worktable and handed me a piece of paper with a list. The bounce in her short blond hair and her excitement was refreshing.

I noticed that all her pink and white bunny collection was heaped in her wastebasket; its sides bulging as if she'd stomped it all down. I didn't ask why.

Her list..., I glanced at it quickly....

"You've been busy with the internet I see."

I helped her pick out some of her older clothes that didn't hang off her recovering body. While slack, they were all too short for her gangly legs and arms; my how she'd stretched. I made a mental note that a shopping spree was in order. We found something suitable for her to wear the next day and I went to place out our meal.

I was sure Chaste was being polite while eating my attempts at cooking; my abilities in the kitchen were no match for Elizabeth's.

My cell phone rang just as Chaste sat down to eat.

"Dr. Schumacher? My name is Ferry Dunavin."

It was a pleasant voice, not what I was used to.

"I'm taking on Mr. Shoemaker's clients and I wanted to confirm our meeting at two o'clock tomorrow afternoon at our law office in Phoenix, if that's convenient with you."

"We're planning a trip into Phoenix tomorrow. That would be perfect for us."

Ferry…, what an unusual name.

"Good, I'll see you then."

The phone rang off without the customary goodbye. What a strange lady.

I walked into my office and shut the door for a moment of privacy.

"Hello, My name is Dr. Kress Schumacher. I need to speak to the person in charge of my family's move to the United States."

"Case number please…."

Ferry Dunavin extended a chilly hand in greeting, then quickly apologized, rubbing her palms briskly.

"I took a walk during lunch. I didn't realize how cool it was until I was back inside. Well, Dr. Schumacher, it's good to finally meet you. What can I do for you today?"

It seemed our new lawyer was both distracted and very distracting. She seemed more preoccupied than rushed.

"I need to set up a provisionary Trust Fund for my daughter Chaste and update my Will."

Chaste sat down with her usual smile in the seat next to mine; her sudden glow hiding the gaunt circles under her eyes.

"You must be Chaste. How are you doing young lady?"

"Very well thank you."

Ms. Dunavin smiled warily at the lanky child swallowed by the enormous wing back chair and then it was back to business.

"Can't your bank or your broker do this more efficiently? Don't you have a financial advisor?"

"Yes, in London, and most of our resources will remain in

London, but we reside here now. It's just my daughter and I now and I want to make sure that in the event something should happen to me that she would be amply taken care of without any lag or complications."

I handed her my latest financial statements and Ms. Dunavin's eyebrows arched painfully and her voice stressed.

"Well.... How much of this would you like to include in the new Trust?"

"All of it."

"All..., all of it?"

"All of the local assets immediately."

She ran her slender fingers through the light brown hair over her left ear as she stared at the numbers and back up at me. This seemed to be the icebreaker that garnered her full attention.

"I want my Will to be the fiduciary that populates the remainder of the Trust Fund upon my death. I still need access to my other assets, obviously."

"Your daughter could live comfortably on the interest alone..., both of you...," her eyes flicked up, "...but you already know that."

As our new lawyer began pouring over our financial records, I couldn't help but notice the abundance of framed collegiate and law certifications proliferating the wall.

Ms. Dunavin was admitted to the Arizona Bar in 2004, but she was a member in twelve other states, including New York, New Jersey and Washington D.C. and the U.S. Supreme Court. She was also a member of the Association of Prosecuting Attorneys, and spent two years as Special Council for the Federal Bureau of Investigation.

Her Harvard Law MBA was dated 1994, roughly two years after my own doctorate degree.

I had to do a quick reevaluation as to my uneducated guess at Ferry Dunavin's age; she was either not the early-thirties she appeared or she'd been an extremely focused and determined young woman.

All these framed accolades were centered around a graduate certificate from St. Mary's School for Girls; obviously something she was particularly fond of.

"Dr. Schumacher, you need to realize that while I don't specialize in Wills and Trusts, Theodore Glass, one of our partners is more than qualified to set this up for you. He's also our CPA and tax expert, he'll explain the details."

I nodded, then my curiosity peaked, "What exactly do you specialize in Ms. Dunavin?"

A slight grin edged up one side of her lips, "I have the unofficial title of being the bulldog of litigation for our firm, especially now that John is no longer with us. Now..., I know enough to lay out the terms, but Mr. Glass will have to draw up the forms and complete the process for you."

We haggled out the terms of the Trust, converting an enviable fortune to a child that I was determined to build a bubble around. A tremendous weight lifted from my shoulders as soon as I realized that should anything happen to me, Chaste would be just fine. It was as if I'd beat some imagined closing gate just before a ship set sail.

"Have you picked a guardian yet?"

I hadn't quite reached that point in my thinking just yet.

"Can I let you know in a day or two?"

I signed a few documents, insisted on a temporary form allowing Ferry Dunavin power of attorney, and thus began the legal machine shifting the family fortune to Chaste. It was all old money, from both sides of the family; generations old, and the entire process made me feel stuffy and pretentious.

Before letting me go, Ms. Dunavin ushered me into the privacy of an adjacent room, just out of earshot of my daughter.

"Dr. Schumacher, do you mind if I ask you something personal?"

How much more personal could baring all my family's considerable financial assets to a stranger be? She took my silence as a yes.

"Are you dying? Is there something else that I should be aware of?"

Apparently she didn't know about all the events which John and I had wretched through. I explained that because of certain recent events, I had re-evaluated my needs. It wasn't a lie, just wonderfully vague.

"It's just that John..., Mr. Shoemaker, did the same thing only a week before his.... I'm sorry, I shouldn't have mentioned it."

I hadn't fully considered how attractive Ms. Dunavin was until that moment. It must have been the vulnerability I saw in her bright green eyes and her expression when she mentioned John's death.

"Quite all right Ms. Dunavin, we're all deeply saddened by John's accident."

I watched for and I saw a twitch, there was a glimmer of doubt when I mentioned the word accident. She suspected.

She wanted to talk to me and tell me something about the circumstances of his death. I assumed that sudden insight was a side effect of Pitre.

"Chaste and I have some business in town for a few hours..., would you like to catch a bite to eat with us this evening?"

I felt like such a dolt as soon as the words left my mouth. I hoped I didn't give her the wrong impression.

Her eyes unconsciously brushed her concerted thoughts for an excuse.

"Of course if you'd rather not, I completely understand. I thought you might want to discuss John's passing, with a mutual friend."

Her expression softened even further.

"I might be able to get free after five."

CHAPTER TWENTY-NINE

Chaste was taking her time going from shelf to shelf. I had picked up a copy of Runners World magazine and a cup of coffee then buried up into one of the cushioned chairs where I could observe my daughters every move in the bookstore.

Paranoia barely hinted of the protective mode I was in. I was still considering purchasing something as vulgar as a gun despite my recent acquisition. While I despise the idea of using a weapon of that sort on another human being, especially after seeing the resultant carnage on a body on several occasions, I'm quite proficient with firearms. A doctor's steady hand can be an advantage for more than a mere scalpel.

My cell phone blazed a loud awful tune and it was a strange number. I remembered the last time I'd received a call from an odd number and dismissed the call. Minutes later, I noticed that I had voicemail and my phone began growling that same music once again.

I looked at the screen and it was yet a different number. I ended it also and reluctantly checked my messages.

A man's voice I didn't recognize came on.

"Dr. Schumacher, I understand that you were instrumental in recovering my daughter. I don't want to invade your privacy, but I would like to thank you personally. I also have a reward I want to offer you if you'll accept it."

He left his name and number and there was a beep....

Another strange voice came on. A desperate voice that bled my heart in an instant.

"Mr., Uh, Dr. Schumacher, I was told that you know how to find lost children...."

The woman's voice broke down into sobs...,

"I can pay you, handsomely. If you can help me find my little girl please call me at...."

Another name and number.

My cell phone rocketed into revelry once again.

"Bloody hell."

I startled myself as I grumbled out loud.

This number I recognized.

It was the number of my contact at the State Department returning my call.

"Hello Doctor, I received your message, it's good to hear from you. I was so glad to hear about you recovering your daughter Chaste. Such a miracle. Now, how can I help you?"

"Mr. Contrata, yes thank you, not as pleased as I am I assure you. I know you're busy, so I won't waste your time. I'm interested in knowing the process of creating a situation of dual-citizenship."

There was undue silence; enough time to make me wonder how he'd heard about Chaste Ellen.

"Hello?"

"Yes, yes..., why would you want to do something like that?"

It was a fair question and I expected it.

"It's not for me personally. You see, after everything that has happened to us over the last year, I want Chaste to be able to visit where her mother and I grew up. I also want her to attend our old school in England when she is of age. It's only a formality for the dual-citizenship."

"Oh..., of course then. I completely understand."

He was lying. I don't know how I knew it, but he was lying through his teeth; his voice like fingernails across the chalkboard of my mind.

"It's really not necessary to have dual-citizenship for her to attend school in another country. A simple VISA will do."

I was fully aware of that.

"It would be if she decided to live at my family's old home place in Cambridge afterwards."

"You still own property in Great Brittan? Oh, yes, here it is. I must have missed that somehow."

Another irritating lie and it took me aback until his voice shook me awake once again.

"I understood that you didn't have any surviving family in Great Brittan."

"That's correct, but when the time comes, I want Chaste to be able to decide for herself where she wants to live."

"I see, I see…. You haven't received any more threats have you?"

What an odd question considering we moved here to get away from all that.

"No, unless you consider almost losing my daughter a threat."

"Yes, that was unfortunate."

A cold or the flu is unfortunate. A flat tire is unfortunate. Having your only child stolen was a life-altering catastrophe.

"Can I ask a question? Have there been any other missing children during the same time as my daughter?"

I knew I'd get the truth even if he lied.

"None that I'm aware of Dr. Schumacher."

Smarmy bald face lie.

"So you didn't know anything at all about my daughter's abduction?"

"Only recently. Is there some reason you wanted to know?"

Another blatant lie that sent me reeling.

"Just curious. I was recently made to understand that there might have been other children in similar circumstances. It doesn't matter."

This brought an undue amount of silence that spoke volumes to the questions formulating in my mind.

"Dr. Schumacher, I understand your concerns. Your first months in the States haven't been paradise."

The understatement of my lifetime.

"Why don't you give it a few more months and see if that's what you really want to do?"

I had the information I wanted and the conversation was going nowhere.

"Yes, I believe I will. Thank you for returning my call, Mr. Contrata."

I pressed end call on my phone so hard it's a wonder it didn't break its delicate glass screen in half.

As soon as I slipped it in my jacket, it broke into that same vile song, vibrating in my hand.

165

Another unknown number....

I ended the call, dialed my cell carrier to learn the procedure to change my phone number, and began looking for Chaste.

My daughter was walking back toward my seat with an armload of books while I begrudgingly listened to an unruly amount of recorded menu options on my telephone. Chaste sat beside me, not knowing she had some serious explaining to do about her mischievous choice of ring-tones on my telephone.

At my request Ferry Dunavin chose a suitable place where we would be able to have some quiet conversation while dining.

We ended up at an anonymous looking Steak and Ale'ish restaurant with a dark atmosphere, not far from downtown Phoenix. Chaste slid into her seat first with a questioning look. There weren't many children in the dining room, mostly older patrons.

My cell phone buzzed in my pocket – a new trick I learned, then another unknown number appeared. I ended it quickly.

As soon as we were seated, Ms. Dunavin took a few minutes whispering something to our waitress.

Her smile turned soft as she looked at Chaste and I.

"I didn't mean to sound so mysterious about John earlier. We worked closely together and I guess my imagination was running away with me."

The screech in my head wasn't quite as vivid. It was a white lie. A protective one. It sounded vaguely familiar to the one I'd used to fend off Brent.

"I understand. You probably worked closely with one another for quite some time."

She blushed, notable even in the dim lights.

"Our relationship was strictly professional."

It wasn't a lie, but she had personal feelings for her co-worker. Completely understandable; John was a good man.

"What made you think there might be foul play?"

There; the question was asked, right out in the open.

She stared me in the eyes and all at once, I knew how I must have glared at Thomas when he read my mind.

"I'm very sorry, Ms. Dunavin...."

"Ferry, please."

"Kress…, pleased to meet you."

I smiled and stuck out my hand in a reaffirming gesture trying to lighten the mood. Her laughter may have eased the tension, but didn't kill the question. Her congenial smile faded slowly while she chose her words carefully.

"John was on edge for a couple of days, some case he was working on was upsetting him. He was always taking on more than he could handle, especially after his wife's accident. Anyway, out of the blue, he had me help him set up a Trust for his son, and a rather large life insurance policy."

She was being very liberal with confidential information.

"Ferry, it was my case he was working on."

"I see."

She already guessed that. I needed a way to let her know that I was trustworthy or this would take forever.

My cell phone buzzed again, unknown number. What a nuisance.

"Looks like you're a popular person…, Kress."

The waitress came and took our orders before I could respond, dropping off our drinks.

I could tell Chaste was bored beyond tears with the conversation and I suggested that we get one of her new books.

"It's time for my medicine…, and I want the angel book."

As I rose, about to leave, Ferry looked relieved to be seated across from Chaste instead of me. She felt it. Just as I felt the probing mind of Thomas when he was around. It was probably the underlying reason Chaste didn't like Thomas.

I hurried to the Range Rover, grabbed her medicine and dug through the heavy stack of books in her plastic sack. About midway was "A History of Angels" with a photo of a magnificent angel statue on the front cover. It looked remarkably like Pitre, albeit with wings attached.

I pulled at the glass door to go back inside and saw a reflection and spun. Another tall grey similar to the watcher outside our fence was standing in the parking lot, staring at me, observing. My spine stiffened and I walked briskly toward it. I had to know its purpose; and of course, it faded from sight in a wisp before I reached it. I was now standing in the middle of the parking lot looking lost like a fool.

Our food was on the table when I returned and the two ladies had waited on me before eating. To my surprise, they both waited to say grace over the meal. Interesting. Chaste and I always blessed our food at home, but rarely when in public.

My cell phone erupted once again and I immediately tried to power it off. Frustration was fouling my logic and I handed the thing to my daughter.

"Chaste, would you mind turning this off for me."

Ferry threw me an interesting glance. It seemed that nothing escaped her intuitive eye.

The food was admittedly good; well to be honest, anything was better than my cooking and Chaste ate like there was no tomorrow.

I didn't want to spoil the food or the atmosphere, but I still needed to know any information or concerns Ferry might have.

"Ferry..., if you think there is some offhand chance that you might be in danger by taking over our affairs; I can go to some other firm."

Ferry almost choked on her bite of steak.

"No. I don't believe that... John's accident... was related to handling any of your affairs."

How sad. I had become a dollar value for her firm that was worth risking her life for.

"Was there an inquiry into his..., untimely..., accident? I asked.

I didn't want to say the word 'death' at the table for some reason. It seemed so cold.

"The usual badges, and there was an official with a U.S. Marshall's ID asking questions, but he didn't stay long."

Must have been someone from Brent and Carl's group.

"If you ever feel threatened or coerced by anyone having to do with myself or Chaste please let me know immediately."

"I don't understand, Kress. Why would anyone threaten me? Is there something more I should know about?"

I didn't bring up the GPS correlation. There was no need to place her in undue danger. Knowledge of its existence was most assuredly the reason John was no longer alive.

"No..., I suppose not. We've had a bit of a struggle since moving to this country. I just assumed that you may have heard particulars from John Shoemaker."

She didn't know anything about us? How was that possible?

That was probably for the best at present.

"You'll have to forgive me. I just returned from a lengthy case with a client in another state. I haven't been back to my office for more than a week and then John..., died..., and I've been handed all his clients. But..., having said that, John was a stickler for attorney – client privacy. Unless he needed help with a case his door was usually closed."

I nodded through most of what she said listening closely for information she wasn't intentionally offering, but there didn't seem to be any. Ferry Dunavin was being as clear and honest as could be expected.

"Now that you're my client, I'll make sure to look over John's notes and try to catch up..., just to make sure there aren't any loose ends."

"Of that I have no doubt," I mused.

A few minutes passed while we were finishing our meal and the waitress came by with a piece of some type of exotic cheesecake with strawberries bearing a burning candle.

Instead of some raucous song and revelry, she simply handed it to Chaste and whispered, "Happy Birthday."

What a kind gesture. Suddenly I felt silly for not offering my own sort of post celebration for my daughters ninth birthday.

"I hope you don't mind. John had it on top of his calendar to do something for Chaste's missed birthday. We always do something special for our clients."

Chaste smiled and said thank you as I slunk even lower inside.

"That was very thoughtful, thank you."

"Thank John for marking it in red on his calendar or I'd have missed it."

I supposed we wouldn't be changing law firms anytime soon, but I needed to pay special attention to make sure that nothing happened to Ms. Ferry Dunavin.

"I'm glad it wasn't buried somewhere with the group of notes that went missing from his planner."

CHAPTER THIRTY

Pitre, my new internal companion was strangely silent that evening. Our observing tall grey was gone and the atmosphere felt lighter. After my evening run, my new obsession, it felt as if our lives could possibly fall back into the mundane. Thomas was gone, I'd received no blatant opposition to my plans for Chaste, and our new lawyer was set in place. Just having the security of her future well within grasp was a major milestone of relief, considering my accumulating unknowns.

The time together with my daughter was actually pleasant. We watched some television together, looked over the half dozen books Chaste had purchased, and finally we both headed off to our rooms to bed.

A short time later, there was the tiny rapping of knuckles on my door. Chaste came in and sat on the end of my bed and waited patiently for me to drop the journal in my hands.

"I want to now more about Pitre."

"Chaste dear, I'm not too thrilled about the subject of Pitre and its getting late."

It seems Pitre was not to be ignored.

"But Dad, I keep having so many strange dreams."

It was the curse that Thomas had endured. Anyone near those touched by Pitre was subject to lucid dreams of the strangest varieties.

"My new book says there are good angels and bad angels. Which is Pitre?"

Ah, the honesty of children.

"The jury is still out on that question."

She looked at me strangely, so I rephrased my answer.

"I haven't figured out the answer to that just yet."

"I knew what you meant…, but don't you think he must be a good one? He helped me get home. And what about all the others like me?"

But for his own selfish purposes. Was I not seeing something that was obvious to my child? Or was I being manipulated into helping Pitre through my daughter's innocence?

"I hope you're right, Chaste. I hope he is one of the good ones. When we use bad things to make good things happen, isn't that a bit of a conflict?"

I didn't want to bruise her new inspiration but I needed to let her see that the would-be hero Pitre might be a wolf in sheep's clothing.

"But didn't you let him sting you? That was bad. Sooo…."

"Chaste…, it was my desperation to find you…."

I wanted to argue the point, but had no ammunition. She had her mother's tenacity and logic at nine years old.

I couldn't imagine her cunning at sixteen.

"Dear, let's not be hasty, either of us, in making a judgment for or against Pitre."

That seemed to be efficacious enough to placate her reasoning; however, it still left her on the 'innocent until proven guilty' side of the fence. I didn't like that. It made her vulnerable to ideas…, that's when it hit me. Pitre was not being silent at all. He was shoring up his trenches, becoming ingrained in our lives.

"Can we talk about this tomorrow? It's getting late and we both need our rest."

Even with our mild disagreement, I still received a healthy hug and kiss before she left the room.

I reached over to the nightstand and powered on my phone. I had twenty-seven new messages. Good heavens. I fumbled with the buttons and listened to each of them on speaker as I dressed for bed.

All were from people asking for my help in finding their lost children, lost loved ones and even one missing poodle. I still didn't understand how I had become the new hotline for the missing. It meant another trip into Phoenix to expedite getting my number changed.

"Okay, Pitre. Please show yourself."

There was silence.

"I know what you're doing."

The room effused white, more brilliant than I remembered.

"I know what you're doing too. I suppose you have more questions?"

I had demands.

"I need you to stop bothering Chaste."

"Kress, I am what I am. Humans are naturally drawn to us. I'm not manipulating her. It's her own curiosity and intuition that has her mesmerized."

He was telling the truth, despite his choice of words. His..., our..., proximity to my daughter was non-negotiable. And how did I come to this understanding? I was finally getting it. Pitre was part of me. Blast it all.

"Why are the tall greys watching us?"

"They're interested, they're observing our activities."

Now that answer was iffy, it was definitely an incomplete truth.

"What are you hiding from me Pitre?"

There was more silence.

My cell phone buzzed. I stuffed it under a pillow out of frustration.

"You should use what Thomas has done, together we can rectify the wrongs that have been done. I can tell you where every one of the missing children are."

I was temporarily blindsided.

"Thomas is the one responsible for all the messages on my phone?"

"He has been charging a substantial fee for your phone number. The people are desperate."

I wanted no part of it. I was about to protest when my bedroom door opened and I heard Chaste gasp.

Too late for me to stop her, there she stood in the entrance, partially shielding her eyes from the brilliance in the room.

"Are you the angel I saw in my dreams?"

I had tried to keep her isolated from Pitre until I could find a way to rid myself of him.

Pitre sat quietly looking at me as if asking for my permission to answer my daughter's question.

"You're so bright."

Why hadn't I locked my door?

"How can she see you?"

Pitre lowered his voice.

"Children are pure."

The meeting was inevitable, yet I wished for someway to protect her from Pitre. Now, it was too late.

"Yes…, this is he."

Pitre bowed politely from his seated position and sat back up.

"You're the one that made my chains fall off?"

"Yes."

"…and told my Daddy where to find me."

He nodded.

"Thank you."

I found their exchange different. Pitre turned to me.

"You fear me. People learn to hate what they fear. Your daughter does not fear me. The less you fear, the more you see."

He looked kindly at Chaste.

"Would you sit with your father?"

I wanted to protest her presence during our discourse.

"Why did you become a pediatrician?"

Immediately I sensed what he was up to. That wasn't a fair question and he knew it, so I lied.

"It was my career choice. I had to do something with my life."

Pitre laughed piteously at my puerile reply so I confessed.

"Because I wanted to help unfortunate children. There; are you satisfied?"

If it was possible, Pitre glowed brighter; it was becoming hard to look at him and I shifted my eyes.

"Can you tone it down a bit?"

"You're responsible for it. It's you that's making me brighter."

How utterly absurd. How could I make him brighter?

"That's why the fallen ones watch us. It's why they hate children. Children are pure. The fallen are jealous of anything pure and do anything in their power to defile them. The fallen are gray because their glory has been stripped away."

"But you're white…."

"Haven't you been listening? I didn't join them."

My daughter looked on wistfully.

"Where are your wings?" she asked.

Pitre turned his head away, from either shame or sadness, I couldn't tell. I answered for him.

"The others, the bad ones, took his away."

I couldn't believe the words that I had just spoken. Did that mean that I believed Pitre was one of the good?

"They did it to keep me earthbound," he injected.

Ah, now we were back to the crux of the matter! The reason for our new partnership.

"You helped me. If I help you, what do I have to do?"

He seemed further saddened.

"You wish to be rid of me."

We sat looking, rather staring at one another.

"Don't let your selfishness rob you of much better things Kress."

"Selfish? How dare you accuse me of being selfish."

Immediately my mind snapped to the incidents with the other stolen children and the young lady. I had to repent of my tone.

"Right then…, I suppose I can be a bit self-centered."

My voice had lost all of its self-righteous indignation.

"I don't see how I can help you, but I guess I can try."

"Thank you. Remember Kress, the more you see, the more you'll know."

Pitre vanished slowly, leaving the room aglow from his presence.

Chaste seemed awe stricken; so taken in by Pitre.

I could see how it would be easy for some malevolent spirit to defile an innocent child.

With a quick hug, Chaste left off to bed. Her smile said her curiosity was satisfied, "I like him."

She hadn't been impaled seven times by the bodily creature the tall greys had given Pitre. She wasn't attached at the soul with a stranger, listening in on every thought. I still didn't completely trust Pitre.

"Say your prayers, Daddy."

Such innocence. I nodded. Then more enthusiastically.

Yes, I believe I would.

By morning, I had a total of thirty-six voice messages to weed through. Didn't these people sleep?

The answer to my question was so obvious it hurt me to my depths. When Chaste was missing, I scarcely slept two hours each night, for months. No these people didn't sleep; they couldn't sleep.

Very carefully, I transcribed each message with their names and telephone numbers, but for the life of me didn't know what to do next.

Then I heard these words clearly, "The less you fear, the more you see. The more you see, the more you'll know."

I looked at the list and two names on it were glowing.

Eleven names were darkened. Sadly, I knew what that meant and drew a line through each of them, including the missing poodle.

Petrified, I called the first glowing telephone number and hung up before anyone answered. Then I gritted my teeth and hit redial.

A gravely voice that didn't sound anything like the message answered.

"I'm returning your call about your missing child?"

I listened non-stop for a solid ten minutes while I was informed of every detail, pertinent or not and scribbled some of it down.

Then came the dreaded question; Do you think you can help us find our daughter?

I absolutely didn't know how to answer....

"I believe I have enough information to get started. Why don't I call you back this afternoon?"

There was a profuse silence. Had I said something wrong?

"Thank you."

It was so muffled and breathless I could barely understand it. I remembered grasping at the vapor of hope.

What next? I looked over my scribbled notes that were barely legible.

...a five year old girl.

...last seen with the parent at shopping mall.

...the time was approximately 2 p.m.

...it was last Tuesday.

...in Kansas City, Kansas.

The list went on...

I called the other number. I recognized the name from the news; it was the father of the young lady I had rescued in the City of Juarez, the one I'd disavowed any knowledge of.

The call answered so quickly I didn't hear the ring. The man's voice was very professional, very educated, and most of all overwhelmingly grateful. It was then I knew why I was supposed to call.

I told him about the possibility of an implanted GPS device being used to track his daughter like a stray animal, then warned him of my own experience of the theft from my bank.

He grew inordinately quiet and asked me wait while he placed me on hold.

Moments later the phone clicked and another voice heralded through my speaker.

It was baby-soft and kind, making me shiver inside.

"Mr. Schumacher? I want to thank you so much for helping me."

It was all she could manage to say before the gent came back on the line.

"You're right. There's a small lump just where you described. I promise you, I'll get to the bottom of this. You'll be receiving a certified letter in the mail; it's my way of saying thank you."

I was about to mount an argument when he hung up abruptly. How strange the phone etiquette is in the States. Pondering how he was supposed to send a letter without my address, I looked back at my list. No more glowing lines.

Who was I kidding? I closed the leather cover to my notepad and pushed it away like something filthy.

I walked from my office back to our open living area where I didn't feel so stifled.

Chaste had finished breakfast and was standing looking out at the boys by the front entrance, chatting away at their attentive ears. She looked so much healthier and happier. It was time to get her a tutor. Impossible, constricting fear crushed me at the mere thought of it.

No school, private or boarding, could I bear at the moment. I never wanted Chaste out of my sight even for a moment.

I snatched a piece of cold jelly toast off a platter and walked behind her. I've never been one for dramatics, but what I saw made me summarily drop it on the floor, jelly side down.

Out in the road were roughly a dozen tall grey spectres mingling about and staring with vacuous eyes toward the front of our house. *The Boys* had retreated from my daughter's attention to seat themselves near the fence side by side, with the faintest white glow about their heads; deputized with some strange angelic power.

"They're there aren't they?"

I barely heard Chaste's question.

"The bad angels…. You can see them can't you?"

She tugged at my sleeve and I woke from my stupor.

"Y…, yes…, a few."

At some point, I would have to stop lying. It was becoming a bad habit even if it was to protect Chaste. At least she was calling them bad angels instead of what they were; the diabolic essence they exuded.

"They don't like the boys do they?" she asked.

Pitre seemed to be correct; the tall greys were interested, but it seemed as if it was something much more; worried, or angry, or plotting - maybe all of these.

"You're very intuitive today, young lady."

"The boys didn't come in when I put out their food. I knew something was wrong."

That had me wondering how much we humans were already aware of the spiritual activity around us and spent our time ignoring it. A child could tell something was amiss.

"I'm sure they'll go away, sweetheart."

"I think there'll be more of them," she mumbled.

I hoped not.

"What makes you say that Chaste?"

"Something Pitre said last night."

I had forgotten that she was now privy to the open communication with my new parasite.

"I'll speak to Pitre about it, for now, let's you and I talk about your future and your education."

Chaste looked stunned.

"You didn't think I'd forgotten did you? It's important we try and get back to our lives as usual."

"Where are you going to send me?"

She looked pitifully downcast. I suppose her fears were causing her intuition to run aground. All this talk about Trust Funds and the like probably had her thinking of stuffy boarding schools in places far away.

"I'm not going to send you anywhere without your approval. I want to talk to you about getting a tutor, or maybe a governess for the time being."

She didn't look all that enthusiastic.

"Why can't you home school me again?"

So much for my own intuition.

"I'm still leaning toward a tutor, besides, you must be getting tired of my company, cooped up in this house the way we've been. I'll find out what I can and we'll discuss it together later if you'd rather. I suppose we had better make sure you're healthy and ready for all that before we do anything."

That finally earned me a hug and I hefted her into my arms.

The sallow gray was almost gone from under her eyes and she seemed much more chipper; it was hard to believe how well she was rebounding.

"We'll set up another visit to Doctor Cort tomorrow and see how you're progressing, alright?"

"Do I have to?"

She was definitely feeling better.

CHAPTER THIRTY-ONE

The usual stack of letters was begging to be sifted through; something I regrettably only gave into twice a month.

The usual bills I tossed into one stack and the rest were sifted unopened into the wastebasket.

Interestingly enough, I received a rather thick envelope from the headquarters of the European Medical Association. We usually received a quarterly correspondence from them at our medical clinic, but it had been so long.

I remembered the gloating threat from the FBI Agent that I would never practice medicine in my new country and slid it open with some disdain. Inside, on an official letterhead was a personal handwritten correspondence.

Dr. Kress M. Schumacher,

It is with utmost regret that we have not been able to contact you since we were informed of your wife, Dr. Elizabeth Ellen Schumacher's death. We also apologize for the delay in correspondence due to the lack of a verified address from the U.S. State Department.

Please accept our deepest condolences on both counts.

Elizabeth was a highly respected member of the EMA and we will miss her and her monthly articles to our journals as well as your excellent photographic record of events.

It was also recently brought to our attention about the loss and recovery of your daughter Chaste Ellen Schumacher – thus this correspondence.

We on the council could not imagine undergoing such an ordeal. We are however happy to hear that all was not lost.

Which brings me to the following good news:

It was our unanimous decision of the board at the EMA to extend your membership with the EMA for another ten years.

This also affords you a continuation of your Diplomatic Envoy status with whichever country you decide to practice your medical profession in the future.

We truly wish you all the best.

Please fill out the enclosed forms, post-haste, and return them to our headquarters for immediate processing.

With deepest regards,

I lifted the letter high in the air and shook it until it crackled.

I had assumed that my status of Diplomatic Immunity ended the moment we left African soil. This changed everything.

I made a note to mention the good news to Brent and Carl.

Then I remembered I needed to call them about Thomas.

If I had only known what I would find out, I might not have placed that call.

Thomas *Whitefeather*, indeed. How quaint.

"That's how he's advertising himself."

Brent sounded as disgusted as I.

"Advertising?"

"One of my men found him in a shoebox office in the same town where you said you met him, Sedona. The shingle over his door says 'Finder of Lost Things' and his phone is already ringing off the hook.

"I hardly think lost children are things."

"That's where it gets even more strange. If it's lost or stolen, he's claiming he can find it, but if it's a person, he hands out your phone number at two hundred dollars a pop. Our man went in as a prospective client and even though he didn't mention your name, Thomas claimed that you were the one that found those kids in Mexico. It seems that everyone has seen that news clip on CNN. He is very convincing."

That was why I was getting all the messages.

"How do I stop him? I only went to rescue my daughter, the rest of the children were coincidental. You of all people know that I was extremely lucky I didn't get us all killed in the process."

"He says he wants to talk to you."

I did not want to talk to Thomas Whitefeather, ever again.

"Is that how I make him go away? I've received almost forty inquiries already…."

"Shouldn't he be handing out the number to the person from your anonymous tip?"

My anonymous tip. So that snake was going to try to turn around and bite me.

"That's impossible. I have no way of knowing the number."

It was the truth in a divisive sort of way. The other end of the conversation became a little quiet as if Brent were trying to make the determination to believe me or not. There was another undercurrent…, something hidden he was unwilling to share.

"I'll give you the address to where Whitefeather setup business in Sedona. Do you want one of us to go with you?"

Their added presence might be that little extra push needed to rid me of Thomas.

"Doctor?"

"I…, I suppose not. I think I can convince him to go away peacefully."

"A piece of advice? Record your meeting with Thomas. If the FBI gets wind that Thomas Whitefeather is peddling you as some kind of psychic or medium that finds lost kids, you'll always be on their list as a 'person of interest'. Do I need to explain to you what that means?"

My mind instantly conjured images of small, filthy, dank interrogation rooms, with two-way mirrors and blinking cameras. Let's not forget the pair of devilish beady eyes.

"Use that fancy phone of yours."

I realized at once that I was nodding my head in silence to answer my advisor.

"Oh yes…, yes I understand."

I ended the call, feeling almost as dreary as before; before I received my letter from the EMA. I forgot to mention it.

I feared that my life was already being herded down a long narrow chute that would have me praying that I had never met Pitre. All at once, I repented of my heresy. That would mean that I would have lost my daughter Chaste to some unknown fate and possibly never seen her again in this lifetime.

Pitre, my enemy, my friend, ...my parasite.

"Is that really how you see me?"

The voice and the question inside me caused me to jump.

"Am I actually a parasite and an enemy?"

I was quickly reminded of the instructions Thomas had given me, the truthful part, 'After Pitre, you will never be the same'.

He did warn me and it was back when I believed what Thomas was telling me. I walked in this door with my eyes open.

"I didn't know...."

"The whole story?"

"I didn't know you were also a mischievous liar and manipulator."

I didn't care if he crushed the life from me for my accusations. I felt the truth pour from my mouth like clear water. Pitre didn't refute me.

"Would it have altered your decision to face the evil creature I used to test you? You came to me of your own free will. I didn't force you. In fact I was going to let you leave when I saw how ill prepared you looked when you met me. You were almost pitiful."

"Pitiful, really..., thank you for the vote of confidence Pitre."

I remembered that moment, the precise moment of our altercation. I knew that I could have walked away unscathed, back to my lonely existence and he would have allowed it.

"Yes you looked pitiful, comparatively. For several generations, the local Indian tribes sent their bravest hearts to face me.

"At least when they faced me, they were painted, hardened and ready to do battle. They were willing to die to possess the power to lead their tribe and become a Shaman."

I also remembered Thomas saying that many died or went insane from the experience. Pitre went on to answer internal my conjecture.

"They were the ones that wanted to use my power to brutalize and destroy all the surrounding tribes to gain land and power. When I resisted them they...."

His voice trailed off in my mind. I knew the rest of the story. I was living that part of their experience.

"Then why me, Pitre? If they were so wonderful, why did you pick me?"

"I've already explained about the grey ones and how Thomas was the instrument that chose you to face me."

Yes, we were back to Thomas once again. I remembered the pitiful story of his son Steven and yet Pitre had purposely evaded part of my question, still hiding something he knew about me.

"Why didn't one of your Indian braves help you in your escape to freedom?"

"They were brave, but they saw me as a way to rule and lead. A few saw me as a powerful spirit, others as diablo, the devil."

I understood that concept perfectly.

"They were incapable of helping me, even though we were somewhat attached until they passed on. And so it went, generation after generation."

I let his 'somewhat attached' slide past momentarily. This voice inside my head was becoming exasperated so I shifted our joust in another direction.

"What became of Steven?"

"Thomas had a son named Steven. His captors ended the boy's life long before Thomas failed his test with me. After my creatures first sting, I knew his son was gone. Thomas never got over his losses; his status, his wealth, his family, and finally his health were all gone. I took pity and offered to repair him if he would help me find a successful candidate, which he did."

That seemed to explain the piece of leather, the boy I had seen in the vision and the Steven that Chaste knew.

"The Steven you saw does exist and we will free him in time."

So many diversions, so many half-truth's and gaps to fill....

"Pitre, how do you propose we get these missing children back with their parents? My friends Brent and Carl have posed an interesting scenario. I will be misconstrued as playing some part in their abductions. Answer me that and I'll leave you alone for the present."

My mind and body was tired of haggling, listening for pieces of lies and unfinished truth's.

"You did the first part already. You contacted the ones that I instructed and marked off the ones too late to help for now. If you'll be patient with me, I'll show you how we can do this and you'll see why you're being mercilessly persecuted by your oppressor."

In that moment, I felt so incredibly torn. It all boiled down to my one concern.

"Will Chaste be safe?"

"I will personally protect her."

I wanted to believe him, really I did. He hadn't lied or I would have known it, but what if he couldn't protect my daughter?

"Yes..., well I want guarantees," I mumbled angrily.

From this point forward, I fully intended to test every word that came from Pitre.

"What do we do next?"

I could try and get on with our lives; arrange to accept the onslaught of speaking engagements I had been offered or possibly some internship. After the personal threat from the FBI, I was uncertain if I would be able to practice my vocation. Yet, the news of my renewed license and affiliation with the EMA may have changed that. But even with that renewed hope, so much was still uncertain. With all the recent developments, everything concerning our lives was tossed high in the air.

For a fleeting moment, I reconsidered a boarding school for Chaste in Cambridge and a local guardian to watch over her.

After I'd secured her financial future and after I was assured of her health, that would be my next step.

"What do you get out of all this, Pitre? I don't understand how this all fits into your plan. How does this help you?"

Pitre was silent. He desperately wanted to tell me but something was holding him back. Finally, I could tell his internal struggle was not going to allow it, so I changed the subject.

"What do I tell the poor lady that called with the missing little girl? Is she yet another one that Thomas is involved in?"

"No, their ordeal has ended."

"Ended! They're dead?"

"No Kress, the ones you found with Chaste are back with their families. You asked about Thomas."

Would it have been too much to ask for him to let me know that already? The vague ambiguities of Pitre's answers were almost more than I could take.

I caught my breath, "Alright..., then explain to me in simple terms how we..., are going to help these children."

"When the dark ones steal a child they always leave a thread that can be followed. It's an arrogance they display to show one another how stupid humans are."

"Then we really can help all these people recover their children?"

I felt chills replace my tired shaking nerves.

"Call this first one back and tell them to look at the calendar entries on their refrigerator door. This one has become a very short thread, you should call them now."

Somehow, I felt the urgency Pitre was feeding me, then put aside my concerns as to how deep the waters and plunged in.

After looking up the number on the list, I misdialed twice from nervousness.

The lady that answered was also nervous and still in shambles. I explained that she should do what I said immediately and I held the phone while she did so.

After a few minutes of scrabbling noise, I heard her voice quiver.

"Daddy's coming?" she whispered.

Her ex-husband had called the child and the little girl had written, 'Daddy's coming' on the very day of the calendar that she went missing. It was a tiny scribble written by her daughter. The lady knew what to do and promised to let me know the outcome.

Relief flooded me, for the lady and the life of the child.

"Why can't we call each one, right now?"

"Most of the threads are only valid for a tiny window in time. When that passes, we cannot interfere."

I didn't like the sound of that one bit. It gave new meaning to 'time is of the essence' and a horrible weight fell on my shoulders, crushing my heart.

"We won't need to travel then? We can take care of each one from here can't we?"

"Yes..., we can, for now."

More ambiguity, I didn't like the sound of that. Before I could protest his open-ended answer, he continued.

"You'll need a special monetary account for our future work together; think of it as an expense and travel fund. I'll let you know what to do with the rest when the time is right."

"The rest of what?" I demanded.

"There are many things I want to share, but you aren't ready to understand."

Yes, I knew I could be belligerent and hard headed; anger and frustration does not breed trust. A cycle I didn't know how to break.

"It's hard for you to understand, but I am tethered to your soul, and ...as I heal.... It will grow easier for both of us."

It was truth, an attempt at opening up to me, but then I considered his abrupt termination. What did he mean, '...as I heal?'"

CHAPTER THIRTY-TWO

If Pitre hadn't instructed me to open a special account, the entire two hundred fifty thousand dollars in the certified check from one Bartholomew Hall would have immediately been added to the Trust Account for Chaste.

Ferry Dunavin, our new lawyer, seemed overtly suspicious but handled the transaction after passing me along to one of her tax savvy associates to deal with the mish-mash of tax liabilities. My daughter Chaste seemed stirred at the prospect of seeing new territories, after she heard me explain that it would be used for travel and business expenses.

I on the other hand had lost all of the imagined charm of my past holiday fever. I was becoming the proverbial stick in the mud and didn't care who knew it. Pitre had suggested purchasing some mobile behemoth, which I utterly rebelled against. I had no intentions of cavorting about the country in a house on wheels.

Today, I was thankful for my Range Rover even after watching the odometer turn over 200,000 miles. Considering the Rover was brand new when we arrived in the country, the mileage was probably some type of record. It barely sat idle the entire time Chaste was missing.

I forced all my concentration on my new grievances against Thomas as I watched the pavement slither past.

On the way to see Thomas Whitefeather, Pitre poured more salt into fresh wounds. He instructed me to leave Thomas to his referral service, which needless to say infuriated me to no end. It was a sort of vague penance for his evils, playing a part in the retrieval of other lost children.

Thus, we squabbled with each other like two elder sisters all the way to Sedona Arizona.

When we entered the downtown area of Sedona, all was quiet. The foot traffic was also sparse even though today was relatively warm for the end of February.

As we passed the mission, the bell cote began a series of deep mellow tones announcing the hour. It felt as if they were the warning chimes of some medieval village, signaling our approach.

Finding the sliver of a storefront where Thomas had setup shop only a short time ago was a simple task. There were two people standing outside on the sidewalk in queue waiting to get inside. Apparently, his grand opening was all the rage among his local peers as well.

That wasn't how I located him however. There were dozens of tall greys standing in little congregations everywhere, but the most pronounced were just outside his door.

Even though they parted and moved to a distance as we approached along the sidewalk, I was none too comfortable being that close to them even with my child's hand firmly clasped in mine.

We received dreadful glances when we attempted to cut past the line of two women outside the puce colored doorway and were almost forcibly ushered to the back of the line with chattering rebukes. So there we stood, Chaste and myself, and of course the ever present Pitre cowering inside.

It was unnerving with tall greys milling in the distance, staring at us with empty eyes. They seemed bolder somehow, more confrontational and all their attention changed focus towards us. I ducked my head in feigned ignorance, not letting on to Chaste as we waited for our turn just outside Thomas Whitefeather's shop of horrors.

By the time we reached the front of the queue and the door jingled open, there were three more patrons in line behind us. The hovel sized office was barely the size of a closet, without room for even so much as a bench for waiting patrons.

Silently, we stepped inside and my old conniving friend was seated with his back turned.

"Hello, my name is Tom, how can I help you?"

His chair spun around and his expression must have been as priceless as was mine.

I felt Pitre lurch inside me. He somehow restrained me from mutilating the man that played some integral part in my daughter's abduction.

Tom was radically changed. His sickly putrid gray hair was now white as an albino rabbit and plaited into a single string down the small of his back with a single white feather entangled, dangling lewdly. His farce made me want to gag. The most prominent change was the absence of the gray mist surrounding his body that had been visible since my first encounter with Pitre.

His leg was obviously healed, twenty pounds heavier, and his voice was no longer the dry rasp…, but it was still Thomas there underneath the façade.

"Hello Thomas."

He stood and inched his way toward the door, not to escape, but to turn his sign to 'closed', lock the door and draw the shade to the one large window.

"I see you've made up for lost time since I last saw you."

"Fella's got to eat, Kress…, uh, Dr. Schumacher. Hello Chaste, good to see you. You look really good."

"How dare you speak to my daughter."

Again, Pitre shut me off, then asserted his own agenda with Thomas.

"I'm not here to upset your applecart, Thomas. I don't appreciate your giving my number out as a lost and found for people…."

"Yeah? Well, talk to your new boss about that. He agreed to go along with it; in fact, it was partially his idea as a way for me to pay my dues so to speak. I just sort of added my own flair to it you see."

I could feel the silent tugging inside me, wanting out.

"Pitre isn't exactly ecstatic about how far you've taken the business…, Tom."

"No. No, I expect he's not too happy. Try losing everything you have and then hopping around on one leg that looks like a dried grasshopper for two years and see how that affects your view on life, Doc."

"And here you are…, finder of lost trinkets. While I on the other hand have been turned into…."

Pitre shut me up, pinching off my sentence, so I returned the favor and didn't let him have a go at Tom.

Tom Whitefeather laughed at me while sliding back in his chair. It wasn't a gloating, scoffing or jeering laugh, which is the only reason I didn't flatten his nose with my knuckles. It was pure pity.

"I see you're having to give the wingless wonder equal time. I feel sorry for you Doc, really I do. Has he explained all the rules yet?"

I was speechless, choking back my parasite's efforts to shut off Thomas from giving away their secrets.

"Hmm, guess not. Well, just make sure you don't accidentally let out any curse words with God anywhere in the mix or you won't be able to talk for a week. And suicide has also been taken off the menu."

Thomas stood back up, idly marking some notes on the large wall calendar behind his chair while he continued.

"See..., forgiveness is pretty much all new to him, and Pitre didn't get the memo. He's..., more of a..., well, Wrath of God, Old Testament kind of guy."

I was angry, not at the implied restrictions, but that there were most likely other attributes of my relationship with Pitre of which I had no inkling. I would definitely take this up with Pitre at some point in the near future.

"I'm not here to debate religion or discuss my contract with Pitre. I'm only here to deliver a message.

"Unless you want to go to prison for the rest of your life, for the four abductions you took part in, including my daughter, you will not give out my number again. You will call me directly. If you comply, you can keep doing business as usual, much to my disapproval. In return, Pitre will make sure that all your phone calls to me are not recorded or traced.

"Do we understand each other?"

Thomas Whitefeather stood there, thinking, considering ways to further sweeten the pot in his favor. I saw the surly look and so did Pitre.

"However, if you do not agree, Pitre says to tell you that he will visit you in prison everyday until you are one hundred years of age."

When we walked away from the tiny storefront, the window shade did not go back up immediately, nor did the 'open' sign flip back around. Tom Whitefeather was now our very silent partner.

"Kress, I'm beginning to like you."

"I wish I could say the same Pitre. Tom Whitefeather indeed."

My daughter looked at me wearily, while her father was having yet another seemingly one-sided argument with himself.

"Can Pitre sit in the back seat so that I can listen too?"

I felt his immediate answer.

"He says there's not enough room in the Rover, dear."

"Then make it where I can hear him too. I feel stupid listening to you talk to yourself the entire time and I don't like the secrets Daddy."

"Can you do that Pitre?"

The decision was tossed right back into my lap.

What kind of a father was I turning out to be? I nodded and it was done.

"Thank you Daddy. It was really driving me crazy."

I didn't like it one bit. I felt Pitre nod inside as I amended how much she would be privy to.

Diversion time - I needed to think.

"I called Dr. Cort to confirm our appointment for you."

It somehow helped me anchor to my old reality, something closer to normal, if only for a brief moment. My vocation as a children's doctor was my life, all I had ever known; that and Elizabeth.

Chaste sat in a huff, in the new uneasy silence, realizing what I was doing.

The car in front of me on the highway swerved past some debris, waking my mind to the immediate.

Chaste and I were virtually hostages to the whim of a self-righteous de-winged angel and in league with Thomas, the one that pulled our random names out of some cosmic hat. How could I be angry with Thomas without being angry with Pitre?

In my eyes, they were both equally guilty, each with their own selfish agenda; and he'd had the gall to call *me* selfish.

"With everything I now know about you Pitre, I have to ask myself if I should help you at all."

"You wouldn't have volunteered, Kress, which is what made you perfect."

"You're absolutely right. No sane person would have volunteered. And quit calling me Kress, as if we're best of friends."

"Okay, Doc."

He imitated the voice of that insipid fool Thomas Whitefeather exactly, knowing it would chap me. I was so furious I could barely speak.

"Pitre, why are you trying to make my father angry at you?"

Ah, finally silent thought. Pitre had to actually think before answering Chaste.

"I'm trying to get all the anger out in the open so we can get past it. We have to work together if he intends to get rid of me."

"Bottom line, Pitre. What will it take to get rid of you?"

Actually, I was terrified of what the answer might be. But because of my attachment, I would instantly know if he was lying or holding something back.

We waited while he deliberated his version of the truth.

"My wings. I need my wings to go home."

I shrank inside, not just because it was pure truth, but because of the pitiful desperation in his tone. Still, no matter how pure, it was still an incomplete truth.

"No one can carry me through..., not even being attached to you Kress. I have to enter through an open portal under my own power."

"I..., I don't understand. Why the elaborate ruse? Why destroy our lives?"

I suppose I should have been even further angered, but instead I was totally confused.

"I hate long explanations I know you won't understand. Connected to you I have my light back. I'm not the burned out angel you first met. I was almost as dark as the ones you call greys. When I attached to you, for the first time in ages, I was filled with Creation's light. The dark ones are afraid of light; that's why they're watching."

Once again, that wasn't the whole of the matter. He was still hiding something. Some secret I couldn't penetrate.

"Ages? You told me there were several others, remember? I'm tired of your lies Pitre."

He turned his blank face toward me in my mind, thoughtfully, then droned on avoiding my accusation and my question.

"Kress..., you and Elizabeth had selflessly given your lives to helping others; your lives, your money, your time. You were exactly where you were supposed to be, doing exactly what you were called to do, willingly, happily.

"Your family was already targeted to be eliminated by the dark ones

the minute you decided to give your lives in service. The very minute you left your home in England, but you were protected by the guardians assigned to you. Then you started making choices to turn from your calling and you walked away from your protection."

Heaven, hell, God, devil, angels, both good and bad..., I was going to have to rethink everything I had believed or the little I'd been taught. Elizabeth and I had rehearsed many episodes of how we had miraculously escaped uncounted life-threatening situations during our eighteen years together in South Africa. It had been a rough existence for us, not one for the faint of heart.

Every answer from Pitre created ten new questions. I felt the weight of my wife's passing, heavy on my shoulders. And what of my daughter Chaste? She sat next to me quietly listening in.

Had we maintained our post for two more years at the medical clinic under the protection of a higher power, would Chaste have endured her recent vile ordeal? Would she have suffered an even more horrid fate? How could we have known? How could I ever know?

"I have to get you back on track, doing what you were put on earth to do, helping others. The sooner you get back on assignment, the better the chance I can heal."

"Pitre, I'm a medical doctor, a children's doctor; not a missing persons investigator."

"The morning we met, after my seventh mark, you saw things Kress. Have you so easily forgotten? Those things were real. I'm real. I let you see where your daughter was, where to find her. You saved her and the other children."

Not with my medical training, but he was correct. The end result was the same.

I was tired of arguing. Pitre knew this chess game far better than I, with only a little over four decades of existence. Pitre had unknown centuries of practice under his belt as a fallen angel. And how much time before that?

Centuries..., and no one else before me was courageous enough? No one else was capable of helping him for centuries? That was my enigma, my internal warning of Pitre's deception. I had already asked twice and was cleverly diverted to walk right past the truth while looking the other way.

"Tell me what you're hiding now or I'll fight you until my last breath Pitre."

I had his full attention.

"I'll know if you lie to me or omit the truth."

We were finally home. I pulled up in our driveway and we sat listening to the automatic gate squeaking closed behind us. There were seventeen tall greys standing just outside our fence in the street; yes, I counted them twice. My anger threshold went even higher at their presence; so much for an evening run. I wouldn't leave Chaste alone for a moment with them glaring or scheming or whatever the blazes they were doing.

Pitre was up to his old tricks again, looking for some answer that was so close to the truth that I would not be able to see the subtlety in his deception.

I parked the Rover in the garage and we went inside.

"Wait Pitre. I don't want to hear your answer just yet."

I wanted him to be so very assured that whatever answer he was devising was perfect to the last minute detail.

When we had settled most of our day's items, I had Chaste sit with me in the expanse of our living room. Without Thomas, there was no distraction or blaring television.

"Now…, Pitre. I want you to answer my question face to face."

Pitre emerged in his usual white brilliance, humbly seated on the floor.

"No. Wait. I want you to stand and tell Chaste, not me."

It was the first time I had seen an expression of any kind appear on Pitre's occluded face. Outlines of his eyes, nose and mouth, barely shades, moved with sudden expression. It was all in the eyes.

He darkened somewhat, dimmed from his arrogant brilliance, and turned his face away from the both of us.

Ah! It was just as I suspected. He could not lie in the face of purity.

"You can tell me Pitre. I won't be angry with you."

If angels can weep, I think Pitre might have been doing exactly that.

The innocence in the voice of Chaste broke him. With his back to us, he bared part of his inner self.

"Since my creation, I existed in the presence of purity. I never considered that my existence would be any different. It would always be that way. Eternal. Forever.

"When I fell, I felt something I had never experienced before; something worse than the pain. I felt…, unclean. Since the fall, I have

been surrounded by the dark ones, polluting me with their games, their schemes, their lies. I've become like them."

Pitre turned and faced us.

"You were the first."

He spat out his declaration quickly, before he changed his mind.

It was the truth and it didn't make a bit of sense.

"I was the first how? I don't understand."

"Before you, no one had gone beyond my third mark. You were the first to receive all seven marks and merge completely with me."

All that talk about how pitiful I was and how brave so many others were, it was all skewed versions of a deeper truth.

Chaste stood and walked toward Pitre and he cowered in childlike fear; as if he were a child waiting for the requisite punishment for his offenses.

"The creature you saw, the one I used to place my marks on you, no longer exists. Once our merger was complete it died. There is no turning back for me now."

One more thing stunned me into humility. Apparently, I wasn't the only one that had taken a leap of faith, of putting all of ones eggs into a single basket.

Whereas I had thrown myself at my one last hope of saving my daughter Chaste, at the same time I was Pitre's long-shot; his one last hope.

Chaste raised one of her hands to his to comfort him.

"It's going to be okay. We'll help you. Both of us will help you."

Pitre took her hand and an effusion of blinding white light burned away every shadow from the room.

Pitre disappeared and as soon as our blinking eyes began to regain their sight, then I heard the boys barking furiously at the fence.

Cringing, I expected to see a multitude of tall grey spectre's clotting the perimeter, reminiscent of the villagers of Frankenstein's monster. Instead, there wasn't a single illicit voyeur standing anywhere to be seen. It must have been the burst of light, that radiant white sun that burned them away.

"They're gone. All of them."

My child hugged my waist, "I still say there's some good in Pitre."

"Maybe there is, Chaste. Maybe there is."

CHAPTER THIRTY-THREE

"Hello Kress? This is Ferry. I took the liberty of filling out all the financial portions of the forms you dropped off and wrote a check to take care of your legal fee's to the EMA. You were right about the Diplomatic status. The United States recognizes the EMA as a qualified political entity of Great Brittan and you are protected under their statutes."

Ferry's exuberant speech hadn't given me a chance to answer her past hello.

"Kress? Dr. Schumacher?"

"Yes. Yes. That is excellent news. Thank you so much."

"There's more. I've had a chance to look over your..., colorful past with several of the law enforcement agencies. I'm beginning to understand why John was so intense the last week before he died. You burned quite a few bridges. How many times were you arrested?"

I immediately wished for the resurrection of John Shoemaker.

"I don't recall."

Had I made a rash decision to accept Ferry Dunavin as our new advocate?

"And, why didn't you tell me your daughter was stolen? It would have helped me understand the serious intent of setting up the Trust. Actually, it would have explained a lot of things. I thought the poor child was going through some awful sickness."

Then she gasped, "Please tell me she isn't going through some sickness, is she?"

"No, Chaste is still recovering. I assumed that you already had enough information on my family to write a dissertation and as you can see Chaste is at home and safe now. I did what I had to do to get my child back. I'd do it all over again regardless of what agencies were disgruntled in the process. Surely you can understand that."

I could hear her breathing into the phone, thinking.

"Yes. I do understand, but we should schedule another meeting soon so that you can fill me in on some of the blank spots."

Bloody hell. I wasn't about to fill her in on anything that wasn't absolutely necessary. John Shoemaker knew our entire story and now he was dead and his son was being raised by one of his relatives as a result.

"Are you still there?"

"Yes..., I'm still here. I'm not sure that's wise Ferry."

I could tell she was getting angry with my answer, but so be it.

"I am your lawyer, I need to know."

When I didn't give her the answer she wanted, she flipped our conversation to another tact.

"I see you're going to make my job..., difficult. I can handle difficult. So..., from what I do know..., I managed to put together a proposal.

"Under the guidelines of your Diplomatic status, you are entitled to litigation against the way the FBI handled your case, your arrests and detainment, it was a life threatening situation when Chaste was abducted. Even with your recent change to U.S. Citizenship, your Diplomatic Status takes precedence and makes it an international issue. They really crossed the line.

"Basically, you can sue the pants off the FBI. It's not groundbreaking. It's been done before with the United States versus Harwick back in 1977.

"Under the Foreign Sovereign Immunities Act, you were still in transition from British Citizenship to U.S. Citizenship when the incident occurred. You were never arrested for criminal acts while under the British umbrella of Diplomatic Immunity in Africa and should never have been held for questioning while under duress of your missing child. Not to mention your 4th Amendment rights of illegal search and seizure, your right to an attorney before questioning and I'm just getting started.

"I've contacted the British authorities and our law firm will be mediating for you on their behalf. We already have enough documentation from the Federal Judge's office to substantiate a generous settlement. Judge Harrison is even willing to go to bat for you and speak in your behalf."

"Judge Harrison is willing?"

I didn't intend to say that aloud, but there it was. With Pitre cohabitating with me, it was becoming second nature to blurt my thoughts for all to hear.

"Yes, especially if we can get a deposition from the U.S. Marshal's Investigative service. With John's notes, as limited as they are, they'll settle out of court; I can almost guarantee it. The last thing they want is a jury of your peers to hear the tale of what you and Chaste endured at the hands of the FBI."

"That is amazing news, Ferry."

"Can you stop by my office this afternoon? Actually…, why don't I bring these forms by your house this evening? I really want to get the ball rolling on this and my schedule is booked for court the rest of today."

"I couldn't ask you to drive all the way out…."

"Nonsense. I need to see where my new clients live anyway. I can get you to sign the forms and then place them in the mail first thing tomorrow."

Ferry actually said goodbye after our conversation.

What was I thinking? Ferry was coming here? Was this some ploy to leverage more information? Then it really hit me.

"Oh blast. Ferry Dunavin is coming here. This evening."

I felt heat rise in my face as I realized what I'd agreed to.

"Chaste. Chaste. Do you feel up to helping me pick up a little or maybe suggest something to cook?"

I saw my daughter's squinty eyes peering over the upstairs banister.

"I guess. Why?"

"We have company coming."

She was thoroughly excited by the prospect of company, but doubly so when she discovered that it was Ferry coming by to pay us a visit, even if it was only for professional reasons.

Then my mind woke up. I hadn't asked Ferry to join our meal. Why was I so bent out of shape?

My cell phone began to announce its presence and I ran to pick it up, thinking Attorney Ferry Dunavin had forgotten something. The number was another unknown, but seemed familiar.

"Oh no," I mumbled, the moment the gears in my mind synchronized.

It was the lady with the missing daughter.

My downstairs office was the closest privacy, so I slid inside quietly and closed the door.

All the confidence from our first conversation floated away down my stream of thoughts. I now stood alone, wondering if I should answer. As if on its own, my finger pressed the button.

"Hello?"

"Is this Dr. Schumacher?"

The voice wasn't the gravely one I'd first spoken with, nor was it the weepy despair riddled one.

"Yes?"

"We found her. We found my daughter. She's going to be all right. If we hadn't found her when we did, she might not be alive. It's a very long story, but in short her father had barricaded both of them in his basement. He had injured himself and was dying; she wouldn't have been able to get out by herself."

"I'm so proud for you and your daughter."

"I don't know how you knew about the note on the calendar, but it saved her life."

"I can't explain it either, but I wish you and yours a happy life."

I was trying to hang up before she wanted a list of detailed explanations – I'm sure I would have.

"I know we never discussed your fee, but whatever it is we are more than willing to pay it."

"I didn't ask for a...."

My throat constricted with a viselike grip.

'Pitre. Let me breathe'.

"Excuse me...," I coughed. "I didn't ask for a fee. But if you wish to make a donation to help find other lost loved ones you may send it to my attorney."

She assured me that she certainly would, so I gave her the address and hurriedly thanked her and ended the call.

"Pitre what the blazes were you thinking?"

My protector nemesis rang my head like a bell causing me to stagger - then he spoke his piece.

"Kress. Please call her back and ask her not to give out your name

or involve you personally with the media. Do it."

I did just that, somewhat disgruntled at Pitre's method yet I wholeheartedly agreed.

She was indeed about to spill the beans to the world that it was due to my Psychic Ability that her daughter was found. Daytime talk shows would all be ablaze with the scandal. Heavenly days; it would have been a train wreck of epic proportions.

I begged her to take personal credit for finding the scribble on the calendar. My premise? The less evil-people know about me, the more freely I can help others.

This seemed to satisfy her reasoning and I made a note to myself.

"Did you want me to cook or help you cook?"

I didn't hear the door open and Chaste made me jump.

I lifted her up and kissed her on her cheek and set her back down on her two feet. After the telephone conversation, I realized I would have given everything I owned to get my child back safely.

"You're gaining some weight! Marvelous."

She looked at me strangely, as I hurried past her into the kitchen to try to decide on something to put together.

I scrambled through our walk-in pantry, pulled out a half-dozen items, sat them on the counter, then stared at them.

"American food, please Dad?"

Chaste was right of course.

"We have loads of brisket left, all you have to do is heat it up."

My mind went blank; What goes with brisket?

CHAPTER THIRTY-FOUR

When the buzzer from the front walk-in gate went off, I remembered slothfully that we had a perimeter fence. It wasn't as if someone could waltz right up to the front door and ring the doorbell. That could only be accomplished if you were some type of clandestine pseudo-government group that liked to kill guard dogs. My renewed paranoia was only so many days old after all.

I dispensed with the table settings and scurried out the front door to the gate, ignoring the remote and the intercom.

"I do apologize for the inconvenience, Ms. Dunavin."

The walk-thru gate clacked loudly and screeched open as I scanned the area for any tall greys, thankful for their absence.

"I'm happy the spring monsoons haven't reached here yet or I'd be drenched."

She turned around and looked up at the fencing; a good three feet taller than the top of her head, then squinted into the lowering sun.

"Are you expecting an invasion?"

I had to force myself not to explain every nuance of the genesis of my beloved fence and its current state of uselessness.

"The contractor gave me a very good rate on the materials and it keeps *The Boys* from climbing over and running off."

The boys were running amuck, prancing along behind us nuzzling and sniffing at her briefcase.

Ferry Dunavin was looking a little antsy at the two large Rottweiler mutts drooling behind our every step.

"Your boys aren't violent are they?"

"They seem to do a good job at keeping the ghosts at bay."

"It's not ghosts I'm worried about at the moment."

Before I realized it, Ferry had siphoned a laugh from some dark recess inside me as I opened the front door and held it.

"You have a lovely home, Dr. Schumacher. Hello Chaste, how are you?"

Ferry hugged her gently and frowned ever so slightly at my daughter's slack frame.

"Would you like to give Ms. Dunavin the grand tour while I make us some tea?"

Chaste grabbed our guest's hand before she could object and began dragging her off through the house. "Well I really hadn't planned on staying more than a few minutes...."

"Dad and I were about to eat; please stay and eat with us."

Couldn't have put it better myself, however I was suddenly at a loss as to why I had assumed Ferry would be interested in more than fifteen minutes of my time.

Ferry didn't answer, but glanced my way for some type of approval, which I instantly gave with a nod and a smile.

I heard their chattering disappear into the back recesses of the main hallway and I stood there dumbfounded as to what I should do next.

I set out what I had hoped would be something palatable for our guest as well as us of course and surveyed the table setting. Tea?

Blast it all. Ms. Dunavin liked iced tea. So did Chaste.

What was I thinking?

The two of them passed through several times, Chaste chattering happily into to the ears of her captive audience.

"You have a spectacular view to the rear of the house. Chaste should consider a career in real estate. She gives a wonderful tour."

My daughter positively gleamed at the notion while tugging our guest to the dinner table.

"Don't worry, I helped Dad pick out what to eat."

I knew my daughter's innocent remark was far too leading.

"I'm so glad you like the house. Did she show you the view from the deck?"

I sat their glasses on the table side by side so the two ladies could choose where to sit.

"Maybe later. I hope I'm not imposing on you."

She sat across from where I was standing and slipped her hand under the stem of one of the glasses.

"Are you joking? Dad hasn't stopped since you called."

Oh God…, Chaste. What have you done? I felt my face blossom from heat and tried to ignore the remark. Something dire was wrong with me…, I never blush, never. That was a feminine response I'd never had to deal with.

Napkins, we needed extra napkins. I didn't dare look our guest in the face.

"Well then, you'll make a fine cook as well, Chaste."

When I returned there was the slightest hint of a grin on Ms. Dunavin's face. I sat as quickly as I could before I felt compelled to explain myself.

Then the silence became awkward and I blurted out the first thing I could think of.

"Did…, did you say you had the forms for me to sign?"

Ferry suddenly turned to her all business expression.

"Yes, they're in my satchel, I'd be glad to get them for you to look over."

"Dad?"

Stupid, stupid man. My daughter gave me an evil look.

"No, no, of course not. I don't know what I was thinking. Please, Ms. Dunavin, sit and relax."

I sat back down as well and rubbed the knee that I had slammed against the underside of the table.

What was wrong with me? Why was I suddenly behaving like some besotted adolescent?

I somehow managed to keep my comments short and the conversation slanted toward my daughter until we were nearly finished with our meal.

I couldn't help but notice how Ferry seemed entranced with Chaste, several times forcing away a furrowed brow just as their eyes met.

Chaste chattered on more than she had in days and actually managed a second helping of food, …unheard of, and her demeanor was brighter, more cheerful.

"I know you'll miss your friends, but I think you're right Chaste, home-schooling would be perfect for you. Are you still considering a governess?"

Ferry's eyes flitted between Chaste and I as if she might miss one of our expressions.

"We've discussed a tutor, home school, and of course a private school," I watched the expression of Chaste go from blithe to black, "...I haven't exactly decided either way."

Ferry saw the cold darkness as it fell over Chaste and placed a hand on top of hers giving it a squeeze.

"Don't you worry Chaste, I won't let your father stuff you in some snotty boarding school."

I watched Chaste's hand turn palm up and grip Ferry's hand. Their quick friendship was interesting to say the least. Possibly some emotional need after all she'd been through.

"Chaste has another doctor's visit tomorrow to check her progress. I don't intend to make any decision until she's physically fit for duty."

"I don't want to go back for another doctor visit Daddy. You're a kid doctor, why can't you check me out?"

"Sweetheart, you know I don't have any of the equipment or the laboratory to check your blood like your mother and I once had."

Ferry saw the potential conversation hovering like a mist in the air and turned to Chaste.

"Your father's right. Would you like for me to go with you to your visit tomorrow? I'd be glad to sit in with you. I don't have anything on my docket until late tomorrow afternoon. When is your appointment?"

How strange. I stared blankly for a moment, "Uh, nine a.m., but I can't ask you to do that."

"If I recall, you didn't ask. I volunteered. What about it Chaste?"

"I'd really like that," she answered immediately.

Something about her answer was a bit too soft, too quiet, and unhesitant.

"If you're sure. I have business in Phoenix tomorrow besides. I suppose we could meet you there so you wouldn't have to drive all the way out here."

"Good, then it's settled."

I refilled our drinks and we moved into the main living area.

Chaste sat crunched next to Ferry's small frame on the couch while she opened her briefcase to retrieve several large stacks of paper.

She handed them to me and began explaining each one and where to sign, then pulled Chaste closer to her side.

"Chaste you're cold honey, are you feeling okay?"

The last evil fighting for a foothold on Chaste was anemia. Her thin blood was slowly recovering with the aid of her supplements.

"I usually build us a fire in the evening; I don't like to keep it too warm in the house. The air is already so dry here."

I placed the stacks of documents on the table between us and busied myself with the fireplace. I could hear them mumbling between one another in some private chitchat as I lit a bundle of starter under the stack of piñon.

Suddenly I felt a stirring inside me, something far away coming closer to the surface.

Pitre. What he was suggesting was ridiculous, but he began to insist. It was only a whisper in my mind, *"...ask her."*

I whispered back, "Are you sure? She's a perfect stranger."

"...Ask her," he demanded.

It would have come out a vulgar belch if I hadn't relaxed.

"Ferry, would you consider being the guardian over my daughter's Trust?"

Both of them stopped their private talk and stared at me.

"Of course I realize that would probably be far too much responsibility for someone as busy as yourself."

She sat there staring at me strangely, some unreadable thoughts.

"Wouldn't you rather have someone from your family or...?"

"There's only Chaste and I. We've no living relatives in our homeland and couldn't fathom my daughter back in Johannesburg with any of our old colleagues."

Still the same stare, almost equal to the one on the face of Mr. FBI. It wasn't harsh by any means, just unreadable.

"It's a little unusual, but I can speak with my law firm associates and see what they think."

I shook my head, "I wasn't talking about your law firm."

"Me?" she frowned.

Pitre must have been mistaken, "If you'll mull it over and at least consider it, I'd be grateful. I'll place a salary stipulation in the Trust so that you can be compensated for your time, of course."

I heard the adolescent fire pop loudly behind me and quickly turned to set the screen in place. Out of the corner of my eye, I watched Ferry pull Chaste's hand up and kiss it before they went back into their private talk.

I realized they needed some actual privacy; it was some kind of girl-girl thing happening and so I went to refill my cup of tea.

Desperation clenched me when I got far enough away from them to relax. What if I'd done that mind reading thing that Pitre always seemed to incur that gave me the absolute creeps?

That would explain why Ms. Dunavin didn't offer much more than a nod in response to my question.

Pitre, what are you doing?

He didn't answer and I was so very glad that he realized it was a rhetorical question.

When I walked back to the doorway, Ferry attempted to explain her feelings.

"I was guardian over my…, niece for about a year, until my…, brother-in-law finished his military duty and remarried. It was a lot more responsibility than I realized at the time, but worth every minute. She and I still keep in touch from time to time."

Still not an answer, but Ferry was actually flirting with the idea. Unbelievable. I walked back in and picked up the documents and began scribbling my signature on each one.

Then I scanned the thickest one out of the bunch.

"What if I don't want to pursue the litigation against the FBI?"

Ms. Dunavin frowned at me strangely, "Why wouldn't you?"

"How much attention would it draw to us? Would Chaste be grilled in front of some hearing about everything she experienced?"

Suddenly, there seemed to be a shift in her motivation. She sat thinking, not as a lawyer responsible for her partners, but as a guardian to a vulnerable nine-year-old child. Suddenly aware of the unbreached subject of Chaste's very recent ordeal.

"Can you guarantee that?" I prodded.

Ferry looked at Chaste for several moments, at the circles just now beginning to disappear from under her eyes.

"No, I can't. But we can place it on the docket and if it begins to look like it will be difficult we can drop it."

"As my attorney, is that what you recommend?"

Again, that unreadable stare, then she nodded.

I scribbled my signature and initials in at least ten different places and handed the whole of it back to Ferry Dunavin.

She quickly stuffed it all away, business concluded, and snapped the folding clasp of her carryall.

The boys began to rabble about noisily at the front of the house.

"Are your ghosts acting up?"

There was a smile on Ferry's face and I was determined not to say something else stupid enough to make it go away.

"I'm sure it's only the neighborhood cat."

Nevertheless, I stood and went to the front glass panes and flipped on the flood lighting. One of the boys was dancing at one corner of the fence and the other was trying desperately to keep a vigil between the front and the back of the house. It seemed to be a little foggy so I stepped out to the front stoop where I could get a better look, closing the front door behind me.

There wasn't a fog. Our enemies had returned, *en masse*. There was what appeared to be hundreds of tall greys surrounding the perimeter of our fence.

"Pitre, what's going on?"

His concerned answer faded into my head, *"They're angry."*

I didn't bother waiting for an explanation. Despite his reticent forthcomings, Pitre was still the King of Vague.

"Are we safe? Will Ms. Dunavin be safe driving home?"

"If you follow my instructions, then yes."

I saw a multitude of glowing pairs of eyes shifting from side to side. Their usual mode of leering made them still as a post, but they were obviously agitated.

"Then be very clear what you want from me and I'll do it."

I saw the outline of Chaste against the glass behind me, peering out into the darkness.

I hurried back inside and tried to brush off the leeching cold on my arms and hide my emotions.

Chaste was already chattering away, disclosing information I wanted to keep far away from Ferry Dunavin's inquisitive ears.

"We had some bad men break in our house. Daddy says they probably won't be back."

Then my daughter looked in my eyes and we passed darker information between us. She knew what was there, lurking in the darkness, watching us.

"Don't you have a security system?"

Bloody hell. Here we go.

Now I was forced to explain with the barest of necessary details, the evolution of our struggle, while we managed to congeal around the fireplace. I managed to avoid any mention of the events connecting Chaste, hoping Ferry would do the same. I was very relieved when Ferry never once hinted of Chaste's abduction or my time alone.

"Now my contractor stocks the exact size glass panes to our house so it only takes them a few hours to replace the broken ones."

"So you don't have a regular telephone and you don't own a gun? What are you thinking? This is America. I'll get you an emergency carry permit and I'll take you to get a firearm."

Little good that would do against a host of dark wispy enemies.

"I don't think that will be necessary, Ms. Dunavin."

"Will you please quit calling me that? I thought we settled that ages ago. If I'm going to be your daughter's guardian, call me Ferry."

"Ferry..., I don't think buying a firearm is the answer.... Oh..., that's wonderful news, Thank you so much."

Such an abrupt turn of events. You'd think I was used to such things by now. I doubted that I would ever be.

"If you don't mind my asking, how did you make such a quick decision?"

She scrunched Chaste to her side, "Do you really have to ask?"

She smiled nervously and looked at her wristwatch.

"It's getting late and I'd better be leaving before my to-do list grows any longer."

Chaste looked at me and back toward the front door.

"I'll meet you a few minutes before nine in front of Phoenix Children's Medical. Chaste and I had a little talk about her first doctor visit."

I was going to ask how she knew where to meet us.

"Fine..., good, we'll meet you there then."

What instructions? Pitre where are you? She can't leave with those creatures milling about. I couldn't bear the thought of another accidental death like John Shoemaker.

Finally, he whispered inside me, *"Touch her hand, kiss her."*

Bloody hell. I barely know her. I can't simply....

Chaste looked at me in some sort of disgusted urgency.

I had forgotten that my daughter could hear Pitre when I was near her, blast it all.

"Thank you for coming Ferry," Chaste said.

She leaned down and kissed Chaste on the cheek, quickly wiping away a hint of pink lipstick.

"It was my pleasure, I thoroughly enjoyed our visit."

It was my turn to look into the warm gaze of Ferry's bright green eyes.

"Thank you Ferry, you've been a Godsend to us."

I took her hand and leaned down and gave Ferry a peck of a kiss on the cheek. Not the overtly romantic kiss Pitre had insinuated with his instructions, but I did exactly what he requested to the letter.

Ferry glowed. No I don't mean..., well in retrospect, I guess she did that too, but she actually had the same light glow about her that I'd seen on the boys. It was that incandescence that seemed to hover like a shield of some sort.

As she drove away, the horde of tall greys parted like the Red Sea for her car.

"I like Ferry."

I was still staring out at the mass congregating around our house.

"I *said*..., I like Ferry," repeated Chaste.

"What? Oh, yes Chaste. I like her too. She's very nice."

"Nice? Daddy, are you blind? She's really pretty and I think she likes you."

She finally had my full attention.

"Likes me? What are you saying?"

"Ewww!!!" Chaste growled in disgust and stormed off up the stairs to her room.

"Pitre, what is going on?"

"Honestly Kress, as oblivious as you are, it's a miracle you have a daughter. Can't you see how well she and Chaste get along? You'd still be looking for a guardian if it wasn't for me."

I was far more interested in the growing mass of enemy outside our home but Pitre ignored that, ...of course.

"Pitre, there are far too many abnormal things going on in my life to consider any type of romantic entanglement."

"Unbelievable," he grunted, almost sounding human.

They were ganging up on me.

"Pitre, you can't guarantee our safety, much less someone else's. Why would I want to endanger someone else's life? Especially someone we care about? Now who's clueless?"

There was a new silence coupled with a feeling of anger.

Then I quickly regretted my own words.

"Will Ferry Dunavin be safe? I don't want someone else dead because of their affiliation with me."

"You did what I told you, almost..., she'll be fine."

"Almost? What does that mean?"

"Unbelievable," he grumbled.

I sensed Pitre walking away down a long imaginary corridor to get away from me.

This whole event opened far too many doors, holding back far too many memories.

After backtracking the evenings events several times, it took me a little too long to realize that this whole Ferry Dunavin escapade wasn't all about me, it was about Chaste. Pitre was trying to please her.

Now Chaste was angry at me as well.

I trailed slowly up the stairs to talk to Chaste. She wasn't thrilled to see me standing outside her door.

"Would you like to talk about it?"

"No."

She picked up her iPhone and made it play some ghastly noise as she flopped on her bed. The music was far too angry for my liking.

"I'm offering to explain myself Chaste."

"No."

She turned her back to me. "I thought you liked Ferry," she mumbled. Conversation terminated.

I was already three steps down the hallway when I heard her voice above her..., vile music.

"It's only natural."

I turned and stood back in her doorway, her back still to me. She didn't want to talk, she wanted to argue.

"It's been almost two years since mother passed on. She wouldn't want you to be alone. You know that. I heard her tell you that in the hospital."

Her open confession was so blunt about what I was hiding that it stung like a hard slap to the cheek. She conveniently didn't add, 'before she died', to the end of her chide, even though her voice was full of emotion.

"Chaste, I…."

"Don't tell me you aren't ready or some other grown up excuse."

"You just met her Chaste. How do you know you like her just yet?"

Her back twitched awkwardly as she shrugged lying on her side and her music changed to something much worse, going from angry to violent.

"Pitre likes her. You asked Ferry to be my guardian and you just met her."

Blast. I had no viable argument even if it was because of Pitre's insistence.

"But you do like Ferry?" I asked.

She tried to answer with a shrug once more and it looked like she was shifting her weight against her pillow.

"I'm glad to hear it. She does seem very nice."

Chaste didn't take my bait to shift the conversation.

"Sweetheart, I doubt that Ferry is interested in me that way."

"She is," said Chaste, with just a hint of defiance in her voice.

I wasn't about to ask my nine-year-old daughter how she knew.

"Well if she actually is, then I should be able to tell without your aid. Why don't we see how things progress after your doctor visit tomorrow?"

I couldn't believe I let that escape from my own mouth. To a child it was almost a contract of commitment.

Chaste turned onto her back and stared at me with her large round eyes, dark intense pupils almost hiding the bright blue scrim of color.

"Okay. We have a deal."

I wanted to cut the tension between us. I wanted to hear…, something besides that blasted noise.

"Why are you listening to that rubbish?"

I watched as her eyes turned cold and dead as week old ashes. She was trying to find a way to tell me because I could see the wheels turning in her expression.

"It helps me relax…, you wouldn't understand."

Chaste let out a deep painful breath.

"If I tell you, you'll put me in therapy. Again."

That was as disturbing as it was blank.

"What if I promise..., no I can't promise. What if I promise not to jump to conclusions?"

She rolled over and scrambled through the top drawer of her nightstand while dangling like an acrobat from the edge of her bed.

"It helps me forget the music I was forced to listen to every day, all day long, all night long; then there were the movies...."

She choked off the last word in a gasp and turned her back to me once again; as if she'd let something secret escape.

Equally disturbing.

She was forced to watch movies? I knew without asking that they weren't Disney classics.

She plugged in earphones and quickly stuffed them in her ears and turned out the light.

Apparently, therapy was the least of my future concerns.

CHAPTER THIRTY-FIVE

The sun had just risen on what promised to be a cold clear bright Arizona day. I was not anxious to look out at the encroaching light of the unfiltered front windows and so I muddled around in the main portion of the house for the first few minutes of my morning.

As far as I knew there was a veritable sea of malcontents weaving their vile bodies side to side in angry protest to some unknown target inside my home.

Strangely, well strangely for me, I wanted coffee and ground some beans to start the brew. I heard the boys whimper through the garage door, their babyish method of begging for yet more food. After opening the door, I determined not to glance out the garage door windows, my way of living in blissful denial for the remainder of the morning.

The two mongrels were seated like obedient children at a breakfast table, with tongues lolling about as they huffed the chilly air.

I filled their food bin and still they sat looking at me. It was then I noticed the scratches and bumps across their massive heads and shoulders as if they had been in some sort of altercation with something stupid enough to challenge them.

"Busy night, eh chaps?"

They whimpered once again in some semblance of canine understanding. I patted their sides, speaking childish nonsense to them and inspected their wounds.

The gouges and clawmarks weren't very deep and seemed to be

healing quite nicely already, but I plastered some ointment on a few streaks that were still raw looking.

"Good job men, keep up the good work."

This opulent gesture seemed to satisfy whatever need they had and they dug into the food with their usual voracious repartee.

I went back inside to the quiet refuge of our home, scrubbed dog off my hands and poured some coffee.

I heard small noises and the shower come on upstairs; it wouldn't be long before Chaste appeared.

Time to man-up. I set my cup down and marched straight for the front windows for a look-see at what was awaiting me.

The streets were as deserted as a scene from one of the old spaghetti westerns I'd seen years ago. There were no cricket sounds.

"Pitre, where did they all go?"

He was silent at first, but I knew he was listening to me.

"They were called back to their posts of duty."

I would have thought that was a good thing, but there wasn't a cheerful tone to Pitre's voice.

"Kress, there's something I should warn you about."

"Is Ferry alright? She didn't have an accident did she?"

I could just picture a horde of evil creatures following her home last night.

Pitre laughed and it was full of good spirits.

"I thought you didn't care, Kress."

Before I could breech a stiff rant, he answered me.

"Ferry's fine. She's getting ready to go by her office before she meets you and Chaste."

"Then what? I don't understand."

"You should prepare yourself for our next level of opposition."

"There are going to be more of the tall greys?"

I couldn't fathom that scene in my head after the hundreds milling about last night.

"No Kress, you should prepare yourself for a visit from their leader."

"Oh God," I almost sank to my knees. "How do I prepare myself for a visit from the devil himself?"

Pitre laughed again, but it was a thin, short-lived one.

"Not the devil Kress. He's far too busy trying to manage bigger things than us. It's their..., regional director of operations."

"Their commander in chief is coming here?"

"Maybe, probably. We've attracted too much attention, disrupted his

workforce."

"What do I do? How do I prepare?"

"You just did. I didn't want him to surprise you. He can be a bit intimidating at first. I can keep you safe."

I felt my gut finally relax from its clench.

"Today, when Ferry asks, tell her the money is a consulting fee. I have to leave for a short while; I have things to prepare for."

I felt an emptiness, a vacancy inside and knew Pitre was gone from the forefront of my mind. Gone where? Gone in what way?

"What money?" I blurted into the silence.

There went my bright cheerful day tossed out the window.

"Morning Daddy."

My bright day reemerged from its hiding place as I listened to the thumping of my daughter's feet rushing down the stairs.

"You're up early. Did you sleep well?"

"No, not really. Was that Pitre I heard?"

"Yes it was. Why didn't you sleep well?"

"Bad dreams. What did he have to say?"

"It was private and you should turn off that awful noise when you sleep. No more…, whatever that was when you lie down. That's an order. Now come eat something so your stomach won't growl at the doctor during your examination."

She giggled and hurried to the kitchen just ahead of me.

"Are they still out there?"

She swallowed one of her pills with a gulp of water and a shiver and looked watery eyed at the other three medicines waiting their turn in dismay.

"They all left before morning. It's a beautiful day outside."

"It's going to rain you know. Buckets."

"Oh, really."

I didn't ask how she knew.

Breakfast came and went quickly. Chaste rinsed her plate and looked around wistfully.

"Where's Pitre?"

"That's an odd question. Still attached to me somehow I suppose."

She looked around quietly again.

"No. I usually hear that low humming sound like music when he's near; ever since you brought me home."

She walked to the front door and looked out at the bright

sunshine just starting to turn the sky its amazing southwest blue.

"You're right, it's nice, too bad it's going to rain."

I don't know why I was so preoccupied with watching her every move, but I managed to break my daze and put the dishes in the sink.

As I turned around, she was suddenly there reaching around my waist from behind in a hug. I heard her tiny muffled voice against my back, *"I'm so sorry about last night."*

"Me too Chaste."

"You too what?"

"I said I'm sorry too. You just said...."

"I didn't say anything, but I guess I am sorry for being such a brat last night. Please don't be angry with me."

I was about to let my mouth say a multitude of things I would probably highly regret in the near future, when she grabbed me once again, pressing her ear to my side.

"Oh, there he is. I hear the music again."

Before I had a chance to offer a question or opinion she darted off up the stairs, I assumed to get dressed for our trip to town.

"I heard her muffled voice again, clearer this time."

"I get to see Ferry today."

I stood there even more dumbfounded as the empty spot inside me refilled itself.

"It was only fair," Pitre barked, making me jump.

"Now you can hear some of what I hear."

"What? Absolutly not!"

"It's one of your seven marks. You can't learn to swim without a little water."

I began to hear soft distant gibberish from Chaste upstairs.

"I'm not sure..., no..., I don't want to hear, Pitre. Make it go away. Make it go away this instant."

I didn't want to hear all the private thoughts of anyone..., this was going to be a disaster of epic proportions.

"Better practice with Chaste and Ferry today."

I detested it already. Just the trip into Phoenix was frustrating as hell. Chaste was looking at me as if I'd sprouted two heads covered in giant warts as I tried to explain for yet the third time that it must have been a father's intuition that made me answer her without her asking.

I'd never get used to this. It was maddening. It sounded like her tiny voice the first time I heard her, before the last blows of the stinger from Pitre's creature.

I understood the need back then, but why now?

Then I realized that in a few minutes I'd have not only her thoughts to contend with, but the doctor and Ferry's and....

"Dad..., Dad?"

I turned to look at Chaste cautiously, wondering if I had heard her voice or her thoughts.

"Are you getting hard of hearing?"

I was about to snap at her for such an insolent question when she reached over and gently placed her hand on my ear. It was then I saw the concern in her eyes.

"I'll be fine dear."

I turned into the clinic and parked.

"Are there any of those bad angels here?"

I scanned the area quickly and turned to face my daughter.

"No sweetheart and you shouldn't be worrying about such things. You're well protected."

She was staring with such wide-eyed glee. I hadn't seen such a giddy smile on her face in ages.

"You heard what I thought," she said, then grinned at me with a sly mischievous twist.

"What are you talking about? What a preposterous idea."

"I love it. I can tell you stuff without anybody else hearing. Awesome...."

She squeaked with joy and leapt from the vehicle before I could offer any further rebuttal. She was still laughing when we caught sight of Ferry Dunavin, standing at the curb by the front door, smiling brightly.

"There's my sweet little angel – Good morning Chaste – Good morning Kress – *In that same drab suit. Doesn't he own another one? And he's wearing that same awful faded tie again."*

Unconsciously, my hands flew to the knot of my tie while she and Chaste exchanged a warm hug.

"Say something daddy, tell her she looks pretty. Hurry, do it."

Chaste bumped me with her elbow and startled me.

"Good morning Ferry, you look very lovely today."

"Thank you – *He smells good, but that suit* - I need to talk to you for just a second about something before we check in at the desk. I went by my office on the way here. Someone wired you a check in care of my office."

She looked around, keeping her eyes and thoughts blank, then she leaned in and whispered.

"There were a lot of zero's after a five in the amount."

I remembered what Pitre had instructed me.

"Yes, a consulting fee. That will need to be added to the account we just…. What? Is there something wrong?"

Ferry stood looking at me dumbfounded.

"He doesn't know…, he really doesn't. The first person I'm attracted to in years and he's doing something illegal – A consulting fee? I obviously need to change occupations Kress."

She's attracted to me? Good heavens. When did this happen? Everything else Ferry said rolled away into a blur.

I stood gaping at her and nervously covered my mouth with my hand, internally begging for Pitre to help. Somehow, my fragile mind came back to attention.

"How much was the check written for?"

Her eyes drew down to slits, a storm ready to burst.

"I knew it, it is illegal – Five hundred thousand dollars."

She stood taller, stiffly, pulling Chaste to her side as if protecting my own daughter… from me. Then it hit me.

"Fuh, fi…, fi…, five hundred thousand? There must be some mistake."

"No mistake. I can count zeros – *but I never expected you to be one of them. Why Kress? I should ask him to get another lawyer – No. I can't leave this innocent baby in this crooks' hands."*

Me? A crook? I looked nervously at my watch, - diversion, diversion, diversion.

"Can we discuss this after Chaste's appointment?

She pasted a blank looking smile on her face.

"Of course, you're right. Honey, let's go inside where it's warm. Go take care of your…, business and we'll see you back here around eleven, Dr. Schumacher – *Maybe I can get Chaste's doctor to help me."*

She regressed to addressing me as Doctor Schumacher.

I stood there feeling far more stupid than usual as she turned and ushered Chaste inside the automatic doors with a whoosh.

I hurried back to my Range Rover and plopped into the seat. The perspiration of embarrassment and anger on my body was turning to ice in the frigid morning air and I shivered.

"Pitre! What have you done to me?"

I don't know how long my forehead was pressed against the steering wheel in self-pity, but it wasn't long enough.

"Kress. Snap out of it. It's going to be okay."

I gritted my teeth.

"No Pitre. It's never going to be all right ever again."

"Then you aren't the man I thought you were when we first met."

What was that supposed to mean?

"Pressure will either make a man crumble to dust or turn him into diamonds."

This wasn't the time for more if his blithering wisdom, besides how much more pressure could a man take? My body shuddered at his insinuation.

I felt that empty withdrawal inside me once again as Pitre receded.

"Pitre... come... back... here... and fix this at once!"

My fists ached from pounding the steering wheel and my throat hurt I yelled so loudly, but there was only silence and emptiness as a response. I cautiously looked around the parking lot to make sure no one had seen me screaming and pummeling my vehicle like a madman.

CHAPTER THIRTY-SIX

There'd been a dozen items on my checklist to do before Chaste was out of her appointment and yet none of them seemed important.

I pushed out of the Rover, slammed the door and marched into the clinic; down the hallway to Dr. Melva Cort's section of the clinic.

The door seemed to fight me as I pulled it open but somewhere in the back of my mind I remembered how those hydraulic suppressors resisted extreme force.

I quickly scanned the waiting room area at the blank faces and saw that Chaste was not there. Of course not.

I walked past the receptionist and pulled open the door to the patient area, ignoring the blaring voice of the rabid lady trying to do her job to stop me.

Off to the left down a hallway of doors I heard the voice of Ferry Dunavin in my head and yanked at the door.

I was greeted by the glaring eyes of Dr. Cort and Ferry in a somber conversation.

Dr. Cort jumped up from her stool and seemed frightened.

"What do you think you're doing?"

The lady guard dog burst in on my heels, "I'm sorry Dr. Cort; he flew past before I could stop him."

"My daughter is here with Ms. Dunavin, my attorney."

I distinctly heard Ferry's muted and distraught thoughts about lawyer-client privileges as I glared right back at her, ignoring the young lady behind me.

"I have every right to be here. Where is Chaste?"

Dr. Cort immediately distanced herself from Ferry.

"I thought you were family. You're a lawyer?"

Then she looked at Ferry's blushing cheeks and back at me.

I didn't hear the doctor's thoughts, but I was soon to realize that it was because she was dumbfounded.

"It's okay," Dr. Cort waved off the receptionist.

"Dr. Schumacher, I should have recognized you. It's good to see you again, please come in. Chaste is in the examining room across the hall. I'm waiting on the results of her blood and urine tests. She's making wonderful progress."

My blood was boiling, but Dr. Cort's calm announcement somehow distracted me into a more sane mode of thinking.

"I'm so glad to hear that, as will Chaste I'm sure. I apologize for bursting in on you like this, but it's very important that I to speak to my attorney for a moment."

This earned me the exact response I wanted from Ms. Dunavin.

Before she had a chance to make some excuse I pulled open the door and swished an inviting arm.

"Ms. Dunavin, if you don't mind? This won't take a moment."

She snatched her purse and pushed past me into the hallway after hissing, "How embarrassing."

"Thank you Dr. Cort, I'll be back in no time at all."

I barely caught the trail of where Ms. Dunavin had hustled off to. When she finally stopped moving, we were both standing outside, just past the automatic doors, her purse gripped tightly across her chest.

"Ms. Dunavin... - Dr. Schumacher..."

It all sounded like angry garbled mash aimed at each other.

"By all means, you first."

She was so angry, even her thoughts were too scrambled to decipher.

"Doctor, what was so important that you felt the need to yank me away from Dr. Cort? You made me look like an idiot."

"I didn't appreciate the implications over the money you received in my name, Ms. Dunavin."

"That's why you came in there and got me? You..., you were angry over what I said about the check? It couldn't wait until after the doctor visit? Dr. Schumacher, I don't know if I can represent you as your legal council any longer."

Right.

"And I don't know if I want someone representing me that doesn't trust me."

Bloody hell. What was I doing?

Almost everything I was blasted about was from what I'd heard in her thoughts. There's no way I'd find another lawyer that I trusted nearly as much as her.

She was already walking away. I had to stop her somehow.

"I..., Ferry wait. I told you that there must be some mistake and..., and you stood there with your judge and jury eyes ready to pass sentence on me. Don't deny it."

"That's it you... you crook. Oh, why can't I be mad at him? – Of course I was upset over the money! Wouldn't you be suspicious if your client received a wire transfer for a half million dollars? And then explains it away as some consulting fee? I may not be the brightest lawyer in the southwest, but I'm certainly no fool, Doctor. Are you caught up in some money laundering scheme?"

She looked past me, almost frantic, into the double doors of the clinic.

"Oh..., I can't leave. Chaste is still inside there all alone."

I lowered my voice as much as I could effectively control.

"The first check I received was from very wealthy family in which..., I played a role in recovering their lost child. This last one offered to pay me some ridiculous fee, which I refused. I told them they could make a donation to help with other such endeavors. I gave them your information since you now have power of attorney over my accounts. There. Are you satisfied?"

It wasn't one of the actual children I'd imported, but....

"What lost child?"

Heavens..., was she ditsy?

Then it hit me like a load of freshly baked bricks. Ms.... Ferry didn't know anything about the other children. How could that be?

"Ms. Dunavin, Ferry..., did you not read the circumstances surrounding the recovery of Chaste and the other three children in John's notes?"

"That's what they took... - All I know is that your daughter went through some terrible ordeal, but the written details I had were sketchy at best."

Ferry looked bewildered, something I'm sure wasn't the norm.

"And you say there were others? I don't have a clue what you're talking about."

"Surely you talked to Chaste."

"No," she spat. "No, of course not. I didn't want to upset her, she seems so fragile."

At least I knew where Ferry Dunavin's sensibilities lay hidden, she didn't seem the least put off when drilling me for information.

"Don't you barristers confer information about your shared clients?"

Ms. Dunavin stared at me, in shock I suppose. We couldn't stand out on the curb and argue all day. I knew one quick way to end all the confusion.

"Come with me."

I spun on my heels and glanced back to make sure she was following me to my Range Rover, "Well…, come on."

I rifled angrily through a file box in the back storage area and pulled out one of several copies of my sworn affidavit of the events concerning the redemption of Chaste from Mexico. It was very hard not to show some emotion when I saw my friend John Shoemaker's signature on the cover sheet above the federal judge's signature and finally mine.

"Have you seen this before? It's one of several copies John made for me."

She took it and looked far too long at the signatures, the same way I had, rubbing her finger and thumb across the crumpled notary seal.

"No, I haven't, someone from the FBI took a box of John's…, files after he…, they said it might have something to do with his death – *those liars*."

"John Shoemaker's accidental death?" I asked, unsuccessfully fighting away my burgeoning sarcastic tone.

She stopped reading just long enough to give me an interesting and piercing look into my eyes.

She read the first two pages very carefully and flipped it back shut. From somewhere magical her cell phone appeared in her hand and she dialed a number.

"Trice? Ferry. Cancel all my afternoon appointments today and have…, uh, have Barry take my place in court, you sit in with him."

I heard a squeaky high-pitched voice as Ferry held the phone away from her head, "Barry? Me? Are you crazy? Barry's only a second year intern and I'm only a first year."

"It's just a hearing, he can handle it. Besides…, I trust you. You keep him on track. Something's come up. Thanks."

"Thank you Dr. Cort. Say thank you, Chaste. No more pills or syrups for you."

"No refills. Chaste needs to finish what's left and then we'll do a final workup to make sure all is well, but it's nothing short of miraculous. Her blood was a playground when I first examined her and now it's perfectly normal other than a slightly low red cell count. I expected to see her for another six months at the very least. Her teeth and gums look healthy, her skin is healthy and the new growth of her fingernails have their color back. Now she's still a little thin, but I see no reason why she can't resume public school next month if all goes well."

I forced myself away from the baited public school conversation and smiled. There was another heated conversation usurping my faculties, awaiting me somewhere in the lobby of the Medical Center.

Chaste squeezed my hand and twisted her head looking through the outer office window into the waiting area for Ferry.

"I still want to see her every two weeks, then set her up on a schedule."

Chaste pulled away and walked through the door looking for her new friend.

I met Chaste moments after concluding my chat with Dr. Cort and she gave me a grimacing scowl.

"Ferry's out in the main lobby. I didn't run her off."

In an instant, the sunshine was back on her face and she began to tug me into the hallway.

Ferry was seated close to glass walls of the main lobby, still buried in the brief, with a notepad in hand, busily scribbling notes.

Chaste sat down next to Ferry and received an exorbitant kiss on the top of her head as she held her tight.

"You precious little girl."

Ferry's eyes flitted quickly to me, "You did all this? By yourself?"

When I didn't answer, Ferry dropped her eyes and continued.

"The brief didn't mention any other children, or the GPS device in the back of Chaste's neck, but the case notes from U.S. Marshals team tells quite a different story."

She held up a twenty-page document authored by Brent and Carl that must have been attached to the brief.

I ducked my head in frustration and wanted to curse the sky at my stupidity. I didn't care if she knew about the others but....

"Why didn't you tell me about the GPS device? Or the other children you helped?" she gasped.

Oh, bloody hell. There it was. The beans were not only spilled, they were scattered all over the floor, and kicked a few times.

"Because I didn't want you to know. I assumed it was the reason John was murdered. I couldn't bear the thought...."

Chaste finished my sentence when she saw I was about to trip over my unruly tongue once again.

"We didn't want you to get hurt."

Ferry looked back down at her notes.

"Incredible. You did all this... – *I knew there was a reason I liked you Kress Schumacher. What a brave, brave little girl.*"

Ferry's face flashed at me in terror and she snatched at her phone once again.

"Trice? Yeah, me again. Can you call Judge Harrison and set up a short meeting as soon as possible? And set out those forms for an emergency concealed carry permit. No, of course not for me. I already...."

Ferry looked up at me and turned her head to whisper into the cell phone, "I already have a permit, you know that."

Thunder made all our bodies shake and my head jerked toward a bank of darkening sky. It seemed my daughter's prediction of rain was true.

"Let's leave before the monsoon wave starts. Can I keep this copy Kress?"

I truly wanted to say no.

"Only if you promise not to use it to get yourself killed. I suppose you can use it to fill you in on most of what happened."

"Most?"

The lawyer in Ferry was poking its head up. Why did I keep tripping over my own tongue?

"Yes..., most. As much as you need to know."

I heard myself struggle to spit out the words. She gave me her best frown and turned a sly happy face toward Chaste.

"How would you like to come to my apartment for lunch?"

Again, the lawyer was searching out an unfair advantage to manipulate me.

"Yes, that would be terrific, wouldn't it Daddy?"

I saw exactly where this road was headed and fought to loosen and strip off my *ugly* necktie.

"What are you doing?"

I ignored the question, balled up the tie in a knot and pitched it in the trash bin next to the door. If it hadn't been near freezing outside and if I weren't wearing my favorite sport jacket, I would have thrown it in the bin as well.

It was my turn to give Ferry a scowl, which she seemed to ignore.

"I need you to follow me to the SouthWest Telephone building on our way. You're getting a landline to your house even if they have to run the entire circuit inside steel pipe."

Having Ferry Dunavin as a lawyer and friend was akin to following a bulldozer through a thicket; I was genuinely happy to be following and not in her immediate path.

Eighteen years in the remote bush regions of South Africa had stripped me of the nuances of daily civilized life. Where we had lived was ruled by the weather and the current mood of the leadership surrounding us. There was no need for law offices, no parking tickets, no credit checks or cell phones. Arguments were settled by personal negotiation or at the end of a rifle, whether human or vicious animal.

The pending sheets of rain held off until we were leaving the parking lot. At the parking exit stood a single tall grey deathly still with its back to us. This was the first one I'd seen since Pitre gave me notice of a most unwanted future visit. Even though it didn't seem interested in us, it still sent a shiver down my spine.

Up ahead of me, seated in Ferry's silver Lincoln, I could just see the top of my daughter's head. From their frequent twists, I could tell they were deep in livid chatter. I cringed at the thought of the bits and pieces of our lives Ferry was garnering from Chaste without her knowledge.

I begged Pitre once again to turn off the influx of voices, which he ignored. Evidently, there would be some lesson to be learned and despite my misgivings, it had helped me smooth things over with Ferry. How could anyone get used to something like this?

Minutes later, we were in the parking lot of a familiar bare white brick building with SouthWest Telephone etched into the ornate brickwork. Ferry exited her car, towing Chaste in a dead run for the door. By the time I'd parked and caught up, Ferry was already leaning over a counter in a heated discussion, similar to four conversations I'd already had with a stalwart looking lady. I almost felt sorry for the clerk, …almost.

We had a written promise of immediate reinstallation from her, her supervisor, and their southwest regional supervisor before we left. I stood, nodded a few times and signed the order.

Outside the building under the tiny front shelter, Ferry looked down at Chaste, "That's the only way to handle some people," just before they took off in a mad dash back to her car.

CHAPTER THIRTY-SEVEN

The rain continued 'in buckets' as I followed Ferry to a gated complex of apartments with a guard seated inside a tiny office waving us past.

Ferry's apartment was near the front of the complex and seemed more of a small bungalow than an apartment, in my opinion.

A large tile covered breezeway, bordered with native rock and cacti, kept most of the rain from drenching us as we hurried inside.

As soon as I entered Ferry's doorway, a different type of flood nearly strangled me.

The strong scent in the air was some cinnamon apple spice with another hint of pumpkin pie. A tall puffy sofa with a colorful throw was in the center of the large room, with an ornate dark wooded curio against one of the walls filled with trinkets.

A few tasteful paintings were here and there with profuse flower arrangements at every turn. The recessed lighting was warmer than the clinical white fluorescence and sunshine of our home. It had a cozy feel..., the feeling of a home.

Chaste felt it too and was walking around slowly, wide eyed, with arms crossed over her chest.

I stood near the entrance with my back toward the door for several minutes collecting my emotions, deciding on whether or not I should stay, if I could stay. The feeling spilled Elizabeth all over my skin; God how I missed her in that very moment.

"Help me Pitre, God help me."

Ferry's voice from the adjacent room shattered the glass of my frozen memories.

"Well..., come on in, the kitchen is this way, and the bathroom is straight ahead down the hall. Make yourselves at home."

Chaste looked at me and I melted. She was feeling the same intensity and we seemed to gravitate toward each other's side before following our invitation.

I looked down at my daughter before we moved from our spot and whispered, "Me too."

I didn't need to read her mind to know what she was thinking. She gripped my side tightly in a severe hug and then began to pull me behind her into the kitchen.

We heard the clatter of dishes and silverware before we saw Ferry flowing about in a mad rush.

She suddenly stopped and looked at us.

"You two look as though you'd seen a ghost. Is everything okay?"

I forced a smile as quickly as I could, "Of course. You have a lovely home, we were just admiring your..., decorations."

My voice gathered in my throat like a slipknot and Chaste saved me.

"Can I help with the table? We usually eat at the kitchen counter."

Ferry's eyes both brightened and drew to slits as she glanced my way.

"Of course you can. I hope leftovers are okay with you. I always seem to cook too much and end up giving it away or throwing it out – *I wonder what possessed him to throw away that ugly tie? Thank goodness. Why is he staring at me like that?*"

Ferry smoothed her dress with open palms and checked her hair in a quick motion as I snapped my head away. I hadn't realized that I was focused so intently while listening to Ferry's thoughts. I turned away; small talk Kress..., small talk....

"We do the same thing. The boys eat all our leftovers when we get tired of them."

I felt strange and muted. Besides my nickname of 'Dr. K', my wife always called me her 'chatterbox' and now I couldn't think of a single clever thing to say.

"Kress would you like to fix our drinks?"

Thank God, something to do, "Yes, I'd be delighted."

"Now, tell me more about what really happened, from the time you…, - *No, Chaste is right here, I can't ask him that* – got your…, anonymous tip and went looking for Chaste."

I quickly finished filling glasses with ice and given a subject to talk about, felt more comfortable as I began repeating a congealed mix of my sworn testimony and the written brief from my investigators.

"I hope you like pot roast. Would you say grace?"

I lost my breath…, and managed a quick, two-sentence prayer.

I heard, *'Good job Daddy'* and cleared my throat before resuming my practiced dissertation of events.

"That's what the reports said. Now I want to hear what really happened."

So much for light conversation over a meal.

"Ferry, that's all I can tell you. I already feel I've told you far too much for your own safety. I firmly believe John is dead relative to his knowledge of certain events. I'm thankful that the Judge didn't know everything or he'd be exterminated as well."

We ate salad, fought over wonderful dinner rolls and I thought for a short while that we might be past the inquisition.

Ferry scooped another small helping of beef and potatoes into her bowl as if contemplating, but I didn't hear anything from inside her thoughts. Gleefully, I almost believed that the dirge was past and Pitre had disabled my curse.

"Do you still have the GPS device?"

I closed my eyes and exhaled. Did she really have some misguided death wish?

"Ferry…."

"You might as well tell her."

I wanted to bonk Chaste on the head. She'd been such a good quiet girl up until now.

I suddenly felt Pitre filling me with his presence, filling that emptiness he had occupied inside me and almost gasped at his return.

Chaste smiled and I heard her happy thought, *'The music is back'*.

I heard, 'learn to trust' from somewhere inside, not Pitre, at least I don't think it was him.

"It was stolen from our bank the evening after John was…, killed."

"I knew it. I knew there was foul play. All I had were suspicions and I couldn't prove anything after the FBI confiscated several boxes of his records."

She reached to the counter behind her for her cell phone and I managed to stop her.

"Ferry, no. You can't. I won't let you put your head on a chopping block. It's insane."

She was still pondering, still plotting to postpone her calls until after we left.

"I'm willing to take that chance," she grunted.

"There's no evidence. You're a lawyer Ferry, everything is circumstantial, think about it. You can't prosecute someone based on suspicions, unless the laws are different here."

She was still angry and unconvinced.

"Ferry, if you make those phone calls it will put Chaste and I back in their sights once again."

I heard Pitre speak softly and slowly inside me once again, as if trying not to startle me.

"Tell her you're already working on dismantling the network of people responsible for the abductions. That's what the checks are about. Tell her. Tell her she can help. Go ahead."

Why, oh why couldn't things just be simple?

I did exactly to the letter what Pitre asked of me, all the while watching the expressions and wide eyes on Ferry's face. The food had grown cold and the iced tea had an odd oil and vinegar look when we were through.

"Who is this anonymous helper Kress? He is the key to exposing them and putting them all in prison. Or is he some kind of competitor? Uh…, like another kidnapper, using you to get rid of the competition for him?"

Amazing. She must have spent her entire childhood buried in mystery novels.

"No, it's nothing of the sort. I assure you."

My cell phone buzzed. Saved by the…, oh no, not now.

I'm sure my face turned either beet red or stark white as I pressed the button to silence the call from Thomas Whitefeather, probably giving us yet another client's information of a missing child.

"That's him isn't it?"

Ferry hurried from her seat to get a glimpse of the incoming phone number, just as I pocketed my phone.

I'd never seen anyone in such a hurry to place them self in harms way.

"Why don't you trust me, Kress? I only want to help?"

I couldn't take any more. I stood and dropped my napkin.

"Bloody hell, Ferry. I've never seen such a tenacious woman in all my life. Can't you see that the more you know, the more danger you could be facing? I won't be party to some evil coming your way. Chaste, it's getting late, we should be going."

Chaste didn't bother to move. Instead, she sat there staring at me, eyes swelling on the verge of tears.

I wasn't the only one that saw the change come over Chaste.

Ferry sat back down nearer me at the table and shrank, making herself look smaller, if that was possible.

"Please…, don't go. I get that way. I'm a digger. I get hold of something and I can't let go. It's what makes me a good lawyer, but…, it doesn't work as well with friends."

She grasped my hand firmly; I felt her warmth as she pulled me back to my seat at the table.

"Please…."

I stood there in the uncomfortable silence, listening to the insistent rain battering the windowpanes above her sink.

My body slid back down into the chair and I glanced at Chaste. I heard her thank me in my mind.

The subject changed in an instant. She and Ferry resumed some small talk over a future shopping expedition and busied with refreshing our tea, while I sat measuring boundaries.

Such a tangled web of personalities; so many walls of safety to keep firmly standing, so many pockets of volatile information between them. My head began to ache as I tried to sort the imaginary lines of demarcation and their intersections. I saw flashing road signs ahead on my path to schizophrenia.

Pitre arose into my thoughts like a mist.

At least he was learning etiquette instead of making me jump like a puppet on a string every time he spoke.

"Kress, it will get easier. Ferry is good for Chaste; you didn't meet by chance. She is a very good person. If you open your heart just a fraction you might find she's good for you."

Bloody hell. That's all I needed; Pitre playing matchmaker to a brooding old bachelor like myself.

"I realize I kept you from your list of things today Kress, can I help?"

None of them seemed important but one, "I was going to see if I could hire the local Boy Scout troop to take down all the posters of

Chaste in the National Forest. My phone number is on them."

"You've got to be kidding? You used your personal phone number on the posters? You're supposed to use the FBI hotline."

Her voice trailed away in recognition of my dilemma; at the blunder of her very own words.

I shrugged and blinked, what was I supposed to do? I gave Ferry my best blank stare.

"I'm sure the rain will take care of them over the next few weeks. How many are there?"

"A couple thousand..., maybe a few more, at the Tonto State Park. Then there's Scottsdale, Phoenix, Albuquerque..., I don't remember..., all told..., a little over twenty thousand."

I couldn't remember exactly.

She laughed and banished all the ghosts from the corners of my mind.

"...*and he called me tenacious. That must have taken him months. —*I know a service that will take them all down for you for a very reasonable fee."

I felt myself blush.

"Okay Kress, tell me, what I need to know, about the checks...."

Ferry and Chaste were busy with some nonsense in an old chest back in Ferry's bedroom; pictures, memorabilia and such. Their chitchat gave me a chance to breathe and be the nosey one and have a look-see into the life of Ferry.

The first thing I noticed was what wasn't. Photographs.

Not the decorative ones, but the familial ones. No parents, siblings, children, nieces, nephews or that sort of thing were anywhere to be seen. Maybe we weren't the only ones that had gone through the biblical Job experience and had everything ripped away from us.

I looked for other signs, keepsakes, trinkets and that sort, but nothing revealed itself to me. Even her cabinet of curiosities seemed to whisper anonymity.

"Pitre, where are all Ferry's family photos and such?"

"Why don't you ask her?"

"Don't be a bore, just answer my question."

I felt the sensation of a sigh, *"She was an orphan; she has no family. Before you ask, she was never adopted."*

Alone?

"What about her niece? Her brother-in-law? She admitted she was guardian over her niece," I asked.

"It's her self-adopted family from St. Mary's, where she grew up."

That explained a world of things. How could I have been so dense? My heart sank for her.

I heard muted laughter from the back bedroom and resolved myself to resist temptation and join them. Instead, I let the two ladies bond.

My phone vibrated, just an alarm, three o'clock. I remembered the phone call from Thomas Whitefeather, then pressed voicemail and listened.

"Kress? Thomas. I got a visit yesterday from the FBI. I just got away from them. They had a lot of questions about you. I told them I didn't know anything. Now I'm on their permanent radar. They wanted to know how I found things. I told them the truth…, well mostly. I passed their polygraph so they think I'm a bonafide loony. Ha! Tell our buddy they might pay you another visit. Oh, hey I got three more missing cases. Call you tonight."

He was talking so fast I had to replay it twice just to get a clear picture of what had happened.

"Pitre?" I needed to ask a question, but was interrupted.

"Kress. Do you have a minute?"

I turned my head and looked behind me toward the open hallway, but I didn't see anyone.

"In here, Kress."

I turned and looked the other direction toward the kitchen and still didn't see anyone, "Hello?"

"In the back room. Would you be a sweetheart and bring me my glass of tea?"

Like the obedient creature I am, I dumped fresh ice in a glass, poured tea and walked inside the spacious bedroom.

"I don't believe it," hissed Ferry.

Ferry was grinning from ear to ear and positively shaking with glee.

"Don't believe what?"

"You read my mind."

She was holding my daughters hand, who incidentally wouldn't raise her eyes my direction. She had been needling Chaste for information. Such bad form.

Ferry still didn't know the tea was hers and I smiled inside. I quickly took a sip from the glass of tea and stared at her.

"What in the world are you going on about?" I asked, using my best dumb look; possibly my usual look.

Ferry glanced at Chaste, her expression, then back to me, "But..., you brought my tea."

"You wanted tea?" I asked, sipping the glass of tasteless liquid. "I'll be glad to get you a fresh glass."

I turned to leave, grateful and amazed at my sudden brilliance.

"Not so fast, Mr. Schumacher," she grunted, her smile back on her face. "You don't drink iced tea. You hate iced tea. You were bringing that to me, weren't you?"

I sipped the glass, rattling the ice, "Just trying to fit in."

Her face finally fell to a soft frown, "Chaste? I thought..., I can't believe you'd lie to me."

My daughter is no liar, not even the sort we adults consider white ones. I had to bury this quickly before my anger spread to Ferry.

"What other absurd information have you managed to niggle from my daughter? Of all the nerve. Chaste, are you all right? Why would you tell Ferry such a wild thing?"

"It was an accident," she whispered.

"And you expect me to trust you Ferry. That's not the way you go about gaining trust; coercing information from my traumatized daughter. I believe it's time for us to go home Chaste."

Ferry smiled, "Me thinks he doth protest too much."

After all the good will and sharing, it was the only way I could think to remedy the breach, yet I was now twice the fool. Such blatant denial only means one thing; some measure of guilt.

What a fool. To make matters worse, all I could do was stand there trying to conjure some other means of denial.

And now, I'd made such a blunder of denial Ferry knew her trick had exposed some inkling of truth as her expression shifted into a sly grin. I hoped that her rational mind would eventually see how ridiculous the notion that I could hear her thoughts actually was and forget the entire matter. Knowing Ferry..., not bloody likely.

We gathered our jackets and we left despite Ferry's lighthearted protests all the way to the door.

My phone rang no less than a dozen times on the way home, with Chaste apologizing to me after Ferry's every attempted call. With her every apology, I explained to Chaste that it wasn't her fault. Anyone could be tripped up with enough persistence.

"Pitre, what do I do about Ferry?"

A stoic response was instantaneous.

"I can erase her memory of the event, but it's like tearing out a sheet of paper from your notebook. I wouldn't be able to erase one line. It could cause damage, unless she is close and asleep."

"No! No, don't do anything that might harm her. What do you suggest? Why didn't you warn me?"

I felt my shoulders shrug as if they were his, shrugging inside me. Very unnerving to say the least.

"You needed to learn. Use it. What's done is done."

"I'm not in a forgiving mood, accident or not. What if she had somehow tricked Chaste into mentioning you, Pitre?"

I felt an icy chill rake my body to the core and an awful silence.

"Pitre?"

"That would be very unfortunate. I would have to erase Ferry's memory of the event, in its entirety."

Chaste slid over in the seat close to me, listening quietly. That would place the blame on Chaste if Ferry managed to scratch the information from between the lines of one of their conversations.

"That's a lot of responsibility to place on a nine-year-old child, Pitre. Especially a nine-year-old child you care so much for."

I knew I was stepping out on a limb by playing that card.

Pitre was silent until we pulled through the gate at home and shut off the vehicle.

"Yes. I do care about your daughter."

We sat inside the car close to one another as the noise of the rain became muted by the closing garage door.

He had something else to say that was causing him pain, pain that I was feeling as a physical reaction inside my body.

"I would give up my quest before I would harm Chaste."

I felt the tension leave along with several tense emotions.

It was the first sign of self-sacrifice he had ever offered. He seemed to withdraw as if he had bared information he was not ready to share but did it anyway.

"Thank you Pitre."

Something changed in me in that moment. I felt a new respect for our would-be angelic Pitre. All my hatred, contempt, and mistrust I held in reserve for Pitre slipped away. For the first time since his occupation, I truly wanted to help him.

Together Chaste and I fed the boys, then changed from our rain-soured clothes and collapsed on the couch, ready to blot out the day with some mindless movie on the television.

Darkness was already upon us at 6 p.m. and the weight of the day began to slide away. I had no more than powered on the television when my phone rang again. It was Ferry. Blast it all.

Tenacious woman.

I started to mute the call. I fervently wanted to mute it, but after a dozen calls already, it was time to end our hullabaloo.

"Ferry, See here, I don't want to discuss...."

"Kress. Thank God. I'm so scared. I'm just outside at your front gate. Can you let me in?"

I ran to the front door and peered down the end of the path by the front walk-through. I could barely see her silhouette in the downpour.

"Yes, of course, get out of the rain and pull your car inside the garage. I'll open the main gate this minute."

She hung up immediately and I saw her running to her Lincoln. In the distance, in the downpour, just past the steeply sloping intersection, I saw one of the tall greys, standing, pointing at the Lincoln. Not a good sign.

I met Ferry inside the garage, dripping wet, and sobbing uncontrollably.

"I'm sorry. I didn't know where else to go considering.... I think someone was following me."

"Tell me what happened? Are you hurt?"

"Right after you left, I got two phone calls, from a blocked number, but nobody said anything. Then I saw someone looking in my back window, by the garbage pickup lane. The person was dressed in solid black with a black mask over his head. I called the guard at the gate, but he didn't answer."

"Did you call the authorities?"

"I tried to call the cops but suddenly my cell phone lost all signal and my main phone went dead. I wasn't able to reach them until I was blocks away."

It sounded like she was visited by the same chaps that paid us a visit recently.

"Please, come inside and dry off. I'll get Chaste to help you."

I all but carried her inside as her panic turned into shivering sobs.

The strong willed, assertive, even arrogant person I'd seen in Ferry was gone. This had truly shaken her.

Just as we entered the door, her phone chirped in her hand. I gave her some privacy and asked Chaste to walk Ferry to one of the spare bedrooms while I stepped back out to my own seclusion of the garage.

"It was them wasn't it Pitre?"

"The same."

"Are we safe?"

"Perfectly safe."

Pitre's words sounded strange, powerful, controlled and certain. I wanted desperately to discuss this sudden change but it wasn't the right time.

"How do I help Ferry? Why did she come here of all places?"

"Encourage her to stay here. Go before she gets suspicious."

I hurried out of the garage into the house. I found Chaste in one of the back bedrooms and heard the shower running. Together we scrambled through some boxes of her mother's clothing, looking for something warm for Ferry to wear. I had to close my heart's eyes as I pulled out a thick cashmere sweater and tweed pants that looked like a good fit for Ferry.

"Tell Ferry to look through these and use whatever she needs."

I handed them to Chaste before I could change my mind and went to make some hot coffee.

I hurried past the front door to look outside and was not surprised in the least at the dozen or so tall greys milling about the front in the rain. The boys didn't seem upset with them; as if they had proven themselves and secured the line of territories. It seemed they understood they could somehow inflict damage if the enemy came past the fence into their domain.

I was pouring the first cup of coffee when I heard low mumbling chatter from the downstairs hallway.

"Do you think it's safe for me to go back to my apartment? How is Bob? I see. Yes, I can get a room somewhere else tonight if you think…, yes, I will, thank you."

Ferry slumped into one of the tall chairs by the bar in the kitchen. I tried to keep my eyes focused on pouring coffee, but the sight of her thin frame in clothes I'd been reluctant to carry off was too compelling.

She looked exceptionally nice; almost human, considering our recent differences.

The contrasting chocolate cashmere made the golden highlights of her hair sing and there were curves in all the right places. I shook my head and forced myself to turn away from my unsolicited adulation.

"Thank you for letting me in. I would have understood if you sent me away."

"Don't be ridiculous. What did the authorities say? Did they find anything amiss?"

I handed her a cup and pushed some sugar and creamer her direction.

"They found plenty of stuff *amiss*. They found the guard knocked on his…, knocked unconscious. My back door was broken down flat and everything in my apartment was turned upside down. The police seem to think it was a disgruntled litigant, given my reputation. Anyway, I managed to get my briefcase before I left, with your two documents and my notes intact. Thank goodness I didn't bring my laptop home from the office."

I heated some milk and cocoa, with Chaste in mind, while I listened. It would be a matter of minutes before she would be seated next to Ferry like two birds on a wire.

"You're staying here for the evening. I don't want to hear a single word of argument. We have four spare bedrooms or a very comfortable sofa for you to choose from."

Her eyes drew to that uncomfortable slit, scanning me. Of course, I'd done it again without realizing it, absently listening to her thoughts. How stupid of me.

Her mind said that she didn't like the disadvantage of having to guess my thoughts.

"Thank you. I was hoping you'd invite me to stay. I didn't want to be alone."

She sipped her coffee and stared down at the counter while I stirred the hot cocoa.

"I take it you're not the type that's easily put off by hooligans. I'm glad you're taking this serious."

She grinned at me, studying me over her cup of coffee and her thoughts taunted my choice of vocabulary.

Another critic....

Chaste walked in and as predicted, crunched up on the stool closest to Ferry and I shoved her cup of hot cocoa in front of her, while Ferry studied us.

"You two really get along well together, don't you?"

Chaste looked at me and nodded with her thin smile, "Want some hot cocoa?"

"Yes, I'd love some."

Ferry slid her nearly empty cup of coffee away and looked at me expectantly. I couldn't help but smile.

CHAPTER THIRTY-EIGHT

"**Brent Rand?** Yes, this is Kress Schumacher. Yes, Chaste is doing marvelous, just had a checkup and all is going splendidly.

"No, you're right, this isn't a social call. I need to see what your schedule is like for the next few days.

"No, I'd rather wait for you and Carl if you don't mind. You remember our discussion about John Shoemaker? Of course you do..., what am I thinking. Of course, I know you did everything you could.

"Actually, the reason I'm calling is to try and prevent a repeat performance with my current lawyer Ferry Dunavin, one of John's associates."

I looked over my shoulder and saw Ferry making small glances, straining to listen to my conversation. I made it easier. I walked back to where she and Chaste were seated, finishing their cocoa, just before I was taken off hold.

"Excellent news. Really..., unbelievable. Yes, Ms. Dunavin is right here at the moment."

I handed the phone to Ferry.

"This is Brent, one of the investigators from the U.S. Marshal's team I told you about. He wants to ask you a few questions if you don't mind."

Chaste and I walked to the living room and absolutely flopped down in the sofa next to each other. I felt my daughter sink next to my side as we both fought away the exhaustion. I kissed the top of her head and she looked up at me; worry in her eyes.

"Everything is going to work out just fine."

Ferry walked in and handed me my phone.

"It went dead. Don't worry, we finished our conversation before it died. Brent said that he …and Carl, I think, would be here the day after tomorrow."

I nodded tiredly.

My phone clicked into the charger and I noticed that it had plenty of battery left.

"That's strange. My cell phone is dead too. It did the same thing earlier," mumbled Ferry.

She shook her phone and popped the battery out and back in.

"Maybe it got wet…."

"Daddy?"

Chaste was sitting tall, looking at several bright multi-colored lights flickering through the hazy front glass panes of the house.

Bloody hell. When it rains, it pours.

I heard the buzzer from the front gate fire off just inside the front door.

The three of us hurried to the intercom and peered out into the gray evening light. The floodlamps revealed two black SUV's parked in the street just in front of our house, with blaring red and blue lights destroying the peaceful landscape. Six men were standing by the gate in the downpour under umbrella's, with a dozen tall greys at their backs, pointing in the direction of…, us.

I pressed the intercom like a good fellow.

"Can I help you?"

"Special Agent Lilly, FBI. We need to speak to you, Mr. Schumacher."

I instantly pictured another night in that blasted filthy interrogation room and ducked my head.

"Let me handle this one Kress."

Ferry stepped up to the intercom and pressed the talk button.

"Agent Lilly? Do you have a warrant?"

"We need to speak to Dr. Schumacher."

"Not what I asked. Do you have a warrant?"

"I can get one."

"That's doubtful or you would have brought it with you. My name is Dunavin, Dr. Schumacher's lawyer. Call my office and make an appointment. I'm sure you already know the number. I'll make certain my client is present. Have a good evening."

We watched them leaning into one another in conversation, just as the boys trotted up to the gate and sat down in the drenching rain.

God bless the boys.

Two of the men, one with an arm in a sling, anxiously slid back from the fence pointing at the dogs, with exaggerated nodding heads, then quickly made their way back into the rear SUV.

Ferry slid her hand across Chaste's shoulders and nudged her.

"Let's move away from the door. Let them know we're not going out and they're not coming in. Kress, you should probably check the back door."

I flipped off the front flood lamps and left our guests standing in the pitch black downpour.

"I trust the boys, no one's back there."

Ferry and I sat up late that night, bits and pieces of conversations flowing. Neither of us had any desire to attempt sleep with the anxious adrenaline drip injecting our veins.

It was a nightmare jolting Ferry that woke us, stretched on opposite ends of our large sofa sometime just before daybreak.

We went our separate ways and returned for coffee soon thereafter.

I convinced her to stay put and make her inquiries where I could keep an eye on her safety.

Her reluctance was noted, but she seemed very settled and very much at home during the early morning. Chaste was beside herself with someone to socialize with, especially Ferry Dunavin.

Our houseguest steeled her nerves sometime before noon and found a suitable cubby to work from.

"Hello Trice? Yes, I'm okay…. How did you find out? Really? Yesterday?"

Ferry looked ashen, then glanced at me.

"Good girl, no one gets in our records without a warrant. I'm so proud of you I could sing.

"Trice, before you go home this evening tell everyone to lock their laptops in the floor vault, stuff mine in there too, and set the alarm, …no exceptions. Can you do that for me?

"Shift the rest of my schedule around to the gang, tell them I'm working a live one. It's gonna be big."

Apparently, the rogue unit's first stop was to the bottom floor of the banking complex in Phoenix where Ferry and her associates were located.

My mind and body wandered aimlessly toward the back deck. I didn't dare ask what next for fear of an answer I wouldn't like. The glass panes felt cool to my open palms as I leaned to look outside at the gloomy day.

"Pitre, you say you can protect us. For once, I believe you. What do I do about these men that persist in causing us grief?"

"That was odd. Talking to himself..., or praying maybe?"

In an instant, I saw Ferry's reflection in the glass. Blast it all, I'd been thinking out loud again. I ducked my head and turned to face Ferry who'd obviously walked up at the end of my musing.

"A little of both."

Ferry backed up a step or two and studied me. The cat had more than it's head out of the bag now. She knew for sure I'd heard her thoughts and I'd have to trust Pitre's judgment to let her into our tight circle.

I watched Ferry study me with added fear and anxiety.

Finally her head wobbled in little shakes, "I don't like it Kress. You can't lie to me. You're mind reading; it's like having somebody look up my dress. It's not...."

I hurried and raised a hand to stop her and give me a chance to explain as best I could.

"My apologies. It's not something that I particularly relish either."

"Is that how you're helping these people find their kids?"

Pitre spoke up and for the first time, it felt natural, easy, almost like my own thoughts.

"Tell her yes."

Actually, since Pitre and I became attached, I was. It was as good an alibi as any.

"I know it makes you feel uncomfortable Ferry. Heaven knows it makes me uncomfortable. For that I am sorry. But to answer your question, yes, I'm a bit of a human lie detector."

"My God, I sure could have used that in court."

I smiled and she blushed, just a little, then her eyes rounded, her face blossomed red and she turned her back to me and her thoughts went blank except for one short phrase.

"Oh no."

That single phrase repeated itself over and over inside her head as she stepped a few feet away. Then she began trying to recall everything she had rolled around inside her head since she met me.

"Back at the clinic; that's why you threw away that ugly faded tie of yours isn't it?"

She walked away, mumbling to herself, "You're an idiot Ferry…, you are an idiot."

I was learning more about this new necessary evil the more I interacted with Ferry. Her thoughts were sometimes the instant result of what she spoke.

Telling the difference between the truth and a lie was all Pitre's doing.

What was I thinking?

That was simply absurd on my part.

All of it was Pitre's doing; detecting a lie had become so second nature to me, that I'd subconsciously accepted it as myself.

"I don't like it Kress. I don't like it at all. It's…, I think I'll…, go talk with Chaste for a little while – *at least she can't…, oh God, Ferry, shut up…, shut up."*

Her bare feet pattered away as she headed toward the stairs.

I watched her, almost uncontrollably until she reached the top landing and she turned and caught my gratuitous gaze.

Good heavens! What was wrong with me? It was my turn to blush and contain myself. I was overwhelmingly glad Ferry Dunavin could not read my thoughts.

My phone chirped some growling ghastly tune Chaste had punished me with that particular day; the caller was Thomas Whitefeather as promised. I hurried to my office and locked myself inside.

His conversation was lengthy, but thankfully to the point. I had four, not three, more prospective clients and carefully dictated all their information down on a notepad. As I finished, I saw three of them glow, and one name darkened to a harsh smudge. Back to three.

I told Thomas I couldn't help the second one from his list and he drew very silent. Did he suddenly care or was it something else? He wouldn't tell me.

We said our goodbyes and prompted by Pitre, made three difficult phone calls to three highly distraught parents with missing children.

My new standard disclosure statement to the highly emotional adults was to keep me out of the spotlight at all costs or I could not help them.

After looking at the dates, locations, and time constraints, I was reminded to flip back several pages on my notepad. There were twenty-three more hapless families from my previous list still in dire need at the very same moment.

There were several unused day planners Elizabeth and I had purchased in hopes of a fresh start after we settled in. They were stacked in a box, all out of date, but still usable. I dug through them and found one abnormally large one with lots of room for notes and began transcribing each of the cases into some type of sequence.

As I wrote them down in the planner, like some idle grocery list, I felt the weight of their anguish stack on my shoulders, one by one.

As soon as I finished my task, one of them drew a line through itself. Now twenty-two; a total of..., twenty-five little lives depending on me.

I fell to my knees with the burden of that knowledge and wept for the one lost, then the rest of them.

I was their thread of hope. For some of them, Kress Schumacher was their last and only thread of hope. I prayed to God that my efforts wouldn't be in vain for all their sakes, for all our sakes.

With great difficulty, I forced myself to focus and got back up into my chair.

I skipped ahead on my calendar and noted the phone repair date, a carry permit for a weapon upon confirmation of my EMA status – date unknown. What else?

Brent and Carl's visit in two days....

Trying to focus on every detail was getting more and more difficult. I needed help.

The knock on my office door was not good timing, nor was it welcome.

"What!?"

I heard my voice, loud and sharp as a razor.

"Food's ready if you're hungry."

I heard Ferry's distinct footsteps padding away from the door.

I looked at my watch, almost eight. I'd been so consumed I'd completely forgotten about feeding my daughter and my guest.

Chaste had updated her forecast to include even more buckets of rain early this morning. I on the other hand could only prognosticate a volley of profuse apologies in my immediate future.

I unlatched the door and slunk to my groveling.

Chaste and Ferry were seated at our dining table with a banquet of items dotted around.

"Where did all this come from?"

"You have an entire grocery store in your pantry; you should look in there once in a while – ...just sit down and eat okay?"

Ferry was giving me the look again, then she smiled; an evil sort of smile.

"Now that you're in my head, I have a few things to say to you...."

I needed to preempt her volley of justified anger.

"Ferry, I'm sorry – for the outburst. I'm not usually an ogre. I can't remember the last time I blurted something hateful without any provocation whatsoever."

She sat in silence, both inside and out, watching me, listening. Chaste was bouncing her eyes from her plate of food and back to me in silence.

"Since...," I tried to build my list.

Since what? Since when? Since Elizabeth died? Since Chaste was kidnapped? Since I was fused with an angelic being? Since dark forces were seeking me out to destroy me? I didn't know where to begin.

"Since...," I muttered, struggling with what to say.

"Just eat. We can talk later - ...*but you're not getting off that easy mister – Why does he look like he's been crying?*"

Then Ferry grimaced and clacked her plate with her spoon and her thoughts went forcibly blank.

"Ferry. Please try and relax."

"Says the doctor as he pops on the rubber gloves."

Then she smiled and I realized it was a joke.

"Would you please pass the... um, what exactly is that?"

Our night could have been a continuous exchange of hand grenades, but for some reason Ferry did an about face. I began to see a different side of Ferry slowly emerge. Bits and pieces of her personality easily displayed as she lowered her professional defenses. She spoke of her years at law school, her MBA, bragged how she'd passed the bar examination on her first attempt. I did notice that she never referenced St. Mary's or talked of her childhood. It was as if she'd skipped that entire segment of her life and vaulted straight into adulthood.

Chaste was asleep with her head in my lap while Ferry sat and listened to me prattle on of my college years, random incidents while living in Africa. Soon Ferry had me talking freely about the outdated medical department in Johannesburg where Elizabeth and I were forced to keep up our continuing education once a year. Memories both good and bad seemed easily forthcoming to her attentive ears.

It was near midnight, while I was still rambling on like a blathering twit, when I noticed Ferry's fingers absently touching mine on the back of the sofa. I had no idea how long we'd been sitting there connected, absently, yet intimately.

Apparently, she was just as surprised as I when she noticed and we decided to end our soirée for the evening.

Ferry followed me up the stairs as I carried Chaste to bed and shoed me out of the room so that she could change my daughter into her bedclothes. I would have had to wake Chaste from her natural rest or left her in her day clothes. It served as my subtle reminder of the missing element in our small family.

CHAPTER THIRTY-NINE

Something stirred me from my sleep. It wasn't the ever-present Pitre. Actually, it was almost bothering me when he went on his jaunts into seclusion, rambling about somewhere inside my recesses. Where exactly was he going?

In any case, I was wide-awake and there was nothing left to do but get up.

I peered into Chaste's room and she was a lump of contentment purring beneath her covers.

Ferry was in one of the downstairs bedrooms. It would be easy to avoid an incident, especially at..., five in the morning.

Another fleeting item presented itself to my mind and I hurried to jot it down in my planner, then possibly a hot cup of tea to start my day rolling on an even keel.

The house was utterly silent and peaceful, not the silence of loneliness or dread I'd come to bear during the several months without Chaste. That in itself filled me with hope.

I was about to open my office door and noticed that I'd left the desk lamp on.

I slipped inside and found Ferry sitting in my chair, buried in my planner, with a furrowed brow.

She looked up, not with the shock of me catching her flagrante delicto in my privacy, but from what she was reading.

"These are all the children you have on your list to help?"

She said it so matter of fact, without so much as an apology of her invasion.

I was tired of the arguing and pulled up a chair next to hers. I didn't want to start yet another day off kilter.

"Yes."

"But there's so many. What's this one with the line? Should I expect another mysterious certified check?"

I had hoped for a better start of this day than the last.

"No Ferry, there won't be a forthcoming check for that one."

She looked back at the list, at the name of the child, and the circumstances noted.

"Oh. I see," she sighed at her moment of understanding.

She drew a deep breath and swiped away something I couldn't see from her eye.

"Ferry, I'm tired of arguing with you. I'm trying to protect you. The more you know, the more danger you put yourself in. I wish you could see…."

She leaned over and kissed me, my morning breath and all.

Blazes. I didn't see that coming.

I surprised myself and let it happen, well not exactly; truthfully it was more of a mutual effort. Her hand was both warm and soft on the side of my face.

She sat back up in the light of the little desk lamp.

"You're a good man Kress Schumacher. Weird as hell…, but a very good man."

It was a strange compliment, but in lieu of the circumstances, I wasn't about to protest.

"I feel the same about you Ferry Dunavin, all except for the weird as hell part, of course."

She kissed me again and I decided to put off making my morning tea. Maybe the day was looking up after all.

I expected a flood of emotions of missing Elizabeth, years of memories of our lives together, but instead it was peaceful bliss, without any guilt.

When we finally composed ourselves, she sat back looking at me, and seemed very pleased with herself.

"Good morning Kress, how about some coffee?" she whispered.

This time when we sat across from each other at the kitchen bar the tension was lifted and for lack of a better description, …easy.

"Your two boys didn't do their jobs last night. You know, keeping the ghosts run away? I had the most vivid, disturbing, dreams last night. I don't think I've ever had dreams like that. It must be the stress of someone trying to...."

She looked at me with a little renewed distress.

"Kress, do you think that man at my apartment would have tried to kill me?"

I'd stalled, still pondering the powerful effect of Pitre on other people's dreams.

"Quit trying to candy your answer and tell me the truth."

"Yes. I think that if you hadn't had the presence of mind to get out when you did, we'd be devastated and mourning your loss; and looking for another lawyer."

Her eyes darted and flashed, flowing with a rain of thoughts the Great Mesmer couldn't have followed. For a fleeting moment, I envied the brilliant abstract mind inside her.

"This is crazy. How do you get protection or a restraining order against someone posing as law enforcement? If I didn't know better I'd have guessed they were SWAT or even FBI.

"I'm going to have my associates file our suit against them and give it a little nudge, some publicity. It'll be a diversion that gets them in the public eye. I suppose that's as good a start as any."

"Ferry, they can't all be bad. We can't lump them all into one basket and throw out the baby with the wash."

She fixated on that for a few minutes, not entirely agreeing with me, then amended her decision.

"I'll meet with everyone today and see if we can narrow the focus of our lawsuit. The problem is, I don't know how it will affect the court's ruling. Plus, I don't know how deep this goes or how high up the ladder?"

I instantly thought of the chap from the state department and how many times he'd lied to me.

It was Pitre prompting me to share.

"There's more you should know then," I mumbled.

Unexpectedly she took my hand and donned a curious expression, "You'd be devastated?"

When I heard the buzzer from the gate, my heart squirreled in its cage. I envisioned a slew of black SUV's, a dozen men in black, weapons raised, as I inched to the edge of one of the glass panes.

There was a brown UPS truck parked in the street and a plastic covered deliveryman waiting in the steady drizzle, impatiently prancing at the covered gate. The self-loathing from my cowardice turned to anger as I hurried to the front door.

The boys sat side by side far away, by the garage door, watching the deliveryman as intently as he was watching them.

He heard the buzzer and latch of the gate engage and hurried with a large box on a two-wheeled dolly down the narrow little twisting path.

When he dropped the heavy box in the foyer, he glanced up, "Nice place…, sign here," then he was gone in a trot, back into the rain.

I looked at the box as if it was set to go off any minute. Was it a Trojan Horse sent by one of my many enemies? I hadn't ordered anything. Overnight Delivery was pasted on every side of the box like Christmas streamers.

Once the plastic wrap was removed, I looked at the label, addressed to Ms Chaste Schumacher c/o Ferry Dunavin at our address.

What the blazes?

It was an express package from someplace named Academic Training Academy, Affiliated Department of Education.

Despite my inclination to push it back out on the front stoop, I stripped off the wet plastic wrap and opened it. It was full of books and instruction packets.

Chaste heard the ruckus and joined me as I was dragging the oversized mass through the house.

She quickly poked her head inside the box and dug around.

"My books! Yes!"

She picked one up and danced in a small circle holding it in the air.

"Ferry promised to order my home school kit. I have to call her and let her know its here."

She began an excited frenzy of taking each one out and stacking the text with the matching workbook on the coffee table. She didn't seem at all disappointed that most of the volumes were teaching aids.

Suddenly she pulled out a VHS cartridge still in the wrapper.

"You'd think they'd at least send their media on DVD. I don't think we have a player for that."

Chaste's face became drawn, her eyes dead as a floating halibut, as she dropped it back in the box. She slid backwards and had the sofa not been behind her she would have fallen flat of her back on the floor.

"Chaste. Are you alright?"

I didn't hear her thoughts so much as I saw them.

My body clenched and I wanted to vomit.

The VHS cartridge triggered some latch to a door in her mind. A forbidden place Chaste had locked away.

A dirty hand was forcing one of many tapes from a small stack into a crusty silver VHS player. There was a whir of noise as it snatched into play.

Vile orgiastic scenes of brutal torture and sex too extreme to begin to describe began flickering on a tiny television screen. With several pairs of innocent glazed eyes peering at the images for nights and days and more nights on end. Then I heard slurry voices cheering as hands and sticks prodded into their cages, forcing them to watch. All the children were made to believe that this was their ultimate future.

When I tried to reach out to Chaste, she fought me like a wild animal drowning in depths of dark images.

When I backed away, she crunched her eyes closed and began to breathe in heaves and mumble the end of some nursery rhyme from when she was just a tiny thing.

Then it was ended, just as it began.

"What happened?" she asked, frowning at me as I hovered over her.

I was so shocked at what I'd witnessed, I couldn't answer.

Chaste stood up, brushed herself off and went back to the box and finished sorting the books to her liking.

I felt as useless as any one human being can feel, living the illusion that I had my daughter safe at home. She was still lost to me, still a prisoner in a cage, lost in the dark recesses of her mind.

The doctor's report said that she had not been violated physically. But in every other aspect, she had been subjected to far worse redundant iterations of abuse.

I felt my soul rip to pieces inside me.

Just last night, I had knelt and wept over a list of anonymous children that needed rescue and now I had not the resource to help my own precious child. No antiparasitic or antibiotic would ever be able to rid her of the corruptive disease forced into her impressionable young mind.

I woke from my deluge to the cheerful voice of Chaste on her phone, talking to Ferry, announcing the arrival of her books and thanking her profusely.

Without realizing it, I found my way inside my office. I had one good fight left in me. One to end all fights.

"Pitre! Show yourself at once!"

The prepubescent warble in my voice made my demand sound broken, misplaced, and I was about to repeat it with a violent scream.

I felt the empty void inside me filling up, brimming over with his presence.

"I demand that you show yourself."

The room glowed dimly at first, then was flooded with a brilliance that blinded my eyes. My eyelids were insufficient to filter the painful effusion and I found myself turned, with both my hands covering my face.

"Did you know about what they did to my child? Answer me! I'll know if you lie to me Pitre."

My answer was barely a whisper.

"No. I did not."

I was terrified of my next question, terrified of the possible answer. My own anger and destruction hid the compassion I should have felt flooding from Pitre.

"Can you help her?"

"In her sleep, in her dreams. It will take time."

"Then you'll help Chaste?"

"I exist to serve; I'll do everything I can."

Anguish flooded from his voice. Recognizing a lie had become my second nature, now truth and pain joined in.

I felt waves of relief that spilled me out like a puddle of water. In the middle of my relief, my mind allowed me to take notice of this being I was in the presence of.

Pitre had changed. This was a different creature altogether.

My hundred questions could wait. His very presence comforted me. Crouched there on the floor with my back to Pitre, I became a child basking in the warm summer sun without a care in the world, peaceful.

"Kress. I received the answer to my petition."

253

His voice vibrated through my body; strummed all the strings of my being with perfect harmony. I heard the music Chaste spoke of; a thousand voices humming, all merging like a soft spring shower.

I suddenly felt the craving to swim in it, exist in it.

"Your petition? When? Tell me."

"I've been seated with your soul, next to our Creator. I'm healing, thanks to you Kress."

That must be where he was going when I felt that deep emptiness of his absence. That didn't make a bit of sense and at the same time it made perfect sense.

My mind emptied. I couldn't babble another question.

Then just as quickly, I felt the intensity wane and uncovered my eyes. The room was now empty, but the very walls still radiated that brilliant pure white as if it were glued to their very substance.

I stood up, felt rejuvenated, refreshed, energized. Twenty hours of sleep and a good meal couldn't compete.

Chaste knocked on the door and entered, looking around.

"I thought I heard Pitre."

The understatement of the century.

"So did I."

She looked at me strangely, which was understandable.

"Daddy, you're glowing."

Before I could say or do anything, she touched my hand, closed her eyes and her shoulders fell slack. I barely caught her before she fell limp to the floor.

I carried her into the living room and lay her on the sofa. I thought she had fainted, but after checking her vitals, she seemed to be simply sleeping. I remembered Pitre's promise and covered her with a throw and watched her there, so thin, helpless.

Somehow, I knew she would be all right. I resisted the urge to kiss her, to touch her brow, anything that might risk waking her up from the work going on inside her.

I stood there, resisting the urge to pace the floor, finally looking for something to occupy me. I felt compelled to stay near, something to do with my connection with Pitre. Since technically, I was his residence, it seemed to make a little sense. The view from the back deck seemed to be safe and began pulling me toward it. The burst of refreshing chill air promised more rain as a mist peppered my face. I tried to relax, to think of anything else; I was now the parent in the waiting room, anxious over the hands of the skilled surgeon.

As I stepped back inside, memories from the vision of degradation tried to replay inside my head.

What of the other children? How could such horrid demented people live with themselves?

I felt the answer, saw the answer, remembering the scenes from my experience in that time after the seventh stinging blow from Pitre's creature. Unseen entities herding humanity like cattle, tempting them, luring them, the ones unprotected. Multitudes of tall greys pointing, coercing, and orchestrating the degradation of humanity.

I dismissed all the questions that were building and felt the urgency to save the remaining children on my list. I couldn't save the world, but I could save these few.

I felt a fire inside me with the same faith filled intensity that had driven Elizabeth and me to the bitter war-torn region of South Africa.

CHAPTER FORTY

Back inside, Chaste was still sleeping peacefully. I had no idea how long she lay there; it was irrelevant. Once again, I resisted the urge to sit and watch her as I peered over the back of the sofa.

I sensed or heard or felt…, I don't know which…, the boys at the garage door. I'm sure their bin was out of food. I'd been preoccupied all morning and hadn't been out of the house since Ferry left to go to her office.

I opened the door and flicked on the lights and they didn't seem to be working. I reached behind me in the hallway, into my emergency cabinet and grappled for a torch, …a flashlight.

It clicked loudly and flared and I pointed it at the breaker box on the opposite wall.

The light was suddenly too dim to illuminate the far wall only forty feet away. I almost blinded myself as the glare pointed back at my own face. It was most definitely working.

I heard growls from the boys, then whimper's, and more growling deeper still as they sat side by side, their backs pressing to my legs; finally the hackles arose on every nerve point of my body.

Feeding the dogs didn't seem quite as important as it had moments earlier.

Even the rain outside was muted by the physical presence of dark. How do you fight dark? The only thing I knew bright enough to burn through this inkwell was busy at the moment.

Pitre was busy with reparations inside my daughter and I wasn't about to interrupt him. Surely, I could handle a little darkness until he was through.

Our two huge watchers whimpered and retreated outside.

Sliding back in from the garage door, I closed and locked it, as if closing a door would prevent ingress of this sudden malady.

It didn't.

The door itself turned odd shades of brown until finally it looked as if it were the charred remains of a fire.

Thick blackness like ruined oil spilled slowly on the floor toward my feet and human nature forced me to start backing up.

My hands slid along the wall of the hallway, my grasp on reality; daring not take my eyes off this strange enemy.

It had to be the visitor Pitre warned me of; the underling of evil, a supervisor from hell making an unannounced visit.

One by one, the recessed lights above me darkened and disappeared.

I found myself standing beside the entrance leading to both the kitchen and main living area and something inside me told me where it was headed.

Over my dead body.

I hurried to Chaste, still asleep on the couch, and stood between the encroaching black and her gangly thin body.

The kitchen with all its excessive lighting was now dark and I was running out of space to retreat.

I scooped up Chaste in my arms and backed toward the front door. There was no neighbor within shouting distance and even if there were, they had proven themselves my enemies over the last ten months. I wasn't about to turn to one of them for assistance.

It was suddenly all an absurdity; what could they do?

I glanced outside, through the several rain pebbled glass panes, through the rain, to see exactly what I suspected. An army of tall greys just beyond the fence, with the boys barking and pacing from one end of the frontage to the other.

"God help us."

"You should have asked sooner."

I thought the answering voice was that of the blackness scoffing at me, because of the menacing vibrancy of its tone.

The dark stopped and I could sense thought and emotions coming from somewhere deep inside the mass. I sensed fear.

"You have no right to be here!" I yelled.

"How is it that you see me human?"

This voice made me jump inside and out.

There was no frame of reference. It sounded nothing like a human voice; more like huge claws grating on hollow metal.

"She is covered by her father."

Pitre's voice echoed into the void of the room; it no longer sounded like the simple angelic creature I'd come to know. I was terrified by the authoritative voice of him.

"I have come for what is mine."

Pitre answered with the same loud fury.

"The child is protected by me."

Roaring laughter spilled through the house, making it seem like a small tin can instead of the four thousand square feet of structure. I heard murmuring laughter outside among the gathering mass.

"Protected by you? And who are you?"

Pitre emerged in all his brilliance behind me and the chattering laughter ceased.

"You...? It is not possible."

The darkness became a dusty mist, pierced by the light from Pitre, and I saw the creature hidden inside. For the lack of a better term, it was a tall black. The same in appearance as a tall grey, only a filthy black.

"My master shall hear of this!"

There was intense anger in his threat, but something else was there, something far too familiar encased in thick raw fear.

"Yes rebel..., and I look forward to hearing your screams as he punishes you for your losses," Pitre's voice echoed.

The silence was thicker than the blackness that had forced its way inside my home. Something about the truth of Pitre's statement, struck the tall black like a blade and he retreated.

"Maybe I've been too hasty. Maybe..., we can bargain for my possession?"

He was talking about my daughter, my Chaste, as if I weren't there.

"You can't have her!" I yelled.

It came out of my mouth before I could rein it back.

Pitre nodded toward me, "Then it is settled."

Quickly, he replied to the creature inside the misty dark void, "You shall not have her."

I thought for a moment that I saw the tall black flash an ebony jagged blade.

I felt Pitre tell me to cover my eyes.

With both my arms full of my limp daughter's body, it wasn't the easiest thing I'd ever done. I rolled Chaste up in my arms and hid my face against her stomach, quickly backing us both away.

Instantly there was an intense heat and I saw light so brilliant it felt as if it was glowing right through my skull, through my daughter's body. Rumbling thunder shook my very core as I gasped for breath, twisting to shield Chaste with my body.

As quickly as it started it was over, my body cooled and relaxed.

"Lay her to rest so I can continue my work."

This was the soft voice of Pitre that I had come to know and recognize.

I lowered Chaste, uncovering my eyes and all the darkness was gone, only the fresh scent of ozone lingering in the air. I spun and looked outside at the vacant rain drenched street. It was just another pleasant rainy day with the refreshing sound of clear pellets playing some melody, tapping the ground outside.

Oh yes, I had questions and not one of them mattered.

I lay my daughter down and covered her, then sank to the floor beside her, letting the day flow away.

It was the sound of Ferry's car and the bump of her horn that awakened me. I went to the door and pressed the control to open the large gate that lead to the garage; then stood there watching the rain bouncing into a mist off the top of her Lincoln.

It was then I heard Chaste yawn and saw her feet spinning the cover from her body in mid air.

"Daddy?"

"I'm here."

"It's so late. How long did I sleep?"

She looked bright, clear; I was hopeful.

"We both took a long nap."

The door from the garage opened and Chaste jumped to her feet, "Ferry's here!"

"Hey! Some help?"

Chaste all but tackled Ferry above the waist as she tried to turn and close the door behind her.

I took several sacks from Ferry's hands and she finally conceded to a backwards kick to shut the door. Then her shoes slid down the long hallway landing together in a lump.

"Oh..., that's much better. I brought food with me. Hope you didn't cook anything, really... hope...," she saw my blank expression. "Think you can put up with me for another day or two?"

I couldn't believe she felt she had to pose that question.

"The more the merrier."

I sat down two sacks of deli-cooked treats and waited.

"Okay, here's what happened today; in no certain order."

The paper sacks were rattling as Ferry started a fire brigade of food into Chaste's nimble hands.

"I went by my apartment at noon, right? I wanted to see what was left of my things. Well, I pull up to the guard shack. Bob wasn't there of course..., still in the hospital with a bump on his head. I called to check on him this morning; he'll live.

"Anyway, there's this new guard sitting inside the shack, and he steps out and wants to see my drivers license. He says it's because of blah, blah, blah..., he's new..., blah, blah. The arm on the gate lifts up and he waves me through, but before I could move, he picks up the phone and calls somebody and I got this vibe. You know, like something wasn't right? He's staring at me and it gave me the willies. So I put my car in reverse and backed out of the entrance.

"This new guy nearly broke his neck to get outside the guard shack and stop me.

"Well! The new guy found out not to get in front of Ferry Dunavin's Lincoln Continental. The point is..., I think someone was there waiting for me."

Ferry folded the empty sacks and clutched them to her chest.

"Think I was being silly?"

I waited a moment to see if it was a rhetorical question before I answered.

"No. I doubt there's anything silly about Ferry Dunavin."

I helped her shrug from her long coat, which seemed to earn me some sort of brownie points.

"Wanna see my books?"

Chaste was staring up at her with wide pleading eyes.

"Oh, that's right! Your books came! Absolutely. Why don't we stuff ourselves with this food while it's still hot first?"

"You just want to talk to dad."

"You're right I do, but I'm also starving. I didn't have a chance to eat today."

She kissed Chaste on the cheek with a loud smack and instantly the world was right in her happy eyes.

Ferry scrambled through three cabinet doors, "Uh, where's the plates?"

I opened the one behind me and drew out a short stack of dishes.

As the food zigzagged across the table, Ferry picked up where she left off.

"We had our staff meeting today. This whole lawsuit over domain boundaries has the whole office buzzing. We came to an agreement to streamline our target, the way you suggested Kress, which will most likely set another precedence. There's going to be a press release tomorrow with our law firm's officers standing together; one of the pictures with John Shoemaker still in the lineup. They'll get the message."

She took a pause and a bite, but her mind was in full motion.

"Special Agent Lily called early this morning and made an appointment to see you. No warrant, big surprise. He wanted to meet today, but I set it up for Friday, three days from now, we'll make the...," she looked at Chaste, "...uh, agent...," cool his heels and see the news release before we meet."

She stopped and looked at me, *"Are you okay?"*

I almost answered aloud, before I met her gaze and nodded.

There was concern on her face; some part of me liked it, the other parts were afraid, for her.

Ferry smiled a very mischievous smile, then glanced at Chaste and back at me.

"Kress..., I like that name..., I have a list of questions I want you to ask Special Agent Lily and I want to prepare you for the meeting, okay?"

Ferry was much better suited for this new supposedly altruistic gift of hearing thoughts than I suspected.

I frowned and took another bite of oven-roasted chicken. She planned to use me, use the meeting as a way to garner information for their lawsuit.

"Remember, Kress, the meeting with Agent Lily will be at our office, on our turf. We'll control the venue and he'll be the one in the hot-seat."

Come to think of it…, I had a short list of questions I wanted to ask the Special Agent.

"Brent and Carl will be here by tomorrow or Thursday. Is there a reason why they can't sit in on the meeting with us?" I asked.

"Yeah, I like that. I really like that. So will the rest of the crew."

Ferry's thoughts went from the calm to the tornadic and the conversation died down. When she was energized, it was as if she were a storm inside that needed to blast forth in waves. It was obvious when a calm was reached.

"Now can we look at my books?"

"Are you ready Kress?"

Pitre was patiently needling me to get started.

Chaste was excitedly pouring over a stack of new books in her room, while Ferry was sitting at the table overlooking the back deck, phone in hand, scribbling abstract notes on the open page of a binder in front of her.

I locked my office door. I couldn't afford to take any chances with Ferry meeting Pitre. I opened my planner to the list of missing children and sat down, staring at the names. Suddenly I didn't see just a list of names; it was a list of scrambled lives, destroyed ambitions, perverted fears, and in walked that amazing desire to help them. The same desire that Elizabeth and I had shared for over twenty years.

"Start with the top three…, they were just moved to a cargo crate all together. They need to be found first before they get loaded onto a freighter. You'll only need to call one of the parents with instructions; the other two children will be rescued by proxy."

I looked at the first name, Carrie Florence, and imagined her circumstances, felt the urgency.

"But the other parents need to know. Trust me Pitre, they need some hope."

I felt him nod in agreement inside me.

"Call the Florence girl's parents and ask them if they remember their trip to San Francisco two months ago. The man on the boardwalk that walked up and took their picture and then their daughters, accidentally dropped his business card and the husband picked it up. He still has it.

That man knows who took her, which will lead to the shipping container their daughter is in."

I called immediately and gave the information, with a reminder of my requisite anonymity in the situation. Then I called the other two parents and informed them to have hope; their children would be found safe in a day or two. It was difficult not to answer all their questions, but I explained that finding one would be finding theirs and to pray for the safe return of them all. They agreed. It seems the old adage that there are no atheists in foxholes is true.

Together, we went in some strange random order down the list of the missing.

Pitre seemed to know the most urgent ones and the quickest link to their locations. After the last call, I felt Pitre smile inside me. He didn't share with me what it was about and I didn't ask.

"You should rest. We will work together again tomorrow."

I looked at the time…, just after eleven p.m. and cringed.

I eased my door open and most of the lights were off in the house. Ferry's things were stacked neatly on the coffee table, ready for the next days business.

I ambled up the stairs, my mind still reeling through all the phone calls, all the turmoil in the missing children's lives.

By nature of habit, I peeked in on Chaste and found Ferry asleep on top of the covers beside my daughter, with various books scattered at the foot of the bed.

I quietly picked them all up and looked for a blanket to cover Ferry.

"Kress? I must have fallen asleep."

Ferry stirred then turned her head and extended her hand for me to help her sit up.

"She's…," Ferry lay a finger to her lips and looked down at Chaste. *"She's such a wonderful little girl. A brilliant mind."*

I helped her stand and we quietly walked out of the room.

"I noticed that you're getting very comfortable with my hearing your thoughts."

Ferry smiled, "Glad you noticed."

"Please remember, it has to remain our secret. You mustn't let any allusion seep out that I'm cursed with this."

"Cursed? You have to be kidding. I don't see that as a curse."

She picked up her pace walking down the stairs ahead of me.

"You didn't think so yesterday as I recall."

She stopped at the turn of the stairs and looked up at me.

"You've got me there."

She took my hand and walked with me to the sofa.

"Don't be surprised if you don't see Chaste much tomorrow. I gave her the first weeks suggested assignments from the home school pack. She was so excited. You should have seen her face light up."

She looked a little distraught for a moment, "Chaste needs to be around other kids her age. She needs a social life."

She quickly put up her hand, "I know why you're keeping her isolated for the moment, I understand. Just keep it in mind for the future, okay?"

After the incident with the tall dark lord, how could I ever let her out of my sight again?

"Kress…, is there…, is there anything else you want to tell me?"

Something inside me drew up in a cinch, a tightening panic. Had she eavesdropped through my office door and heard me talking? It would have sounded like I was chattering on with myself, but still.

"It's okay. Don't worry about it. I was just curious."

I didn't hear her thoughts betray any covert actions, or depictions of her ear against my door and relaxed.

"Only that I'm quite fond of you," I offered.

Her eyebrows arched in that way that only a woman's can.

"I'm surprised to hear you admit that, Kress."

"So am I, quite honestly. I never expected to have feelings for anyone again."

This time I expected her to lean into my kiss.

CHAPTER FORTY- ONE

Ferry was already drinking a cup of coffee when I dragged into the kitchen at six a.m.; another early riser but obviously earlier than I was used to.

I received a warm hug and a kiss before she sat out a cup before me.

"There's toast in the oven if you want some."

"Do you ever eat real food for breakfast?" I asked.

She swallowed and shook her head, "I never have time. My head's always spinning and ready to go by the time I'm awake. And these dreams are driving me crazy...."

She pressed her palm to the single furrow on her brow.

"That's probably my fault. I seem to have that effect on people..., the dreams I mean."

It wasn't entirely a lie, it was Pitre's fault, but he was after all a part of me now.

Her eyes drilled into me, "Really.... Huh...."

She finished her cup of coffee while staring at me over its brim hiding the tiniest hint of color high on her cheeks.

"There's a lot more to you than meets the eye, Kress Schumacher. I would have never guessed it."

I felt heat on my face and wished it away as I quickly turned to pour a fresh spot of coffee in my cup.

We shared our days' plans and said our goodbyes as I handed her a house key and one of the spare remotes to the main gate and garage.

She held up the fob as a spectacle in front of her face, hiding something, deliberately pushing it away from her conscious thought. "Huh…. Thanks…."

Then she blinked a smile, somehow pleased with herself and stuck it out her window with a soft click before she started her car. The garage door crawled slowly upward and at the same time, the main gate began to whir open.

Suddenly her thoughts were dead quiet and she looked at me and smiled. What was Ferry Dunavin up to now?

The gate was closing as she drove away and I could have sworn I heard a few faint disjointed words…, *"Ferry… Schumacher… Is he the one?"*

I should have panicked for any number of reasons, but was the idea of having someone in my life so impossible?

I stood there dumbfounded until I heard the electric lock slap tight on the gate and the overhead garage door engage.

Pitre what the blazes have you been up to?

While waiting for Brent or Carl to return my phone call, I almost forgot the original need for the request.

I quickly rehearsed my panicked reasoning for bringing them onboard again; it felt good to have people I trusted know what was going on in case things didn't go as planned. At least there would be no mysteries or sudden accidents and illnesses that befell us without someone else having the facts.

Not that it mattered of course.

Of one thing I was certain; rich or poor, King or Pawn, in this confusing game of life, when the game is over, all the pieces are put into the same box.

Dead is still dead.

And there went my comfort, dashed out the window.

When did I become such a worrywart? Those types of thoughts were easily traced back to when Elizabeth announced that she was carrying Chaste. The moment it was no longer just she and I against the world; the moment we knew we were responsible for another life other than our own.

The phone call didn't last long after I'd settled my thoughts and asked my questions.

"Would you be willing to sit in as an observer during an interview between myself, my lawyer, and the FBI agent you've already met?"

Brent seemed worried, "You know their procedure won't allow an outside party near an interview."

I wanted to smile, but didn't want to nix the meeting.

"The interview won't take place at a government facility, it will be at my lawyers office, and they have already extended a welcome to you and Carl. I promise it will prove to be most interesting."

"Really…. How did you manage to make that happen?"

This time I did smile, but tried to hide it from my voice.

"You haven't met my attorney Ferry Dunavin yet."

"I'll get the time and address when we meet Thursday."

After he hung up, I pondered why he would lie about arriving Thursday instead of Wednesday. I told myself to trust.

"Kress?"

Before I answered Pitre, I realized how much different our relationship had become. He wasn't the ever-present alien and agitator he once was. Had he truly changed or had I? Maybe both of us had given just a little.

"We have much work to do; we need to finish this list today."

I hurried to my office and opened my planner. Only a dozen names were marked off; so many left to attend to.

Stolen children were scattered like the wind and all with one single common denominator other than wealthy parents – someone took their photograph, either blatantly or covertly.

From the best that I could tell, scouts catalogued this particular group of children and logged their images as if they were items in some store flyer of commodities to be distributed for advertisement.

I wondered about their ultimate destinations, if they received the same programming that Chaste had, and most of all, who was in charge of it all.

Hearing so wide a foray of emotions from the parents brought back my own memories of fear, anger, despair and every imaginable intense feeling a human is capable of.

If not for Pitre calming me, I would have been a bundle of raw nerves when we reached the last name on the list.

"This one is special Kress. You need to follow my instructions exactly for this last one."

If I hadn't been so exhausted, I would have asked why. Instead, I listened.

"You cannot call the parents for this one."

"Who the blazes am I supposed to call?"

"The FBI."

I physically felt my jaw fall slack in shock.

"Are you daft? They'll put me away for…, for as long as I live."

"Kress. This one is meant to be a trap for you."

I grabbed my pen and scribbled a mass of dark lines through the name.

"There! Done! Case closed."

I smacked the cover closed on my planner and sat back in my chair.

"This is a real child, not a decoy. I thought we were past this Kress. Have you really not changed?"

I folded my arms in defiance.

"Don't you want to stop them from taking other children?"

"How is stepping into their trap going to stop them? No, I won't participate in my own downfall."

"You love Chaste. You loved the children you helped. You and Elizabeth loved and cared for hundreds that came through your clinic over the years – sometimes at gunpoint."

I didn't remember standing until I heard my chair slam over onto the floor. How dare he use Elizabeth or Chaste as a prod!

"Not fair Pitre."

"Love is self-sacrifice. Remember the other children that were captive in the desert? When you went back and rescued them? Remember the relief you felt inside? Imagine how it would still be eating on your conscience if you knew you could have saved them but didn't."

Was I destined never to win an argument with Pitre?

"I didn't say you would be giving yourself up. I said you needed to follow my instructions so that you can save a child. In their own arrogance, they abducted a child to draw you out and implicate you as the one responsible."

I felt heat rise in my cheeks and my hands began to shake uncontrollably.

"Thomas Whitefeather knew this didn't he?"

"They threatened him Kress. You of all people should know how weak Thomas truly is."

I stomped from my office looking for something to kick, unrepentant at the anger inside. Instead, I went to the nearest restroom and gasped at the cold splash of water on my face. The shock seemed to refocus my mind when I settled to the fact that the life of a child was hanging in the balance and my past grievances against Thomas were meaningless in comparison.

The door to my office was stuck at an odd angle when I returned, even though I didn't remember slamming it open.

"Forgive me. I trust you Pitre. What do I need to do?"

"That's the Kress I know."

"Yes, well…, don't push your luck on that just yet. Tell me what I should do before I change my mind."

Chaste and I were seated close to one another on the sofa as she rambled on about her new studies and asking my opinion on several of her answers.

Despite Ferry's outlay of her lesson plans, Chaste was determined to catch up to where she should have been at the beginning of the school year. She had sneaked a view inside the semester schedule and was arguing answers with me concerning the week-three lesson plan.

Both of us heard the unmistakable clatter of the large gate as it sprang into action outside. Chaste was the first to go to the front and peer out the glass to confirm Ferry's arrival.

Admitting to myself that I was just as anxious to see Ferry actually surprised me. Chaste was getting used to her presence as much as I. What would become of this arrangement when Ferry was able to go back to her apartment? And furthermore, what would become of…, so many things I wasn't certain of?

I recognized the worrywart bobbing his head up and crushed the thoughts down just as a cheerful American voice began chattering into the house. I heard her scrunch Chaste into a tight grunt of a giggle and smack her with a quick kiss without missing a step down the back hallway. Then came the familiar clop-clop of disembarking high heels tumbling to the end of the hallway, hailing the eminent arrival of Ferry.

"…and could you please look over my assignments before you and Daddy get started?"

I had made my way to the kitchen by the time the two of them marched hip to hip into the living area.

"Kress?"

"In here, Ferry. I hope you're hungry."

The casserole was spitting around the edges as I sat it on the stovetop. Her smile was glamorous as she peeked in the doorway.

"Starving...."

She tossed her baggage and coat on the nearest chair, walked right up to me and kissed me; as if it were our usual greeting. I didn't complain, you understand.

"Did you miss me?"

Chaste stomped a foot to the floor, "I knew it."

She dropped her small stack of excitement to the floor in emphasis and hurried off to run upstairs.

"I'd better go do damage control. I think Chaste had other plans. Don't you go anywhere Kress Schumacher."

Ferry seemed all the more pleased when I answered her with, "I'll be right here."

She picked up the scattered pieces of paper Chaste dropped and shuffled them evenly, then hurried upstairs.

I heard the squabbling all the way downstairs in bits and pieces.

While I had been worried that Chaste was upset with the new 'certain familiarity' exhibited between Ferry and I, not that we were behaving inappropriately of course, Chaste was actually distraught over her newfound academia. She had after all waded through her first weeks assignments in a little over ten hours. It seemed it was becoming an obsession and although I was excited for her ambitions, it worried me that she wasn't obsessing over the latest fad or some other typical nine-year-old behavior. I wished some modicum of normalcy for her, even if it was only typical childlike silliness. That was probably being overambitious of me after the incident with Chaste and the triggered memory brought on by the VHS cassette.

I heard a gentle reminder from inside me, reminding me to be patient – all in good time.

I was relieved to see them come back down the stairs together, smiling and chattering away as if the whole dramatic scene had never occurred.

CHAPTER FORTY-TWO

I couldn't believe it was Friday already. Pitre had been living in the forefront of my mind since my first thoughts upon awakening.

"Now if you're asked a question you're unsure of, all you have to do is defer to me."

"Ferry, you don't understand. This…, this… person has a way of sliding underneath my skin like a hot splinter. He enjoys it. He's good at it."

It wasn't as if I were confessing some weakness. I was afraid that I'd hear Mr. FBI utter something that would make me throw myself across the conference table to address…, personally, physically.

"Ms. Dunavin, we appreciate your Firm's invitation and we don't want to overstep our boundaries. Will we be permitted to ask a few questions also?"

Brent and Carl nodded discretely at each other. Such guarded thoughts. Brent's secrets were buried somewhere deep and inaccessible.

"As soon as Special Agent Lily and his counsel are done, then it's our turn. I don't think they'll be expecting questions from any of us and I'm hoping that we'll catch them off guard. Even if the agent doesn't answer, ask your questions one at a time and wait for their council to respond."

I heard Ferry clear as a bell in my head, *"…and you make sure you write down everything that weasel is thinking after each question Kress."*

I nodded her direction before I knew what I was doing and Ferry flushed a little pink.

"We want our questions to insinuate we have foreknowledge of certain events."

Ferry started to place her hand on mine but quickly subdued any outward affection in front of those present. Instead, she turned her affection to Chaste already scrunched up close to her side.

"Chaste honey, do you mind staying in my office until we're through?"

Suddenly Chaste and I shared a secret as she glanced at me; a secret that made the burden of hearing the thrush of thoughts worthwhile. It was always welcome to hear my daughter say *"I love you"*.

A rather charming young lady poked her head in Ferry's office and flashed a grim smile, "They're here."

"Thanks Trice, show them to the conference room. I want them to sit and stew a few minutes."

Brent stood and shook my hand and wished me luck followed by the enormous grip of Carl's double-handed shake.

"We'll be recording the entire time. Just make sure everything we record is to our benefit gentlemen."

To describe everything that happened when I entered the conference room, exactly as it happened is nearly impossible.

A tall black was crouched below the low ceiling of the room, directly behind Special Agent Lily and a tall grey behind his advocate. Their nondescript faces barely visible from underneath the death reaper's cowl covering their heads.

The instant I walked in the room, the spectre behind Agent Lily placed his hand on Lily's shoulder and disappeared..., almost. Lily now had a diffused misty dark outline surrounding his entire body.

It was as if the vile entity had jumped right inside an empty host. In an afterthought, I guess I shouldn't have been so overtaken, since I was cohabitating with angelic Pitre.

I'd seen this type of mist only once before.

Agent Lily didn't seem to be put off in the least by the intrusion of darkness nor the presence of Brent and Carl as they seated themselves at the far end of the table, posing as observers.

When I was able to remove my eyes from the already disconcerting stare of the cold-eyed devil in front of me, I noticed that the room was much like the interrogation rooms that I had become so acquainted with recently. A camera was in the upper corner, blinking a steady red dot and of course, there was the familiar mirrored pane of glass directly behind me. It seemed both men accepted the fact that the entire staff in the law firm were standing on the other side looking on.

Pitre was right; several things made sense all at once.

As soon as I was seated, I smelled some type of strange but familiar medicinal odor. It had been over twenty months since I had set foot in my clinic, but some things you never forget. I was about to shirk it off when Pitre spoke inside me, *"Don't touch the water bottles."*

In the center of the table was an iced container of several plastic water bottles standing half-submerged, each one sweating inviting droplets of humidity.

Before introductions were offered, Agent Lily propped his elbows on the table and clasped his hands together, "Mr. Schumacher, what is your affiliation with Thomas Whitefeather?"

Ferry flashed a smile and answered on his last breath.

"Well..., aren't we anxious to get started? I need to remind everyone that these proceedings are being recorded. Our two guests, Smith and Rand, at the end of the table you already know Agent Lily. I'm Ferry Dunavin with Kohlner, Dunavin, Shoemaker, and Glass."

She deliberately included the deceased John Shoemaker with her introductory lineup. I'd learned that nothing Ferry did was by accident or without some predetermination.

Agent Lily only blinked; his thoughts were an empty cave.

I scribbled the word 'empty' on my pad to that effect which actually did get a reaction from him.

"I'm Special Agent in Charge, Amos Lily, this is Mr. Fred Blauche, attorney for our local Missing Children Detachment of the FBI."

I sat there in shock and began to write on my notepad as fast as I could scribble legibly.

Then the agent smiled sarcastically, "Would you like for each of us to go around the table and tell a little about ourselves?"

"I think we can dispense with any congenialities, Mr. Lily. Please state the reason for your visit and begin."

"Good."

He turned and stared at me for a moment in silence. For some reason I couldn't breach that one arena of his mind, although I was digging like a crazed badger. Of one thing I was now certain.

I tried to tap my notepad to get Ferry's attention, but she was already three steps forward in her game of chess.

Mr. Blauche opened a folder in front of him, "Recent investigations have repeatedly intersected with Mr. Schumacher indicating some type of involvement, including the rescue of his daughter Chaste Ellen Schumacher and several other missing children. As a person of interest, we requested this meeting with Mr. Schumacher to get a better understanding of that involvement."

"Just for clarification; is there a reason why you didn't subpoena Dr. Schumacher before a grand jury?"

Blauche unmistakably glanced over to the Agent, "We wanted to keep these proceedings as low key as possible, so that we didn't impair our ongoing investigations."

The thoughts of Blauche were as simple and bland as reading the Sunday paper; he was pure puppet.

I scribbled down, …because the federal judge refused.

The agent leaned forward on the table once again, attempting to glance at my god-awful version of penmanship.

"For the record; we at Kohlner, Dunavin, Shoemaker, and Glass agreed to this meeting as a reciprocating venue to interview Special Agent in Charge Lily and Council concerning our recent filing of Schumacher vs. The Federal Bureau of Investigation. The federal court has agreed to visit the abuse of Dr. Schumacher and his daughter's Diplomatic Rights."

I almost smiled, …almost, as I realized the Agent hadn't seen the press release concerning the pending litigation.

"The floor is yours Mr. Blauche," mumbled Ferry.

Again I nervously tapped my notepad; another attempt to get Ferry's attention.

The Agent's arrogance continued unscathed, "Should I repeat my question for the record? What about Thomas Clay, alias Thomas Whitefeather, Schumacher? What's your affiliation?"

It seemed stupid to answer a question he seemed to already know the answer to. It seemed droll to play along with this sideshow.

"I have no affiliation. When we met, he was a homeless

mendicant living on the streets of Sedona and pretending to have some knowledge of my missing daughter's whereabouts. I took pity on him for a few weeks and after I found my daughter, he left voluntarily."

I didn't bother to write down specifics of his thoughts to my answer; my only entry was, …much swearing.

"When did you last speak to him, Doctor?"

I had actually spoken to Thomas only once in days. I'd received voice messages, which I'd transcribed.

Pitre answered inside me…, and I repeated it.

"It could have been the day you followed my daughter and I and watched us walk into his office in Sedona."

I wrote his thoughts on my notepad, …he couldn't have seen us watching.

Finally…, Ferry looked down and read my notes.

Not Amos Lily – Not FBI – Shadow something… Dangerous.

I'd underlined it so many times the paper was nearly gouged in half. I knew Ferry would want his real identity, but I couldn't see past that blasted smirk on his face and the black wall erected in his mind.

I didn't understand how he got past the lie detector living inside me. Then…, I understood. He hadn't. He was pure evil, completely possessed by that darkness I was unable to scratch past.

A terror of cold chills slithered slowly down my spine.

Ferry read my note and her expression never changed.

"Dr. Schumacher has already stated the extents of his relationship with your suspect. For the sake of time please keep your drilling expeditions to a minimum."

The man posing as Agent Lily leaned back comfortably smug, "Are you using a scrambling device on your cell phones? – *'Answer that you limey bastard'*."

If not for Pitre snatching control of my temper, his provocation would have sent me reeling.

Instead, I frowned at the question and shrugged, "I barely know how to use this new phone, much less do anything that ridiculous."

I produced my cell phone and lay it on the table beside my notepad, but not after twisting in the air for a show.

"Your phone records indicate that both incoming and outgoing data as well as your voicemail is scrambled and overlaid with static."

Pitre's music, no doubt. I wanted to kiss him.

"How did you subpoena Dr. Schumacher's phone records when he has diplomatic immunity in the United States?"

Mr. Blauche fumbled to produce some typewritten correspondence and slid it across the table.

The Agent leaned over the table and glanced towards Brent and Carl, "You're not the only one that can get a writ from DHS. Do you want me to turn this investigation over to them?"

I wrote, …bluffing, he's very angry, and shoved it where Ferry could see.

"I believe I have DHS on speed dial," said Ferry.

She scooted her phone on the desk past the decanter of water bottles, taunting his response.

"Call them," she added calmly.

Ferry started to take one of the enticing water bottles and I reached and stopped her. There wasn't time to communicate why, but thankfully, she didn't squabble over my rebuke.

The Agent definitely saw what transpired and glared at me with his piercing dead eyes.

The tall grey behind Mr. Blauche began pointing at me, menacingly.

As I lowered my gaze and scribbled, …*he knows*, I both heard and felt Pitre laugh inside me.

It was my own written drivel 'they know' that made my head spin. I understood so many things my head began to ache. Pitre had been hiding inside me…, those long disappearing acts weren't just to distance himself from me. All the army of grey assumed he was still tucked away in a hole in the ground, diminished, beaten and waiting to demand yet another human. The dark lord, the tall black that visited our home, the one that fully expected to just waltz in and whisk Chaste away, Pitre had obliterated him, he hadn't relayed back who was causing all the problems. I had assumed it was the presence of Pitre that had been attracting all the attacks.

It was Chaste Ellen. They had been after Chaste all along.

Until this very moment, Pitre was just any other ubiquitous being in white, just another anonymous guardian protecting his charges.

I had to force my mind to stop the flood of knowledge and rejoin the meeting where I sat.

The agent leaned over and whispered into Mr. Blauche's ear and it wasn't necessary to record their secret.

Blauche closed his folder and announced, "We have no further questions at this time."

Ferry looked at me with that single furrow in her brow.

"You arranged this formal meeting with only two or three questions for our client? What kind of show are you running Agent..., what did you say your name was?"

They were about to stand, when Ferry violently flipped a cover page from her own notepad, not waiting for an answer.

"Agent Lily, when and how did your detachment gain knowledge of the GPS device extracted from Chaste Schumacher?"

Ferry was including the death of John Shoemaker in her vendetta. It was far more dangerous ground.

Both men settled back in their chairs as if the session might not be at a total loss just yet.

The Agent smiled, "From the doctor at Children's Medical, the initial examination of the subject."

I scribbled, ...a lie, which wasn't entirely helpful.

"...and you bypassed doctor patient privacy by...?"

"The doctor offered the record to us of her own accord."

Another lie.... I was tapping my previous notation vehemently.

"Interesting."

Ferry looked at her notes, then over her shoulder, "Trice?"

The door opened and in walked the bright young lady I'd seen only a few times beforehand.

"Call Children's Medical. Set up an interview with their administrator as soon as possible. Inform them we'll be prosecuting Dr. Cort and the hospital for breaking doctor patient privilege concerning the February seventh examination of an underage child, Chaste Schumacher."

Trice scratched it all down and hurried back out of the room.

Ferry smiled, "Thank you for your testimony, Agent Lily. It's not every day we're handed a free ride by the FBI."

I wrote on my notepad slowly, ...he's very angry, be careful.

Pitre spoke inside me, *"And now the kingdom crumbles."*

I didn't have time to ponder the cryptic message before my cell phone began to sing some horrid tune and vibrate across the table.

I quickly grabbed it and apologized as I fumbled to mute it. Just before the cell phone's screen flashed its exit, I recognized that the call was from one of the missing on my list.

The tall grey behind Mr. Blauche stood as erect as the ceiling would allow as if listening to some unheard call in the distance, then it disappeared like a wisp of vapor before my eyes.

Brent spoke up from the end of the table using the sudden lull in conversation as an opening.

"Agent Lily, I have a question as a matter of departmental courtesy."

Mr. Blauche seemed a little disoriented for a moment and nodded at Brent and Carl.

"Did you have any foreknowledge of the abduction of Dr. Schumacher's daughter?"

"I'm not at liberty to answer questions concerning open investigations," said Lily, forcing a grin.

Brent and Carl looked at each other, "So the case of Chaste Schumacher is still open and pending?"

"Agent Lily has already answered your question," said Blauche.

"For the record, where is your main office located?"

Agent Lily scrunched up his face, "I don't understand the need to know. We cover a tri-state area in our investigations."

Carl spoke up, his voice irritated, "Let me rephrase the question. Where is your desk? Where did you drive from to come here today?"

Lily pulled out a business card and flipped it across the table toward Carl.

"Tucson, but we have offices locally in Phoenix and Flagstaff, Albuquerque, Las Vegas…."

Carl glanced quickly at the card, "This says your office is in Washington D.C."

Lily shrugged.

Carl opened his notepad of secrets and flipped through a few pages.

"According to the Scottsdale Police records, you arrived on location…, in Scottsdale…, ten minutes after the local authorities arrived to investigate Dr. Schumacher's missing daughter. How did you manage that?"

Blauche spoke up, "We're not on trial here."

Ferry spoke up to try and ease the tension, "Neither is Doctor Schumacher."

This didn't divert the fact that neither answered the question. My hand was now shaking as I fought back the anger, I wrote: …they knew.

Brent opened a thin package he had been fondling since well before we were seated together.

He flipped out several large grainy photos for everyone present.

"Ever see these men before, Agent Lily?"

He smirked and scooted them away to the center of the table without so much as a glance at their content.

"Screen shots from the internet?" asked Agent Lily.

I wrote down, …Williams …Hatcher, before the Agent's thoughts went silent.

I felt the heat flowing off Ferry's arm, "Could the names Williams or Hatcher be associated with these photographs?"

Ferry was digging for blood. I wanted to warn her she was treading on no-mans-land.

Brent and Carl snapped their heads our direction in shock then back at Agent Lily.

He only shrugged again and smiled, "Could be anybody – *'I guarantee they won't miss the next time, you freak of nature…'.*"

I neglected to write down the expletives he added. Regretfully, I must add that I wanted to do irreparable harm to this human fraud with my bare hands but from the look on Carl's face, I would have to stand in line and wait my turn.

"I realize their faces were covered, but we have a better angle on their vehicle. Maybe this will jog your memory."

Carl flipped over a photo of a black SUV with a squat multicolored light strip over the top. In the corner of the photo was an enlarged square of a blacked out government license plate. Some sort of opaque smoky cover was obliterating the identification.

Agent Lily smiled, "Again…, could be anybody. Surely you're aware of how many compartments there are to the Bureau."

"It's a civie photo, but it'll stand up in court," Carl leaned forward. "The plates were blacked out. Standard procedure during covert ops; and you're right, I should know."

The tall grey behind Mr. Blauche suddenly reappeared. It seemed agitated and Blauche slid back his chair nervously, making room to stand, "We will not be answering any further questions."

The grin slowly faded from Agent Lily as he positively yanked Mr. Blauche back into his seat.

"This compartment raided a civilian's home," barked Carl, "…but it looked more like a snatch and grab mission."

The Agent rolled his eyes, "Conjecture. For the record, I have no knowledge of any agency operations in Phoenix."

Carl sat back angrily, "I didn't mention the location."

Agent Lily's cell phone rang and he stood, hurrying to the corner of the room, the smoky billowing haze following him. The phone was practically plastered to his head.

"What? When?"

Pitre whispered to me, *"Careful."*

Agent Lily slapped his phone shut and pocketed it. His thoughts went completely blank as he slowly returned to his seat.

His eyes were unfocused in a glassy stare.

In an instant a tall grey behind Mr. Blauche began pointing somewhere outside the room.

Agent Lily smiled thinly, looking across the table. The overhead fluorescent lights chose that moment to flicker above our heads and that same crawling black I'd seen in the sanctity of my own home began to spill in all directions.

I took Ferry's hand and scooted back a few more inches from the edge of the conference table, "Bad news Agent?"

Mr. Blauche leaned over to Lily, "Are we done here?" and was angrily waved away.

Lily took the opportunity of the silence to cast his eyes as if thinking of some clever reply to all the insinuations.

I wrote, …he's thinking about his weapon.

The florescent lights flickered once again, this time completely off and back on as the black began to slither across their plastic cover.

The agent looked at me directly, "How is your daughter doing since her miraculous recovery, Schumacher? I bet you don't let her out of your sight nowadays do you?"

There was a very distinct threat in his tone.

Needless to say, I didn't answer his foul question.

This time Mr. Blauche succeeded in standing, "We're through. We'll be in touch, Mr. Schumacher."

We all took our cue to stand and Ferry leaned over the table near Mr. Blauche.

"You will not be in touch with Dr. Schumacher. You will not attempt to contact him in anyway until our pending case is…."

Her words faded from my mind while I watched in horror as the tall black reappeared behind Agent Lily, submerged in a moving black cloud. It held a cadaverous hand over Lily's head, twiddling its long spindly fingers, causing Lily to jerk facing me. I saw..., God help me, I saw a face from another continent, dark skin, adorned in brilliantly colored feathers about his head.

The next thing Lily spoke, I was not prepared for. Loosely translated, "I am going to pay you a visit."

It was in Afrikaans.

I heard myself belch out a reply, "We'll be waiting," in the same dialect.

As if time were slowed down, the lights flickered dim and I saw the Agent's intentions. There was no time for polite interludes; I grabbed Ferry and thrust her into the corner behind Brent and Carl just as he pulled his gun and aimed toward where the tall grey had been pointing. The gun was aimed somewhere past the mirrored wall - toward the onlookers - toward Ferry's office – toward Chaste.

"Bloody hell!"

I lunged across the table at the gun forcing it upward before he managed to fire four deafening blasts into the ceiling.

The tall black had disappeared, but Lily's eyes spread impossibly wide looking up in his struggle, then he simply wilted as I forced him across the table. Brent had already thrust Mr. Blauche into a corner, scrambling to help me while Carl had Ferry behind his massive body, with gun drawn.

I heard Pitre say, *"You can thank me later."*

The terrified voice of Trice screeched into the room, "We called 911."

Unbelievably, she walked inside.

The limp body of Agent Lily was dangling across the end of the conference table, unmoving and unconscious. I quickly moved to block her entrance.

"You shouldn't be in here. He seems to be having some sort of a seizure, but it might be something worse."

That stopped Trice in her tracks, just as the Agent's mouth flew open eructing white foamy spittle across the table and onto the floor. The instant splatter made her chirp and exit the room. This warning seemed to work with everyone else except Mr. Blauche, as he inched forward wiping his hands briskly on his lapel.

I placed a cautious finger to Lily's carotid artery and felt the slow faint thumping of his heart.

"He's alive, only barely. He appears to have suffered some sort of seizure and passed out."

I dragged his limp body around until flat across the far end of the table; splaying him over on his back. His pale complexion gave the appearance much like a cadaver waiting for autopsy. It was a little unnerving even if I did abhor the man.

"Seems you did our job for us Kress. I didn't see that coming," boomed Carl, his voice amplified by adrenaline.

CHAPTER FORTY-THREE

Carl Smith was seated in front of the computer screen clicking the mouse, "See. I almost missed it. Just before they sit down, Lily sprays something over the tops of the water bottles. If I'd known it, I would have searched him before the paramedics arrived."

Ferry and the others crowded around gawking in amazement.

Trice walked up quietly, "You didn't really want me to phone the Clinic did you? Even I could tell Agent Lily was lying."

"No, Trice. The testimony of a liar could have destroyed the reputation of Dr. Cort," said Ferry, shaking her head.

Levy Kohlner, one of the two partners spoke up, "None of his recorded testimony will stand up."

Theodore Glass chimed in next, "Someone in the frame of mind to commit murder would not be deemed a competent witness, Ferry."

Ferry looked upset; not wanting to yield to the age and experience of the two older men. "We don't know if he was trying to commit murder or suicide."

Levy raised an educated hand, "Doesn't matter. The testimony is tainted. With that controversy alone it would be dismissed or stay in litigation for years."

Ferry didn't seem put-off by her partners' opinions.

"Unbelievable. Can we still have the water bottles tested for chemicals?"

Apparently, Carl was of the same mind, "We'll send them off before the end of the day. That was a good catch Dr. Schumacher."

Brent nodded, "I saw you stop Ms. Dunavin from grabbing one of the bottles."

It wasn't an accusation, but it was as probing as Brent had ever been despite all the strange events surrounding me.

"It was the scent," I assured him.

"By the way," I continued, "you should ask Mr. Blauche for the name of Agent Lily's Director. I have a feeling he won't be available."

I was about to continue on and venture a guess as to the sulphurous nature of the chemical on the bottles, but Pitre stopped me. If correct, my guess would cast even more suspicion my direction, *"Let them do their job, Kress. We have other issues to prepare for."*

That didn't sound like the victorious announcement I was expecting from Pitre.

I suddenly needed a diversion for my own nerves, "Frankly, I'm excited that the good agent is going to be behind bars instead of making my life a living hell."

"I'll amen that," mumbled Brent.

"Seconded," said Carl, with quick Queen's wave above his head.

"Speaking of good catches, Carl did a most excellent job with the surveillance photographs. They were bloody brilliant."

Carl, still seated with his back turned, raised his large hand and gave another wave before his focus returned to viewing the recorded meeting.

"That must be why you didn't let me know you arrived early Wednesday," I muttered, the epiphany came out before I realized.

My diversion succeeded but not the way I'd intended.

Brent and Carl both turned to face me, then looked suspiciously at Ferry. She was up to something.

I couldn't distinguish between either of the men's thoughts, 'She told him? Does he know about her apartment?'

Ferry picked up on my blunder and covered for me, "It must have slipped out, sorry guys - Kress?!"

I looped my arm through hers and coerced her into her private office away from the chattering group.

Chaste was seated at Ferry's desk, looking a little anxious, book open and scribbling on paper. She seemed to be the only one in the office nonplussed over the noise and confusion.

Ferry hurriedly pushed me aside and closed the door.

"Ferry, is there something you need to tell me about your apartment?"

She pinched her lips, "Can't you turn your radar off once in a while?"

"I'm afraid it's a two edged sword. You'll have to take the good with the bad Ferry. Are you going to tell me or should I go ask Brent?"

She lowered her voice to a whisper, "No!"

The door eased shut and she pressed the lock.

"Look Kress. I asked Brent and Carl to come a day early and check out my apartment for me, that's all. I was afraid to go back there and I can't keep staying with you and Chaste. I knew it might upset you. You understand. Don't you? You've already got more than you can handle."

It wasn't a lie, but it wasn't the complete truth.

"Of course I understand your reasoning. Now tell me the rest.... What's a full sweep?"

I could tell I'd struck a nerve; the thin line of her lips said she wanted to stomp a heel, possibly on top of my foot.

"There's no getting past you is there, Kress Schumacher?"

I turned and clicked open the door.

"That isn't an answer. I'll get it from Brent...."

"They found a bug in my apartment."

She saw the dumbfounded look on my face as I turned.

"A..., listening device..., an electronic bug..., a transmitter," she said, clarifying my astute ignorance.

I scratched my head reeling at the implications.

"How long do you think it's been there?"

"Days..., weeks..., maybe since John's funeral."

It's never simple, "Then they've been listening in to your home?"

Ferry's face pinked, "It's possible, I'm always on the phone with Trice."

It wasn't her telephone conversations that had her frightened.

I heard Pitre's usual calming voice inside, *They know nothing.*

"Thank God...," I sighed in automatic relief.

"What? What's wrong with you Kress Schumacher? You want them to know our plans, or that you can...," she lowered her voice to barely a whisper, "...you know..., hear thoughts, ...have you gone crazy?"

"All is well. I assure you."

Ferry looked at me, her head cocked sideways, eyes squinted to smiling slits, "…and just how do you know this?"

I smiled, almost laughed because of her queer expression, took her cheeks in my hands and quickly kissed her forehead, "Trust me Ferry. You heard what the agent said about my telephone. I'm some sort of human static generator."

We'd begun our usual staring contest until we heard Chaste rattling her things into her backpack.

"You really should trust Dad," Chaste mumbled. "He has a way of knowing these things."

Ferry snapped back my direction, "Kress, how did you know about the water bottles?"

"I've already explained. They smelled strongly of solvent. Call it intuition, a hunch. You sometimes run with gut feelings don't you?"

"Yes and right now my gut is telling me…," her entire frame relaxed and she exhaled, her eyes became fixated on mine. "Why are we arguing? It must be the sound of that gun still ringing in my ears. I'm sorry Kress. You're still a hero in my book. Who knows what would have happened if you hadn't manhandled that lunatic?"

We heard a soft tap - tapping on the door and realized just how close we were standing to one another.

"Yes?" asked Ferry, opening the door.

"Better come take a look at this," said Trish.

We heard Carl grumbling some choice words from the next room and Ferry looked at me in dismay.

Carl was backing up the video replay over and over with the same result, strange warbled lines and dark shadows at the segment just before Agent Lily went berserk. Through the static, a milky slur of white followed my arms as I pushed Ferry to my right and lunged to wrest the gun upwards out of harms way, all of it a blur of motion.

"It must have been caused by the power flickering and the lights," said Carl in disgust. "Nobody moves that fast, not even you Dr. Schumacher."

CHAPTER FORTY-FOUR

It was a marvelous feeling sitting in the warmth and faux privacy of our Rover. The pouring rain and my thoughts were usurping too much of my attention, so instead of fumbling with the screens on my phone, I handed it to Chaste.

"Will you check messages for me?"

'Yes sir,' she thought as she slid the cell into her open palm.

"Darling, you really shouldn't make that a habit," I began, but my chide was cut short with the sound of the first message rattling the invisible speaker.

"You did it! You did it! God bless you!"

It was the same general beginning with several other messages from worried parents, terrified parents, and already grieving parents of missing children. One by one, each message heralded a mixture of unrestrained excitement, joy, and relief. It was that crumbling thing Pitre spoke of during our volley with Agent Lily.

Chaste leaned timidly over against my arm when all the messages finally finished playing and lay the phone down. Her feelings were much the same as mine. We were happy to have done our part, but all the children still had a long journey ahead of them before they would truly be home.

"It's good to see you back on mission Kress."

"Pitre!" chirped Chaste.

"Hello Chaste."

Without a physical body to respond to, she hugged my arm tightly in proxy.

"Your obedience has almost crumbled an entire working domain."

"All I did was place a few phone calls, Pitre. You did all the work."

"Together Kress..., the domain lord has been spoiled. Now we wait."

It was the same feeling I got when Pitre informed me of the imminent visit from the tall black. I knew not to ask the question I must and Pitre knew not to breach the subject with Chaste's intuitive and inquisitive mind listening on.

"Will we ever know about the child that was abducted by the FBI as a decoy?"

Pitre was silent.

I didn't say it out loud, but my thoughts whispered, 'oh no...' as I stared down the highway.

"I don't know if I can ever get used to this 'win some - lose some', battle plan."

"The FBI's self-policing methods aren't working. The real agency team didn't arrive in time."

"If their system is broken, why did we even try to use them?" I asked.

"All we could do was try. I didn't understand at the time that the child was never intended to survive, Kress. You would have been implicated."

I almost didn't care if I was implicated. My heart was broken. I would rather the little blank face in my mind were still alive.

"We will talk more later. We have much to discuss."

With that, Pitre slipped back into silence.

Chaste spoke up immediately, "Will Ferry be over tonight?"

Another issue to consider.

"Yes dear, I'm sure she will as soon as her days' responsibilities are done. Tell me..., exactly how do you feel about Ferry?"

Chaste crooked her head at me, smiling, "I like her of course."

"I know you like her as your friend. Are you comfortable with her as your guardian?"

"What's the difference?"

Suddenly, it was me asking myself that same question.

"None, I suppose. How much do you think we can trust her?"

Chaste looked at me strangely once again, "How do I know? I'm just a kid."

I laughed, "Sometimes I'm not so sure about that."

The main gate began its slow crawl to allow us inside our

sanctuary and I noticed the boys lying side by side only lifted their big heads to watch us drive inside.

Too much food was making them lackadaisical in their duties but they worked so hard when evil was afoot I couldn't complain. I parked our vehicle outside one of the three closed bays, leaving room for Ferry to park beside me and paused to look at my wondrous little girl.

"Yeah, I trust Ferry," Chaste answered. This time she seemed sure after given time to mull it over in her mind.

"Me too."

"I don't want her to leave," she mumbled sadly.

We stopped in our tracks and I knelt in front of Chaste.

"Neither do I sweetheart."

She hugged me tight, something that was becoming a regular occurrence, not that we were standoffish by any means. This conversation, this baring of souls, was destined sooner or later.

"We'll know what to do when the time is right, agreed?"

The garage door glided up with a silent whir, then began to close behind us.

When we walked just inside the door, the walls seemed to echo with silence. I didn't like the emptiness I heard.

"Kress, wait…. Be very quiet."

Thank God, I didn't have to repeat Pitre's request aloud to Chaste. At Pitre's request, we both backed from our hallway entrance in the garage.

Pitre emerged, an enormous pure white statue, bent on one knee. Despite his height, he made the strange position look effortless.

"Is there someone in our home?" I asked.

"No, follow me and don't talk, don't make a sound," he said. *"Chaste please stay here. Don't call out no matter what you hear. Don't let the dogs inside."*

He pointed at my shoes, until I understood that I was to remove them.

Now I was worried, even a tiny bit of explanation would have been appreciated.

"What?" I whispered.

He only looked at me with his blank stare then bowed into the door to the hallway. Once inside the main living area he stood to his full height and looked around, then pointed at our coffee table, more precisely to the large floral display.

Pitre spoke inside me, *"Pick it up carefully, don't make a sound, ...do not drop it."*

The baked ceramic hexagon was only twenty inches or so across, rather squat, and filled with a variety of artificial long stem flowers that made it seem much larger. I scooped up the simple white planter, expecting it to be the usual light delicate object I'd moved a hundred times to dust around.

It now weighed at least fifty pounds, no..., definitely more.

Dumfounded, I gave Pitre my best 'What now?' expression.

Pitre nodded and grasped my arm.

We were instantly standing in the middle of nowhere, a stiff north wind roaring across desolate sandy terrain, canyons and red rock. There had been no sensation of movement; one moment I'm in my living room, the next I was somewhere else; like flipping the page in a book or changing a channel on the television.

Pitre motioned for me to put the planter down carefully. I fought biting dust carried along with the wind as I bent my knees into a squat and set down my best and only effort at a feminine touch inside my home.

Pitre grabbed my arm once again and we moved, shifted actually. At first, it seemed only a few feet due to the redundant landscape, but then I saw a landmark and my gaudy floral decoration, a dot nearly an eighth of a mile in the distance.

"Very good, Kress," he whispered.

"Can I relax now?" I asked.

He nodded, *"Would you please give me your best yell?"*

I'd done everything else without question; I saw no reason to second-guess him now.

I cupped my hands to my face and gave out a good loud noise.

In an instant, there was a bright flash of light in the distance and a resounding concussion that positively knocked me off my feet. A small mushroom cloud of flame and ash rose into the air, roiling with heat on my face, as I sat there deafened and numb. Even the wind was sucked into sudden dead stillness. I hurried to my feet and watched as the orange glow dissipated high into the air.

Pitre took my arm without a word and we were instantly standing behind Chaste in the garage.

"You may talk now," said Pitre, from his recess inside me.

Chaste chirped and jumped around, looking at me.

"What happened? How did you get out here?" she asked. "You were just there," she pointed.

I knew without asking that Chaste didn't need to know what had just transpired.

"I presume we have no more surprises inside?" I asked.

I needed to know even if it opened the can of questions that Chaste would ask. She'd probably ask them anyway.

"I wouldn't let you inside unless it was safe," muttered Pitre. *"You'll need to replace a section of fence along the back. The animals were drugged, you should have noticed."*

Chaste turned to open the garage door, "Are the boys okay?"

"Only sleeping, Chaste. Let them rest," said Pitre.

"Are you going to tell me what happened?" Chaste grunted angrily. "You're not are you?"

"No," he answered for me.

The finality Pitre put into that one word ended the discussion. If I'd tried that, there would have been fifteen more minutes of prying questions.

CHAPTER FORTY-FIVE

Before Ferry arrived, I'd managed an hour or so locked away in my office with Pitre. We'd both agreed it would not be wise to mention the sound-activated dirty-bomb placed in our home to anyone.

After all, what would I tell anyone? How could I explain knowing about it? How could I explain disposing of it? I didn't have a clue where Pitre had whisked me off to; where we'd watched it detonate, nearly singeing my eyebrows flat.

I still didn't know what to make of the vision I'd seen of my African nemesis, his image hovering over the face of Special Agent Lily, fraud FBI. I'm sure Pitre would have an interesting explanation for that as well. Then my interrogation with Pitre was cut short, when we heard the front door-chimes gong. I'd forgotten that my Range Rover was still blocking the inlet to the garage bay doors.

"A little help?" Ferry grunted, kicking the sack by her feet. I took her keys from between her teeth and received a smile and a kiss.

"Thanks, I was about to drool. What's up with the boys? They didn't try to slobber up the backs of my legs today. Are they sick?"

"I'm sure they're just tired and full," I grunted, lifting the heavy sack. "What is all this? Smells good whatever it is."

"I hope you like it," she mumbled. "Deli to the rescue."

Her high heels clattered against the coffee table as she hurried off to the kitchen with bare feet.

"We're having company tonight!" she grunted loudly. "Oh! I'm sorry, I didn't know you were right behind me."

All I saw were more complications. Who'd be visiting us?

"Company? What kind of company?"

She struggled with the rest of her burdens and turned to me.

"You performed most excellently today, Mr. Schumacher. Did I tell you I'm proud of you?"

She hugged me, then frowned at me with an upturned freckled nose, "What have you been burning? I smell..., ew..., something acrid..., nasty like burned plastic. It's awful; you better change before they get here."

I held each of her shoulders to get her attention, "Ferry, who's coming here?"

"Brent and Carl," she said, with a shrug, as if it were the most obvious thing in the world.

That was good and I felt some relief.

She finally smiled, "Don't tell me you're the antisocial type? I never pictured you as one of those hermit bachelor types."

"No, not at all. I have a few questions I'd like to ask them."

"If it's about them getting here a day early, that's my fault. I didn't want to worry you. You trusted them, so when I talked to them the other day, I hired them to go through my apartment. That's when Carl came up with the surveillance photo's you saw today. The photos were from the line of stores at the strip mall across the street."

"Yes, well, the security cameras didn't stop your visitors from wrecking your home or trying to harm you, did they?" I asked, with my best smug tone.

"No, but it will help with our court case."

Ferry turned and started emptying sealed items onto the counter.

"Good heavens, there's enough food here to feed and army. Are we expecting someone else as well?"

Ferry laughed. I suddenly wanted to wrap my arms around that laughter and bathe in it. I had to turn away before I could get a grip on reality. What in blazes was wrong with me?

"Have you taken a good look at Carl? I bet he can eat half this all by himself."

At roughly six foot five and a chest like an oak, she was probably right.

My thoughts drifted back to some recess I didn't quite know how to handle. When I came to myself, blinking, I was turned back around standing still and staring into Ferry's green and pepper speckled eyes.

"Everything okay?" she whispered.

I took a deep breath and nodded, not daring to try and speak.

She ran her fingers through my dirty blond hair, "You need a haircut Mr. Schumacher…," then curled her nose, sniffing like the boys. "And a bath. Go change before they get here. Where's Chaste? I can use her help with the table."

I'd already started walking, not wanting to have to explain the scent I'd obviously ignored, to the trained olfactory glands of Brent and Carl. No doubt, they'd immediately recognize the scent of explosive after-burn and all bets would be off.

"She's been napping. I'll send her down."

"No…, don't wake her," Ferry frowned. "I can do this."

When my feet reached the top of the stairs, I passed Chaste, a full smile on her face, "Ferry's here, isn't she?"

Chaste didn't wait for an answer, her bare feet spattering down the steps at a frightening pace.

I quickly dumped all my clothes into a rubbish sack and tied it off to stifle their scent. They were a liability now, despite being one of my best pairs of slacks, a dress shirt and tie.

"You can thank me later," said Pitre.

"Thank you for what? What happened this time I don't know about?" I asked as I flipped on the shower.

I heard him laugh quietly, "I turned off the voices for now."

I felt the shock, then smiled, "You did! Bless you Pitre."

"Don't bless me quite yet," he warned.

"This was a training exercise. You're going to need to get used to dealing with…, wait…, let me finish…," he scolded me.

I was about to raise a rant above the noise of the shower.

"Soon you'll be able to turn it on and off by yourself," he said smugly, then I felt him smile inside me.

I knew without asking. The bloody prankster knew my curiosity would have the voices turned on at every occasion, especially when I saw certain expressions come over Ferry; or something else was brewing. Blast it all. I was becoming just as addicted as if it were a drug.

Our guests were running late so after a quick private chat, Ferry ushered me aside and had me sign the last of several documents.

We brought each other up to speed with our individual concerns, while Ferry seemed especially concerned about Chaste.

"Ferry, there's something else you should know."

After wrestling with this new information I needed someone to share it with that I could trust. It was difficult.

"I think I know what these people are after."

How could I tell Ferry without letting her know where I'd received my revelation?

She listened with sudden professional caution, waiting for me to divest myself of some hidden illegalities; at least it was what I guessed from her previous suspicions.

"They're still after my daughter."

Ferry sat back in unbelief, covering her mouth, waiting to hear my reasoning. I did my best to recant dissected pieces of the threats we'd received without including the private interactions of my angelic helper. I spoke of foreign soil, its political upheavals, and my family's involvement, finally throwing in the threat issued in Swahili, blurted by Lily that day. It would have been so much easier if I could have bared my soul in confession of my enemy's sudden presence.

She seemed much clearer as to why I was working so desperately to shield Chaste. She assured me that my daughter was well protected financially, and the guardianship was in place. With her legal blessing, I was going to tell Brent and Carl my concerns as soon as the subject was opened that evening.

I listened to her fascinate me with her years of knowledge while I watched her every expression, her movements and motions. Her eyes darted and flashed in expectation of every thought as it erupted. How was I so fortunate to find someone like her?

Without Pitre's boisterous recommendation to have Ferry Dunavin fill that office, I'd still have been lost. It was amazing how Ferry was able to keep pieces of our interesting relationship clearly defined. She may be tenacious and tedious, but she was caring, concerned, and in my corner.

Our guests finally arrived and Ferry moaned over the ice cold food, grumbling that we should have already eaten. Nevertheless, she shooed us away while she and Chaste hurried to redo her well-planned meal.

Brent and I were standing at the back corner of our yard, a little over three hundred feet from my back door, inspecting the ruined section of tines in my steel-barred fence.

"They used a special-ops device," he muttered, flicking his little light around. "A mechanical spreader. It'll rip through chain-link like scissors and just as fast."

He shook the heavy steel bars on my wounded fence, "This is some heavy duty steel fencing you have here, Doc."

"Please, just Kress," I frowned. 'Doc' was far too indicative of my old friend and enemy Thomas Clay; alias Thomas Whitefeather.

"I'll call my repairman and get it fixed tomorrow," I sighed. "He'll probably see my call and bring a pane or two of glass as well."

"You've had a rough go of it…, Kress. What did they do to your house this time?" he asked.

I chuckled inside…, not much, just installed a bomb.

"Nothing that I can tell. We must have startled them."

It wasn't a lie; it was 'nothing that I could tell him'.

Brent shook his head side to side, "You didn't startle these people Kress, whatever they came for, they finished, or they wouldn't have left."

I gestured an arm toward the house and started walking. I didn't want to argue. I knew he was right. My silence was better than some sad attempt at misdirection.

"I think I know what they were after," I sighed.

There was no time like the present.

Brent, stopped walking and blocked me with an arm, "You know what they're after?"

I almost smiled at his many-faceted insinuation, "It's not what you think. They're after Chaste. That's what this has been about all along."

"You're daughter? That little girl? I don't understand," he hissed.

We sat down on the steps of the back deck. This would take some time to explain.

"It all has to do with the original threat. Do you know why Elizabeth and I left South Africa?"

Brent nodded. I'd assumed he'd already read our recorded transition. God knows every other federal and news agency knew bits and pieces of my family's lives. At least I wouldn't have to explain every last detail.

"Evidently the feathered aborigine that threatened us, that threatened Chaste, has connections with the State Department. I know that sounds utterly ridiculous, and before you ask, I don't know how they are connected…, yet. But I intend to find out."

Brent nodded, thoughtfully, "Please, let us help. That's what Carl and I are best at. Does your lawyer know?"

I was almost stunned that he didn't instantly refute my accusations, or barrage me with heated questions about my suspicions.

"Yes, and she thought it best I mention it to you."

"Good, 'cause if you keep trying to do this on your own, you're going to dig a hole neither of us can't pull you out of."

He sat thinking for a moment, "So when your clinic was burned to the ground and littered with all the body pieces, someone was sending you a message."

I felt my insides drop like water, "Body pieces?"

I heard myself from somewhere else, some distant echo.

Brent caught my shoulder, "You didn't know?"

He wouldn't tell me details, despite my insistence, which was a good thing in retrospect.

"That young man, Satiiri; the one you saved, the one that someone tried to murder, how does he figure in all this?"

I shrugged, "I don't really know. He was such a kind young man. It was a miracle he lived at all. What do you know about him?" I asked. "Is he able to walk now?

"More than that. His name has been all over their local news. He's already leading some protest for a group called Unify South Africa."

Brent's face lit up as if his own words filled in every piece of some large puzzle.

"You boys come inside," said Ferry. "The foods ready."

Brent nodded to me and his face seemed clearer about something. Now would have been a good time for Pitre to turn on my 'radar' as Ferry called it, but the moment was lost with no way to reclaim it.

When we walked back inside the house, Carl was standing in front of the fireplace, leaning over.

"That's what we were smelling," he mumbled.

He grabbed the iron tools by the hearth, then prodded around in the ashes until a black glob emerged onto the ash shovel.

"Looks like an old VHS tape," he grunted, as he frowned in disgust. "You shouldn't burn these things, especially inside your fireplace. They give off dangerous chemicals."

Ferry was staring at me from the table and I didn't try to explain or formulate another story. I followed him quietly to the front door and we threw out the remains of one of Chaste's Department of Education training videos.

It was then that I noticed the stack of large plastic cases, with flip-over latches sitting in the foyer by the front door.

Before I could form the question, Ferry placed a hand on my back. She obviously had questions of her own.

"Come eat," she whispered. "Please?"

CHAPTER FORTY-SIX

We were all seated at the dining table, stuffed to the gullet, Carl eating his second helping of dessert, when I finally managed to bring up a few of my questions.

"What are all the suitcases by my front door?"

Carl grinned, but thankfully kept his mouth closed.

"They're equipment cases," said Brent. "We're installing a security system around your perimeter. Ferry told us that you're getting your phone line reinstalled tomorrow, so we brought all our toys with us. We're going to work on it tonight and have it ready to sync up whenever they arrive tomorrow."

It all seemed like a waste of time, "What good will it do if it only records someone in a mask shooting us in our sleep? Even if your system calls the authorities, we're miles from any real help and there's no one left I trust…, present company excluded of course."

I felt a nudge from Pitre, it was time to hand over my only evidence. Brent was trying to offer some type of rebuttal when I excused myself and walked away.

"…at least an alarm will sound and you'll have time to get in a secure room until someone gets here."

I didn't tell him that there is no secure room that could withstand the bomb blast I'd seen and felt earlier today. Instead, I handed him the white cloth from my hall pantry and sat down.

Everyone around the table frowned as Brent unfolded my mystery object. After a few turns of the cloth, there lay one of the weapons intended to cause us irreparable harm.

"A Glock 40," chimed Carl. "Nice. I thought you didn't like guns."

Unbelievable, "No I don't. Without going into detail, it was dropped in my back yard after one of the boys attacked one of our intruders."

And of course, they asked all the questions anyway, despite my weariness to the whole subject, and I sparingly answered them all without telling a single lie.

Brent pressed a lever and ejected the magazine from the pistol grip.

"Is that what I think it is?" asked Carl.

Brent flipped out one of the unspent cartridges into his hand with a flick, then held it up and shook it, letting it fall several times into his open palm.

Brent nodded, "Mercury tipped and Teflon coated."

Carl caught it in mid air and examined the end of the shiny brass object.

"Unmarked," he grunted. "Spec-op ordinance. It's illegal for a civie to own armor piercing ammo. A couple of these can punch a hole through a cinderblock."

"Technically, I don't own it," I spat, "and I'm giving it to you to dispose of."

Brent looked at the side of the pistol, "Still has its serial numbers? What an idiot."

He tossed the pistol to Carl, "Here's your next project."

Carl grinned from ear to ear, "I'll know who the owner's grandma is by tomorrow night."

Ferry and Chaste had been amazingly silent throughout the entire exchange, both looked worried and with good reason.

"Should Kress and Chaste be somewhere that's safer?" asked Ferry.

"I'm not going anywhere," I blurted. "I refuse to live in a bottle."

Chaste gasped when she heard me repeat her mother's pet phrase and sank next to Ferry, then her timid voice spoke out.

"I'm staying with Daddy."

"Then we've got our job cut out for us. You ready Brent?" asked Carl.

In minutes, the two men had all the cases opened and were sorting tiny cameras and matching them with infrared floodlights, motion sensors, all independent of any conventional electrical source. Even though each item seemed to be smaller and better camouflaged than what I'd seen in a catalog, before deciding on the live protection of the boys, I wasn't impressed. It wasn't until I saw the ceiling-mounted, automated pulse taser system that I became interested; activated by motion and body heat. Then other toys of sufficient interest began to surface. An alternating halogen and infrared strobe system, designed to frustrate even the most sophisticated night vision equipment.

Then I remembered that most of the events had taken place in broad daylight. There was no secrecy involved.

I held my peace and walked away.

Ferry and Chaste were seated side by side quietly whispering over their glasses of tea. I sat across the kitchen counter from them not wanting to interrupt, but such is life with the female of the species. They both hushed and stared at my intrusion.

"Are you sure you won't consider going to a safe house for a few days?" asked Ferry.

I wanted to tell her about the explosive device and ask her if there were any true safe houses; but I didn't.

Instead, I shook my head.

She stared at me, then she focused on my eyes until I was almost mesmerized, then frowned angrily and stood in a huff.

"What?" I asked quietly.

"Aren't you listening?" she asked.

"Of course I am," I said, returning her frown.

Then it hit me.

"Ferry, I can't always hear what you're thinking. It comes and goes as it pleases. I have no control over it."

'Not yet at least,' I thought.

Her frown instantly vanished and she closed her eyes.

"Chaste will you excuse your father and me for a few minutes? I promise I'll be right back. I won't take long."

Ferry refilled both tea glasses and left hers sitting on the counter with Chaste.

I'd seen the serious frown. Anything that was this private to Ferry was going to be yet another obstacle. I was so very tired of the growing list of obstacles. I had to rethink my strategy to protect my daughter. I needed to talk to Pitre to hear him reassure me once again that he could protect her.

Ferry managed to tug me into my home office and locked the door behind us.

"You didn't tell me it comes and goes," she whispered.

Her arms slipped around my waist and tiptoed up for a kiss; so much for my drab expectations. It felt good to hold her close. I could have spent the rest of the evening right where we stood. When our lips parted, Ferry laid her head to my chest, lost in some foray of thoughts.

"What are we going to do?" she asked.

That took me off guard. Ferry was always the assertive, self-confident sort. Even with the dreamy muse in her eyes, she sounded like I felt..., tired.

"We're going to live our lives," I said, trying to reassure both of us.

"It just keeps getting more and more complicated," she mumbled. "Normally..., I actually like a challenge, but I can't seem to sort this out like I usually do."

Since Ferry had become our lawyer, all she'd done was sacrifice; her job, her safety, her home. It was time I reminded her of my original warning, before she accepted us as her responsibility.

"Anytime you feel you should separate yourself from our dilemma, I won't hold it against you. You've already gone far above and beyond Ferry. I don't expect you to sacrifice yourself...."

"What? Is that what you think I'm talking about?" she frowned.

She immediately distanced herself from me, facing my desk, then sat down in my chair.

"I'm such a fool," she whispered. "I was...."

I thought I heard her curse, then she stopped mid-sentence and drew a deep breath.

"You're right. I'm going to get my things and get a room at the Hyatt for a few days, until my apartment is repaired. I can follow Brent and Carl back into Phoenix when they leave tonight. I need to go over your case tonight so I can brief the others about the new information."

She hurried to the door, fumbling nervously with the lock, then left without another word. I wasn't sure what had happened, but everything inside me told me it wasn't good.

I quickly locked the door.

"Pitre?" I hissed.

I felt his presence emerge inside me, there was tension.

"Kress. You're an idiot. I don't know if I can undo this."

It was as if he were standing there glaring at me from my insides. Instead of feeling his long slow disappearing act, Pitre left my presence so abruptly that it took my breath from my lungs, made me dizzy, nauseous.

I was so taken aback I couldn't seem to focus clearly enough to replay the conversation I'd just had with Ferry. I resigned myself to go find out what I'd done and make some sort of reparations for my ignorance.

Chaste was still seated at the kitchen counter staring at her glass of tea as I passed.

"Sweetheart, did you see which direction Ferry went?" I asked.

Chaste turned suddenly and looked at me; blind rage in her watering eyes, "You're such an ogre!"

She jumped from her barstool and stomped off up the stairs toward her room.

What in blazes was going on?

"Chaste Ellen, you come back here this instant!"

Both Brent and Carl stopped mid-stride at the front door to watch the drama, then hurried outside and shut the door.

CHAPTER FORTY-SEVEN

Chaste Ellen met me at the top of the stairs, then suddenly bolted down past me, ducking underneath my arm.

"Young lady! What's gotten into you?"

She was already at full speed running down the hallway by the time I reached the bottom of the stairs.

Why couldn't things be simple?

By the time I found her, she was inside the bedroom Ferry had been using. I felt as it were, a hand yank me backwards and plant my back to the wall just outside the doorway.

What the blazes?

"Please, please don't go Ferry," whined Chaste.

I heard her crying softly. That seemed to explain the fit of emotions from my daughter. Ferry must have told Chaste she was going to a hotel for a few days. Their bond was already much more progressed than I'd realized.

"It's for the best."

I heard Ferry whisper out the words, now it sounded as if she was also crying. Blast it all.

I tried to move, but that same force had me pressed firmly against the wall.

I heard Pitre, angry, rise up and speak to me, "Listen."

"I'm sorry Ferry," said Chaste. "I was so sure Daddy liked you too; I wouldn't lie to you about something like that."

"You're a sweetheart Chaste," sighed Ferry. "Don't be angry with your father, he's..., doing what he thinks best to keep you safe at the moment. Besides, I don't know what came over me. I promise to have you come visit me as soon as everything settles down and I can get my apartment back in order."

"But I don't want you to go," hissed my daughter. "Daddy's very smart at some things, but he can be really stupid sometimes."

She gritted out those last words like coarse sandpaper.

"I know you want me to stay. And I was the stupid one, as usual. I took way too much for granted…."

"What about my lessons?" asked Chaste. "I'll have questions, I'll…."

"That wasn't meant to be my job sweetheart, I was only getting you started," said Ferry, "but I'll still help you. I promise."

She sounded clearer now, more contained and I could tell she had hugged Chaste to her, preventing more arguments.

I felt the giant hand release me and I fell forward, peeled off the wall.

It appeared that both Chaste and Pitre were right; I was an ogre, an idiot, and stupid.

I couldn't bring myself to go inside the room, to apologize for my one-track mind, my blind ignorance. Of course, I cared for Ferry; of course, I felt more than casually for her. I heard Pitre, once again, but I already assumed most of what he was going to say.

"Get in there and fix this now. You cannot allow Ferry to leave here tonight."

Instead of being thrown forcibly through the bedroom doorway as I expected, I managed to knock and peer inside like a gentleman; albeit an idiot gentleman.

Ferry hurried from the floor at the foot of the bed, trying to hide the two streams of black mascara on her cheeks.

"Please wait," I managed. "Ferry…, I…, I need to…, wait, please."

She darted into the restroom and shut the door; at least Chaste no longer looked angry with me.

I knocked on the door, "Ferry, before you make up your mind to leave I need to have a talk with you."

"Not now. Go away Kress."

"Ferry…," I opened my mouth to speak when the shower and the sink both came on drowning out my efforts.

I turned to talk to Chaste, to find out more, but she was already gone. Blast it all; contrary women.

"Fine. I'll be sitting out here waiting when you give up this…, this…, whatever it is," I barked through the door.

I pulled a chair by the bedroom door and sat down in the silence.

"What did you mean, I can't let Ferry leave here tonight?"

There was more silence from Pitre.

Blast, no one was speaking to me.

"Pitre, I'm sorry. I didn't understand," I whispered.

His voice rose up, softer, less angry.

"That's exactly what you were supposed to say to Ferry."

From somewhere in the main room I heard, "Dr. Schumacher? Kress?"

My eyes closed in despair, "Yes…, yes, I'm coming."

I deserted my post and walked back down the hall to where Brent and Carl were standing.

"We've installed all the instrumentation, but we're going to make a little noise attaching the entry deterrents. We won't take long."

I nodded; both men gave me second looks.

"We can handle the rest of this. Take care of your family and pretend we're not here," said Carl.

My family. My two friends saw more than I did.

Carl picked up a spool of thin steel wire and walked back outside with Brent close on his heels carrying some odd looking contraption.

I felt even lower as I trod back down the hall.

Before I made my way to the door, Ferry hurried out, dragging her wheel endowed luggage behind her.

"Ferry, wait," I begged.

"Kress…," she sighed. "Dr. Schumacher, its better that I go so I can do my job the way you intended."

Her face was clean of the smeared war paint and she was back to her usual professional, distant self; the Ferry Dunavin I'd met in the law office immediately after John died.

"I'd rather you not leave tonight," I said, then felt a painful prod inside me. "I'd…, I'd rather you not leave at all."

Ferry stood staring at me as if she were trying to understand. I knew that if I'd been listening to her thoughts, they would have been a blur of contradictions and evaluations, unreadable.

"Please," I whispered. "I'm sorry for misunderstanding you…, more than anything, I want you to stay."

She closed her eyes and shook her head, as if whatever I'd said had clenched her decision. Blast it all; tenacious woman.

I blocked her path to rush past me, "Ferry, you know I care about you, don't you?"

She stopped her persistent advance and looked up at me, "Do I?"

"Yes Ferry, you do. Very much."

Always the unexpected, I felt something inside me break loose, rendering me into irrational jello. The old Kress would have said, 'I understand', then I would have politely shown her the door and rid myself of the confusion. Instead, I heard myself profess an unbridled spew of emotion.

"I misunderstood you. With everything happening at once..., surely you can understand that?"

"What I understand is that I let myself get caught up in circumstances and act unprofessionally," said Ferry.

Blast it all, she was making the same mistake I had.

"I..., I've just found you. I won't stand by idly and watch you waltz right out of my life. Don't be as blind as I was Ferry. I won't stand for it. Chaste loves you..., and..., and..., so do I."

The boys were happily groveling at the feet of my two security consultants, providing the requisite 'background noise' needed to set up their devices.

Brent and Carl were fine-tuning the aim of some cleverly concealed items at the corners and eaves of the house, while I was being used as their practice target. Somehow, this was all too familiar of Thomas and his tortures.

I'd needed the fresh air to clear my head, but my heart was still inside the house; still rehearsing its confessions.

I squinted again as my retinas were painfully blasted with a single 'low intensity' blast of light; I couldn't imagine it turned up to full intensity while looking through night-vision equipment.

"We're done," said Brent. "I put all the stuff from your cow pen in a box. It was pretty much useless."

I noticed that the high-voltage box and all the old mangled wire I'd had installed was gone and there was different wire atop my fence replacing it.

"What is this wire for?" I asked tiredly.

Carl nodded to Brent, "We figured..., that if your visitors were used to cutting the useless electrical wire every time they broke in, if they come back, they might not look as close before cutting these."

Now there were two strands of steel wire running parallel to each other about ten inches apart. I still didn't understand, but I was confident in their work and let it drop.

"We'll have to come and take it down, after we're sure you're safe. It's a little too dangerous so leave up in a residential neighborhood."

I took the bait, evidently I needed to understand, "What does this wire do? Is it electrical?"

"It's blade-wire, stretched to one thousand pounds per linear inch. It's strung in looped sections; cut one strand and its reciprocal recoils and removes a hand, or..., whatever else is in its path."

The idea of dismembered limbs was a little too fresh in my mind I suppose.

"You do realize that I'm a doctor?" I grunted. "I repair people, I don't want to maim them."

"Neither do we Kress, but these people seem hell bent to gut and filet you and your daughter, and your friend Ferry," said Brent.

My memory refreshed as I recalled the flash of heat on my face from the bomb blast.

I nodded, "I know..., of course you're right..., it's very late and I'm not thinking clearly at the moment. Do what you think is best."

I wasn't thinking clearly at all it seemed and hurried back inside the house ahead of my friendly experts, still dizzy from the unexpected flood of emotions unleashed earlier. There was no way I could have known how much I'd repressed inside my heart..., no way I could have known....

Ferry was seated next to Chaste where I'd left them, an hour after I'd fallen to pieces in front of Ferry, both of them in pajamas.

"Hey Dad, come sit with us?"

Ferry stretched out her arm as I fell into the lineup and I didn't bother to tell Chaste it was hours past her bedtime.

"I'm sorry Dad."

"It's no one's fault, Chaste, least of all yours," I answered. "How can anyone know what's hidden inside themselves until the door is unlatched?"

I remembered the day Chaste picked up the instructional video and the ensuing chaos she'd suffered. Our minds try to protect us, keeping all these life-altering events hidden away in little compartments and eventually let them out a little at a time. Unless some unplanned event hits a trip wire, a default switch that turns all the little rabbits loose from their cages at once. Then each memory, happy to be free, runs amuck - uncaring of the damage inflicted to our inner garden.

Ferry was silent, her hand sliding up the back of my neck into my hair; watching me.

"Thank you for not leaving," I said once again.

"I'm warning you. I can be very hard headed," she whispered. "I guess you already know that."

Her reciprocating smile bandaged our common wounds.

One of the mass of cell phones on the table began to dance in a circle; it was Ferry's.

She looked at the caller's name and shook her head.

"Dunavin," she answered.

"Yes, you have the right number," she said, sitting up tall on the edge of the sofa. She quickly gave the universal motion for a pen and paper and scribbled down some information on a wrinkled envelope.

"I see. No, it wasn't too late at all. I requested the callback. Did you fax the information to my office? Very good. Thank you again."

After ringing off, Ferry handed me the makeshift notepad, which read: Nitrazepam with an even mix of lysergic acid in a base of Dimethyl sulfoxide.

"That was the lab that did the chemical analysis on the water bottles. Care to decipher it for me?"

"I knew I smelled the DMSO, but it's only a solvent. Possibly a delivery system, but the rest is interesting. Nitrazepam is a powerful hypnotic especially when mixed with LSD. I'm certainly glad you didn't get that on your skin. You would have been of no use to anyone for days, maybe never if both hallucinogenics set up residence in your central cortex. Did they tell you what kind of concentration?"

"It was refined, potent enough to knock down a horse."

She looked at me a little puzzled, "I take it this isn't a prescription drug?"

"Absolutely not. It's pea soup. Nitrazepam is a tranquilizer, a sedative that would let your brain cells accept the LSD without any restrictions. I'd have to look at the chemical bond, but I'm certain it could have reduced you to a vegetable within minutes," I mumbled.

Suddenly, the scissor wire on my fence didn't seem such a bad idea after all. Suddenly I saw the resolution of the hideous creatures after my daughter. They were willing to risk being caught in some Kamikaze act of desperation to kill Chaste.

"Elizabeth...," I whispered, wondering.

Then I remembered the bottle of water Agent Lily had tried to thrust upon me in his interrogation room nearly a year ago.

CHAPTER FORTY-EIGHT

Brent and Carl were gone at last and my family was asleep, yet my duties were only beginning.

"Pitre, why didn't you just tell me? Why didn't you turn back on that..., that radar thing and let me hear what was going on inside Ferry? I could have avoided the entire drama this evening."

"It would have been a disaster," he replied. *"You were blinded by your own heart."*

I suppose I was. If I'd understood that Ferry had been sharing her feelings about us, about how she felt about us, I would have closed my own doors without hesitation.

"Kress, how can you know if someone is in love with you when you don't know you're in love your own self?"

After all we'd been through together, I still hated it when Pitre was right.

"I understand why you handled the situation the way you did and I accept it, but I don't have to like it Pitre."

We had much else to discuss and I could tell he was tired of my rant over personal issues.

"Was it too early to leak my suspicions to Brent? I know I mentioned it to Ferry, but I suppose I should have asked you before I spilled the beans."

"No, and you need to keep them busy. During the interrogation, you were too obvious while giving Ferry information to notice that both of them were watching you. They have their suspicions."

Too many things were happening at once.

"Then help me," I griped. "You're the one that nudged Ferry and I together; it's becoming harder for me to concentrate on the business at hand."

Ferry and I, our relationship had the hint of Stockholm Syndrome written into it. Thrust two people together under dire circumstances and instantly you have a deep co-dependant relationship, much like infatuation, even love.

"I wasn't the one that put you together," said Pitre. *"Your rational thinking is trying to blind you again. Have some faith."*

What was he trying to imply? Who did he think put us together?

"Yes, well you certainly had a hand in it."

Pitre broke a short frustrating silence.

"While I'm still allowed an opinion, I'll share mine. I believe that both of you deserve each other. You're both stubborn and hardheaded. Now stop arguing with me, we have important items to discuss.

"Inform Ferry of the release of the other children on the list, then be prepared. The next list will be much more important."

More children. Of course, there were more. The local post office was littered with the faces of proposed runaways and the lost. It hadn't been that long ago I'd taken down the flyer with a photograph of Chaste.

"The donations from this last wave will cover expenses for the next. You must trust me Kress, everything depends on it."

He didn't make any sense at all; I'd only spent a little time on the telephone. What donations? What expenses?

He was hiding something once again; vague about the next phase.

For once, I didn't question, I listened and made notes. If only to prove to Pitre that I wasn't the obstinate prate he accused me of. His instructions were helpful, made logical sense, and reassured me that what I was doing was right. He'd always been short and to the point, but not this night, even though I could tell he was keeping some new secret, one that had him disturbed.

When we were through I looked at the clock, it was nearly four in the morning and I felt myself droop. Ferry was an early riser and I now had a full day ahead of me. My cell phone beeped once, a missed call. I didn't bother to look at the name.

"I won't be able to function tomorrow…, I mean today, unless I get a few minutes rest."

I felt Pitre nod inside me, *"It's time you reap the other benefits of our cohabitation. Go take a nap, then wake Ferry."*

Wake Ferry indeed; I'd be lucky to hear the alarm when it went off in a couple of hours. I yawned, painfully; one of those jaw-wrenching stretches that tell you that you've exceeded every limit.

I counted every step up the staircase and finally fell across my bed. I must have fallen asleep as soon as I crushed the covers, because it was the last thing I remembered until the alarm clock startled me awake.

Six a.m. blared at me across the dim morning light of the room. I rolled up and stretched.

As promised, I felt as if I'd spent untold hours asleep.

Ferry; I was supposed to wake her as soon as I hit the floor.

As my usual morning practice, I peered in to check on Chaste. The covers were tossed, but she wasn't there.

I'd been allowed the luxury of sleep, so I trusted Pitre that my daughter was safe.

Wake Ferry; the words prodded me once again.

I trotted down the stairs, clear headed, with an agenda to take care of; a renewed sense of purpose and direction. It felt wonderful.

I knocked on the bedroom door and waited. A bleary-eyed Ferry opened it after a few minutes.

"I overslept," she yawned and turned around.

There underneath the covers was Chaste, just as I suspected.

Ferry saw me looking, "I didn't have the heart to send her back to her room. I hope you don't mind her sleeping here with me."

"Of course not. Good morning," I mumbled quietly, turning her back to face me.

She smiled and lay against me, arms pulling us together, "Yes, it is a good morning."

We stood there for several moments, until I felt her warmth seep through my clothes. I felt my heart stir, ancient and foreign inside me.

"I have to get ready," she whispered, but didn't hint of turning loose.

"What do you want for breakfast?" I asked.

"This," she mumbled, still clutching my waist.

"You." I heard her think inside; the voice was clear and simple; not rushed or jumbled with some other scattering of morning thoughts. Evidently I'd flipped some internal switch without knowing any of the how's or why's or any of the rules.

"Morning Daddy."

Ferry didn't flinch as we turned to say good morning.

"I had the strangest dreams," whispered Chaste.

"So did I," said Ferry. "I dreamed a little girl came and curled up beside me last night."

Chaste grinned and lit up the room.

"I really do have to get ready," said Ferry. "Get out, make me some coffee, go fix us food, since you're so ready to go."

Her voice followed me down the hallway as I was leaving, "Fix extra, remember Brent and Carl will be here early."

"With everything that's going on, you expect me to drop it all and go with you and Chaste?" asked Ferry.

She yawned delicately before taking another sip of coffee.

"Not drop it all. It's only for a couple of days," I argued. "It is business related. I'm sure your partners won't mind after I explain what we'll be doing."

"I don't like Washington D.C.," she frowned. "I hate the smog as much as the politics. I'll hate having to part with my weapon; they don't honor the concealed carry law there."

"You won't need a gun," I frowned. "You'll be using a much better weapon after we meet with the American Consulate, Mr. Jernigan."

Ferry saw the concerned look on Chaste and grimaced.

"Okay…, okay…, I'll make plans. You know I did have other clients up until I chose to represent you, Dr. Schumacher."

"The phone line is up," blurted Carl from the other room. "So is the security system."

Suddenly I heard ringing echoing in every room of the house. Ferry rolled her eyes and picked up the closest receiver, "Schumacher residence."

She closed her eyes and nodded, "Yes, it seems to be working fine. Why is there so much noise on the line?"

Brent and Carl walked into the kitchen where we were seated. Ferry waved at one of them to pick up another receiver.

"Yes, I'll call back and place a repair order as soon as I hang up."

She hung up the call angrily, about to dial the phone company,

"Stupid people."

"Wait," said Carl. "Don't make your call. Give us just a few seconds. We'd like to check something."

Brent walked into the room nodding, with a grim expression, "I don't know who or how, but you've already got an interrupt in the line. Someone is listening. I checked the line twice with my test equipment and confirmed it. This is insane."

I saw Carl's big frame slump in defeat, "I've never seen anyone dogged like this, not in this country."

"You'd better keep using your cell phones for now until we can setup a cell service to the security center," said Brent. "I'll do what I can to see where the line is tapped. It may take some time."

First, I heard it inside me, then repeated it aloud.

"No, why don't we let whoever it is listen for now?" I whispered. Misinformation can be just as useful as privacy. Besides you'll only be wasting your time."

They both nodded thoughtfully, "As long as you don't forget and slip up. We can put lock switches on all the handsets so they can't eavesdrop on a cradled phone set. You'll have to press a button when you speak, but it's better than someone eavesdropping on every word you speak in the house night and day."

That would be preposterous; there were dozens of phones in the house. I couldn't stand the echoing rings as it was.

"Don't bother, just fix this one. I'll disconnect all the others in the house."

Ferry's cheeks were growing pink from an impending explosion, "This is ridiculous. How can these people masquerade themselves as FBI right underneath the noses of several law enforcement agencies?"

"There's only one way that I know of," said Carl.

He received a harsh rebuking glance from Brent, but it was too late to stop Carl's open conjecture, "They would have to be connected to some Special Operations group or Shadow Company working off the grid."

"Shadow Company," I murmured to myself, suddenly remembering a note that I'd jotted down in haste.

"A group like that could easily pose as any agency and get away with it if they're taking orders from someone high up in the political food chain."

Brent ducked his head as Carl finished, as if something was spoken that should have been left alone. It was then that I began to ponder where Brent's loyalties resided over myself, Chaste, and now Ferry. We were after all placing our lives in their hands.

I all but begged Pitre to turn on my inner hearing and received a null response. Trusting him, trusting my new associates was becoming one of the hardest challenges I was facing.

Ferry's cell phone rang and she snatched it angrily staring into space.

"Dunavin."

Her frown deepened further, then she paled, "What? Who? Whitefeather?"

She covered the phone, "The news, somebody turn on the news."

"Which one?" asked Brent.

Ferry ended her call quietly, then shrugged, "Take your pick."

There on the large television screen, channel after channel was a still photo of Thomas Clay, alias Thomas Whitefeather, with a torrent of vehicles outside his Sedona Arizona office. Just above the screen in bold letters was *Breaking News*.

"...connected with the abduction and murder of countless children across the southwest. The FBI served a no-knock warrant for his arrest at 3 a.m. this morning and were resisted with gunfire. The man known as Thomas Whitefeather, was shot and killed after critically wounding two of the officers during the raid. His business, 'Finder of Lost Things' is being processed as we speak and according to an unknown source, a list of names was found matching several recently recovered missing children. Several of those same children were recovered after paying a finders fee to his business. According to an FBI spokesperson, in what may soon be known as one of the largest organized abduction rings in history..."

We all sat in abject silence and listened while the screen of the television displayed a foray of teargas, gunshots and violence. The blood slowly drained from my body, waiting for my name to be mentioned.

The warrant the FBI served was in connection with the one faceless child, abducted by the rogue FBI unit. The one used as bait. The one they'd intended on pinning to me. Instead, when it backfired, they'd turned on their ally, Thomas, making him their scapegoat.

Of course I was silent, as was Ferry as she gripped my hand nervously, her palm damp with worry.

Brent and Carl tried to hide their questions by keeping their gaze between each other and the newscast. I hoped that they saw the serious intent of those targeting us.

I needed to speak with Pitre in private. Strangely, he seemed peaceful and quiet inside me, much to my distress.

Ferry broke the silence, "Kress, I need to go to the law office and swap notes with everyone. Do you still want me to take off Thursday and Friday?"

Apparently Ferry had made her decision to follow through with our trip to Washington D.C. When I didn't hear a peep out of my angelic advisor I nodded in agreement.

"Carl, you're going to search out the owner of that Glock?" she asked. "...and Brent, you'll talk to your connections in Washington to see if there really is a link to what's going with Kress?"

Both men agreed with a silent nod.

"Before we go any further...," said Brent, "Doctor Schumacher, Carl and I need to know if there's anything you need to tell us. Anything that we don't already know."

They were worried that they were being dragged into illegalities so deep the world was going to vanish before their eyes. There was no way to reassure them of my motives. Honest denial would seem just as injurious as complicity of wrongdoing at this point.

"Nothing," I muttered, shaking my head.

CHAPTER FORTY-NINE

Within the span of fifteen minutes, Chaste and I were alone once again; standing quietly, holding hands and overlooking the quiet street in front of our home. I wanted to pack up everything; no, I wanted to leave it all, get on a plane with my daughter and leave. If it not for my sketchy obligations to Pitre I might have done just that, but then there was Ferry Dunavin pulling at my heart strings and I didn't know what to do.

"Pitre?" I mumbled. "What do we do now?"

Our host emerged, white and brilliant as always, somewhere behind us, probably seated, *"It's not as complex as it seems."*

His voice sent a shiver through Chaste, her hand tightening its grip in mine. Pitre was changing..., something was different; we both felt it, even in his calm mellow voice.

I felt myself relax, as if his very word held some unknown mystical power capable of sedating our very will. Neither of us felt the urge to turn and face Pitre, and at the same time it felt as if we were saying goodbye to the view in front of us.

"One more list Kress and you will have saved countless more innocent lives, future lives; far more than in your entire effort with Elizabeth at the clinic."

Another list. Impossible. Thomas was dead.

"Play the message on your phone, make your next list, then destroy the phone and get a new one."

I'd forgotten the message from last night. I hadn't known it was Thomas. I couldn't fathom listening to a dead man's voice, reciting a new list of missing names and numbers.

Pitre dissipated leaving the house with the aroma of fresh rain and his signature glow on everything around us.

"I'll help you," whispered Chaste, tugging on my hand, drawing me from the glass portal.

The voice of Thomas was just as disturbing as I'd expected.

"This is it Kress. They're on their way to come get me, so listen close. I want you to know…, you and your daughter…, I…, I'm sorry, for all the lies, everything. Tell the big guy that I'm sorry I tried to pull the wool over him with that one missing kid. They told me…, they…, well, they told me lots of things. I should have known he'd catch that, maybe somewhere inside I wanted it. Anyway, here's your list…."

Thomas coughed heavily to clear his emotional state and began to recite a relatively short list of names, seventeen in all, with their requisite telephone numbers.

Among them was a teenage boy named Steven.

He ended his message with,

"They're here…. Goodbye Doc."

I replayed the sad message once more, double-checking the list, then I deleted the message, took my phone to the garage and pummeled it to bits with a mallet while the boys looked on with inane curiosity. In a matter of minutes, I'd obliterated a several-hundred dollar iPhone and felt no remorse for the gratuitous violence whatsoever.

My curiosity instantly turned toward Pitre and I could tell Chaste was just as interested, but it was time for us to leave.

I filed away my questions for him as we left off to Phoenix for the day; among other things to purchase a new cell phone. It was as if I had become a blind man being led about on a leash, taking each and every step by faith in my internal companion.

My daughter was unusually quiet in the seat next to me.

"Dad…," mumbled Chaste, then aborted her comment or question; leaning against my side in silence.

In the grand scheme of things, I didn't know why…, about anything. Her multi-pronged thoughts were no doubt a child's version of my own insufficiencies.

"Would you like to stop by Ferry's office after we're done?"

She nodded her head quietly against my side. Of course she

wanted to, so did I. I tried once again to get her conversing.

"You're hair is already down to your shoulders. You know you're getting prettier every day. Did you know that?"

I muted my sentence before admitting she looked like her mother, then tried another approach.

"I know your mother would be very proud of you."

"You mean mama *is* very proud of me," she corrected.

One of the good things we'd both acquired from Pitre was our renewed faith in something more than this fleeting and sometimes disappointing life. If angels, both good and bad were this prolific, hiding just out of view our whole lives, there must be an entire universe waiting for us.

"If you could choose anyplace to live, where would it be?" I asked.

She shrugged in silence, "I don't care. As long as it's with you…, and maybe Ferry."

Well that certainly put things in perspective for me. Chaste had bonded with Ferry Dunavin more than I'd realized.

"I'll try to make that happen," I sighed. "But you have to understand I can't force Ferry along. She'll have to make that choice on her own."

"Kress?"

I jumped inside, gripping the steering wheel tightly.

"Good heavens, what on earth are you…?"

"Kress do you remember the present you found in your house and our short trip together?"

The bomb. Of course.

"Yes, that trip."

He answered my thoughts, keeping Chaste in the dark.

"Ferry has a present at her apartment similar to that one."

"Oh, dear God," I muttered. "Where's Ferry?" I asked, stomping on the gas pedal.

"At her office, but…," he stalled.

"But? But what?!" I gritted.

"Slow down Kress, we have plenty of time to get to her apartment before she does," he finished. *"Chaste, I need you to do something very important for me. I need you to keep Ferry in her car and keep her talking. Don't let her go inside her apartment where your father and I will be. Can you do that for me?"* asked Pitre.

"Yes, but tell me what's happening. I'm not a silly twit. I know something's there, inside her apartment."

It was Pitre's turn to handle her inquisitiveness.

"Do you trust me Chaste?" he asked.

She looked up at me with a deepening frown for her answer.

"I suppose," she grunted.

"It's something that needs to be carried away so that Ferry won't get hurt," he answered.

She sat bolt upright, "Like a bomb?!"

Welcome to the infernal workings of a precocious young mind.

"Like a bomb," he answered. *"Help me keep Ferry safe?"*

When we arrived, I came to a halt and parked against the curb just outside the draw gate of Ferry's apartment community. Less than five minutes later she turned past us only a few feet away, deep in thought, never seeing us. Luckily, the guard didn't raise the gate immediately and I honked my horn to get her attention.

Ferry looked over our direction with a sour expression, then her face lit up with happy recognition. Chaste jumped out of our Rover and ran to get inside Ferry's Lincoln.

Moments later, Ferry waved at me and the large lever raised vertical to admit both our vehicles inside.

So far so good; I breathed a sigh of relief.

When we rounded the first turn in the gated community, I gasped in horror.

The perimeter of Ferry's home was encircled by a horde of tall greys milling about, tattered angry wings slightly unfurling and drooping to the ground, pointing enthusiastically at Ferry and Chaste.

"Pitre!"

"I see them. Act normal."

They were packed as thick as a concert in hell and I was supposed to act normal and walk right through the middle of them? I'd seen them part like water for Ferry and stiffened my spine. I wasn't about to let them do something to harm Ferry or Chaste.

"Tell me what to do and I'll do it."

I jumped out of the Rover and hurried over to Ferry's car door.

"Hey Kress! How did you know I'd be here? I was going to call you and get you to meet me for lunch but you didn't pick up your phone."

I smiled best I could, "It's broken..., one of the things we're in town for. We were coming by your office to get you for lunch. Great minds must think alike.

"Actually Ferry, I'd like to know what you're doing here as well? Do you really think it's safe to be here alone?"

I saw it coming, the instant she frowned.

"What am *I* doing here? What were *you* doing sitting by my front gate? I have about twenty-four other questions to ask you...."

I didn't have any good answers. Pitre made a sad attempt at saving me.

"Ferry, you know how sometimes I hear others thoughts. You must have...."

"That smoke might work with somebody else," she spat. "Now tell me the truth."

She started to get out of the car - blast it all.

Chaste grabbed her arm, pulling Ferry back into her seat.

"Do you trust my Dad?" she asked.

"Of course I do, but...," Ferry grumbled. "Oh okay. What's this about?"

I sighed, "Tell me what you came here for and let me get it for you."

"No way Mister," she smiled, a faint blush on her cheeks. "I've got to get clothes for our trip this week. I need too many personal things to have you digging around."

"Fine," I grunted. "At least let me go inside and make sure it's safe, then you can get your things while we wait for you."

She squinted her eyes, that intrepid look that always preceded some lengthy argument, "Here."

She handed me her keys, "Don't take all day; I have to get back to the office before two this afternoon. I still have questions for you, Mister...."

One obstacle averted, I turned quickly and stared at the mass of tall greys blocking my path.

"Chaste, keep Ferry busy," Pitre reminded her.

I made a few steps and halted, sizing up my opposition.

The dark angels weren't moving aside, in fact they were congregating into what appeared to be a dark gray wall.

Before I could form the question, before I could think, Pitre emerged in full display before me.

If he looked massive in my home, it was because of the limited space, but out here in the open parking lot, there was no excuse.

Pitre had grown. In the span of only a moment, the elements lit in brilliance, then I saw something so spectacular my breath left my body.

Pitre unfurled a set of enormous white wings and there was a flash of light so brilliant I was blinded where I stood.

An immediate resounding rush of thunder shook my body, deafened me and the world faded from view.

CHAPTER FIFTY

"Kress? Kress? Can you hear me?"

I heard my name being called from somewhere in the distance and soft warm hands patting my cheeks.

When my eyes focused, I was on my back in the parking lot with Ferry huddled over me.

Her frown turned into a smile and she pecked me with a kiss, "That's better."

"What in blazes happened?" I grunted, as I sat up.

"Maybe heat lightning?" she offered, looking warily up at the sparse clouds overhead. "I still have goosebumps on my arms."

She laid her palm on my face and instantly gooseflesh stood to attention on her entire arm. She jumped away, eyes wide.

"I think you were struck by lightening," she gasped.

"Nonsense, I feel fine, but you'd better get back inside your car just in case," I said, pointing to her Lincoln.

Needless to say, there were no more tall greys challenging me, only oddments of dark tattered wings littering the ground, all roiling up in heated spirals.

I swallowed painfully, stepping around the spectacles and opened Ferry's front door; Pitre quickly emerged, kneeling with one palm on the floor.

'Should I keep silent?' I asked in my thoughts.

Pitre ignored my question, *"Beside the sofa, the briefcase. Same as before. Hurry."*

I carefully slid my hand through the handle and as before. He grasped my arm, transporting us to some God forsaken emptiness in the middle of nowhere. A different nowhere, but desolate just the same.

I set the briefcase down in the same position I'd found it on the bare ground and we shifted away. Pitre seemed content with the location and touched my arm, bringing us back inside Ferry's home.

"It will detonate on its own in a few minutes."

"Pitre, you've changed. Why didn't you tell me?"

He nodded, *"You've changed, you've healed. I have my former glory, thanks to you. Because you healed, I am healed."*

Even his voice was warm and soothing.

He dipped his body, partially bowing before me, and I felt awkward, an angelic being thanking me for something I certainly couldn't have been responsible for.

He faded as I heard him whisper, *"Ferry is waiting."*

There I was, standing alone in the silence, with more questions than answers. Nothing new.

Ferry was listening to Chaste blathering on, trying to be polite, while constantly gazing toward her front door. She didn't see me until I was standing in front of her car and she hurried out the driver door, Chaste hot on her heels.

"Well?" she asked.

"All is clear," I said smiling.

She brushed my unruly hair down with her fingers and smiled back at me.

"We're not through, Kress," she chirped. "You should go by the hospital and get a check up. We need to know you're okay."

Her voice faded as both ladies hurried inside.

I was thankful that they couldn't see the aftermath of destruction all around them.

I wandered about, marveling at the few lingering remains of the horde of tall greys.

Leathery pieces of thin membrane turned to spiraling dust at my touch. Suddenly, I felt a memory rise up inside me, one of my memories following my hillside joust with Pitre.

Now I understood why all the beings I'd seen during that transition, all the unmentionable creatures, fled the ones in white at all cost.

Unbelievable. So many things had changed in such a short amount of time. Then my mind readjusted; for I was the one that had changed; this unseen world had possibly been all around us for millennia, at our every turn.

"A little help?"

I turned to see Ferry standing in her doorway with that quizzical look on her face.

I carried out three large luggage; surely enough for a month's travel's, conceivably half her wardrobe, and stuffed them in the trunk of Ferry's vehicle. We looked at the ruined back door that had been nailed helter-skelter back in place and several broken treasures littering the floor.

"Guess I'll have the rest put in storage," said Ferry. "I have to start looking for a new place since the lease is broken. Kress are you sure you don't need to see a doctor?"

"I'll be just fine."

Chaste looked at me, then as our smiles passed along a secret, she walked away.

"Our home is open to you for as long as you need it," I said. "You don't need to feel rushed into anything."

"After this morning, I might just take you up on that offer, Mr. Schumacher," said Ferry. "Let's lock up and go eat so we can discuss a few new details that might influence my decision."

Of course she'd thrown me another curve, something I was getting used to. I didn't have the foggiest clue what she was going on about.

I followed Ferry's car, Chaste's blond hair twitching side to side in the passenger seat, all the way to one of the multitudes of authentic Mexican restaurants.

I saw no dark entities, felt no ill omens, other than my growling stomach, as I turned off my vehicle.

Ferry was all smiles and chatter with Chaste by her side until we were about to be seated, then Ferry made a fuss and had us relocated to the farthest, most secluded table in the restaurant.

"Alright Mr. Schumacher," she grinned. "I want to see you explain your way out of this."

She reached in her purse and pulled out a dozen Xerox copies of some kind, then tapped her finger on it menacingly.

I picked them up and looked at each one; they were copies of bank transfers and certified checks, each name vaguely familiar. More specifically, those names recently rescued from their abductors.

"They're the contributions from…."

"Yes. I'm well aware of what they are and whom they are from," she hissed. "Look at the sum total. What do you expect me to do about that?!"

Just under nine million dollars; twenty-one donations.

"I believe four are missing, but they may have made their contributions elsewhere," I shrugged. "Deposit them in the account we setup. I need to write a few checks as soon as…."

She leaned forward in disgust, placing her face in her palms on the table for a moment and I hushed.

"Kress. We watched the newscast together," she whispered. "Have you already forgotten? You can't keep these. You're already being hounded like a criminal. You could be implicated in all the abductions. I might be a good lawyer, but I'm no miracle worker."

Pitre answered me before I could ask, then many things made perfect sense. I saw the last piece of a huge puzzle in my hand about to slip into place and smiled so hard my eyes watered.

"As soon as we receive all the donations, I'll tell you what is to be done with it all. Trust me Ferry."

"Oh, Kress…," she whined. "What are you involved in? There are real people out there trying to kill you…, excuse me, kill us. Is it about the money?"

"It's more than just the money. Do you remember the telephone call Agent Lily received during our meeting?" I asked.

She looked up, her eyes puffy and dazed, but she nodded.

"That was when the cookie crumbled. That was when all these families were reunited. When I knew we'd won. When Lily knew he'd lost. That's part of the reason he went berserk."

It was my turn to tap my finger on the stack of paper, "Do you want all these family's angst and pain to be for nothing?"

Pitre forced me to hold my revelations, warned me that any premature celebration could cause our work to fail.

"How many more Kress?" Ferry asked wearily.

"Seventeen, which I know of, so…, twenty-one total."

"Oh God…. That's a lot to ask of me, Kress. My whole career and reputation are at stake. I could be disbarred if I'm implicated in any wrongdoing. That's if I don't go to prison or get killed. I don't have a small fortune to fall back on. Most of my extra money goes to St. Mary's at the end of each year."

"All I'm asking for is trust," I said, taking her hand.

She stared at me for several seconds, "Oh Kress."

I pulled her hand closer and gave it a kiss.

"At least you aren't inside my head," she mumbled. "Are you? Please tell me you aren't...."

"No Ferry, your secrets are safe," I smiled.

Ferry actually tried to force herself to relax.

"Where's our waitress?" she hissed, tiredly looking across the empty expanse.

Chaste began an incessant chatter as soon as we left Ferry Dunavin's office.

"I saw him Dad," she shrilled. "Pitre got his wings!"

I nodded, "Sweetheart, I believe we've both witnessed a miracle. What do you think?"

"Did you get rid of the bomb?" she asked.

Right back to the things I'd rather she forgot.

"He did," I answered. I wasn't ready to tell her about the unnerving travels into some remote desert and back.

"So when we came home...," she began slowly.

"Yes, Chaste, we removed one from our home as well. Another secret between the three of us, agreed?"

She nodded, suddenly quiet, "Will there ever be four of us?"

"Sweetheart, you're rushing things again. You know I can't predict the future. No one can."

"Ferry's so worried all the time now," she sighed. "I hope she doesn't get sick of us."

"Ferry's a very bright person. I'm sure she'll make the right decision for herself."

"But Daddy, what if she decides...?"

"Now who's being a worrywart?" I asked, cutting her off. "Remember to include Ferry in your prayers. You've already lived through several miracles already. What's one more?"

Chaste brightened, "You're right."

"By the way, I can predict ice cream in our future. Are you going to help me pick out a new phone?"

"Another one like mine," she answered quietly.

As I've questioned many times before; why can't some things be simple?

Chaste and I hurried in the retail store, picked out a replacement phone and I went to the counter to pay. That should have been simple enough.

My old iPhone was insured, which meant there were forms to fill out. I purposely destroyed my old phone; I had no desire to defraud the insurance. I wanted to pay, get the new one turned on with the old number, then leave.

It was not to be so. Only in America.

What should have been a simple sales transaction turned into an hour-long fiasco of forms only a lawyer could decipher.

I did get to leave with my new cell phone and a new number, but not before canceling my old contract, paying the early termination fee, then starting a new contract. All I'd wanted to do was buy a new phone; utterly ridiculous. When we left, I looked to see if there was a tall grey in charge of the establishment.

As soon as we were in our auto, I handed the new phone to Chaste and asked her to insert the list of contacts and numbers from my notes. A small feat for a brilliant young girl with lightning fast digits.

We had just left the local grocer market when Chaste received a call from Ferry on her phone. At first, my daughter was elated, then frowned when she handed the bedeviled thing to me.

In two short sentences, Ferry summoned Chaste and I to appear at her office, posthaste. From the inflection of our short conversation, rather her short dialogue, our meeting wasn't about another disaster.

Ferry met us on the curb outside, waving us inside the tall banking complex where her office resided.

There was much to-do and happy chatter when we walked inside her law office. As soon as we shuffled past a crew of repairmen in the front hallway, Ferry erupted.

"They settled!" she shrilled.

"Who settled what?" I asked, dumbfounded, my usual state.

"We won't have to go to court, Kress. The Federal Court and the Director of the FBI reviewed our charges and they plead no-contest."

"But you only filed it days ago," I argued. "How is that possible?"

"They're settling out of court because they know they have an internal problem. It's an even seven figures, Kress, as long as we don't embarrass them and go public about the unit impersonating their officials within their organization."

No, we wouldn't want to embarrass them, would we? It was good news of a sort, but it wouldn't bring back John Shoemaker, and a long list of other grievances. Who was responsible for Thomas? Was this the rogue Shadow Company or the FBI cleanup crew eradicating all traces of an embarrassment?

I heard Pitre try and comfort me, *"Pick your battles Kress. This isn't the one."*

"Kress?"

Ferry brought me back around from my harried thoughts.

"Yes…, yes," I shook my head. "That's wonderful."

I tried to smile, but my face wouldn't comply with my wishes.

"I know it's not perfect, but we held them responsible for their actions," said Ferry.

Her hand pressed softly to my back and led me around the office.

The other partners shook my hand in congratulations, some shook Ferry's for setting a new precedence against the FBI; apparently a notch for their firm and Ferry's reputation.

In finality, I signed the requisite papers, acknowledging my settlement.

"What are you going to do with all the money?" asked Ferry, looking over at my silent daughter's face. "Will it go into Chaste's Trust Fund?"

I couldn't think, I still wanted to shove the sword deeper, yet this part of the battle was over. Once again, my unseen partner helped me with an amicable resolution.

"Split the award three ways; one third to your law firm, one third to you, one third to John Shoemaker's son."

Pitre was right. I wanted no part of it, not a cent; no reminder of their effects on my life. It was blood money.

Ferry took both my hands in hers, "That's…, John would be so proud, but I…, I can't accept that…," said Ferry.

"Then give it to St. Mary's School. Do with it what you will," I answered. "But if anyone has earned the money, it's you."

"Kress, don't let your emotions get the best of you," said Ferry. "You don't have to decide right this second."

I knew what I'd heard inside me and I had peace with it.

"That's my decision," I said, finally smiling. "Would you do Chaste and I the honor of joining us for dinner this evening? Now that your case load is lighter, I'd like to get to know Ferry Dunavin a little better."

"Can't think of anything I'd like better, Kress."

CHAPTER FIFTY-ONE

Chaste was excited beyond words when I suggested she stay with Ferry until our rendezvous later in the evening.

I dialed Brent and Carl to share the news of the FBI's acknowledgement of wrongdoing.

When Brent picked up the phone there was a horrible mass of noise in the background.

"Rand, who is this?" he asked brusquely.

"Dr. Schumacher, I wanted to…."

"Kress! I've been calling your number for two hours, your house almost burned down. Hold on a second…."

After a few moments, it was quieter.

"Sorry Kress, I didn't recognize the number. Your guests came back and triggered the alarm, which sent a message to my phone. When I got here, your asshole neighbors were standing around in the street watching your house catch fire. Everything in the back yard was in a blaze; the back deck was already catching, so I sprayed it down with your water hose. The fire department managed to contain it, they saved your home, but the entire back yard is charred bare."

"Are the boys alright? They weren't harmed this time were they?"

"This time? What do you mean this time? No they're fine. I put them in the garage as soon as the fire department got here."

I knew it was all too easy.

I could sign settlements all day long, but whoever this was didn't care about the law, or courtrooms, or lawsuits. All they were consumed with was my annihilation.

"Do you know who it was?"

"They shot out three of the cameras, but you remember how many we installed. It was a tactical team of six, all regulation black, masks, Kevlar vests, no way to ID any of them. They were driving a black SUV with a cover plate similar to the photos you saw at the inquest. Only one tried to get over the fence."

It was exactly as I'd expected, the cameras would only record our deaths by unknown assailants.

"The fence worked though; probably what saved your house. One of them tossed some camp fuel over the back and shot it. It was a real botched job. I got DNA; actually I got half a finger in a baggie on ice."

I wasn't excited. I'd seen what these types of men did with someone that could threaten their identities.

"Your fingerless man is probably dead in the bottom of the canyon beyond my house."

Brent was suddenly very quiet, "What makes you say that?"

"Something I learned from years living in the bush country. Hyenas always turn on their wounded," I gritted. "I'll be there in ten more minutes."

My only consolation was that in a few weeks this might actually all be over. Chaste and I might actually get to live a somewhat normal life…, somewhere.

Then there was Pitre to consider, what he was, what he was becoming; more importantly our attachment. It suddenly dawned on me why our home was never attacked while we were present.

Our enemies were now wholly terrified of Pitre. He was the one being, the one wildcard they should have never let get out of the bag after centuries upon centuries of torture and humiliation.

The proof was lying in tatters all around Ferry Dunavin's apartment. It was why the tall greys stood around the circumference of our property looking on wistfully. The only creature bold enough to actually enter our boundaries while we were there was the tall black creature, his realm and authority threatened.

Then I wondered if even that evil entity would have tried to enter the sanctity of our home had he known Pitre was awaiting him, even expecting him.

Against my better judgment, I called Ferry and filled her in on the latest development; asked her to wait until I called again before coming over. I needed to assess the situation before I could allow either of them on the premises.

She and I were still talking on the phone when I drove up to my home; her inquisitiveness knows no bounds. The front road was littered with emergency vehicles of all sorts and Brent met me at the curb as I ended my call with Ferry.

"Hey Kress."

His voice and sooty face was grim and he was looking at me strangely, "The County Sheriff has some questions for you."

"For me? I wasn't here when my home was torched."

Brent still had a queer gaze and it began to worry me.

"Brent, is there something else that I should know before I speak to the Sheriff? Do I need to call my lawyer?"

Once again, he thought before answering, "They brought out their canine squad. I found a blood trail after what you suggested to me; it looks like you might be right about the body in the canyon. I gotta tell you Kress, you're beginning to worry me."

Pitre had warned me about Brent and Carl's curiosity.

"I worry you more than the people that possibly killed my wife Elizabeth? More than the men that killed Thomas Whitefeather? Do I worry you more than the ones that are trying to kill my nine-year-old daughter and Ferry?"

At this point I couldn't care one spit about our friendship, especially if he turned his suspicions on us. Brent stared at me with his eyes blinking furiously for a moment or two.

"Of course not Kress. I'm not blind."

The Sheriff walked over slowly to where we were conversing, trying to listen in on our heated dilemma. His rotund stature didn't allow for stealth, but I had a feeling he wasn't a person to trifle with.

"Dr. Schumacher? Sheriff Al Gonzales."

He stuck out his weathered hand, then went straight to business.

"Close call on your home. You have some..., uh, charming neighbors. Good thing you have an alarm system or I think the whole place would have gone up in smoke."

He watched my expressions closely, but it wasn't the demonic stare I'd encountered with Agent Lily.

"I need to ask you about a few things. There's no question that this was arson, the fire marshal found a pierced container of accelerant in the yard and your friend Mr. Rand let me see the surveillance recording.

"You must have some idea of who did this. I saw your security system. It's better than the one we have at my office."

He hadn't actually posed a question and more than likely, he couldn't help me, but I didn't need any more inquisitive enemies.

I took my time and explained the ruling we received in Federal Court that morning; about the responsible parties. I told him as little as possible without violating my nondisclosure agreement, then watched his list of questions building until someone yelled from my back yard.

"We found a body!"

Brent ducked his head tiredly, shaking from side to side.

"You don't seem too surprised about this Dr. Schumacher."

"At this point Sheriff, nothing would surprise me."

"You could have warned me today you know? About everything."

The scorched back deck was getting sore on my posterior as I sat trying to force a conversation with my benefactor. The water and scorched earth scent was beginning to sour in the afternoon sun, making it all the more unpleasant.

"I didn't want to frighten you," whispered Pitre.

What had happened to the arrogant, evil, cunning, devious, and even petulant personality I was accustomed to?

"I've found that the more I try to answer all your questions and placate your needs the more conflicted you become."

Now I'm the one that's being difficult?

"I…, I was…, struck by lightning today you dolt."

"No, I shielded you and your family from it."

This was becoming tedious. I liked the chatty version of Pitre, the 'I know everything' version. This 'patient, kind, and understanding' version was driving me to madness.

"About that. How did you get your wings?"

"They were a gift."

There was more silence; I was determined to wait him out this time…, but that didn't work.

Blast it all.

"Well..., they're... magnificent, to say the least. Chaste was impressed as well. She told me as much."

Even the reference to Chaste, his weakness, didn't excite a response. Then it hit me.

"Is something bothering you?"

I thought he was going to ignore me once again or give me a single-syllabic response.

"Kress..., it's becoming more difficult for me to know pieces of future events and not want to change the outcome. There is an order to things, which cannot be altered. With greater power comes greater responsibility and now that my station has changed, I have to obey."

This didn't bode well.

"Are you trying to tell me something without disobeying some higher orders?"

I felt him relax inside me and he seemed pleased with himself, and me. I'd been right in my assumptions.

"Tonight we will work on the last list of children together. I enjoy watching the darkness give way to light. Thank you for your patience."

Before I could protest his plaintive scrupulous dismissal, he'd done that disappearing act to, according to him, somewhere deep inside me and I was left alone in silence.

Deep sadness made me ache at the implications I didn't want to address. Something I wouldn't like was going to happen. Something Pitre could not reveal or shield me from.

It was nearly dark when Ferry and Chaste arrived. I was mopping up the remains of melted ice cream from the back of my Rover, trying to be thankful that all the peering neighborhood spectators had retreated to their hiding places farther down the road.

"I talked to the Sheriff," said Ferry. "He seemed satisfied with what I told him."

Once again, I shoved my sticky washcloth into a bucket of warm water, tired of the whole subject.

I felt her arm wrap around my waist, "It can't last forever Kress. We'll beat this."

I gave her a quick kiss and thanked her for her optimism, then noted the glow about her.

Chaste leapt into the back of the Rover and began stacking the strewn groceries at the edge of the back door.

"You said there'd be ice cream in our future," she chuckled, looking at my mess. "Ew, yuck! Help me down please. No, not with your sticky hands."

She walked away carrying an armload of goods into the house, humming some tune playing inside her head. Ferry watched her until she was inside, then turned up her nose and winced at the stench of wet charred grass and stubs of ruined shrubbery.

"I can't remember many days I enjoyed more than today."

"I wish I could say the same," I grumbled.

She didn't know there'd been a bomb planted in her home; something I couldn't tell her. Pitre had his secrets and I had mine.

I looked up from my self-pity at her contagious smile.

"Chaste is such a handful. She's bright, she's quick on the draw; she's one of the few people that can blindside me with something totally unexpected. Are you sure she's only nine? I had the best time with her today."

I took my soap bucket to the edge of the drive and gave it a dash before I spoke, trying to see things from her perspective.

"Then I suppose you'll enjoy being her guardian for the next few years, should anything happen to me?"

Her smile turned a little plaintive, "If that's all I'm allowed, then yes, I'll enjoy every second of it."

This time I wasn't quite as stupid, at least I hoped not, even though I could hear what she was thinking clear as a bell inside my head.

"Ferry, there's something I've wanted to settle between us for several days now. You know how I feel about you; surely you must by now? Blast it all. Why is this so difficult? I don't want you to think I'm rushing things along...."

Ferry's smile returned, "One thing at a time."

"Ferry, I'm not afraid of commitment to you. It's just that I can't bear the thought of making promises and then something happening to me. Such as what happened to John Shoemaker."

"None of us are promised tomorrow Kress," she smiled. "Wasn't it you that just told me we were going to live our lives?"

How frustrating. Especially after Pitre's odd warning. Here I was trying to bare my soul and she turns my own words against me.

"I love you too, Kress; and your little girl. If something was going to happen to you, don't you think it already would have? Kress. You were struck by lightning today and you're still here. Don't you think that's a sign?"

Well, not actually struck according to Pitre; all I'd seen was the familiar flash..., then my mind went awry.

It seemed to be heat lightning. It was a bolt from the blue, but this one instigated by an angel. How many similar exhibitions of electricity had I seen in my lifetime? Hundreds? Thousands? It was a common occurrence in the Kalahari Desert regions south of our clinic. Was that some battle raging between good and evil? Some unseen confrontation similar to what occurred today?

Something about that seemed to fit, like a piece of a puzzle I'd worked as a child.

Obviously, some things could be changed, or I'd not been able to save Chaste from a horrible future. According to Pitre, some pieces were preset into position, immovable icons, directing future events so that the 'big picture' wasn't altered. Well, no matter; if an angel couldn't alter it, who was I?

Ferry was right, today was a good day and I could certainly enjoy what was left of it.

"Kress? Do I need to take you to the doctor?"

Ferry was holding my cheeks with her open palms, testing me.

"Are you okay?"

I smiled and scooped Ferry up in my arms, "Better than I have been in years. Let's go make some dinner, shall we?"

CHAPTER FIFTY-TWO

"Yes, of course I understand. We'll be perfectly fine and thank you again for rescuing our home."

The telephone went dead and I stared at it; seems I'll never get used to the lack of a simple goodbye.

I now had a list of telephone numbers at the ready for any emergency imaginable, thanks to Brent and Carl as well as the County Sheriff.

"No more phone calls."

My daughter was giving me a stern look to make sure I agreed. So far the evening had been wonderful. The only part that was difficult for me was pushing away my heart's desires for Ferry.

"No more phone calls," I agreed.

Chaste looked back down and rolled the dice to some horrid little board game bent on revenge, which she and Ferry had picked up earlier in the day.

She gleefully tapped her game-piece across the board and sent my only survivor back to Start.

"Chaste, if you keep doing that your father is going to make up some excuse to work."

Chaste glared at Ferry, then at me, "You wouldn't be a sore loser would you?"

"The game isn't over yet," I grumbled.

"I'm afraid it is for you Kress. You don't have the killer instinct Chaste and I do."

Ferry rolled the dice and moved another game piece into her

Home. There were smug giggles between them, which I enjoyed far more than winning the board game or some jackpot at a casino.

They made a marvelous pair. I was so very happy at all the decisions leading up to Ferry Dunavin. I saw a bright future..., between them.

"Are you going to play?"

Both ladies fought to hand me the dice. I rolled and let my subconscious play out my last few turns while my mind searched the possibilities of Pitre's warning. It didn't take a bloody genius to figure out the implications.

I was certain my personal timetable was moved up now. I needed to press Mr. Jernigan at the American Consulate for help at our meeting this week. The private jet was chartered for Thursday morning to Washington D.C. and our bags were packed. Phone calls, I needed to make phone calls; especially to the European Medical Association. If only these blasted attacks would stop and give me a moment to plan like a normal human being. I chuckled to myself; I'm not a normal human being, not any longer.

Never would I have believed I'd be thankful that Pitre had turned on the awful gift of eavesdropping on others thoughts. Admittedly, I still hated it and left it turned off most of the time. I felt that pull once again to get busy, to get my ducks all in a row.

My angst dissolved when I remembered the list of missing children I'd yet to negotiate with Pitre later tonight, the ones we'd save alive.

Chirps of laughter brought me back to focus.

Chaste had won, with Ferry's one remaining pawn sitting on the brink, while three of my four pieces were still seated inside the Start. Killer instinct indeed.

Apparently, they thought it all brilliant, which was good enough for me.

"Who wants ice cream?"

I groaned, "It all melted today when...."

Ferry's eyes sparkled at some other victory, "Relax, Chaste and I bought lots of ice cream."

We raced like children into the kitchen and began scraping out assorted flavors of Ben and Jerry's into coffee mugs.

Unfortunately, I let the deluge in my mind slip out.

"Ferry, did you ever receive a notice from the EMA as to when

I'd get confirmation of my Diplomatic status?"

She mumbled and pulled the spoon out of her mouth.

"So that's where your mind's been all night. You missed out on a really fun game with your daughter and I."

I think she was trying to scold me; duly noted.

"It came days ago. We had to submit a copy with the lawsuit we filed…, remember the case we just won by default?"

She grinned, instantly hiding yet another spoonful of homemade vanilla.

"Good. I need to carry a copy with us Thursday, that's all."

"Any more questions…?"

This was a trick question; cheese set on a mousetrap, so I shook my head no and took a bite from my cup.

"Good, because we rented movies and you have to watch them with us."

She must have seen my face twitch even though I was smiling.

"Kress, you can spend this evening worrying, or you can spend it happy, with me…, and your daughter, like you promised."

I felt a physical kick in my belly from the inside. Was this a remnant of the old Pitre having his last say at me?

"What are we watching?"

"Chick flick and an action movie."

"Do I get more ice cream?" I asked.

"As much as you want…."

I heard her distinctly call me a *'little pig'* in her thoughts before she winked at me. How did she know I was listening? I'll never understand the female of our species.

We piled on the couch together underneath a heavy blanket and watched adolescent sparkling vampires cavort with pony-sized werewolves for nearly two hours. Near the end of the movie, I felt Ferry's weight shift even closer against me and noted that she was fast asleep. Chaste had her head in Ferry's lap, asleep as well.

I slipped away after stuffing a pillow under Ferry's head, but they looked so uncomfortable stacked together on the sofa.

I fed *the boys* and made a quick jaunt around the perimeter of the house in the crisp cold Arizona night air with both of them walking lazily by my side. There were no unwanted visitors tonight and the world almost seemed normal.

I wanted to go for a run in the clean air, something reminiscent of my time spent with Thomas, then decided against it. Pitre had made it very clear that the single-most important question I now harbored was off limits, which in retrospect was a good thing. I wanted to be alone with my thoughts, something as foreign to me as a passing comet now that Pitre was in residence.

My nervous energy drove me back inside and I looked at the food still on the table. I scraped and rinsed, idly wondering about my future, most notably, how much I had left. My heart sank when I thought of how I'd allowed Ferry into my inner sanctum, at the damage I might do when I left her alone, with the continual reminder of my daughter in her care. If I truly loved her, could I continue on without drawing Ferry in deeper still?

With the dishwasher stuffed and humming, I walked back to where the ladies were, still together, stuffed and stacked on the sofa.

I stood there for a few moments watching their peaceful rest.

Torn between hurrying to my office or doing the right thing, I carried Chaste upstairs to her bed.

When had she grown so long? Her slim body was still feather light in my arms. How many more nights would I get to tuck the covers around my daughter? I fought away the ache in my chest and hurried back downstairs.

Ferry was still there in some god-awful position…, so the decision was easy. I carried her to her bedroom just down the front hall and stretched the comforter over her.

"Kress?"

"Yes?"

"Thank you…, that was a first," she mumbled.

Her hand slipped behind my neck and kissed me goodnight.

I heard her thoughts drift away after, *"…love you Mr. Schumacher."*

How could I give in to this wonderful woman with my own life dangling in the balance? The answer wasn't easy; I couldn't. If only by proxy, Pitre had made that decision very clear.

I was minutes away from retiring for the night when Pitre gave me a gentle nudge. I hadn't forgotten the necessity of our planned rendezvous, but he'd been so quiet and removed since the evening meal.

It was actually good to have Pitre seated and present in the privacy of my office, even if I did have to keep my vision directed away to aid my concentration. In no time we'd gone over the details to each and every name listed in my planner.

"You have to make the phone calls first thing in the morning to each of these Kress. We only have one opportunity or we lose them all. Our adversary will dispose of them if we don't, do you understand?"

"Then I'll call them tonight," I mumbled, scratching down another note for in the morning. "These people wouldn't care if I called them at 3 a.m."

"Kress, it is 3 a.m. Six o'clock will be perfect timing. None of these abductions are connected with each other directly, none were photographed or cataloged the same way as your first group. The boy named Steven has already been moved to an estate in Brazil, working as a house servant. He'll be the one most at risk."

I had so many questions, both selfish and unselfish.

"Pitre, why can't you take me there and we'll bring him back together?"

He shook his big bright head slowly, *"Haven't you noticed that it's only you I can transport from place to place? We are as one; I am tethered to you now. Remember, I severed my old ties with the earthbound creature when I merged with you. I am limited not by power, but by my..., leash to you and by authority. You are my highest priority now."*

It seemed like doubletalk. I tried to devise some loophole in my mind, to circumvent the unknown rules in Pitre's playbook.

"Kress, please. The boy must be found where he is before his captors can be stopped from taking another. In this world, as long as there is a demand for something, there will always be someone that will try to supply that demand."

I fought with that but it was the simplest rule of commerce. I wanted to ask my next question..., but I was afraid of the answer. I wanted to know if I should say goodbye to Chaste, but how cruel would that be? It would be like leaving a suicide note far in advance. I'd have to live through explaining to my daughter's weeping eyes why events happened this way, even though both our lives had been spared numerous times only recently.

"No more questions. You must sleep at least an hour for me to rejuvenate your strength and I have my own business to attend to inside you."

There it was again. Some secretive eventuality I wasn't privy to even though I was host and recipient.

"One more item I am permitted to tell you."

He stood and stretched out his hand, *"There will be more opposition, but you must not fear."*

I felt my arm reach out to take his hand as he disappeared.

Mere moments later, my alarm clock began to chime.

Blast it all. Why couldn't Pitre warn me when he was going to do something off the scale?

I sat up in bed, brushed away the crust from my eyes, and flipped on the light. True to his word, I was refreshed and ready to take care of the new day's business as if I'd had a full night's rest.

I had many phone calls to make. The first sixteen of which would be most difficult. The most terrifying part was that unknown factor, how the thread would play out when the time came. Pitre had never been this secretive to me about how events would unravel. His final word to me was one of mutual trust.

The bedcovers fell away and I looked down at myself. I was in my pajamas. Yes, well…, we were certainly going to have a talk about this.

There wasn't time to dress properly, so I hurried through my morning ritual and rushed downstairs to my office.

It was time for me to take my own advice, so I took the time to say a prayer before I made the first call.

"Hello my name is Dr. Schumacher. I was given your number to help you find your missing child."

The voice on the line spilled out a desperation I'd heard in my own voice months ago. It was the same pleadings I'd heard time and time again in our clinic by a desperate parent over their sick or injured child. Whatever it cost me, this was worth the price.

The parents and grandparents, aunts and uncles on this list were frantic, after hearing that Thomas Whitefeather, the man they'd made a deposit to, had been killed in a skirmish with the FBI. They'd given up all hopes of ever being contacted or receiving the help they were promised. I had no problem convincing any of them to keep our relationship as mute as possible.

Pitre offered me no hint of their locations or how they would be rescued, but the call was still necessary to build each of the family's hopes.

The last on the list was the hardest for me to understand, it was the boy Steven; no last name.   There was no phone number referenced except the one to Thomas Whitefeather himself. I grieved over the boy as if he were my own son. Partially because it reminded me of my time spent with 'Charles, Chuck, Thomas' and his own lost child with the same name. The evil that invaded him, that drove him to becoming the man that I first met, still haunted me. I still didn't know how each of these people had known to contact Thomas…, unless he contacted them. In any case, he was gone now, silenced as a traitor in some vile army.

That feeling of regret over Steven crept in once again.

One of the reasons for my trip to the American Consulate, Mr. Jernigan was to petition for help to get the boy returned. It would be no less of a miracle than the other children. I had not the first clue how to explain myself or how I knew of the young man's general whereabouts; only that I was to speak to Arthur Jernigan in absolute privacy.

"Are you through?" whispered a voice from behind me.

My heart leapt cartwheels in my chest. Ferry Dunavin had been sitting in my only other comfortable chair in the dark corner of my office; listening…, for how long?

"There is no mystery informant is there Kress?"

I shook my head, "I suppose not, not anymore."

Had I spoken something out of turn? Had I mentioned Pitre in idle question? My one dire secret I could never share with Ferry for fear of the consequences.

"How long have you been listening?"

She yawned and stretched, "About an hour. Chaste is still asleep."

I focused to listen to her thoughts, to turn on my radar as Ferry liked to refer to it.

Good, she wasn't concerned with….

"Kress, how much longer are you going to keep this up? Until someone with more money that God hires the right people to kill you and your little girl?"

It hurt listening her heart ache.

"This is my last group of children to help, you'll understand everything very soon Ferry. Please don't hate me for my passion. I couldn't bear it."

She nodded, "Your last…."

I watched her get up slowly.

"No Kress..., I don't hate you. How can I when you barely let me in?"

She silently walked out of my office and closed the door.

Her thoughts slipped away as if a whisper, '*I hoped he was the one*', about some vague cherished childhood memory.

If I ran after her, if I bared my soul about Pitre..., she would surely believe me mad. We were forbidden to mention him and with good reason. My only choice now was to keep my silence and allow her heart to break.

CHAPTER FIFTY-THREE

"I'll have everything you asked for ready to go first thing in the morning."

Ferry hadn't eaten a bite at breakfast, but after her brief announcement, she sat dully brooding over her cup of coffee.

I'd turned off her thoughts; afraid I'd hear something that would sway me from my final duty. Too many lives, too many futures were at stake.

"The movie was great last night. Sorry I fell asleep. Maybe we can watch the rest tonight?"

Chaste took another sip of orange juice sensing that something in the atmosphere was growing stale.

"I finished this month's lessons. I'll need some help to check my answers before we send it all in today."

"I'll go over it today and send it in," I sighed, then immediately regretted my attitude.

"Ferry usually goes over my answers…, with me…, in case I have any questions."

Ferry only glanced back out at the scorched steps of the deck in silence, ignoring the building vehemence in my daughter's expression.

Where was Pitre when I needed him? My internal companion was peacefully silent somewhere inside me on his 'mission' of our fates.

"Ferry, can I come with you today? I promise I'll work on this week's lessons and I won't be a bother. I'll be as quiet as a mouse."

I saw a sparkle of life rekindle in Ferry's eyes, then she glanced my direction, I believed for approval of my daughter's request.

"Did I tell you Carl called me?"

Blazes; knocked me off my game yet again, "No. Something that I should know?"

She'd ignored Chaste's plea to join her. She must have been pushing chess pieces around in her mind for a good part of the morning and decided to move the first pawn.

"The Glock you gave him was issued from a U.S. Government arsenal in D.C. a year ago. Interesting how that's where we're planning to go for the weekend."

She left that chess piece pushed forward and sipped on her lukewarm coffee, waiting.

"We already supposed who it belonged to, didn't we?"

She nodded, a slight smile.

Blast, I'd taken the cheese; the arm on the mousetrap was about to fall. I stabbed another bite of French toast with my fork, shoved it in my mouth and prepared to take it like a man.

"It belonged to a protection detail assigned to an unknown State Department official. Carl said that he used up every favor he had to get that much information."

The imaginary trap slapped down over my neck as I tried to swallow my bite. Now my suspicions were confirmed; I needed to divert Ferry from the danger she was unknowingly asking for.

"Carl couldn't discover who the official was?"

She shook her head, "More smoke and mirrors."

That was at the very least some good news. I prayed that Ferry wouldn't go charging off pellmell to clear smoke and break mirrors as was her usual tenor. Finesse wasn't her forte when it came to garnering information.

Chaste was looking between Ferry and I, watching some dark battle she didn't understand as Ferry tucked her head back to her cup in more silence, staring out the window into the ruined expanse of our back yard.

Ferry wanted to argue her point she'd begun in my office early this morning, still seething with anger that I hadn't given her every last iota of private details. She saw it as a breach of trust; I saw it as protecting her very life.

My chest breathed in the swell of a breath that was Pitre and he spoke clearly in my head, but not to me.

"Chaste?"

My daughter looked up at me and her horrid frown slid away as she heard our angel's voice.

"Remember how you helped me with Ferry before? Would you do it for me one more time? All you have to do is go to your room and get all your things together and wait for Ferry to come get you to go with her today."

Chaste looked up at me and smiled, then took off in a flash from the breakfast nook, her footsteps pattering quickly toward the stairs.

Ferry turned her head, listening, then heard the bedroom door close upstairs.

"What the... *hell*..., are you trying to prove Kress?"

Her empty coffee cup fumbled from her fingers and rolled off the table to the floor with a loud bounce.

"Do you have some death wish? You..., you..., you don't make any sense at all."

She stood up, wringing her hands, looking away from me.

Ferry was mostly correct, I didn't make sense, but I didn't have a death wish. I had no defense other than keeping her safe and if there's one thing I'd learned in my forty-four years; never argue a woman when she's right.

"Well I've thought it over Kress, more than once now. If this means so much to you, more than your own life, more than Chaste, more..., more than..., me..., us, then it must be important enough for me to join with you to the end. As much as I disagree with you, I can't keep fighting against you. There's enough confusion without you and me at each other's throats."

I sat dumbfounded, stupid with nullified assumptions.

"If the ship sinks..., God help me, I'm on board with you."

My body moved her direction in an immediate response; extremely grateful that Chaste was in her bedroom.

It's difficult to kiss a crying woman, but somehow we managed. If I was given leave of this world, I'd leave it a man loved by a beautiful woman.

The sky was a glistening cerulean abyss and cloudless over Phoenix Thursday morning. I scanned every direction, expecting a gathering of tall greys pointing our direction. There were no enemy stanchions in sight, not even a lone scout anywhere to be seen. Why didn't I feel relieved?

"Are you waiting for someone else?"

The voice behind me was the pilot, standing at the top steps of the entry galley, his eyes following my field of vision.

"Is it time?" I asked. "We're the only passengers."

He looked at his wristwatch, "Then we're ready when you are."

Ferry was seated comfortably in one of the plush leather seats in the center of the private jet, fumbling nervously through her attaché.

Chaste had chosen her preference of a window lounge seat, busy taking photo's out the portal with her iPhone.

"Did you forget something?"

"I..., don't think so," Ferry mumbled as she flipped through another enclosure.

The co-pilot slammed and locked the galley door and Ferry chirped and looked up his direction.

He smiled at us and pressed a button and the Seat Belt sign lit up.

"Are you alright? If you've forgotten something, now is the time to say something. Our schedule isn't so firm...."

"No. I didn't forget anything," she said hurriedly.

She latched the cover quickly, slid the leather pouch underneath her seat, and sat up stiffly looking around at Chaste just as some unseen orifice began to hiss, pressurizing the cabin.

She snapped back to me and patted my hand, "Would you mind getting me something to drink?"

The engines rose to a high whining pitch and the plane shuddered and inched forward. Ferry snapped her seat belt and stared straight ahead.

"Ferry, why didn't you tell me you were afraid of flying?"

She didn't break her stare to look my direction.

"Because I'm not."

"Now who's not being truthful?"

"Well, I'm not normally, not with a 747. It's these little planes, you feel every tiny gust of wind, like you're some piece of paper being tossed around with the breeze. I hate little planes."

"You've never flown in a private jet before?"

"In a little Cessna, once, years ago. I hated it."

I smiled and held her hand, "This isn't a turbo prop, it's a jet. There's a world of difference. Let me get you a soft drink to settle your stomach."

Ferry looked back over at Chaste still casually taking pictures as I hurried past the short row of empty seats to the food galley, ignoring the Seat Belt warning. We began to taxi and the voice of the Pilot clicked on inside the cabin with our itinerary.

I sat down just in time before the full force of our taxi onto the airstrip. Elizabeth had hated flying as well, but all our experiences were with bush pilots landing on hellish dirt runways in remote little villages. This was a far cry from a modified crop-duster.

Ferry took a long gulp of clear soda and screwed the lid back on, resuming her white knuckled grip on the armrests.

"How does she do that?" hissed Ferry.

I looked over at Chaste, her face glued to the blur of scenery passing by the window.

"When you're nine years old, everything is an adventure. You don't have time to be afraid how deep the water is."

She leaned over my direction to rest her head against my arm.

"You always seem to know how to calm me down, even if you are wrong."

She quickly smiled and pecked me a kiss moments before the engines whined to full speed and we shot up into the sky.

I will admit it was an uneasy feeling, pinned to the back of the seat as the plane rose at what seemed to be at a 45-degree angle.

When we leveled off Ferry exhaled a loud sigh of relief, ready to talk and get her mind off our altitude.

"Are you going to tell me what our meeting is about before we arrive at the Consulate's office? I hate walking into meetings unprepared."

Ferry was doing an excellent job hiding her inward turmoil; I supposed controlling her emotions was an asset in her trade.

"We'll be speaking to Arthur Jernigan, the gentleman which tailored my family's transition to the United States. He's one of the few people I trust that knows every nuance of why we left South Africa."

"I know who we're going to meet Kress, why can't you give me some particulars?"

She was already hiding pent-up fright; I couldn't afford to throw another emotion into the mix.

"For two reasons, the first is to plead with him to help with a boy named Steven. He's an orphaned fourteen-year-old boy, which was stolen when he was twelve. He is now living in forced servitude in Brazil. Some tyrant using him as slave labor."

I felt her hand quiver and suddenly remembered that Ferry was raised an orphan at St. Mary's School for Girls.

"Steven..., that isn't the same Steven mentioned in the U.S. Marshal's Investigator brief I read? The Steven you looked for in Mexico?"

"Very likely and before you ask, I don't know his last name."

She slid her head back against the seat, staring at the ceiling.

"That's going to be like looking for a needle in a haystack, Kress."

"Not really..., I have his location in Sao Paulo. They won't be expecting anyone to come asking for him."

Surprisingly, she didn't ask how and where I'd acquired the address of Steven's current whereabouts. Another refreshing attribute of the abstract thinking process inside Ferry's mind.

"And the second reason we're meeting?"

I pulled her closest hand from its torrid grip on the armrest and held it in my own.

"And the other reason I have sworn not to reveal, even to the air that surrounds us, until I'm in his private office with no other witnesses to our conversation than our small group."

She nodded, even though I knew she didn't agree with me.

"There's no one else here but us Kress," she whispered, barely above the hum of the jet engines, hinting for me to give her a tiny ingress.

I'd come to expect the tenacious nature of one Ferry Dunavin, even see its charm.

"Ferry Dunavin, I've learned to appreciate all aspects of your personality, even the ones that drive me insane. If you'll be patient, in a couple hours you'll know everything that I know."

She frowned for an instant, then stretched over to kiss my cheek.

"Fine."

CHAPTER FIFTY-FOUR

An hour had passed and both Chaste and Ferry were dozing to the hum of the aircraft. Chaste was lying flat on the window lounge seat, her latest novel of choice still dangling between her loose fingertips.

Ferry had created a warm niche against me, drifting in and out, her terrors pushed far away.

I sat in silence, rehearsing my plea for the one child on my final list of the missing with no parent or advocate to come forth and save him.

I heard a familiar click followed by the muted voice of the pilot.

"I trust you've enjoyed the flight so far. We've just been informed of an approaching storm front over the Mississippi valley. I'll be turning the Seat Belt sign back on in a few minutes, so expect a little delay and some turbulence while we plot a course around the thick of this mess. I'll let you know when you can unbuckle again."

Ferry sat up and I could tell she wanted to rail a list of - I told you so's - but was too frightened to do anything but cast an envious glance over at Chaste, still fast asleep.

"I'd better go buckle her in one of the center isle seats so she doesn't roll off onto the floor. Want something else to drink?"

Ferry shook her head then transferred her sudden grip of my hand back to the armrest.

Chaste smiled at me when she woke, then stuffed her things into one of the compartments.

"I'll sit beside Ferry," she whispered. "Maybe that'll help."

I took the seat directly in front of Ferry and Chaste, nearer the front galley just as the Seat Belt sign came on. Chaste was already chattering in Ferry's ear about the characters in her latest novel as I tried to relax.

Outside the window there were towering puffy clouds glowing brightly in the distance, flashing darts of lightening as they boiled upward into the atmosphere. Soon the morning sun was obliterated, with only gray darkness filtering in through each of the small portals on either side of the cabin.

Nothing seemed unusual other than the fact that our chartered Gulfstream was flying at nearly forty-one thousand feet; normally far above the caps of even the most active thunderstorms.

A flash of thunder-less lightning flared through the bank of windows on our port side, then there was the slightest shiver of the aircraft as we began a gentle turn toward the starboard side.

There was the click once again, another announcement.

"Attention all passengers. Please remember to observe the Seat Belt warning. We'll be making some small adjustments in our course to avoid the brunt of this storm. Please try to remain seated and relaxed. Remember, in the event of an emergency the oxygen masks will deploy automatically. We'll be past this momentarily. Thank you."

Chaste resumed her conversation with Ferry at her point of interruption as I sat back in my seat.

There was another flash, this time with an instant report of thunder and I heard both ladies behind me chirp.

I knew this was normal, but it was time to dredge Pitre from his solitude for other reasons.

I called out inside me, but was interrupted by another flash of light and an abnormal whine of the jet engines, just before we were thrust upward a few feet in altitude. Evidently we'd passed over a rising wind-shear boiling up from beneath us.

"Kress?"

"Dad?"

I spun in my seat to see two pairs of round eyes glaring at me for consolation.

"Try and relax, we'll be past it soon."

I heard myself finish the sentence to myself as I turned back around, "I hope."

Pitre's reassuring presence filled my mind and settled me in my seat.

"Kress, Remember the opposition we spoke of?"

I nodded my head like a dolt to answer Pitre.

"Our new adversary has certain 'legal rights' when it comes to the air surrounding us. Don't worry, we can also rightfully resist."

"Are you telling me we are under attack?" I whispered.

Another flash of light filled the cabin and the plane jilted both left and right in a horrid shutter. I suppose that was the answer to my inane question. Both passengers behind me seemed too afraid to make a sound, then I heard Ferry uttering a prayer into the increasing din of howling turbulence.

"Be ready to do what I tell you exactly when I tell you."

That didn't bode well.

"Pitre, I'm strapped in a seat so that I don't bounce off the walls. What could I possibly do?"

"Kress, do you see the two handholds on either side of the door in front of you?"

There were two shoulder-high stainless steel grips on either side of the doorway leading inside the forward galley hallway. I nodded, hoping that he wasn't going to suggest something stupid.

"In a few moments you'll need to go to them and grip both with your hands."

I shook my head vigorously, "I won't make it three feet."

"Kress, do you want to save those you love seated right behind you?"

There was another flash of light and the cabin went dark. Suddenly, I noticed that both the turbine engines whine began winding down, not a good sign. In another instant, we began to plummet like a rock. I watched my suit jacket slide across the ceiling above my head, followed by Ferry's attaché.

"Now. Go."

I heard Pitre, and I wanted to obey, but I couldn't seem to get my hands to release their grip from the armrests.

I heard a loud click and my seatbelt loosed itself. I felt as if I were a young bird being kicked from its nest for its first flight. I lifted, almost floating from my seat and pulled myself along the two rows of seats in front of me, my legs flailing aimlessly in the dark.

I felt myself launch from the front seat, sailing through midair, and was suddenly gripping the two shiny supports on either side of the galley.

It was then I heard the shrills of Ferry and Chaste from somewhere in the distance.

"Hold on tight."

I didn't have it in me to argue with Pitre. I gripped my only supports for dear life.

There was a brilliant light around the outside of the aircraft, glowing in through the windows, spearing the black void inside. It felt as if an electric current were jolting through me; I couldn't have released the two metal grips if I'd tried.

I heard the two engines whine back to life, past the crackling in both my ears and slowly my feet settled back to the floor. The light outside dissipated, just as the interior lights flickered back on.

Both Ferry and Chaste were staring at me as if I was a ghost; through rows of dangling yellow oxygen masks swaying every which direction from the ceiling. I smiled at them as best I could.

The loudspeaker clicked once.

"We momentarily lost power."

The pilot's voice was stressed and he had to begin again.

"We…, we lost power, but we're past the worst of it."

There was another blinding light, but it was the sun as we breached the darkness of the stacks of thunderheads behind us.

"We just entered Virginia airspace and should be landing in about forty minutes."

"Did you see that?" hissed a voice, then the intercom went silent.

Moments later the Seat Belt sign went off and I staggered to pick up Ferry's leather case from the floor in the center aisle. My hands were scorched and tender, forcing me to make several efforts to lift its handle by my fingertips.

"What did you do?" hissed Ferry. "What did you do? I saw you do something up there at the front of the cabin. Show me your hands Kress."

I stuffed her attaché back underneath her seat in silence. After refusing to reveal my secret and since I didn't have my usual glib answer for her, I walked about the small cabin in search of my errant jacket. It was dangling and strangled by clear plastic tentacles of tubing at the rear of the cabin amongst an obscene garden of twisted oxygen masks.

Ferry's voice cracked, "I'm not flying home…, not in this."

I sat down in a seat behind them trying to clear the buzzing in my ears.

My daughter leaned across to Ferry who quickly wrapped her arms around Chaste.

"That was terrifying..., you barely made a peep."

Ferry kissed the top of her head and hugged her close once again.

"Weren't you scared?"

"No..., not terribly."

"You're kidding. I'm still swallowing my stomach."

Ferry looked over her shoulder at me once again.

"What is it with you two? Am I the only one blessed with sense enough to be scared?"

Ferry was about to withdraw into her shell of cogitation, but she hadn't planned on Chaste.

"Don't you believe in angels?"

Ferry's head snapped my direction over the back of her seat and back to Chaste. I could feel the painful furrows that suddenly appeared on her forehead, in her heart.

"I..., of course I do, I suppose. At least I did..., once upon a time."

"I heard you pray, surely you believe something."

Ferry ducked her head below my field of vision and I could barely overhear their mumbles, even though her thoughts couldn't escape me.

"When I was a very little girl, much younger than you, I thought I saw an angel."

Chaste turned excitedly, "Did you? Tell me, please?"

"Well..., I remember being really sad over something that happened that day."

"And?"

"I'd almost cried myself to sleep when I saw this person, glowing and white, standing beside my bed."

Ferry had been overlooked once again by prospective parents visiting St. Mary's orphanage. They'd interviewed Ferry and decided on a younger child to adopt. I couldn't believe she was baring this much to Chaste. Near death experiences do tend to loosen someone's constraints.

"He told me that one day a shoemaker would come and change my life completely. Later, I thought I dreamed it or made it all up because of the stories we were reading at the time."

"What a wonderful story..., a shoemaker?" asked Chaste. "It's almost like a fairy tale."

"We can talk about it later, okay sweetie? I'd like to give that some more thought."

I heard and felt Chaste wilt inside, pleading with me to let her tell Ferry about her experience with Pitre, though she didn't turn to face me.

Even a whitewashed version would be too close to exposing the truth we were bound to keep. I too wanted to bare that truth with Ferry, despite the gentle warning rising up inside me.

CHAPTER FIFTY-FIVE

The limousine ride to downtown Washington D.C. was at first riddled with unanswerable questions. Chaste was unusually quiet through Ferry's barrage, but she didn't seem overtly frazzled by our near miss at another stroke of the grim reapers blade. Ferry gave up her quest much sooner than expected and tried to make small talk with Chaste for a short while.

My hands were still a little numb, but didn't show any physical signs of being some sort of electrical superconductor for Pitre to jumpstart the huge twin turbine engines on the aircraft.

At least we were alive, which is what I stressed to Ferry. Now she was seated in silence as our driver navigated the miserable downtown traffic of Washington D.C.

"Will we meet the president?"

"No sweetheart, I doubt as we'll even get a glimpse of him. I'll make sure you get to take some pictures of the Capital Building. Would you like that?"

Chaste nodded reluctantly just as our driver swerved into another lane of traffic, nudging her against Ferry. She seemed to jostle free from some internal private conversation and wrapped an arm around my daughters' slim shoulders.

"Thank you Chaste."

"You're quite welcome. That's what friends are for."

What an odd discourse. Now my curiosity was peaked and for just a moment, I wished I'd been eavesdropping on Ferry's private thoughts.

The privacy divider slid down slowly and the driver announced our arrival. I felt my stomach knot, worried that I'd make a muddle of everything I needed to say; reassured only by the fact we'd made it thus far and were still breathing.

"Please, stay inside the limousine until I have a look-see around us."

For once Ferry didn't ask why, but sat patiently holding my daughters hand.

I hurried out and shut the door. My eyes scanned every direction, expecting to see hordes of tall greys *en masse* pointing our direction. There were none.

"Pitre, where are they hiding?" I whispered.

"You're only allowed to see the ones assigned to you. Otherwise, it would not be a pleasant sight."

"But we're here."

"We put up a strong resistance and they were forced to flee."

"Sir? Is this the right address?"

The driver was suddenly standing beside me. He was looking at me strangely, probably wondering why I was standing there spinning around and talking to myself.

"Will the ladies be joining you?"

I opened the door, "Yes, I was…, just making sure I'd given you the right address."

The wary look on Ferry's expression was palpable as she took my hand and slid from the vehicle.

We walked up several flights of bleached white steps while considering the unknown facing us once inside. A young lady, I assume a secretary, announced us and escorted us down the main hallway at precisely eleven a.m.

The door poured open and a short squat fellow emerged with a crown of closely cropped gray hair that glowed against his coffee brown skin.

"Dr. Schumacher! It's such a pleasure to see you again. Please come in."

As soon as the door closed, I tried to hurry though the cordialities.

"Mr. Jernigan, I'd like you to meet my very good friend and attorney, Ms. Ferry Dunavin."

"It's a pleasure to meet you Ms. Dunavin, and how are you doing young lady?"

Chaste blushed, "Very well thank you."

"Please everyone take a seat, I have another meeting in an hour and I know you want to make the most of our time together.

"Mr. Jernigan...."

"Arthur."

"Arthur..., I'm..., not sure I'll be able to convey everything I need in an hour, but let me start with my first concern. You know of course about Chaste and our previous circumstances?"

"Yes, I was recently made aware of the most recent details. But, please don't be concerned about that. I like to keep up with such things when it concerns families I've helped. I trust you're getting settled in? You are past the personal attacks?"

"Actually, no, not really, but that's not why we're here."

He leaned forward and laced his fingers in somewhat of a fatherly expression of concern.

"There is a young man who goes by the name of Steven...."

As quickly as possible, I reiterated the barest of necessary information, leading to the location where Steven was being contained as forced labor in Sao Paolo, Brazil.

"Kress, as you probably already know, my office doesn't have any direct jurisdiction in such circumstances. However, given your recent past experiences and your daughter's involvement, I'll turn this over to Xavier Contrata in the State Department. We do have an excellent relationship with the Brazilian heads of state as well as an extradition treaty with that region. That's more tuned to Mr. Contrata's office. I don't suppose you know the name of the boy's assigned caseworker here in the U. S. or the names of his currently assigned caregivers?"

I shook my head in a panic.

"Mr. Contrata should be able to open a line of communication and I'll attach one of my staff members to the project to follow the progress. It's the best I can do with the sketchy information you've given me."

Immediately, I felt the crushing blow at the mention of the name, Xavier Contrata. The lies I'd been told, the evil.... For yet another time, I was ever so thankful for an internal source of peace to control certain emotions. If Contrata was involved in the multiple abductions, this could possibly help serve to expose his activities. It would definitely serve as a distraction to my next final mission.

Mr. Jernigan finished making some notes and looked up at me from above his reading glasses, "You said that was one of your concerns?"

I looked at Ferry and nodded as she hurriedly folded a new page on her notepad in personal anticipation of my secrets.

"I need to explain some things to you in confidence. I'd rather that no one outside of your office know of my plans."

I let that settle and waited for him to at least nod his ascent before I continued.

"I've recently been on the telephone with several council members of the European Medical Association. I've convinced the EMA to allow me to make a sizable donation through their organization, to a South African group known as U.S.A. Unify South Africa is an organized effort of local leaders attempting to bring an end to bloodshed and intertribal differences. Their financial resources have recently ceased due to personal attacks against the families that were their regular donors. Several of which are in this country, myself included.

I suppose you know my wife and I lived through the last brutal years of Apartheid...; we saw the damage of political unrest first hand. Our humanitarian efforts were intended to be directed toward the native children of the region. Then, about the middle of our second year, it became widespread that we had surgical facilities. It was frustrating to see our medical clinic turned into a triage for wounded dissidents. Especially when we spent days or even weeks helping a group of patients only to hear that they were killed a few weeks later."

Ferry handed Arthur Jernigan three different various journals published by the EMA depicting Elizabeth with multiple victims of war; not a pleasant sight.

"As such, I intend to make the donation in honor of Elizabeth's eighteen years of sacrifice as a diplomatic icon. I'm sure it would mean a lot to her to see that our years together in service weren't wasted. Also, I intend to make the offering on what would have been the anniversary of our twentieth year of commitment. The exact date if possible.

"The EMA has agreed to allow me to place the check in the organization leaders hand personally. His name is Owasu Satiiri, a local tribal leader."

Mr. Jernigan nodded, "I know the name well. He's all over the South African news media lately. Does Mr. Satiiri know your intentions?"

"Absolutely not and I want to keep it that way until the last possible moment."

He sat back, looking at the ceiling, "I don't understand Dr. Schumacher, what do you need me for? You could make this donation without any intermediaries from my office."

"I realize that. What I'd like for your office to do is negotiate the meeting and the ceremony as a token of diplomatic good will. I believe it would serve to bolster the worldview of America if the actual event took place here and was leaked to certain local news media."

Mr. Jernigan was obviously stymied at my hidden accusations as much as my request.

"You want the ceremony to take place on U.S. soil?"

I felt myself blush, "I suppose. Is that not possible?"

"Wouldn't it be better to make the donation there?"

I felt my stomach twist into a hard knot at the very mention of traveling back and reliving all the emotions. I felt my internal advisor, reluctantly nod inside me. I was flooded with a dreary insight, not of Pitre's revelation, but of my own enlightened suspicions.

"Yes..., yes I suppose it would."

Ferry's hand settled on my arm, bringing me back to focus.

"I can offer you temporary diplomatic status during the hours of your visit, which would guarantee you an armed detail to protect you and your envoy."

"No.... No thank you. Actually, we already have Diplomatic Status through the EMA and our own security team."

I was desperate not to enlist anyone remotely connected with the office of Xavier Contrata or his security detail. We were already stepping into the mouth of danger as it was; a veritable Daniel in a den of lions. Hopefully Brent and Carl would accept the assignment I hadn't even mentioned to them for obvious reasons.

"I'd like to keep my involvement as low key as possible."

He studied me for several seconds and looked at his notes.

"You don't care much for Mr. Contrata do you?"

I caught a glimpse of Ferry's eyes beside me, the heat on my very skin from her gaze, "I'd rather keep our involvement in the donation anonymous until the last possible moment."

Mr. Jernigan made another note, never breaking his eye contact with me as he finished out his thoughts onto paper.

There was a soft knock at the door and the young lady that had escorted us stuck her head inside, "You're noon meeting sir?"

"Cancel it. Tell them something came up. I'll share war stories with them next week."

She smiled and closed the door behind her.

"Ms. Dunavin, you wouldn't happen to have a copy of your recent court finding against the FBI."

Ferry looked shocked by his request as she suppressed a glance toward her attaché. Mr. Jernigan actually smiled at her frozen gaze.

"Don't look so surprised. I keep up with court cases against executive organizations such as the FBI, CIA, NSA as a hobby; especially the ones that win...."

"I assumed you might bring might bring some of that with you, considering the urgency of Dr. Schumacher's request."

Ferry relaxed and opened her vault of secrets, dragging out several documents.

"Here is our original filing in Federal Court, and here is the final concession of the no-contest settlement."

Mr. Jernigan stacked the papers and looked down at the quiet expression of Chaste.

"Young lady, would you look in that cabinet over in the corner and help yourself to a cold bottle of pop? There's plenty of things to explore over there, especially if you like to read."

Chaste hurried off with a trailing, 'Yes Thank You' as we watched his eyes scan the main documents, Judge Harrison's amicus brief, and a few sworn depositions.

"This was very well prepared. You raised more than a few eyebrows with this ruling, did you know that?"

Ferry shook her head innocently but remained silent.

"Well it did. It sent ripples all the way up the hill."

Her expression reminded me to turn on my 'radar'. Listening to thoughts usually served little more than a distraction while people thought of hurrying off to the restroom, trying not to show their angst.

As soon as I began to entertain Mr. Jernigan's train of thought, I knew why Pitre had all but forced me to use his office for our final plunge.

"And these people are still threatening you? The FBI hasn't been able to corral this rouge group even after this ruling against them?"

I understood his interest, but I didn't give a hoot about discussing my enemies. Ferry spoke up before I could redirect the focus back on my primary goal.

"They tried to burn down his house the same day we received the ruling."

I couldn't add that they'd placed a bomb in Ferry's house as well. Forced silence was still better than losing Ferry, my daughter's future guardian and confidant.

"Would you mind if I have a copy of these to add to my collection, Ms. Dunavin? I especially enjoy collecting rulings that keep our executive branch honest."

He stacked them on the corner of his desk thoughtfully.

"How much do you intend to donate, Dr. Schumacher?"

I looked over at Ferry, "I should have close to ten million accumulated at the time of the event."

"And these funds originated from...?"

Ferry jumped in once again, "Donations..., from the targeted families which recently recovered their missing children."

I'd never seen such composure on a man's face while groaning to high heaven inside as he put two and two together. Mr. Jernigan nodded solemnly, his eyes glazed and dry as he took his time reading the accusations listed in the brief.

"I won't ask if you had anything to do with that, considering the unusually long list of personal attacks I have here. You've been ruffling feathers the wrong way for some time now, haven't you?"

Thank heavens for small miracles. He took another long look at me, then at my daughter happily perusing a dimly lit curio cabinet at the other end of his office.

"Very well then, since you're sure you want to do this. I'll give the pertinent information to our Ambassador and contact the American Embassy in Cape Town as soon as I can put together a draft of your request. We've helped initiate a few fund drives together for food, relief and such over the years. I don't foresee any reason for them to reject any goodwill offering from the EMA. However, if I'm not mistaken, U.S.A. is a relatively new organization and there may be governmental restrictions if they are deemed some sort of anti this or anti that. It may take as much as a month or two to negotiate your request. Do you have the number to your contacts at the EMA?"

That would be far too late. There was less than thirty days until the anniversary of the opening day of our Medical Clinic. I knew not to object; we'd come this far on faith, so I handed him my open day-planner in silence.

He raised the stack of legal documents and handed them to Ferry, but she refused, "Keep them. I have other copies at my office."

He quickly rose from his chair and opened a rather large wall safe behind his desk, sliding them inside.

"I'm going to give these people a call this afternoon. Will you be staying in town this evening? I know several good eateries you'd be interested in."

He scribbled noisily with a nub of a pencil and handed me back my notebook.

"Yes, we will. I promised my daughter a picture of the front of the Capital Building."

"Pffff, I'll give her a tour inside tomorrow morning. Be here at ten o'clock sharp."

CHAPTER FIFTY-SIX

"Ten Million? There's not enough in your new account, especially after taxes and our trip expenses. Where do you intend to get the rest of the money?"

Our night together at the Nations Capital had been exceptionally pleasant, however that morning was rushed with more squabbling erupting while Ferry held her most anxious questions as a last resort.

"We have roughly thirty days, besides it was only an estimate, Ferry. I can't be sure which families will make donations with this last list of children. If I have to take it from my personal account to make up the difference I'll do that."

Ferry crossed her arms and watched me as if I were a mouse she had cornered. Chaste was off on her guided tour inside the Capital Building while we sat in the waiting area trying to iron out our wrinkled disagreements.

"You mean money from your daughter's Trust Fund don't you? Well I have a say-so in that now. You made me her guardian and you gave me power of attorney over it."

I wasn't going to add, 'Should anything happen to me'. That would only be more fuel for the bonfire she was building.

"I was referring to my personal Trust Fund in Cambridge."

This was getting ridiculous, "Ferry, you heard everything, you know everything now."

"Do I? What I know is that you're setting yourself up to get killed by these people. I saw the way Mr. Jernigan looked at you. Why Kress? Your daughter needs you…, I need you."

She sucked in some air at her sudden admission and turned from me, those last words hung in the air like a vapor. I'd been trying to hide my emotions, apparently not quite well enough to get past her woman's intuition.

Once again I'd upset her, an easy tell. Her arms flail about in conversation when I've managed to bruise her last restraints.

"If the cards fall right, no one will get hurt and this underground alliance will be broken."

I wanted Ferry to understand and there was only one way to manage it; bit by bit.

"Do you remember the young man I mentioned to Arthur Jernigan?"

Ferry nodded and I urged her back to her seat beside me.

"Well, he and I have a bit of history together. You see, there was one particular clan that lived to the west of our clinic in Zambia, right on the Angolan border. The Satiiri leaders were probably the only ones that openly accepted us. The chieftain was somewhat of an educated man with several daughters and one son, Owasu, a bright boy, fast runner. Fast enough that he was being scouted by a school in Johannesburg as a hopeful for future Olympic trials.

As you can imagine he was the chieftain's pride.

This particular summer it was hot as blazes, dry, very little rain. Our clinic had an artesian well and we shared our water with anyone in need so we received quite a bit of traffic. It had become a point of contention that the Satiiri tribe kept a consistent trail to our unlimited supply of well water. I'd sent word to the surrounding area by some of the locals that our water was free, but I had no idea that it had stirred up such bitter rivalry.

This particular morning…, Owasu arrived at our clinic in the back of a hand cart. There was so much blood, it was dried and matted to the blanket he was wrapped in. Several of the opposing groups had caught Owasu alone and intended his death to send a message to all those around us and rid them of the white devils.

Honestly, I thought Owasu was already dead, but Elizabeth found a slight pulse and we rushed him inside.

He had several lacerations on his body and one of his Achilles tendons had been nearly severed in half. Elizabeth and I managed to close all the gaping wounds and repair the blood vessels, but he needed blood or his heart wouldn't last much longer.

I sent word to bring the chieftain and some of his family as quickly as possible, but the trip was several miles and…, well there was only one thing left for us.

Elizabeth and I…, and Chaste…, all have O-negative blood; the universal donor. We each gave blood…, just enough to keep his heart from fatigue until his father and family arrived.

We had no intentions of ever mentioning our donation. You see, blood is a very delicate subject when it comes to some third-world thinking.

Somehow, someone told the Satiiri Chieftain what we'd done. We honestly didn't know what to expect. He could have easily turned on us and had us all killed. As fate usually manages to twist, he was so grateful for his son's life, he welcomed us into his tribe. After all, our blood was now in his successor's body. Our blood was mingled with his.

I had no idea that the young man we saved was somehow destined to become a unifying force among his fellow tribes and put an end to all the meaningless bloodshed.

So you see…, all this turned into a vendetta against my family. I'm still not entirely sure how Contrata is connected to all of this, but I'm certain it all has to do with money changing hands. So this money that we've collected, intended to bring unity, is finally getting to where it was originally intended."

Ferry slid across to the empty seat beside me.

"Thank you for explaining, Kress…, I understand what you're doing…, and I understand why."

We'd been going at each other all morning with little snaps and bites. I was glad Chaste Ellen was off with Mr. Jernigan and her tour. I held her to me until she managed to regain her composure. It was good to finally clear the air, it felt settled somehow.

"No more harsh words Kress…, I promise…, and I'm buying you a new jacket. I'm picking it out this time. If you're going to represent the EMA at this dog and pony show, you'll need to look your best while you're doing it. You still need that haircut."

It was good to see her smile again.

"Will we charter a private jet again or use a commercial flight?"

"You…, obviously don't care to skip around in an aircraft. I'll make that flight alone. I'm sure you'll enjoy getting a chance to bond with Chaste a little more while I'm gone."

"Nope. As your legal council, I forbid it. Either we both go or you stay. Besides, you obviously lead a charmed life."

Blast it all. There were her intentions - damn the torpedoes, full speed ahead; typical Ferry Dunavin.

"I'm not trying to make this a problem. I need to go with you and we obviously can't leave Chaste here by herself. Do you think your daughter would volunteer to stay here by herself? Of course not. Even in the short while I've know her, I can answer that."

I felt Pitre leap inside me; some strange excitement. It must have given me a start, because Ferry noticed immediately.

"Kress are you okay?"

I hated it when Pitre bounced up into my consciousness, but I also knew that it must be for a good reason. Hardly ever a good thing and now he was silent.

"Yes..., of course.... Why don't we take a walk back around to the visitor area and wait for Chaste and Mr. Jernigan?"

With Pitre being silent, I had no choice but to assume something was going on that I wouldn't like.

"Kress? How long have we known each other...? Only a few weeks?"

"I suppose so, why?"

I gathered Ferry's hand and led her beside me. I was already looking down the long corridors searching for my daughter. I had an instant vision, of my own creation not via Pitre. I pictured Xavier Contrata talking to Chaste in some vivid pretense of friendship and....

"You're obviously upset, even I can tell that. Did you hear something?"

She lowered her voice to barely a breath, "You know..., in your head. Talk to me Kress."

"I can't hear anything above you or your thoughts Ferry. Please calm yourself and walk with me to the visitor area."

Her mouth may have ceased motion, but her mind was gently prodding me with questions.

"Kress? It's back this way. The visitor area."

I could hear Chaste now, down the corridor to our right.

"No, she's this way," I muttered.

We had a short tug of war while I secretly begged Pitre for an explanation. We were suddenly blocked by a cordoned off hallway.

A large red velvet restraint swayed across the corridor with a dangly sign, "No Entrance - Escort Only", with an armed gentleman standing close by, back against the wall.

I was quickly trying to decide whether or not to risk an altercation, when I saw Chaste and Mr. Jernigan turn into the corridor, calmly chatting with each other.

Ferry finally saw her and yanked my arm severely, "There's Chaste."

She was obviously perfectly fine. They ignored Ferry and I, then casually turned down another hallway.

"Kress, what's wrong with you?"

"Ferry, please forgive me. I don't know what came over me."

She walked in a huff, pulling me by the hand behind her.

"We're going to have another talk mister. Follow me."

The visitor area was all a bustle of people, but we managed to get two seats beside each other with a little privacy.

"Kress Schumacher, you'd better spill it. You're not the only one that can spot a lie. Something's up and you're going to tell me or…, or else!"

I smiled at her idle threat, it was the 'because' threat we use on children when we don't have a valid reason.

"Don't you patronize me, Kress Schumacher. I want an answer."

"Ferry Dunavin, have I told you lately how positively fetching you are?"

Her eyes glittered at me unmoving, then she slowly blushed.

"You're not going to tell me are you?"

I shook my head, "Nothing to tell, obviously a false alarm."

"That's not what I meant and you know it. What else is going on inside that head of yours besides meddling with my private thoughts?"

"Is this where you declare me 'weird as hell' once again?"

"No Kress, we are so far…, far…, beyond that now."

She sat back in the lounge chair in a slump, "I wish you trusted me."

"I do trust you Ferry, more than could possibly know. I trust you with my own daughter."

She sat bolt upright again, "But not with you."

"Ferry, you know more about me than anyone else alive."

"But not everything, right?"

I tried silence as an answer, what a foul tactic it proved to be.

"Kress, I'll never be Elizabeth. There's no way I can ever measure up to that pedestal; I understand that now."

My breath left me empty. Ferry believed I was still hanging on to the past. Yes..., I loved Elizabeth as if she were my own life. Together Chaste and I had worked through our loss; now I had only one option and that was to honor her memory by living on.

"Kress..., I'm sorry..., that was uncalled for. I don't know what possessed me to say something so cruel."

I nodded, "It was a fair assumption, even if it was wrong. Elizabeth is gone. Yes, I miss her terribly, but I have responsibilities to myself and our daughter to live..., and now to you as well. That's exactly why I keep my own counsel."

It was my turn to slump, my turn to grunt of her insistent nature. I felt as if I were Samson, being prodded by the inquisitive Delilah about the source of his strength.

"I get it. You can't tell me because I might get hurt. We're back to that. Well guess what? I'm willing to take that risk."

But I wasn't willing. I sat in silence despite her sincerity. I couldn't tell her about my union with an angel. I couldn't risk the damage it would cause if Pitre had to erase her memory. Pitre..., where are you?

"Daddy!"

Chaste's tall slim legs were racing underneath her paisley dress, her face gleaming and bright until she saw Ferry's expression.

"Arguing again?"

Ferry rose from her chair and kissed Chaste on the forehead, "We're not arguing. People that love each other have disagreements from time to time sweetie."

"Really?" gasped Chaste excitedly. "It's about time. Disagree all you want then."

Mr. Jernigan caught up to where we were standing and thanked us for allowing him to give my daughter a tour. He carried on about how delightful and intelligent she was to which I heartily agreed.

He assured me that he would be in touch with me in the next 48 hours to let me know his progress, before excusing himself and walking away.

Chaste looked up at me in a little huff, "I still didn't get to see the president."

CHAPTER FIFTY-SEVEN

Despite her bold affirmations of fearless abandon, Ferry entered the private jet staring intently at each step, her mind ablaze.

It was a different aircraft; apparently, the other was temporarily grounded for some strange electrical repairs.

Ferry took her seat calmly, one against the outer wall facing Chaste, and began pecking the screen of her cell phone.

"Ferry, it's still not too late to switch our flight to one of the commercial ones."

She smiled at me with an unreadable haggard expression and shook her head.

She was attempting to prove to me that she was willing to risk it all, go where I go, do what I do and all that.

Bosh.

"Stop it Kress. Chaste isn't afraid and there's no logical reason for me to be either. Go..., go find yourself a seat."

She waved me off and darted back to her phone.

"...and quit listening..., give me some privacy."

I nodded and there was blissful silence.

She scrunched up beside Chaste and I took a seat in the center aisle, one that could recline. With any luck, my adrenal glands would soon give out and I'd be allowed some true calm.

My last one hundred attempts to get an answer from Pitre had been ignored so I'd resigned myself to sleep during the return trip to Phoenix Arizona.

Liftoff was without incident and we were immediately informed of clear skies all the way home.

It felt as if I'd just fallen asleep when I heard a loud click and the summary announcement of our impending descent into Arizona airspace.

Ferry and Chaste were both awake and chattering like chipmunks; they looked happy together and I felt that uncertain peace again.

My seat made some dreadful click when I forced it upright.

"Look who's finally awake."

Ferry nudged Chaste whose blue eyes darted up at me in a smile, then went back to their banter.

I had to force my eyes away from the two of them just to focus on my own thoughts.

I felt a sudden slow warmth inside, rising up and filling me.

"Pitre, it's about time," I whispered internally.

I had to suppress my relief; now I'd get some answers.

"What was that all about?" Ferry asked.

I glanced over at the two ladies and Chaste had stopped everything to look my way. I was leaning forward in my seat preparing to converse with Pitre.

Chaste and I locked eyes and I knew in a heartbeat that she sensed or heard our friendly angel's return.

Chaste quickly looked back down and seemed flustered to regain her train of thought.

"Chaste? Kress?"

Ferry looked positively dismal.

"Not you too...," she hissed, pulling Chaste to look her in the face. "Please don't tell me that you..., Chaste you can't hear..., you don't hear inside my thoughts too?"

Chaste grinned, "Of course not. That's silly. I don't have...."

She suddenly drew quiet and gasped in a breath at what she was about to say. Her lips already pursed to reveal the angel residing in her father.

"You don't have..., what?"

Chaste smiled again, "I don't have a clue about any of that. I know I'd be rampant with curiosity, do all sorts of wild things. Probably only the most responsible people would be allowed that privilege, don't you think? Besides, we're the best of friends. I would have already told you if I could."

Ferry wanted to believe and she wanted to barrage me with

questions about how it all started with me, then went silent.

"You sound just like your father."

Ferry's eyes were still round as platters and blinking madly, but she seemed sated that Chaste was being honest.

I sat back in my seat and closed my eyes as I heard their conversation begin again, but it seemed stressed.

"Kress, I have glad news to share."

Albeit, with ghastly poor timing. I slid back down in my seat to whisper my conversation and hide from Ferry's inquisitive eyes.

"As much as I want to know, Ferry is getting more and more suspicious."

"Be kind to Ferry, you were the same way toward me in the beginning."

I was probably worse, much worse.

"Tell me then."

"Do you remember Mr. Hall?."

The name was burned into my memory. The young lady abducted and forced into prostitution.

"Karen Hall's father. Yes of course."

"He was successful in locating the manufacturer of the GPS device implanted in his daughter."

Uncontrollably, I sat forward in my seat again barely containing my excitement.

"If he moves quickly enough the entire network could be discovered."

"Yes…," I hissed, then forced myself silent. "Then I was right all along. That was the reason they killed our good friend John Shoemaker."

"Not entirely."

I felt my breath painfully leave my body.

"Please don't tell me John was involved, because I won't believe you."

"Of course not. That is exactly why I cannot give you too much information; your aptitude of jumping to conclusions."

I took a deep breath, forcing myself to relax once again. I was ready to rail at Pitre. What was I suppose to assume?

"Have your two friends, Brent and Carl, contact Mr. Hall and get the information about the GPS tag. Then you'll know what to do next, not before."

After a single moment's extrapolation, I gasped in more air in my excitement. That was why we hadn't called each of the family's back with their thread of information for their lost loved ones.

"This means we can use it to locate Steven..., and the others!"

"What did you say?" Ferry was now standing behind my seat, leering over my shoulder.

Pitre slipped away in silence and I was left with my insistent Ferry Dunavin circling me like a carrion crow, settling in the empty seat to my right.

Suddenly it was very quiet. Only the soft whine of the jet engines, then the familiar click, "We are in final approach, please observe the seat belt signs. We hope you had a pleasant trip."

Ferry was staring at me as was Chaste after my unintended announcement.

"Kress? Are you going to answer me?"

I'd been in such deep thought I couldn't formulate my usual diversion quickly enough to avert her lie detector. Anything I said henceforward would be deemed a concoction of deception.

"Daddy?"

I turned cautiously, afraid of what I'd see; Chaste was standing on my left in the aisle, quivering.

Ferry blinked once..., then again, staring into oblivion..., lost.

Ferry's voice was drawn, "We'd better get our seat belts on."

She hurried to Chaste trying to urge her to sit but she would not. There were tears streaming down my little girl's cheeks, dripping from her chin. She'd heard Pitre, at least his side of our conversation and my unwarranted mention of Steven. Another blasted tripwire in my daughter's memory of her captivity with the boy named Steven.

I looked up at Ferry, at her expression; she was broken.

There was no way to deny that something hidden, something shared and private and unknown had transpired between my daughter and I.

Chaste hurried from Ferry to the seat beside me, still flooded with tears, happy tears, gripping my arm with all her strength. How could I ask her to contain her emotions when it was possibly some final release of her eight-month ordeal?

I heard the seat belt click noisily in the seat directly behind us; then more silence as we began our descent to land.

I tried to hear Ferry's thoughts..., her concerns. All was silent except for some dreaded emotions of sadness and exclusion. She felt as if she was an outsider looking on..., with memories of her childhood crowding in and in a very real sense..., she was excluded. How was I to include her?

"Pitre you have to fix this!"

There was only dreaded silence once again.

On the one hand, we had several reasons to shout for joy, but couldn't share them with our best friend.

Chaste was glued to my side in silence until our aircraft taxied to a halt and the engines sang their closing song.

Ferry didn't ask any questions. Her face was pallid, her thoughts hushed.

Chaste hurried to her side and lifted Ferry's limp hand to hold as we waited for the co-pilot to open the bay door.

We hurried down the steps to the tarmac and through the airport to hail a taxi. Then Ferry knelt in front of Chaste, said goodbye, that she would see her tomorrow and hailed another taxi. When I realized what was happening, I took off in a dead run, but in a flash the yellow door closed and she disappeared into the thick traffic.

Ferry's luggage was still with us.

Next, I made a foolish assumption - one should never assume anything about a wounded and distraught woman. We went to Ferry's apartment building and the gatekeeper insisted that she hadn't been through.

We took the long ride to our house; she hadn't been there.

Chaste and I both left messages on Ferry's phone..., no answer, no return calls.

Pitre was silent, no help whatsoever; as useless as a wet cloth thrown to mop up a spill.

Chaste and I unloaded our belongings into the garage as quickly as we could, fed the two mongrels, then jumped back into our Rover to look for Ferry.

After at least another dozen calls, a visit to her closed law office and several local hotels, we stopped to get a bite to eat.

Outside the restaurant, there we sat in our vehicle, father and daughter for several minutes in silence and worry.

"Chaste..., I'm going to tell Ferry everything."

"Won't Pitre be angry? What will happen to Ferry if you do?"

"I don't know, but I can't bear to hurt Ferry any longer. I'd rather her believe me insane than see that look on her face ever again. I'll be lucky if she speaks to me again. Let's get a bite to eat. We're not stopping until we find her."

Just as we locked the doors of our vehicle, my cell rang. It was Carl.

"Hello Kress, I heard your trip to D.C. turned out good."

"So far…, yes."

"Well, the reason I'm calling, is to confirm that Brent and myself will be traveling with you within the next sixty days as your security detail."

Who had called them?

"I am planning a trip out of the country and yes, I was going to ask you. Tell me, how did you know about the trip?"

"Ferry called us early this morning and said she'd be sending details tomorrow along with our retainer if we accepted the job. She was all worked up about us keeping you from getting killed. You want to fill me in on what's going on?"

I took in a deep sigh and we walked into the restaurant.

After explaining that it would be a baby-sitting job to Cape Town, South Africa on a good will venture, he began to relax.

He seemed to already know some of the details and let it slip that he knew we'd arrived a few hours earlier.

"Have you spoken to Ferry Dunavin? Recently?"

The telephone made several odd noises and he was stalling his answer.

"Carl, are you here…, in Phoenix? Is Ferry there with you?"

"She…. Yes she's here, but she doesn't want to speak to you for some reason."

I felt my tension melt away, just as our waitress waved to seat us.

"Then she's alright?"

"Sure…, she's fine. What's going on between you two?"

"Please watch after her for me. I owe her some explanations."

"Is that on the clock?"

On the clock?

"Oh…, yes…, keep track of your hours and send me the invoice."

Carl chuckled, "That won't be necessary. Besides we don't double bill for the same clients."

His comment must have been some type of jest; I was in no mood for humor, not even with the trustworthy Carl.

"Just don't let her out of your sight. We don't want any more incidents and she's…, Ferry's irreplaceable."

"Speaking of business Kress, the body Sheriff Gonzales recovered in the canyon behind your home is still a mystery. His prints don't show up on any database in the U.S. We're running his picture and prints through Interpol."

I knew where they'd find his identity, but did I dare tell Carl or Brent? I was so bloody tired of all the secrets, so tired of running, guessing.

"Carl...?"

He was silent, listening, waiting. If I told him exactly where to look to find the identity of his mystery man there would be another mountain of questions or more of that dreaded silence.

Then I remembered Pitre's instructions.

"I need to give you the telephone number of a fellow named Bartholomew Hall."

"Sure, let me put you on speaker so I can write everything down."

There was a loud click and instantly I could sense Ferry was listening somewhere in the silence. I visualized her soulful green eyes staring at me across a great gulf..., I missed her terribly already.

"Go ahead Kress."

"Mr. Hall has some information about a GPS transponder you should know about. Tell him I gave you his number and ask him to share what he's learned."

"Hall..., where have I heard that name before?" asked Carl.

Ferry spoke up, "In the news, the software mogul. His daughter was kidnapped somewhere along the southern California border a while back. She just turned up."

Ferry neglected to mention my involvement, considering there was no recorded documentation to link us, other than a check for a quarter of a million dollars. I hoped the lawyer client privilege prevented her from sharing that bit of information.

"You think Hall's daughter had a GPS node similar to your daughter Chaste?" asked Carl.

I had hoped for a tacit response instead of going off on another foxhunt.

"I'll leave that assumption up to you. I haven't had a good record of surmising lately."

Brent's voice crackled above the mixed conversation, "Why do I get the feeling you know more than you're telling us?"

Carl began thinking aloud, "Dr. Schumacher, Where was the

implant located on your daughter?"

"The back of her neck, just under her hairline. Why do you ask?"

"Damn...."

I couldn't tell who'd offered up the swear by the mass confusion.

"I told you the guy was a cut with a blade."

"The M.E. said it was caused by the fall into the canyon."

I didn't have a clue what they were raving on about, nor did I care at the moment. My mind had fallen back on Ferry.

"We'll get back to you on this Kress."

My emotions were exhausted.

"Brent? Carl?"

The chatter finally settled down to a rumble.

"Nothing..., never mind. Just please take good care of Ferry."

I pressed end call. I suppose I was slowly learning that goodbyes were only for polite conversations.

Our waitress came by once again and took our order for food that neither Chaste nor I would finish eating.

CHAPTER FIFTY-EIGHT

Chaste was asleep by ten that night, but I was pacing the floor, not of my home office, but the entire house. Pitre was ignoring my every request, almost as if we no longer coexisted. In the beginning, he'd been an incessant prod into my every thought and emotion, but since his recent changes, he left me alone all the more. It was maddening, but for some strange reason I couldn't find it in me to be angry with him even though I had every right. And why should I be angry? I'd been trying to find a way to rid myself of him for months hadn't I?

Sometime during the night, I collapsed on the sofa and didn't move until the first morning rays of the sun were glaring through the front glass.

A blistering tune erupted on my cell phone jostling me from my morning stupor..., it was Ferry. I hesitated to answer, but I had to end the ghastly song getting louder the longer I waited.

"Good Morning."

"We looked for you."

"I know. I had to leave or..., I promised you no more harsh words, remember?"

"I miss you terribly."

There was no reason to mention Chaste's feelings; Ferry knew.

"Kress.... It was..., necessary.... And I miss you too."

I suddenly remembered the look of abandonment on Ferry's face and what I'd promised myself. I heard my mouth release its clutch.

"I've made a very difficult resolution Ferry. Before you make any more decisions concerning Chaste or myself, you deserve to know everything. Soon if possible, before I come to my senses and change my mind again."

"As tempting as that is Kress, we should keep things just as they are for now."

I felt the lurch in my chest..., I was losing her, had lost her. Was it for the best? Was it the alternative of having Pitre erase her memories and cause her to forget about what I had resolved to reveal to her..., about me? If so, then problem solved. Simple.

"Kress...?"

"Yes..., you're right of course, it would have been a mistake. Well then, I assume you've taken a room somewhere local?"

Time lapsed as we rebuilt the walls between each other.

"I'm right across the hall from your Investigators, but they're leaving sometime this afternoon. It seems they have an assignment somewhere else."

She still didn't tell me where she was staying and her protection was leaving. Blast it all. She'd run Brent and Carl off no doubt, because I'd asked them to protect her.

I somehow knew that if I offered her to return to my home she'd refuse and take that option off her list permanently.

"Very well then, I won't keep you. I know you have your duties."

"Kress..., I'll talk to you soon."

The phone went silent, no goodbyes.

"So are you really going to tell Ferry about Pitre?"

My daughter was curled in a knot at the other end of the sofa.

"No..., yes..., I was going to, but no, not any longer."

Her sudden presence didn't surprise me. Neither did the persistent intent of her suddenly overcast blue eyes, staring into mine. What did surprise me was a completely overwhelming rush of emotions..., not mine..., hers. Anger, frustration, deep sadness, and loss seeped into me, from Chaste. I'd sensed lies, I'd felt singular fleeting emotions because of my union with Pitre, but this was on another scale entirely.

"Will Ferry still be my guardian? Is she still going to help me with my lessons? Will I still get to visit her? I don't understand. What did you do? Pitre hardly talks to us anymore..., to you, now Ferry's gone...."

Chaste hurried off before I could answer or refute her accusations and I didn't stop her.

I told myself it was for the best...; somehow, it felt like a lie.

Maybe half an hour later I realized that I'd meandered into the kitchen as another part of my automatic morning ritual, preparing breakfast.

I'd shrugged my bathrobe higher to catch the drip from my wet hair and set on some water to boil when Chaste walked in and sat on one of the stools observing me. She'd regained some control of herself, still angry about Ferry's absence.

"I'm old enough to make my own breakfast you know."

"I like making breakfast for us, but I'm more than willing to share the kitchen whenever you like."

"I can take care of my own laundry too."

The sudden declarations of self-sufficiencies were confounding. She hopped down from her stool and began cracking some eggs into a bowl. She was getting so tall now; even though she'd never truly regained all her weight from before she was taken from me. It was as if she'd stretched like putty.

Her hand was chopping at the bottom of the bowl with a whisk by the time my mind finished comprehending the changes in my daughter.

Her mind suddenly opened up to me and filled my head with her thoughts. They were concerns of a much older child, not those of a nine and a half year old girl.

"Chaste..., if anything were to happen to me...."

She never looked up or even my direction, but cut me off.

"Will you stop that? Nothing is going to happen to you. You act as if you're going to die any second now; all the time. Why do you think Ferry is always upset with you?"

"For argument's sake sweetheart...," I began again.

"Haven't you been listening dad? I can take care of myself."

She dropped the metal stirring bowl down on the counter with a loud clack and climbed up on one of the stools to retrieve a small skillet from the overhang.

"Instead of making all your plans to die and leave me here alone, why don't you make plans to stay? I heard Pitre. All the missing kids are going to be found; you said that was the last of them."

"They are the last."

I nodded and lifted the skillet off the hook she was struggling to reach with her fingertips. She took it from my hand without a word and placed it on the stove.

"I only wanted you to be prepared Chaste."

"I am prepared. I've been prepared for months now, can't you see that? And you should know I'll never be like other girls..., I'll never be the little girl you expect me to be..., I..., can't."

She spilled the eggs into the skillet and looked away from me.

That gaping door inside her, from the hint of finding Steven and the others, was still open. Reminders of her ordeal, shredded tendrils laced through her mind, flickered through her thoughts. I tried not to listen to her pain; she tried fitfully to block it from me.

"You don't have to do anything to be my little girl. You simply are."

I slid the skillet of eggs from off the heat and urged her to a stool beside me.

"Chaste..., the things we experience, both good and bad, form us and make us who we are, who we become. If we don't use the strength inside us to stand tall, our adversities can crush us, but if you buck up you can choose what you become."

She stared at me some more; some new talent similar to Ferry's piercing glare, then slid the skillet back on the heat.

"I want a piano..., and I want lessons..., please."

She stood on the bottom rung of the stool and scraped at the eggs, looking away again, her father's daughter, looking for a diversion to blindside me.

"Very well. Tell Ferry what you have in mind. I'm sure she'll be thrilled to help you find exactly what you want."

Her arms were suddenly around my waist in a tight grip, then an instant later back to fluffing her scrambled eggs.

"Thank you daddy..., for not asking about... you know."

I finished breakfast with my daughter, pondering the strange conversation, wondering if I'd said too little or too much considering the delicacy of her state of mind. Pitre had done a remarkable job removing the bulk of her memories and fears, but there was no way to pluck all the thistles without damaging the whole of who Chaste was.

CHAPTER FIFTY-NINE

That week dragged along as if it had gained tenure to the rest of my life. My contact with Ferry was sketchy, business only, information about two more checks received, deposits, and tax liabilities. If our severed familiarity was bothering her, she was hiding it well. Chaste on the other hand, chatted with Ferry several times each day and at great length in the evenings.

I envied her sorely. I missed my friend.

Even my evening runs along our nature trail, which had an almost anesthetic effect on my emotions, left me spent and empty.

My sparse communions with Pitre were actually short cryptic monologues, only when I was absolutely alone and all business. He still hadn't told me the particulars of how the missing children were going to be recovered, or my involvement. His repetitious single-syllabic response was 'soon'.

I couldn't discern if he was avoiding conversation to keep me from gathering information about my short future or if it was an old tactic of revenge to somehow punish me for avoiding any intimacy with Ferry Dunavin. I assumed it was a mixture of both.

There had been no reoccurrences of attacks, not a single ominous tall grey lurking about or following us. Was it possible that life could somehow blend me back into its construct?

Not likely.

Friday…, no Thursday afternoon…, I received a phone call from Arthur Jernigan. One of the board members at the EMA informed him that my donation to Unify South Africa would be accepted. The

South African government however, had denied my proposal to organize a media friendly declaration of the event, also noting that there was no rule against showing up at a fundraiser and making a donation.

It seemed nothing more than a splitting of hairs, but if Mr. Jernigan could arrange to get a schedule of such events, it might work out even better than I'd thought.

As was usual, I received another call from the chairman of the EMA, reiterating the same information from Mr. Jernigan. He driveled on asking me to reconsider some speaking engagements in the near future, to present an anthology of our family's years on foreign soil, then spoke of a few more pleasantries. When I rang off it felt as if my life had fallen back into the mundane, as if there might be a somewhat normal future ahead for Chaste and I.

Chaste walked past my office and poked her head inside.

"Ferry's coming by to get me. We're going shopping."

I heard her footsteps galloping down the hall toward the kitchen.

Then my telephone rang.

"Kress? What's your schedule look like?"

There was no hello, my name is, how are you doing, do you have a few moments to talk. The voice was rushed and frantic.

"Who is this?"

"I'm sorry. This is Brent. Did I catch you at a bad time?"

"I didn't recognize your voice. Please…, continue."

"I was running down a cab when I dialed you. Can you fly out to Seattle this weekend? I have something to show you. I met with Mr. Hall and several of his people this week. You keep interesting company Kress."

I wouldn't know Bartholomew Hall if I bumped into him on the street, but there was no reason to try to explain our acquaintance.

"Hardly. Is there some meaning to this madness?"

I heard him chuckle at my reply.

"Yes there is. We've unraveled a spider web and we want you to see it first hand. I can't talk about it over the phone, its classified information. You've just been placed on the need to know list."

Over the last few weeks, it felt as if I'd finally separated myself from problems with everything from local authorities to the FBI and now I was being asked to voluntarily jump back into some foray of the unknown.

"Are you sure it's absolutely necessary?"

"Yes."

Blast it all.

"Very well. I'll make arrangements and call you back as soon as I can."

"Great. Let me know your schedule and I'll meet you at the airport when you get here. Get the earliest flight you can."

The phone went silent..., of course.

My hands were still raised in a stretch when I reached the front windows, looking out at our black eight-foot reinforced steel fence. I heard the large gate click and whir before I saw the Lincoln turn in off the street; Ferry still had her remote, which gave me a hint of comfort. The boys barked happily at the sound.

Chaste ran up to me with a quick hug and kiss.

"Bye Dad. See you later."

"I need to talk to Ferry before you go. Please tell her it's important."

"Aw Dad. You'll get her in a bad mood. We need some girl time."

The hall door to the garage opened and in slid two high heel shoes to the end of the hallway.

"Chaste honey, are you ready?"

Chaste looked at the ceiling with a huff giving off a dull reply,

"In here."

"Oh..., hello Kress. Chaste said she asked you if it was okay for us to hit a few shops today. I'm tired of hearing her complain about none of her clothes fitting."

I looked at Chaste and her face froze just before it blossomed red.

"You didn't ask your father did you?" sighed Ferry.

"He would have said yes..., I didn't see any reason to bother him. Besides, he likes it when we spend time together."

Ferry jingled her keys at Chaste, "That's no excuse...."

"No..., it's quite alright Ferry. Chaste is right. I would have said yes and I do like your influence on her. Can you spare five minutes? I need to ask a favor of you."

Ferry stiffened and let out a slow breath as I waved her towards my office. As soon as the door closed, Ferry began her recitation of our usual business.

"The last two checks, minus tax puts you about one hundred eight thousand above your pledge to the EMA and Unify South Africa. I had our CPA freeze the Ten Million plus the fees and exchange rate, so it's available whenever you're ready to make the transfer."

I sat in my chair and let her stand. She needed no invitation to find her own seat.

"I need to take a trip this weekend and I was wondering if you'd mind it if Chaste stayed with you? You're welcome to stay here or..., wherever you're currently living."

She still hadn't offered her location, nor had I pried into her personal affairs.

"I'd be more than happy to watch her. Is everything okay?"

I nodded, "I'm meeting Carl and Brent in Washington at their request."

"Something's wrong isn't it?"

Her piercing gaze was electrifying and I almost smiled.

"No Ferry. In fact he wouldn't tell me the particulars over the telephone."

"Anytime you mention D.C. after our trip..., I just assumed...."

"Not D.C., Seattle Washington."

For someone unwilling to relinquish something as mundane as her whereabouts, she was still quite diligent in ferreting out every detail she could from me.

"My only request is that if you do stay..., wherever it is you are, that you bring Chaste by to feed the boys and make sure the alarm is turned on."

I heard an unintentional scratching just outside my door.

"Please come in Chaste."

Chaste fell in the door and screeched with glee over the prospect of a weekend with Ferry, scooting over to stand at her side.

"Thank you Dad."

They made a very fine-looking pair.

"The Arms...," said Ferry, staring at me.

"That's where I'm staying. It's a little lodge between Phoenix and Scottsdale. It's half way between work and..., Chaste."

I nodded, "Whatever you decide. The house is at your disposal."

She seemed disappointed, either that I didn't insist on more particulars or offer some sarcasm about her possession of our house keys. Frankly, all the drama had escaped my current thoughts.

"Should you need me for anything, night or day..., call me, or

Brent or Carl. You have access to the account. Use it as you deem fit."

I stood and pulled the door fully open.

"Unless you have anything else…, I need to pack and make my reservations."

Neither of them dared move from their stance, "I hope you have a good weekend together. You have my permission to spoil Chaste as much as you like."

I walked out into the hall and they hurried behind me in a scuttle of bare feet.

"That's it? You're not going to hug your daughter bye?"

"Before I leave…, yes…."

Ferry looked down at Chaste with a deep frown.

"You didn't ask if you could spend the night either?" asked Ferry.

"Consider the matter settled. She will be staying the weekend with you after all."

"No, it's not settled. I won't tolerate you disrespecting your father young lady. You apologize for lying to him or our shopping expedition is off. Do you understand me?"

Chaste huffed to stand in front of me, "I didn't actually lie, I just didn't mention…."

"Chaste!"

"Oh… alright. I'm sorry I misled you father, even though you don't really care what I do, since your not planning to be around anyhow."

Ferry gasped in horror. I was numb when I understood she was hinting at death, not referring to my sudden trip out of town. I wasn't actually planning to leave Chaste; it didn't appear that I had any choice in the matter.

"What has gotten into you? I've never heard you act like this before."

Chaste ducked her head in silence at Ferry's rebuke.

"Kress, I don't know if I can watch your daughter this weekend. Apparently she's not the young lady I thought she was."

Chaste gasped but kept her gaze to the floor in defiance, waiting for a verdict.

"Maybe she should go with me to Seattle instead. I apologize for her actions Ferry. She had no right to mislead you this way."

"That's the most ridiculous thing I've ever heard. Don't you dare apologize for her. When I was a little girl, I'd have been punished severely for talking to my..., elders that way. She should be proud she has a father that cares about her as much as you do."

I looked at the hurt on Ferry's face. I knew what grit it took to manage the content of her scold. She had no parents her entire life.

"Ferry, she's been through so much."

"All the more reason Chaste should respect you."

She turned Chaste by the shoulders to look at her and bowed over to face her.

"You're father is a wonderful man. Any little girl would give her ponytails to have a father like him. Even if it's only for one more day. You should be ashamed."

Ferry stood and slid to my side, "I'll give you one last chance to apologize."

I felt her arm slide around my waist waiting for some acknowledgement from Chaste. The warmth fueled by her fervor and her nearness was intoxicating.

Almost as an automatic response, my arm circled Ferry's waist beside me and she looked up at me in surprise.

"Damn," she whispered, letting her head fall against my arm.

"We've been played."

I looked down at Chaste, her face still to the floor; her draping hair barely hiding a silly grin on her face.

There we stood arm in arm, hip-to-hip, closer than we'd been since our falling out an eternity ago.

"You little scallywag."

CHAPTER SIXTY

Bartholomew Hall owned an enormous sprawling estate engulfed by massive spruce and pines. A storybook drive wound through the thick trees to the front of Mr. Hall's front door.

Brent and I were met, not greeted by any stretch of the imagination, at the front door by a somewhat unfriendly fellow in a tan suit, trying unsuccessfully to hide a bulky holstered weapon underneath his left arm. As soon as we were inside Brent turned my direction, "Don't pay any attention to him, all the security guards here watched too many Bond movies."

I nodded somewhat reluctantly and realized that I'd spent too many years in South Africa away from the shifting cultural changes of the civilized world. Pomp and circumstance as well as common cordialities were obviously a thing of the past.

"Hello Dr. Schumacher!"

A slim fellow with short coal-black hair and dark flashing eyes hurried my direction. When our eyes met, I instantly recognized him as Mr. Hall.

"It's so very good to finally meet you."

I extended my hand and he pressed past my arm to embrace me in a brotherly hug. How odd. In an instant, my experience with Americans had gone to pervasive rude indifference to a capacious show of emotions. Maybe I was too hasty about my societal judgments. Maybe it was the company I'd been keeping.

"I won't settle to shake hands with the man that saved my daughter's life. Please, come on in, make yourself at home. My wife is arranging for some breakfast out on the back lawn. She's very excited to meet you."

I was somewhat taken aback by the faux celebrity status. Brent stood in the background observing our interaction with intense scrutiny.

As distasteful as it was, it was time I began to listen past everyone's outward pleasantries and figure out what was really going on inside.

We followed the chattering Mr. Hall to a pair of double doors leading out onto a natural-stone paved veranda. Old world French patio furniture sprawled everywhere facing an expanse of deep green shorn grass, worthy of any quality golf course.

There sat a young lady in one of the heavy wrought-iron seats sipping at a tall glass of tea. When she turned and faced me, I felt myself smile uncontrollably at her dimpled chin and bright oval face. Her black hair quivered at the sight of me and she hurried to stand in front of me.

"Are you Dr. Schumacher?"

She was crying..., rivers..., and I felt that same feeling when I'd looked through the adobe portal and saw Chaste after months of agony.

"Hello Karen. You certainly...."

I almost choked and stopped myself abruptly. I was about to draw some inane contrast between now and when we last met on the street corner in Mexico.

She hugged me and quickly backed away shyly.

"It's good to finally meet you. I mean..., well I don't remember much, about the night you found me. Just the weird white glow around your face. Drugs..., you know."

Both Brent and Mr. Hall were standing at a distance, watching and waiting. Some questions were floating in her father's mind about how I'd found Karen - If I'd actually been there as her savior or if I'd been involved somehow. There were so many coincidences. I'd been driving Karen's red Volvo the entire time, then happened upon her on a rainy night on a street corner, offering money for her services.

"I'm happy to see that you're safe and sound."

Mr. Hall's questions were suddenly obliterated by more pronounced thoughts from somewhere behind me. I spun on my heel to see a carbon copy of Karen, admittedly somewhat older; her mother. She smiled and stepped forward, her slim hand extended.

"Hello, it's so good to meet you – *you heard me, didn't you?*"

"Yes…," I nodded. "It's very good to meet you as well."

She immediately turned to her husband and nodded. Something unknown passed between them and he visibly relaxed; his thoughts of doubt and conjecture immediately dissipated.

Good. Finally, all the greetings were done and I was becoming emotionally exhausted, not to mention tired from my 3 a.m. flight from Phoenix.

Brent was apparently the only one left out of the loop of 'need to know' information, his mind still grating over our silent transactions.

"Have a seat Doctor, we have a lot to discuss."

I felt a portion of my weariness drift away when Mrs. Hall offered me a hot cup of Earl Grey to go with the brunch just arriving. Her voice was just as finely tuned to graciousness as her husbands was to the business at hand.

"I hope you're hungry," she whispered, then sat down near her daughter.

"You didn't make accommodations anywhere I hope? We have more unused bedrooms than a Motel-6. I have to keep up an image and we have to entertain clients two or three times a year."

Husband, wife and daughter's eyes were all trained on mine, almost pleading, "I'd be honored to stay here. Forgive me, but if I might get right to the point, Mr. Hall…."

"Bart, call me Bart. This is Helen."

"Very well Bart…, Helen…, I'd like to know why you insisted I come here."

"Be glad to. I made you a promise and I'm a man who keeps his promises, but you'll have to sign a few forms before I can share what I need to share with you. First, I'd like to know a little more about your business in South Africa."

I sighed tiredly, but since he wasn't being a brute about how I'd come to find his daughter, it couldn't do any harm. We ate sparingly and chatted freely for over an hour about my Medical Clinic near Zambia and our trials since arriving in the United States.

When I'd exhausted everything I was willing to share due to Brent's quiet audience, Bart sat back thinking quietly.

"My wife and I donate five million a year to various relief funds in

South Africa since Apartheid died. But apparently, some of the old heads are still trying to run the show from an underground. A lot of political heads didn't like the changes as you might imagine; entire fortunes were lost. Vast fortunes."

He let that settle; it was something that Pitre had already explained to me.

"You don't seem very surprised by that."

"My wife Elizabeth and I donated every year as well, before she passed, before my daughter was taken."

"How is your daughter?"

He was fishing, but I couldn't get into his thoughts to see his intent and it began to worry me.

"Much better now, thank you."

"I notice she didn't make the trip with you."

I wasn't about to let on of Chaste's whereabouts.

"She's in capable hands."

He nodded.

"I'm sure she is. It's hard letting her out of your sight isn't it?"

The words stung. It was similar to the ones uttered at the final confrontation with Agent Lily.

"Indeed. This is the first time we've been separated since I was able to recover her from her captors."

Instantly, I regretted my choice of phrasing and returning to that subject, but Bart didn't pursue that avenue of discussion. His own daughter had not only been abducted, but drugged into oblivion and forced into prostitution.

"I realize my daughter isn't a child any more, you know. I'm just now letting Karen go to the local mall with her mother. It's just..., scary as hell."

Bart seemed adeptly averting all mention and commentary of how I'd been involved and Brent was becoming agitated, wanting to ask his own probing questions; something he'd not done when he and Carl were together with me. I remembered Pitre's warning, but I couldn't judge Brent; I'd be doing the same were the roles reversed.

"Well, in any case..., I'd like to meet her. I insist you visit again soon and bring her with you, after...," he cut short his sudden openness and quickly looked at his wristwatch.

"I see it's time for us to venture deeper into the abyss. If you gentlemen will follow me. Our ride should be here any minute."

CHAPTER SIXTY-ONE

Downtown Seattle on a Saturday morning was all a bustle. If not for the cooler temperatures at this time of year, it would have the same feel of a port city much like Cape Town.

The building we stopped in front of was unassuming for the most part. A carbon copy of most the multi-floored complexes in the area, all wrapped with reflective glass sheeting.

Two guards ushered us inside where another uniformed guard sat waiting. I suppose that was my first hint that this was no ordinary place of commerce.

Mr. Hall..., Bart..., stopped at a half-moon shaped kiosk and handed me two legal forms; one a standard non-disclosure statement, another I'd not seen before.

"This is for good old big brother. You're promising that you'll keep what you see and hear a secret. Standard stuff."

The form ended with all sorts of threatening statements should I disclose any proprietary information. I didn't want to sign. I wanted to turn and leave; to rid myself of potential future troubles, to return to my daughter and try to live out what was left of my life. Then I felt that this must be part of Pitre's secret, the beginning of my end, and scribbled - Kress Schumacher, MD.

"Kress?" asked Mr. Hall.

I nodded and handed him my life, for which I received a dangly orange badge reading "Escort Only".

He led the way to the elevator, stuck in an odd round key and turned it to the left. He pressed the 3, but instead of the usual heft, we began to descend to some third floor underground. I tested my gut feelings, one of Pitre's gifts, and felt no alarm or compromise.

The doors opened to a glaring bright room with several desks, clinical looking technicians suited in white laboratory coats, busy with some questionable duties.

None gave us the slightest consideration as we passed through the maze; each enthralled with their duties or well versed in eye-service.

We entered one of the many rooms through another series of security precautions and the room was dimly lit.

"Now that we're through that hurdle..., take a look at this."

Bart hurried to a wall cabinet and took out a small plastic case.

Inside was a GPS node similar to the one removed from Chaste.

"Look familiar?"

"Of course. Is it the one removed from your daughter?"

He shook his head no, "That one is in one of my company safes..., somewhere. You spooked me when you told me what happened after you put yours in a safe place. I promised you I'd get to the bottom of it all..., and I have."

This much I already knew via Pitre's revelation.

Brent threw up his hands in dismay.

"Don't mind Kress, Bart. He never gets excited about anything."

Bart smiled, "Here, let's take a look at something..., Sasha?"

A lady I'd not seen in the gloom stood and pressed a hand held remote and an entire wall beside us lit up. It was a huge world map with blinking red dots in hundreds of places globally.

"What you're looking at is classified Top Secret, please keep that in mind. Each dot represents a live GPS signal from GEO NODES, International; a manufacturer of GPS devices and satellite technology. They make products for most every service that needs to keep track of shipments, pets, people, the Pope, you name it."

I watched in fascination as several were inching slowly across the oceans, probably in an aircraft.

"Okay Sasha."

The screen changed and all the dots shifted to different locations and diminished somewhat in quantity.

"Now, the ones you're looking at are their more exclusive line of GPS devices. These only respond to an encrypted signal, to and from their satellite transponder. The dots you see now are soldiers inserted into..., places where they might need to be extracted from and have no way to phone home. Next...."

The number shrank to maybe forty blinking red dots.

"My staff took the liberty of testing the GPS node from my daughter's neck. It's what put us onto GEO NODES, International in the first place. Now..., GNI did their homework and tried to hide who manufactured them and such.... They didn't exactly stamp GNI on a microdot inside the node, but every technology has its own unique registered trademark built into it's manufacturing design.

It took a team working twenty-four seven for a month to match my daughter's to this manufacturer. Then..., we had to isolate the signal, then decrypt it. Our Cray complex downstairs struggled for a week before it broke the algorithm."

My head was reeling, expectant and pleading for the obvious grand finale.

"These dots..., whose are they?"

"Unregistered GPS nodes..., one of them in Sedona Arizona, in a grave with the name Thomas Clay on the brass marker."

Had my enemy known where Thomas was the entire time? That did surprise me, but I was more interested in the screen set before me.

"You've isolated the signal to the missing children?" I asked, hoping to detour my original surprise.

"The ones you're looking at.... Sasha?"

"Wait..., please."

I walked closer to the screen and sure enough, there was one single red dot in Sao Paulo on the coast of Brazil. Now I was impressed.

The screen changed and was about the same number of dots in various places, several in Washington, D.C. and across Europe. I felt myself quiver inside, my benefactor Pitre no doubt.

"The network..., you've isolated the network?"

"Not just the network.... We followed the money trail past all these drones, right to the top of several organizations."

Bully for you Mr. Hall, but how do you plan to do anything about it? These people are above the law.

"At least we can retrieve the abductees before more evil befalls them," I mumbled.

"We'll do a hell of a lot more than that!"

The screen went dark and the lights came up a little brighter in the room. Several other people appeared that I'd not noticed before in the darkness.

"Let me just say that I have twenty active contracts with the CIA for technologies we specialize in. I took my time and found the right person to show this to…, and as we speak, these people on our soil are all being rounded up."

"That's why you needed me here so abruptly. You wanted me to see this as it transpires?"

My insides turned to jelly, "What about my daughter? What if one of them breaks free and makes another attempt on her…?"

"Ferry Dunavin and Chaste are in a safe place together right now," said Brent.

I shifted against the nearest desk, my mind a whirl. This had been my suggestion to Thomas…, to use the device in Chaste, to find all the missing. Pitre swelled inside me and I closed my eyes.

"Everything all in the right time, Kress. Our common enemy needed a target to keep them occupied."

I was nothing but a decoy? I suppose in this case that the end justified the means. If I'd gone off half-cocked, we may have succeeded in finding most of the children, but the network would have gone unpunished. I had neither the right resources nor the know how.

The beauty of it all? I wasn't implicated in any of the abductions or their recoveries.

"I don't suppose any of this will ever make the news networks will it?"

Bart laughed softly and shook his head.

"When this is all over, we'll both be able to give our daughters and ourselves a little freedom, Dr. Schumacher."

CHAPTER SIXTY-TWO

"I told you that you lead a charmed life. As soon as your flight left the ground, Brent called me and told me I should expect some friends of theirs. He wouldn't tell me what was going on; said he was afraid I'd tell you, that you always seemed to know things. As if it was all my fault. I guess you're not going to tell me either."

At least Ferry wasn't angry with me, especially right after we'd come to an armistice over our differences.

"Soon. As much as I'm allowed."

"Fine. I suppose you think that just because Chaste and I were locked away watching movies and eating junk food for the last two days it makes everything all right. I do have a job you know."

It was nice having a civil conversation, maybe not intimate or romantic, but now that the team of miscreants were either dead or in custody, that could change quickly. Maybe I'd read the wrong story between the lines of Pitre's secrecy. Maybe there was a life for me after all.

"I wasn't entirely responsible for ruining your plans for the weekend together. But as soon as I return I promise to make it up to the both of you."

I heard Chaste giggle her silly laugh in the background. Ferry was learning Chaste's skills of manipulation.

"I'm going to hold you to that, Mister. Come back soon, okay? We miss you."

My heart swelled; I needed no further encouragement.

"The minute I can get away..., I promise."

I lay down the phone and took another sip of my tea.

"Everything okay at home?"

It was Mrs. Hall..., Helen..., seated quietly on the other side of their dining room table. That feeling of overwhelming peace, of filling up inside made me relax as my personal angel made his presence known to me. He only offered his silent attendance.

"I didn't hear you come in.... Yes, everything is just fine."

"I take it you didn't tell your friend about what just took place?"

"She'll wriggle if from me in due time, I assure you. If I offered it up that easily, she wouldn't believe half of what I said."

Helen laughed softly and nodded agreement, "It's a woman's gift."

The room went silent and I began to struggle for my usual small talk.

"How long have you been able to hear other's thoughts?"

Blast it all. I could have offered the usual excuses, but Helen had rooted me out upon our first meeting.

"Quite recently actually. Probably something to do with the stress of losing my daughter for almost a year. I'd rather no one else knows, if that's agreeable with you? It's not something I like to advertise."

She nodded in agreement and placed her hands flat on the table with a soft smile. I started to ask her how she'd figured me out.

"I can hear a little myself, every now and then, since I was a child."

I quickly set down my tea and spun to face her directly, "Don't you hate it?"

She nodded and smiled again; her face transformed into one much younger, the very image of her daughter.

"Just when you think you know someone...," she whispered anxiously.

We heard voices coming down the hallway toward us and shared one last thought, just before the room filled with others.

"We'll have to share more, sometime in the future."

"I trust you'll come back soon and visit my husband and I. Karen thinks you single handedly hung the moon."

Bart hurried in on the conversation, "I have to warn you. What my wife and daughter want they usually get. Our home is open to you and your family."

I stood and shook his hand for the one-millionth time since our first meeting.

"I hate to break up your chat honey, but Mr. Rand and I need to speak with Kress alone for a few minutes."

Helen gathered my empty teacup with a dutifully practiced smile and slid a large retractable door closed behind her, closing us off.

Bart opened a large manila envelope and began to fan out pictures across the table like a deck of cards.

Some were obviously police photographs, while others were photos taken in a morgue; most of them bruised and bloody.

I looked on carefully, one at a time at each face. I knew what he'd ask and offered it as soon as he'd completely covered the end of the table.

"These two…, outside my front gate, but I can't be sure. It's been a while and it was raining at the time. Are you sure this is everyone?"

"I felt you might ask that."

Brent held up one photo and held it for me to see. The pale look of death, eyes already beginning to recede into his skull.

"This one was in the canyon behind your house."

He lifted another photo, "This one was in the same unit as him."

I heard myself mumble, "The unit attached to the State Department official," and instantly cursed myself for thinking aloud.

Brent let out a long labored hiss, but kept a veritable flood of comments to himself.

"Typical Kress Schumacher…. More importantly, do you notice who's missing?" he asked, anger mounting in his voice.

I felt my heart skip as I scanned the pictures once again, then slowly turning each over one by one.

"Lily…?" I mumbled past my confusion.

Brent looked at me in a somber stare, "Yes…, Agent Lily."

"I assumed he was arrested after firing his gun at our meeting."

Brent shook his head, "His ambulance was diverted to the county hospital while in route. He never made it there."

I quickly turned the photos over once again and flipped through them again. Not a single face remotely resembled the man identified as Amos Lily.

"He's still at large?"

"We've given a copy of the video recording to the CIA and there's a man hunt in progress. He could be next door or he could have easily fled the country after all this time."

Brent put his hand over mine, already clutching my phone to alert Ferry and Chaste.

"They're taken care of..., they're safe. I needed to let you know."

He let out a deep breath, "Now do you want to tell me how you knew about the unit's attachment to a State Department official?"

It was only a guess, but Pitre jostled my memory.

"Carl..., it was Carl that told Ferry about the Glock I found in my back yard. He told Ferry that it was issued to a protection detail assigned to a State Department official. I only assumed...."

Brent pointed his finger at me..., "That's exactly what I'm talking about.... There's too many coincidences like that...."

Bart jumped in and saved me from another interrogation.

"Or..., Dr. Schumacher has a better sense of the big picture. He's lived through all this by the skin of his teeth. Take a breath and calm down. Here are our criminals."

Bart waved the stack of pictures in Brent's face and stuffed them back into the envelope.

"Now we get to the most important part of what I wanted to show you."

Bart opened another envelope I'd somehow missed.

Pictures began to fan out on the table..., children..., little innocent faces with dull blank expressions. Through the miracle living inside me, I recognized each one by name.

Then..., there was Steven.

Tanned and smudge faced, long dark hair stretched tightly back into a tail, barely visible in the photograph. His features suggested some Native American heritage, but could easily pass for most any Latin heritage as well.

I had to control myself as I lifted his photograph. Brent was leaning in to strike, already presenting himself as The Inquisition.

"That one mean something to you?" asked Bart.

I waved my hand, "They all do. Every one of them."

Brent was still itching to throw me back underwater to see if I'd float.

"Funny you picked that picture from the pack. He's the only anomaly out of the bunch. All the rest of these kids were from rich families, that one was an orphan. He didn't have penny to his name."

I wanted to grip the photo and hold it close to my chest, would have lost my composure much like Chaste had done.

"If you were going to test a group's skills at kidnapping, wouldn't you pick a subject that wouldn't be missed? Someone no one wanted?"

Bart looked at me strangely and took the picture into his own hands to study it.

"This one means something to you though, doesn't he?"

"Steven…, I've never met him, but yes…, I suppose he does."

Brent became agitated once again.

"I remember him too. That boy had something to do with Whitefeather or Clay, whichever you want to call him. Steven was all that quack talked about when I first met him. How did you know that was the same boy if you've never met him? Did Clay show you a picture?"

I felt my hackles rise; maybe I was tired, losing control.

Then the most curious thing happened. Well curious is probably as much an understatement as 'unnerving' would be.

My body turned of its own accord and hurried around the table where Brent stood. It was as if I were a bystander watching the events taking place, my body a puppet to a puppet master, minus the strings.

Suddenly I found myself standing face to face with Brent Rand and I began to speak violently, following him as he retreated.

"I recognized the boy from a vision. I know about Steven the same way I know about your sudden morbid curiosity to attach me to all the crimes these vermin committed. The same way I know you lean on Carl to keep you from falling back into alcoholism. The same way I know you're family was murdered by some psychotic killer. That you bear the weight of a secret…, one that Carl suspects, but shuns asking you about. That you ended the killers' life with a vengeful bullet from your own gun, not in self-defense, as you told everyone."

I stood there body wavering…, oh how I wanted to shut my mouth and disappear. Brent was looking at me, face pale, beaded perspiration on his forehead, nearly in shock as my dreaded mouth began once again.

"If you're not careful Brent Rand, you'll soon become another Agent Lily, a mindless drone searching for dark things you don't want to find. A drone filled with an uncontrollable hatred driving you from one event to the next. I don't want that for you, neither does your partner, neither does your Creator."

I felt myself slump and two hands grip my shoulders from behind me. Bart Hall quickly guided me to the nearest chair and sat me down.

Brent was bent backward, still leaning against the dining table in a dead stare.

How could Pitre do that to me?

Why would he do that to Brent?

I heard the door to the room slide open behind me. Bart left me seated alone there with Brent staring into space, still silent, in shock.

The door closed again and Bart was holding a pitcher of cold water and some glasses.

"Remind me never to get on your bad side Kress," Bart whispered in my ear.

He handed me a glass and poured another for Brent, who was finally coming out of his stupor.

"That's how you knew what was going on during the interview."

Brent had finally regained his voice and took a drink of water.

"Can we keep this incident between us? I've never lost control like that before?" I asked.

Brent nodded, neither admitting nor refuting anything I'd said during my sudden burst of unwanted clairvoyance. Regret filled me as if I'd slapped a best friend on the face out of petty anger.

Pitre spoke quietly inside me, *"Be at peace. It was necessary."*

CHAPTER SIXTY-THREE

I dozed most the flight home Tuesday, the weight of Atlas removed from my shoulders. Despite our victory, I still couldn't shake the foreboding dread that had perfused my mind since the day I stood in dismal agony on the curb in front of Chaste's primary school.

My heart should have been light as a feather, but here I was, fighting off some unknown gloom.

I believed it some sort of lingering psychological malady due to the length of time I'd groveled in depression. Surely it wasn't still the drear emotions leaking into me from Pitre; our ordeal with the children was complete, our mission together a gleaming success.

Pitre was reclusive and quiet; after his display of bodily possession, it was probably for the best. Still, why couldn't he be honest with about my future and set my mind at ease? Was his secret something that I was incapable of accepting or were the circumstances so drastic I'd try to steer away in another direction? After all, self-preservation is a very strong motivator.

The bright side of it all was that I'd fulfilled this half of my mission. I only had one more viable task before the end of the month..., the donation..., to get the monies back to their intended destination before the anniversary of my twenty-year commitment. I told myself Elizabeth would be proud; her death would not be in vain.

The majority of the responsible were already in custody, several governmental ties under investigation on several continents, but most importantly every last child was located.

For a fleeting moment, I pictured the elusive Agent Lily inside an interrogation room, from the egregious side of the table. That would have to wait. Miami Airport security captured pictures of Lily leaving the country on a flight bound for Venezuela two days after his disappearance. Probably part of the retirement plan for the demonically influenced. His vile threats while under demonic influence seemed to be negated, hopefully it was permanent.

Now all I had to do was present a check, place it in the right hands, and not only would my commitment be fulfilled, but a war could possibly be averted. A tribal war financially fueled and urged on by an underground faction was unwilling to relinquish their hold on the rich continent of Africa, a final untapped resource of global resources. Hundreds, if not thousands of indigenous lives might be saved with the right leadership and influences.

The huge Boeing aircraft bumped and shivered slightly as the wheels synchronized to the speed of the runway beneath me. It was time to let go of my ghosts, Ferry and Chaste would be waiting for me, expecting a lighter happier version of friend and father to greet them.

As I stepped out of the gate, I was greeted almost immediately by two men in identical suits and froze in my tracks.

"Kress Schumacher?"

The man on my left held up a photograph in a quick glance and nodded to his partner, who quickly stuck out his hand.

"We work for Mr. Hall."

He didn't exactly smile, but neither did he scowl at my reluctance to shake the hand of a uniformed stranger.

"We've been assigned to watch over you and your family for the next week as a precaution. You won't see us but we'll be close should you need us."

He handed me a non-descript business card with two phone numbers, nodded and walked away into the crowd. I remained there for a moment in silence; at least I was learning when to appear rude and inhospitable.

"Daddy!"

Chaste pressed past an elderly couple and I raised her up into the air for a kiss.

"We missed you so. Promise to take me with you from now on?"

Ferry managed to get past the same doddering couple.

"Just you, what about me?"

I managed another kiss or two from each of them before I conceded, "I promise to take you both whenever I can."

"I saw you meet the two goons that kept us locked up for the last four days. And I thought the paparazzi were bad. At least I talked them into letting us spend the day at my office today instead of that horrible hotel."

Ferry was back to her usual fervor, a good sign.

"I hear you have good news to share with me?"

"Oh, please Ferry. I want no reminders of this weekend. Didn't I promise to make it all up to you somehow?"

A small opening from the cluster of people presented itself and I began to tow Ferry behind me with a gangly-legged Chaste high up on my hip, chattering in my ear.

"It was just awful Daddy. We didn't get to go shopping..., or to the movies, or hiking, or the bike rides we'd planned."

I heard Ferry's laugh behind me, above the din of chatter around us, just before she managed to make room by my other side.

"Well, I have news for you Mister Schumacher, whenever you come back down to the planet."

"Is it absolutely necessary? I want to let my mind unravel."

I lowered Chaste to the breezeway and felt Ferry's arm at my waist.

"It can wait. I just thought you'd like to know that Mr. Jernigan called about an available date in Cape Town."

Tenacious woman. There was no escape.

"He faxed me a schedule you'll want to see..., sooner than later."

"Tomorrow?"

She grunted submission, "Tomorrow."

"Ferry..., if you've been in lockdown, who fed the boys?"

"That would be Carl. He's been staying at your house, didn't you know?"

I didn't but if he'd asked, I'd have readily agreed, so it wasn't an arguable point.

"Fine then. Take me to the mall, Madam, and we'll go shopping."

"What about the security detail?"

I shrugged, "What about them? Let them earn their keep."

Ferry liked my answer.

CHAPTER SIXTY-FOUR

"Why won't you at least face me?"

I wasn't angry..., I only wanted answers to my questions, simple ones at that.

"As you wish. Shield yourself, turn aside until you adjust."

Suffused with blinding brilliance, all I could manage to do for several seconds was blink in the opposite direction of Pitre.

"For heaven's sake, can't you please tone it down even a little bit?"

"It is for heaven's sake you see me as I am. You will adjust; it is your true nature to see me as I am."

We'd already settled the issue of his using me as his personal hand puppet; already dealt with his long boughts of silence.

Now, it was an humbling experience just to be in his presence. He sat in the corner of my office; wings folded behind him and splayed on either side, more than a head taller than the first time he'd revealed himself to me. Other than the noticeable size difference and the issue with his wings there was one more startling discovery for me.

I could see the features of his face; and there was hair..., long hair down to his wide shoulders.

His features seemed to be in some sort of flux. Just as soon as I settled on the blond of his hair, it shifted to golden brown, then to rich chestnut. I could have sat and watched him in blissful silence without talking, mesmerized by his presence until I saw the sudden smile on his face. I expected some type of stoic, all knowing glare, but instead there was kindness; a softness in his eyes.

Pitre was a work of art..., beautiful, a living sculpture of Michelangelo, yet far more.

I fought to remember my questions after an unknown amount of time had slipped past.

"Can you explain my dread? Can you take it away? I should be overjoyed that our time together has been so fruitful."

"Your emotions are human, they belong solely to you. It would make you less than you were created to be. To remove them would be an ugly smear on the canvas of your life."

An expert sidestep to my answer.

"After all we've been through together, isn't there someway you can tell me what it is that's bothering you or what you're keeping from me?"

My suspicions were confirmed. His emotions were seeping into mine, causing my distress, but I couldn't get him to admit a blasted thing.

"I am bound by a law much higher than our union."

What could possibly be any closer than his attachment to the edges of my soul?

"What you're telling me is that I'm to settle on this unshakable drear for the rest of my life? This unknown is eating me. Everyone is noticing it now."

"What I'm telling you is..., that to remove your emotions would make you vulnerable to unknown events destined in your future. I already explained that some events belong solely to our Creator."

There it was, that answer within an answer once again. Blast it all. "Fine."

I heard Ferry's standard response of frustration flow from my lips.

"Kress, I'm not a crystal ball. I'm you're protector."

Now we were getting somewhere.

"If you're my protector then you can at least warn me...."

"Stop it Kress. I've explained as much as I'm allowed."

His form began to dim.

"Wait..., please...."

Pitre laughed at me, a brotherly laugh.

"Why are you mocking me now?" I asked.

"Forgive me. It's not mockery. I see similarities evolving between you and Ferry."

His laughter drifted away until I only heard it inside me, as he slowly vacated the expanse of my office.

I heard a distant noise and recognized it as one of the overhead garage doors whirring open. It was already after 6 a.m.

I knew it wasn't Carl. I'd sent him on his merry way last night after our impromptu shopping expedition. That left one possibility…, Ferry.

I hurried to the hallway just as the door opened from the garage.

"Morning Kress. A little help here?"

She handed me a double stack of white boxes and sent her shoes sailing to the end of the hallway behind me.

"Is this what I think it is?"

My mind was instantly drifting to a time in my early childhood; waking to the smell of my own mother's kitchen.

"A little bird told me you had a soft spot for them and I have a friend at one of the bakeries in town. He promised to teach me how to make them. Hurry up while they're still warm."

I sniffed once more, before opening the box.

"Hand twisted crullers."

Ferry smiled and I received my morning kiss, something I fully intended to make a permanent routine.

"I'll wake Chaste, you dive in."

I resisted temptation and set out several jams, then scooted the teapot onto a lit burner.

Happy mumbles rolled down the upstairs hallway, quickly followed by a drum roll of footsteps scurrying down the staircase.

We demolished the first half-dozen dainties as we chatted over our last four days experiences.

Not once did Ferry bring up her usual prying innuendos I knew were tickling the back of her mind. She even resisted offering the business at hand rhetoric from her own day's schedule.

It was almost like the family I remembered from not so long ago.

Ferry looked at her phone to find the time then stood and stretched.

"Can Chaste come with me today? We have an empty room next to my office she can use to study."

"Please Dad?"

"Why don't I drop you off around ten or eleven instead? She needs to help me with an errand today…, a rather important one. Also, I need to schedule a short conference with our lawyer today."

Ferry quickly opened her planner with her best fake frown.

"Hmmm, I don't remember any outstanding appointments with you. In fact, I don't have much of anything going on today except playing catch up thanks to my unplanned vacation."

Her friendly rote of sarcasm was noted.

"Incidentally, that's one of the items I need to discuss with you. We need to iron out the details of our trip to Cape Town."

It was one of the few times I'd been able to render Ferry speechless. It was such a pleasant experience, that I made a note to myself to attempt it more often.

She sat in silence, her jaw hanging loose, accompanied by her patented blank stare.

"Does that mean you want me to go with you?"

"I did say 'our trip', but if you're too bogged down with work…."

"No! No…, I mean…, I think I can find a break in my schedule to go with you to South Africa."

"Good. We'll discuss the particulars later."

I took my last bite while Ferry continued her stare.

"What's so important that you need Chaste's help? Is there something I can do to help before I get to my office?"

As planned, Ferry was fishing.

"No, but thank you."

She dropped her planner back in her attaché and began to slip on her shoes.

"Chaste, sweetheart, you'll tell me what your daddy's up to later, won't you?"

Chaste grinned, "Maybe. It depends."

"Now Chaste, you remember our agreement about no secrets?"

Chaste and I stood to follow Ferry out, "Of course. We agreed that there would be no secrets between us, but that doesn't include the secrets between me and my father."

Ferry spun back around, "You sly little fox."

"You said I'd make a good lawyer some day."

Ferry shook her head as she clopped through the garage to her car.

"See you in a little while."

Ferry clicked the remote to the garage door and parked just outside on my drive was a black Crown Victoria with two gents seated inside.

Her car horn echoed loudly in the garage as she tried to force the car to rush out the gate, which was barely creeping open.

"I'll explain later. They insisted on following me. Don't worry, I bought them coffee and donuts."

Both cars drove away down the curved road of our neighborhood and I looked around slowly, every direction.

It had been quite a while since I'd seen the tall peering eyes of a tall grey watching us..., and today was no exception. It was as if they'd all vanished from the face of the planet. Well good riddance. I felt no inward alarms of impending doom and determined that I'd ignore the pervasive gloom still coiled inside me like a pet snake.

It felt good to be inching toward normal.

CHAPTER SIXTY-FIVE

"Okay you have to tell me where we're going."

"You'll see as soon as we get there."

Chaste was wild with curiosity..., with good reason.

"Chaste honey. I need to ask you something very important. It's the reason I wanted to bring you into the city myself."

"A secret?" asked Chaste, almost feverish with anticipation.

"Tell me...; how are you getting on with Ferry?"

Her inquisitive blue eyes darted at me with such intensity it should have burned a hole into my cranium. Possibly afraid I was going to do something stupid again and muck up her hard work.

"We're the best of friends. You know that. Why are you asking me?"

How did she always manage to turn my questions back on me when I wanted to be vague?

"Do you think she's capable of putting up with the two of us on a more frequent basis?"

I didn't dare look my daughter's direction for fear of giving away my reasons.

"Dad, we see each other almost every day. How much more frequent...."

She gasped and twisted my direction in the seat.

"You're kidding me, aren't you?"

I shook my head no.

"Maybe frequent wasn't the proper word. What I meant to say was a more permanent basis."

"You mean have Ferry join our family, to become your..., to be my...?"

She couldn't say the words.

"Chaste dear, you need to know that I'm not trying to replace your mother. I need to know exactly how you feel before I even consider the matter."

Chaste scooted over leaned against my shoulder quietly. All I could see was a mass of blond hair pressed against me. She didn't answer for several minutes, long enough that it was causing me concern.

When I tilted her chin to look at me she was crying. I put on my brakes and pulled into the closest parking lot and stopped.

"I love Ferry, sweetheart, but if you're not ready for this, I can wait..., as long as necessary."

"No..., please don't wait. I'm very happy. Ferry's perfect."

"Are you sure?"

She nodded past her snubs, "Very. Woman's intuition."

"Then you and I need to go find the perfect ring."

"Does this mean you're not going to die?"

The air left me.

"I hadn't planned on it. Chaste, no one is promised tomorrow, sweetheart."

Chaste slid even closer next to me.

"So I've noticed."

"Can you keep this a secret?"

Chaste nodded as I parked across the street from Ferry's office.

We were early and with good reason. I wanted to make sure that Ferry didn't prevail in uncovering our secret from Chaste before our trip to Cape Town.

"I want your promise."

"I promise. How many times do I have to say it?"

"As many times as necessary."

"Dad, you know I can keep a secret. Ferry knows nothing about Pitre."

"That's true, however...."

I muted the end of that matter quickly. I didn't want to spoil our secret by reminding Chaste about the little episode at Ferry's home. As sharp and talented as Chaste was, Ferry was well capable of mining her for secrets.

Now I was concerned about when to pull off my plan.

Ferry had informed me that one of the speaking engagements of the young Mr. Satiiri would be at Cape Town, a few days prior to my desired date in April; for some political event.

My intentions were to give Ferry a guided tour to the scenic southwestern tip of the continent of Africa immediately following the short meeting with Mr. Satiiri.

The Cape of Good Hope seemed a memorable place to offer the ring to her hand; where two oceans met. Closure to one phase of our lives and a new one beginning for she and I and Chaste, together.

"What if Ferry says no?"

Leave it to Chaste to know my one weakness.

It was a very real possibility. It added to the drear I'd pushed away. My chosen location was also rightly called Cape of Storms.

I hadn't yet probed the depths of Ferry's past or her reasoning. Ferry was still somewhat of a mystery to me and not exactly an open book. Most of what I knew of her life and childhood secrets I'd gleaned from Pitre. There were no doubts in my mind that she cared for my daughter and I, but was it enough to make our relationship permanent?

"Then we'll honor her wishes and try our best to stay friends."

"She won't say no…. You're too good a catch."

"Is that more of your woman's intuition?"

Chaste smiled, "I was just curious what you'd say."

Blast it all. Only my daughter could shake my foundations.

"Well don't frighten me like that again; I'm already a bundle of nerves. You're sure you can keep our secret then?"

"Yes…, Dad. I can keep our secret. Dad…?"

There was an immediate hard rap on the window of my Rover that startled me.

A smiling face was peering through the window with cupped hands on either side. Thank goodness I'd locked our secret away in the glove compartment before Ferry peered in on Chaste and I.

She looked both happy to see us and disappointed that she'd missed out on discovering some grand mystery.

She knocked once again and pulled at the locked door handle

insistently.

"You're here early. Good. I was going crazy with a mountain of paperwork. I've been so out of the loop these last few days, my partners have me scanning every new case on the docket. I'm their new prodigy."

She frowned suddenly, "You two are up to something."

We must have looked like two children with their hands caught in the cookie jar.

"Guilty as charged."

"Chaste?" mumbled Ferry.

"I brought my lessons with me. Are you sure I won't be a bother? I can wait until a better day."

"That wasn't what I was going to ask and you know it, smarty-pants. Besides, when are you ever worried about being a bother?"

I watched Chaste smile, taunting Ferry with her secret.

"Oh…, fine. Hurry up and come inside."

The office was mostly silent, even though the few I saw managed to smile and nod our direction. Their half dozen paralegals and secretariats were either milling about or on the telephone.

Once we were inside her private office, Ferry hurried to a golden hued armoire in the corner.

"Here, try this on."

She frantically stripped off a sheer plastic cover from some sort of coat and dropped its hanger into one of her chairs.

"Come on, take off that…, thing…, and try this on."

It was a superbly nice dark navy jacket with hues of gray interwoven, actually similar to the one Mr. Hall sported about in during my visit to Seattle.

"Ferry, you shouldn't have. This must have cost a fortune."

She helped me shrug it on and it was tailored perfectly. Ferry backed away with a smile, obviously quite proud of her accomplishment.

"Well? What do you think? I promised I was going to get you something to wear to the ceremony."

Of course I raved on for several minutes until Ferry knew her efforts were appreciated, all the while wondering what would become of my favorite ugly blazer. She turned and tossed me a fuchsia tie and had me hold it up to cover yet another one of my ties she wasn't very fond of.

"Now..., we have to get you that haircut."

She ruffled my hair like a puppy, then quickly smoothed it back down.

"Alright Dr. Schumacher, what did you need to see me about?"

CHAPTER SIXTY-SIX

The date was set; April twenty-first we would depart Phoenix on a long multi-segmented flight across two continents and an ocean that always seemed to be brooding or angry about something. It was my one concession for Ferry's sake, not taking a private jet.

After double-checking the stops and hotel accommodations, several layovers, and other items of import from a local travel agent, I lay my notes aside, thinking.

The agency had left no time whatsoever for recuperation between flights and certainly no time to explore. We would all be miserable as hell and at each other's throats within the first twelve hours.

I called them back immediately and gutted the entire trip, but despite the agent's first angry rant, she was pleased with my changes and her increased commission.

I did not include a visit to Zambia or the remains of our old medical clinic in the itinerary. It was much too far inland through treacherous territories. Needless to say, that point of interest would have been more than even I could abide. I wasn't willing to risk subjecting Chaste to childhood memories that might further devastate her at this stage in her life.

Our local travels would be limited to Johannesburg, Port Elizabeth and of course Cape Town. I knew the coastal towns quite well and they would provide a pleasant experience, with so much diversity of cultures.

Johannesburg would only be a short visit, after our flight's arrival;

I scribbled a few more notes. There were too many dark memories of our last nights there, when we'd stayed near the University.

I supposed I should prepare some sort of short speech in case I was prodded into saying a few words.

"Daddy, you're doing it again."

"I'm thinking. I do that when I'm trying to sort things through."

"You're thinking too hard then. Your face is all wrinkly."

"I'll try not to think so hard."

"Can I let the boys inside?"

"Absolutely not. They'll crash the whole place," I mumbled.

"Daddy...?"

"Chaste, what's the matter?"

She smiled at me, "That's better."

I'd finally looked up from my planner, from the extensive scribbling and lists on several pages. She flopped down heavily next to me on the sofa.

"Are we still going to live here? You know..., after?"

"We'll have to wait and see. I hadn't thought that far ahead."

"You said you were planning."

"Our trip Chaste. I have to make sure everything goes smoothly."

"You want me to ask Ferry what she thinks about it?"

I dropped my pen in a panic and snapped the planner shut.

"No. I especially don't want you to ask Ferry. Not until.... You know better than to ask such a thing. What's gotten into you?"

"Just curious. A girl needs to know these kinds of things."

She sat there, eyes darting incessantly between me and my planner, daring me to open it again.

"I'm bored."

Finally; the reason for the inquisition.

"I've finished this weeks studies. I predict all perfect grades. Shouldn't I get some sort of reward?"

This malcontent was so not like Chaste, which in this case was a good thing. I'd been waiting to see her open up and break free of her recent past.

Determined not to over-think as my usual trait, I offered a concession.

"Tell me what you have in mind."

"I don't have any friends to come visit or I'd beg until you were sore with me. We've been stuck here for days; maybe we could go see a movie with Ferry?"

It was then I saw something that troubled me beyond words. I watched in horror as the clear blue of her eyes began to scrim, darkened by her pupils expanding dilatation. I hadn't seen that atrocity since Pitre had worked to remove the vile memories of her captivity. Our forced solitude was not helping matters.

"Aren't you feeling well?"

She let me place the back of my hand to her forehead, only for an instant, then withdrew. She was unusually cold and clammy.

"There's nothing wrong with me. I took a nap and had a bad dream, that's all."

Chaste walked all the way to the front door and peered out at the afternoon shadows beginning to form, then slowly wandered back to where I was lounging.

"It's almost four. Why don't you call Ferry and see if she's free this evening. I'll watch whatever movie the two of you fancy. You can wear some of your new clothes we set aside for the trip next week."

Her body relaxed from some tension I hadn't seen. I also foresaw another long chat with Pitre, if I could dredge him from his hiding.

"That's a wonderful idea. Thank you Daddy."

Her phone appeared in her hand just as she bolted up the stairs. Somehow, it didn't matter that she'd made the outing seem as if it were my idea.

Just when I thought things might begin to make some sense.

I pitched my useless planner to the table in front of me and scrubbed the tired windows of my soul with my knuckles.

When would it be enough?

Pitre had already instructed me not to try to contact him; that he would know if there was any danger lurking about well before I would.

I no longer had any reason to mistrust him and quite frankly I was missing our daily chats, even if they had become somewhat one-sided.

For weeks now, we'd not seen so much as a single malcontented tall grey. Of course, my cynical mind assumed our divisive enemy was trying to lull me into a false sense of security. Who could blame me?

After dislodging an entire unseen army bent on initiating some lofty scheme to dissemble a continent of people? An army that was using people as unwitting puppets, turning their inherent greed and avarice into a weapon to keep an entire civilization in the dark ages. Destroying innocents in the process; one of them my own daughter.

I heard the grit of my teeth bring me out of my trance.

My mind had wandered away and I tried to force my focus back on my daughter without much success. Of course it occurred to me to ponder how much of my own thoughts were actually mine now?

Besides Pitre's thoughts and emotions leeching into my own, now I was addicted to probing the thoughts and intents of others. Information wafted into my mind from those nearby with no effort on my part.

It was as if I was being absorbed by some psychic sponge and soon I'd disappear entirely.

Suddenly, I could tell Pitre was listening, weighing some desire to speak or keep his own counsel. Was he afraid he'd uncover his motives; his way of avoiding my repeated insistence?

Little did he know I'd given up on trying to assess the mode of my imminent untimely demise. My list of concerns had absolutely nothing to do with self.

Chaste was well taken care of physically and monetarily; I'd seen to that. If I had my way, Ferry would soon carry my name and her needs would be met as well. The two of them would get along splendidly.

Hiding my impending feelings of termination was not as difficult as I'd previously believed. It was nothing more than a little theatre. A smile and mention of future events and anyone with the slightest qualm wouldn't despair.

This was driving me to madness. Instead of sitting on the sofa and inhaling the oncoming tide of self-pity, I went for a run.

Either the mindless effort of dropping one foot in front of the other or the increased endorphins worked their usual miracle. That and the blast of lukewarm water from the shower had brought me back to life.

Chaste was busy flipping channels on the television when I walked through to the kitchen for a drink.

"Did you call Ferry?"

"Yes..., Sir."

"Would you care to share your conversation with me?"

"She said she needed to come by here after work to change. Oh..., and she said to tell you thank you for the flowers."

Good. I hurried to my room to dress.

Ferry was becoming comfortable again with her regular visits and the constant attention from Chaste and I. That part of my plan, while a little deceptive and a little selfish, was necessary. Even the underlying guilt that I was deceiving Ferry's innocent heart was pushed away; my own conscience subdued.

My newly acquired reasoning was that if I were to somehow be suffering from paranoid delusions of an untimely end then my genuine affections for her would not be a harmful waste of her time.

After crushing my memories, I'd finally allowed myself to love someone again; that much my conscience had no qualms about whatsoever.

"Ferry's here!"

I managed to stuff one foot into the new pair of shoes Ferry had lavished on me. It wasn't that I didn't like them, I did, very much so, even the heartfelt intentions of the gift. The blasted things weren't broken in to the shape of my brogan-sized feet. Blisters or not, they were going on my feet every day until they conformed or I needed crutches. One of us would submit.

"Knock, knock?"

My bedroom door opened just as my other foot overcame the resistant Italian leather shoe. I looked up and Ferry's inquisitive eyes overcame my thoughts.

"Chaste told me you needed to change. I don't see why. You look lovely."

Ferry smiled; something that was getting more regular and natural around me, "Thank you, and thank you for the flowers..., again."

I slipped my arms around her, inhaling the soft fragrance of her hair.

"You've got to quit sending me flowers Kress. Everybody thinks we're fighting and you're trying to make up. I think they're just jealous myself."

She looped a finger in her pearl necklace, one that Chaste and I picked out.

"I'm not embarrassed by any means, I love them, but I don't have any place left to put them. They're all over the office. The whole office."

"Fine." I used her patented terminal response. "Maybe I did go a little overboard. What should I send you then?"

"Please, no candy or I'll inflate like the Hindenburg. What's got into you Kress?"

I cringed; maybe I was overdoing it just a bit, then again…, no. I wanted her to know exactly how I felt about her.

"You. You've gotten into me. What do you expect me to do?"

Her arms tightened around me, "Then I'm going to bring some of them here to brighten up the place."

There was a sudden cough at the door and a grunt.

"Are you going to make us late for the movies…, again?"

Ferry saw her before I turned around and quickly covered my eyes with the palm of her hand.

"Chaste, sweetheart. Why don't we wear something matching tonight?"

I fought past Ferry's blinder to have a look-see, then wished I hadn't. The first thing I noticed…, oh blast it all, I noticed everything at once.

Chaste, my nine and a half year old child, was caked with colorful makeup, black circling her eyes, her blond hair pulled away from her face in a severe twist.

Ringlets of yellow cascaded nearly down to her shoulders; a skintight t-shirt that had shrank to fit a toddler, flaunting her budding womanhood. Then there was the mini-skirt that would make a grown man blush…, I know I did. My heart seemed so shrivel inside me at her bawdy display.

Ferry saw my gawking eyes, "Kress…? Don't. Let me handle this."

Ferry hurried out the door with Chaste in tow and I hurried to watch them disappear down the hall to my daughter's bedroom.

With her sudden spurt in height and developing shape, Chaste, already gangly and tall for her age, could have easily passed for a petite girl of fifteen. Thank God Ferry was there to handle this new development or I'd have broken out in hives and exploded.

After trying not to eavesdrop on their conversation, I hurried down the stairs to a place of distant safety.

Several minutes later, the two of them came trotting down the stairs, in similar summer dresses, chattering quietly together.

The entire evening would have been far different if I'd allowed myself the luxury to light into my daughter for her poor choice of personal decor.

Ferry caught me watching and made a serious looking swipe across her brow, then shook her head.

As we headed to the garage, Ferry whispered in my ear, "I'm really sorry Kress. I don't know where she got the little shrink wraps she was wearing. She must have slipped it in on one of our shopping sprees. I did away with them."

I stopped Ferry in her tracks and let Chaste out into the garage, "Ferry, she's just an impressionable child. But you don't know how thankful I am you were here to moderate. I would have reacted much differently; it wouldn't have been pretty I assure you."

"She must be going through some phase or she's still troubled. Has she talked to you?"

I shook my head, then remembered that Chaste spoke of having some bad dream during her nap. The eight months of constant illicit programming could hardly be redacted in so short a time.

Once again, Ferry proved herself a godsend. I kissed her quickly before she could make light of her good deed.

"Does this mean I'm going to get more flowers?"

"Only if you want them."

A blast of the horn on the Rover shook us out of our embrace and we hurried out the door.

"We're going to be late…, again!"

I barely remembered the picture show, nor did I care, with Ferry's constant mumbling in my ear and holding my hand.

The children's fantasy with scenes of the English countryside and castles was all Chaste talked about during dinner until she finally became frustrated with our lack of common enthusiasm.

When we arrived back home, Ferry hurried to her Lincoln and

pulled out a small wrapped object and hurried to Chaste.

"Here, I know you've read all the other six volumes."

Chaste ripped off the brown paper and screeched, "Thank you, Ferry."

She flipped over an orange slipcover and scanned the first page while we watched. It was another segment of the movie we'd just watched.

Ferry leaned over to Chaste, "Give me a quick hug sweetheart, I'm leaving."

"Oh do you have to leave?" begged Chaste.

"I need to get back and get some sleep before court tomorrow."

I walked out onto the front lawn while they said their goodbyes and waited for Ferry to find me.

"I see you're better at diversions than I am," I mumbled.

"Not hardly. I just know what little girls want."

She let me kiss her for a few minutes before placing both her palms against my chest in a soft push.

"I need to leave."

She said it so seriously, it gave me pause.

"It's getting late, why don't you use one of the spare rooms? You know you're completely welcome."

She pushed further away, shaking her head.

"Because I know what big girls want too, and I need some sleep before tomorrow."

I felt the heat rise in my face.

"Ferry, I promise to be a gentleman. I'll be on my best behavior."

"Funny, I can't promise I'd be a lady. Good night Kress."

She turned quickly and sounded like a hissing balloon as she let out a long breath of air.

My hand caught her car door before it shut and I knelt beside her.

"Thank you for making this a wonderful evening Ferry."

"Thank you too, now let me leave before I change my mind."

Her car began to back away, then she lowered her window and waved.

"Love you Kress."

I watched as the lights of her car dimmed and turned the last corner out of sight down the hill. I replayed visions of our evening as I fed the happy mongrels, locked up the house and reset the alarm.

Chaste was already crushed under her covers reading when I

passed her room.

"Night Daddy."

My cell phone rang before I could offer her any small talk, it was Ferry. My first thought was some protracted scene of malice due to our colorful past and I hurried down the hall to my room as I answered.

"Ferry? Are you alright?"

"Of course I'm alright. Did I catch you at a bad time?"

"Not at all."

She must have heard the relief in my voice and started right into what was on her mind.

"Kress I need to talk to you about Chaste. I..., just couldn't while I was there. We need to talk about what's going on with your daughter. This afternoon..., after I helped her scrape off all that paint and find her something decent to wear, I managed to get her to open up a little. Kress, she's got some really..., colorful..., ideas about what young ladies are supposed to act like around boys. Honestly, after listening to her a few minutes, she scared the hell out of me. She mentioned a few things only..., well..., only..., how do I put this; things a seasoned married couple should know."

"No. I take that back. She mentioned things I didn't know and that's well...."

"Ferry, wait."

This was a conversation I didn't want to have over the phone, but I also understood why it was probably better this way.

"There are some things I should explain to you."

I cautiously went into detail about the rigorous brainwashing technique used on Chaste and the other children during her months in captivity without letting Ferry know how I garnered my information.

"So you see, even though she seems to have blocked most of her ordeal, there are still pieces that I..., we..., are going to have to work on without making her feel...."

"Like she's dirty or abnormal."

"Exactly."

I heard the wind blowing past Ferry's open car window as she was thinking. I could visualize the look on her face as she raced through her options.

"I'm glad you explained. At least I can understand what she's going through. What are we going to do?"

The concern in her voice was more motherly than the role of Chaste's guardian, which made me feel even more at ease.

"We're going to love her and show her patience."

She was quiet for another moment.

"You're a good father Kress..., and a good friend. Well, more than a friend.... I..., I better go. I'm at the lodge.... See you tomorrow?"

"Absolutely."

CHAPTER SIXTY-SEVEN

After dropping the phone on the table, I checked
another item off my list; our commercial flight plans were all
confirmed.

Brent and Carl departed yesterday morning, after they insisted on
flying out before our arrival to take inventory of the outdoor venue
where Owasu Satiiri would be speaking at his political rally. They
didn't seem at all pleased that they wouldn't be allowed their usual
firearms for protection, even on the privately chartered flight. I tried
repeatedly to reassure them that this was only going to be a short to-
do and that most of our time afterward would be sightseeing and
sampling the immense local culture and dining. They were to treat it
as a paid mini-vacation.

The boys were at a boarding kennel in Phoenix, unhappily I might
add. They whined insatiably as I was leaving them, almost like
children being left with a sitter for the first time.

"Dad, where should I put my things?"

"By the garage door…, and no, Ferry's not coming here…, we're
going to pick her up at The Arms Lodge on our way out to the
airport tomorrow morning."

She scooted past me with a sly grin, "Eavesdropper."

I tipped my imaginary hat and she tried to roll the wheels of her
pull behind luggage across my foot. She was smiling again, her bright
blue eyes in full display.

Chaste came back using the same path and I handed her a
sandwich and a drink as she passed.

"You packed warm clothing?" I asked. "I don't need to inspect your wardrobe choices?"

She nodded while chewing her first bite.

"It's not going to be the typical climate you're used to here...."

"Yes, Dad. I remember," she swallowed. "It's only been two years since we visited Port Elizabeth."

That was the day before we left Africa, vowing never to return.

"I wasn't sure if you remembered. You were just a small mouthy little girl back then."

"And now I'm a tall mouthy little girl. Is that what you're saying?" she grunted. "At least your memory is getting better. After all, you kept your promise I could go with you wherever you go, remember?"

"You remind me everyday that you're just a little too precocious for your own good..., but I'm very proud of you nonetheless."

"So you do think I'm mouthy," she mumbled.

"An absolutely beautiful, tall, mouthy young lady. I know you have great things in store for your future."

She rolled her eyes at my admiration; her humility was still intact.

"Does this mean that I can go with you on your run today?"

How odd. I never knew Chaste felt she had to ask.

"I never knew you were interested. There's a chance it might rain."

"You're still going," she mumbled.

"What if you melt?" I asked.

At least the serious rote was gone and a slim grin creased her lips.

"Dad..., please, I'm not a child you know."

Yes she was a little child, but that argument wasn't worth pursuing at the moment.

"Of course you can go, after your food settles. Do you think you can keep up?"

She scurried upstairs to change, shaking her head.

Alone..., I made my way to the sofa, "Pitre have I forgotten anything? I'd rather you remind me now than when we're on an airplane over the Atlantic."

Strange..., this time I didn't actually feel him move forward inside me before his spoke.

"Everything is accounted for, Kress. You should learn to trust your memory; it is one of the marks after all. You've done well with controlling your other marks."

"What others?" I asked, sitting forward.

"The first six of course; listening, sensing, knowing, strength, travel, and sight. I had to give you a nudge from time to time, but you've done well, better than I expected."

I caught myself subconsciously rubbing my arms where he'd laid two of those marks, remembering the pain, "…and the seventh?"

"The first six belong to you…, for your trouble, the seventh is… me of course."

"What's to become of you and I Pitre?"

Instantly I felt that strange loss and darkness as Pitre withdrew, as if he'd allowed something to surface he'd been hiding.

"You don't have to answer. Just promise you'll help me do what's best for Chaste and Ferry when the time comes."

He nodded slowly, so did I; it was a strange feeling. I had my unspoken confirmation.

The thumping footsteps of Chaste jostled me from my stupor just before she began descending the stairs.

She squeaked to a stop before galloping headlong over to where I was seated.

"What did I miss?" she asked breathlessly.

My inquisitive daughter was always interested in the slightest tidbit of information Pitre had to offer.

"Trip plans, boring lists."

She looked crestfallen for a moment.

"You're not running in those are you?"

I looked down at the shoes Ferry bought me, now as comfortable as house slippers.

"Give me a minute to change."

There was still plenty of daylight for us to make my usual circuit down the well-worn gravel trail to the north of our home. I didn't particularly care for rushing past the peering eyes of our neighbor's darkened windows, but it was the only access to the trailhead.

Chaste seemed to sense my uncomfortable emotions as we turned the corner and she took my hand. My head must have been glancing every direction like a ping-pong paddle.

"What do they look like?" she whispered, just loud enough for me to hear.

I knew what she was asking, despite the fact that my concerns were more mundane, not the peering tall greys we'd encountered.

"I'd rather not talk about them."

She squeezed my hand, "Just tell me. Are they like Pitre?"

"Absolutely not! They're hideous, foul, dark empty things…."

Thankfully, she didn't seem phased by my sudden emotional outburst.

"Thank you."

"For what?" I asked.

I stopped walking before we reached the entrance to the trail just ahead.

"For not sugar-coating your answer, for not lying to me."

She took off walking ahead of me, speeding her steps. She didn't ask if there were any of the tall greys watching; she seemed to know we were alone.

CHAPTER SIXTY-EIGHT

Brent Rand called at six a.m. sharp, it was three p.m. in Cape Town and he sounded tired. The meeting was scheduled as announced. Satiiri had no idea that we were coming or of an impending donation to set the course of his efforts back on track. The money would supply new water wells and irrigation equipment to be shared by tribes. Food and yes..., desperately needed medical supplies. All peace offerings to avert the needless hostilities being stirred up by unknown factions.

No sooner than Brent rang off, Ferry called.

"Who were you talking to?" she asked straightaway.

"Brent. Good morning to you too."

"Sorry Kress, good morning. I guess I'm a little antsy. I'm packed and ready to go."

"There's nothing to be nervous about Ferry. This will be a trip you'll not likely forget for some time. I've planned a few surprises I hope you're going to enjoy."

"Tell me a few. Maybe my stomach will stop doing flip-flops."

"I don't want to ruin the surprises.... How do you like authentic Italian food?"

"You know it's one of my favorites.... How sweet of you."

"We happen to have a six hour layover in New York. I did some research on a few of the better restaurants. There's one called Napoli's that has...."

"Oh, no...," she hissed. "I'd better let you go then. I didn't pack anything formal enough for...."

She gasped in some air, "What time are you picking me up?"

"In about an hour."

"Oh gosh, New York is our first stop. I'll have to wear something that's.... I have to go. See you soon, bye."

I couldn't tell if I'd helped her last minute jitters or made them worse.

Most of my plans were not without merit. Our morning flight from Phoenix to LaGuardia International deposited us at our exit gate just before four in the afternoon, New York time. Ferry had little excuse to be flight-conscious while seated between Chaste and I, constantly chattering about our final destination.

The route my travel agency had originally offered was more economical but would have been unbelievably grueling and boring. Our new route would take us first to London, a skip over to Paris, then another to Rome, and finally a non-stop flight to Johannesburg.

Ferry and Chaste looked absolutely stunning as we stepped off the flight at LaGuardia Airport. With a beautiful lady on each arm, together we descended on New York.

We stored our baggage at the airport in lieu of our impending ten p.m. flight to London and hailed a taxi.

Ferry believed our trip would be two consecutive gruelingly long flights with little time to open our eyes outside the airports. It was my pleasure to disappoint her.

The evening traffic in New York was vile and hedonistic. I couldn't fathom driving among such confusion on a daily basis. We were all doubly blessed that we couldn't understand the fits of Hindi our driver frequented at other motorists although his gestures were universal.

It wasn't until we were at our restaurant that Ferry began to relax and badger both Chaste and I to see our tickets or the travel itinerary. It was all in good sport for the first part of our meal at La Pierre's; an extremely formal affair.

Ferry didn't seem disappointed whatsoever that the promised Italian food was put on hold. Our first of several scheduled outings was a splendid success.

After I purposely let it slip that our next stop was London, Ferry began to smile enthusiastically and the battle was won.

We all slept soundly during the flight across the Atlantic and disembarked just past one in the afternoon, London time. It was drizzly and cold, nothing unusual or out of order. We had just enough time for me to show Chaste where her mother and I attended University with a long list of promises to show her our old family estate on the return trip.

I'd never seen this side of Ferry; she looked ten years younger after escaping the stress of her daily duties. She seemed just as overcome and heart-happy as Chaste at every stop; her camera filled to capacity at each venue.

With a night on the streets of London and an early morning flight to Paris, we had no more than four hours of sightseeing buffer before our next short flight to Rome.

Once there, we walked the cobblestone streets of the city until late that evening where we found a perfect family-owned Italian bistro in the main piazza. Thankfully both Chaste and Ferry put away their cameras. Our glaring eyes and chattering persona already betrayed our tourisma.

As we were seated at Mama Cocina, the final vestiges of Ferry's protective shell ebbed away.

"I feel like I'm in some sort of dream world Kress."

"It's probably jet lag," I mused.

"You know what I mean."

"I'm glad you're enjoying the trip so far."

"You're up to something. We could have been in Cape Town by morning if we'd taken the non-stop from Heathrow."

"Sssshh," whispered Chaste, as she nudged Ferry. "Please don't spoil the fun."

"We still have a long flight to endure to Johannesburg in a few hours. I couldn't break up that flight into segments."

Ferry smiled as our waitress opened a bottle of dark wine.

"That's not why you took us the long way, is it?"

Chaste giggled and turned away, pretending to look through the front window at some distraction.

"You did this for me didn't you?"

Thankfully, I didn't have to answer due to a sudden outburst of live music near our table.

Ferry got her authentic Italian food as promised in Rome, sealed with a kiss from yours truly.

New York, London, Paris, and Rome went by without a hitch.

Then came the awfully long flight to Johannesburg, South Africa.

Even with our first class seating, the first half of our voyage was cramped, noisy, and the flight bumpy with turbulence. Our flight was originally booked with British Airways, but we'd been shuffled due to some delays to another airline.

We spent more time affixed behind our seatbelts trying to relax to the idiotic outdated in-flight movies; of which the sound system wasn't working and were pasted with subtitles in French. I quickly tired as verbal translator for my two frustrated travel companions when I noticed that both were asleep against each of my shoulders. I cradled them both with an arm and prayed for sleep that fought me with every noise from the other passengers.

About half way through our late night flight, we were awakened by some loud excitement from the coach section behind us. After asking a distraught flight attendant, we found out that there had been some sort of skirmish between two passengers and our flight was almost reverted back to Rome.

To add insult to injury, one of the restrooms in coach was broken and a steady stream of passengers were being diverted to the first class restrooms.

Gads.

We were now all wide-awake, bleary-eyed and staring at one another. A little later came the announcement of our mid-flight meal; we were ecstatic if only for the diversion. Ferry took a photo of the miniscule portions on our plates and we all had a short, contained laugh. By now, I was ready for anything alcoholic in nature and mentioned it to Ferry. She agreed.

I even considered allowing Chaste the champagne Ferry and I were offered.

An hour before we landed in Johannesburg, Ferry promised to let me charter a private flight for this leg of our return trip; she even offered to pay.

We were drained. The initial fun and excitement of our trip was no match for twelve hours inside the jumbo flying freighter. Luckily, all our luggage was accounted for and we managed a taxi straightaway.

As soon as the vehicle began to move, I caught a glimpse of a tall figure maybe a block away that resembled one of the tall greys that we'd been plagued with for days on end. Then it was gone, as soon as I blinked. My internal warning system wasn't sending blazing jolts of electricity to my mind so I forced myself to pass it off as exhaustion and paranoia. The last thing I wanted to do was let my imagination run away with me and spoil what could be one of the most important defining markers in my family's life.

Upon arriving at the Sheraton, our hotel reservations had been cancelled, we were registered for the previous day.

I hate to admit it, but it was my fault, with the time difference and all. Some international conference was in progress and there was only one suite available at this hotel; a single. At this point, none of us cared. We wanted an actual meal and sleep, even if it was on a floor pallet, but it wasn't appropriate to stuff Ferry and I in the same tight quarters. We walked across the intersection to the Hyatt and found two adjoining rooms available.

We ordered room service and ate like the three little pigs while ignoring the noise on the television. Ferry and Chaste shared the adjoining room and I sprawled to all four corners of my king-sized bed.

Sleep fought each of us like a badger that night in Johannesburg. Street noises below us and twisted dreams robbed us of the rest we so badly needed.

Near morning, nightmares cast me about like a skiff at sea. The first image was a great growing pyre, sparks flying high into a dark starless sky. A faceless, voiceless threat beckoned me closer to the flames just as Pitre appeared and stepped in between to intervene. My dreams never afforded me any sort of speech, even though they were as lifelike as the waking world around me. The powerful torment flashed images of Elizabeth amidst the flames, then the lifeless body of Chaste limp, dashed upon the heap. It was needless to see the face I wrestled with, I knew who was welcoming me home. A dozen more night phantasms punished me for returning to South Africa. By early morning, I was kneaded in sweat and curled in a ball at the edge of the bed.

Back in the burning kettle of my past and seated on the edge of my bed, I looked at the glaring clock in the darkness.

It was four in the morning.

I reminisced of my family's last night in Africa, of my night in El Paso just before my expedition into Mexico, and much, much, more.

Pitre spoke softly, befriended me, convinced me into at least two more hours of dreamless rejuvenating sleep.

CHAPTER SIXTY-NINE

We took the first available shuttle flight to Cape Town and it was as if a heavy blanket had been lifted from all of us. The atmosphere was positive and easy to breathe; we all noticed it right away.

Carl was the first to greet us in the Hilton lobby and thankfully, all our rooms in Cape Town were booked by the travel agent. We were located within sight of the ocean on Africa's southwestern coast. I had forgotten the feeling of my bare feet buried in cold gritty sand with wind driven waves pounding inland.

The first thing I did after we checked in was have everyone shrug into something comfortable, then grab Ferry and Chaste to hurry with me outdoors. We made our way across heavily trafficked thoroughfare and in minutes were standing facing the boisterous Atlantic Ocean. A chill ran through every fiber of my being as I closed my eyes and breathed in the salty spray. It served to reinforce an already good memory.

The predominant wind was brisk with a fresh chill, forcing Ferry and Chaste to huddle into my sides to stay warm the entire afternoon.

The main part of the city was more of a gleaming megalopia of ultramodern high-rise buildings; close to three and a half million people crushing about in their daily pursuits.

Carl and Brent followed everywhere we went and the five of us spent the day at the local markets just outside the main thrust of the city, sampling the local flavors and discussing the particulars of the next day's intended meeting with Satiiri and his organization.

Brent and Carl took me by the outdoor pavilion where the political rally would be held the next day. Cheaply printed circulars announcing the gathering were on every post, shack, and family market in the area. It was conveniently labeled a local cultural event intended to rally support within the mix of local people already co-existing and making a life for themselves away from the strict rule of tribal laws of their origins.

It was a bold move on the part of Owasu Satiiri to gain support of those already living peacefully together; something tangible to bring back to the rigid confines of his native childhood region. It was also a last ditch effort to rally financial support amongst a minority population without the resources necessary to bring about the amount of change that was desperately needed - Financial support that had mysteriously dwindled to nothing over the last twenty months.

As the evening grew late, we found a taxi to take us back to our hotel. It appeared that I was the only one of our assembly ready to find solitude and regroup for the upcoming activities.

Ferry and Chaste were lying on their backs across their bed, tired but giddy, discussing the days' adventures.

"I never expected to see whales swimming right off the coast in front of me."

"I grew up with the occasional lion that wandered in off the savannah into our back yard," said Chaste.

I heard my daughter trying to be the sage of the two women and shuddered at her lack of humility.

"Chaste? That only happened once. You were four years old. Our real problem was the water buffalo that trampled our small garden. They were always an angry lot."

I heard myself usurping Chaste in her one-upmanship and quickly apologized.

"I can't imagine living with all the exotic wildlife in your own back yard. I guess exotic is a relative term. It makes me feel small."

"Ferry you should be happy where you live. Imagine waking up with a eight foot boa constrictor coiled in the corner of your bedroom. The first time that happened, Elizabeth and I knew we were in for a lifetime of experiences."

I didn't mean for the room to get silent by the mention of Elizabeth, but the entire setting was screaming her memories.

"How did Elizabeth handle the change when you first moved here?"

"We were both young and ignorant. The whole world lay whimpering at our feet. After all, we had each other. Both of us had degrees in medicine; we were the educated elite, hah! We were both scared senseless our first entire year, until one of the Satiiri tribesmen befriended us.

"In the first six months of our medical practice, we had exactly four patients. One was a wounded milk goat."

That seemed to lighten the mood with a little laughter. I had a feeling I was going to be reminiscing well into the night.

"Consequently, that milk goat was the best advertisement we could have hoped for. One of the women had died at childbirth and there were no mid-wives to nurse the baby. That nanny goat turned out to be the child's only source of food."

"That's amazing…. That's when you started getting visitors?"

I felt that certain blackness grip my throat and wished I'd not begun my story at the beginning. It was also our initiation into a war zone and the horrible casualties.

"Among other circumstances, yes."

Ferry sat up on her elbows and peered over at me, "What other circumstances?"

"Not a very good memory, Ferry. Let's just say it was messy, shall we?"

She nodded, "Eighteen years…, I admire both of you…, and you too Chaste. Chaste?"

Chaste was lying on her side, mouth open, fast asleep.

"Do you want to do the honors, or shall I?" I grunted, switching off the lights.

Ferry grinned and rolled slowly off the side of the bed.

"I'd better wake her up for a shower. We both smell like nanny goats."

"I seriously doubt that. If you need me, I'll be in the next room. I suppose I should get some sleep too…, we have a long day ahead tomorrow."

I turned away and yawned uncontrollably at the mere thought of actual sleep.

"Kress? What should I do if I need you?" asked Ferry.

"I'll leave the adjoining door cracked open in case…."

I was being stupid again. Where was Pitre when I needed a swift kick in the seat of my pants?

Ferry met me in the doorway and pulled my arms around her waist.

"Let me rephrase…, I'll leave the door open so you never have to ask that question again."

Ferry's lips met mine with an urgency I hadn't expected. I prayed that I was doing the right thing, that there would be several more tomorrow's to share with her. I prayed that if my worst fears materialized, that I wouldn't shatter Ferry's heart.

Then suddenly, I prayed that I'd be able to be a gentleman that night – with hopes of giving Ferry the ice clear emerald cut diamond ring with two blood rubies set on either side.

"Dad? Did I fall asleep?" mumbled Chaste.

Our arms and lips released with a sigh; Ferry buried her face against my chest in frustration. My daughter unwittingly helped keep Ferry and I honest for yet another day.

That night I dreamed of a mass horde of tall greys congregating around the podium where Owasu Satiiri and I stood. All pointing and milling through a raucous crowd of people, whispering into their minds. The blank faces of the people began to move closer and closer, their hands grasping like zombies at our feet and legs.

Quickly the dream turned to the face of the man I knew only as Special Agent Amos Lily, grinning at me with beady eyes set upon me, burning me with perfect hatred.

No words were uttered, but I knew what I sensed…, one word…, *Tomorrow*.

CHAPTER SEVENTY

I didn't dare recant my awakening dream to Ferry. What could I tell Carl or Brent? I had a nightmare. It wasn't akin to pre-stage jitters; dreams of being on stage in your underwear in front of a classroom of your peers.

Pitre was so much a part of me now that I didn't have to ask him what the dream meant. We shared almost every common thought and feeling these last few weeks.

I slipped the knot of my fuchsia tie up to my neck with a sudden angry jerk, pre-noose imaginings constricting my throat. It wasn't until I saw my face turning shades of red that I managed to come to my senses and loosen my perfect Windsor knot from shutting off all blood flow to my seemingly ill-functioning brain. I blinked my eyes until they cleared, thankful for an angel's gift of rejuvenation during my laborious night.

Today was the day....

Two arms circled my waist from behind and Ferry pulled me close.

"You look nice Kress."

Another quick squeeze and she was standing beside me.

"Thanks to you. I never was the GQ sort of fellow."

Ferry was a vision, elegant; worthy of any gentleman's arm. Her tawny hair was pulled high in back, yet hung loose just past her shoulders. The gray wool dress snuggled her features, accenting her every shape. It would be a shame to cover it all up with her knee length coat.

"You are absolutely stunning."

Her eyes pierced mine and my heart sank at the unknown choices facing me as I tried to look away.

"Are you going to tell me what's wrong?"

I smiled instantly, imagining that she was the one with an angel residing within her, exposing my every whimsical thought.

"Jitters I suppose. I haven't given away ten million dollars before."

There was also the little matter of a twenty year anniversary today; one last private matter that belonged only to me, my final goodbye to Elizabeth Ellen Schumacher.

"It's just a symbolic check Kress. Think of it as nothing but a piece of paper with..., an awful lot of zero's lining the right column. On second thought, just think of it as a piece of paper."

She laughed nervously and watched my expression.

"You know you can trust me Kress. You can tell me anything."

I nodded, "I do trust you. If there was anything concrete to tell you, I would."

She made sure she turned me to face her.

"Kress, I'm here for you."

If there was anything left to talk about after today, I'd take Ms. Ferry Dunavin up on her offer for many years to come.

There was a knock at my door, then immediately another at Ferry's door in the adjoining hotel room. Apparently, our two bodyguards didn't want to make any assumptions.

Ferry was peering around me when I opened my door to Carl's bright smile, looking as if he'd won some sort of wager.

"We need to leave here in about fifteen minutes if we want to catch the opening ceremony. Any last requests?"

When I didn't smile at the odd wording of his question, his face became all business.

"Anything you want to tell me before we visit this dog and pony show?"

Blast it all. I'd never make a career out of gambling if everyone around me knew I was anxious just from my clowns' expressions.

Brent abandoned the other door and squeezed in past Carl from the hallway, but not before giving me an awkward glance.

"He won't tell you, but I guarantee he knows something we don't."

Brent cut another knowing flash of the eyes and walked past me wrestling his starchy looking suit coat back into order.

"Can you make sure you keep an especially close eye on Chaste and Ferry today? These public meetings can be a little unorthodox so I'm told."

"Kress Schumacher, you need to quit that right now. You've already got everyone on edge. We're a thousand miles from home and you're still paranoid."

Apparently Ferry had forgotten that this continent was my home for nearly twenty years. This continent was the reason we'd fled to America in the first place.

"Actually, it's closer to ten thousand miles and if the good Doctor says we should watch you and Chaste, I'm not letting either of you out of my sight for a second," said Brent.

Well…, God bless Brent.

Chaste took Ferry's hand and grinned up at her before Ferry could summon some other reprimand from her private repertoire.

Our entourage made it all the way to the front lobby and I remembered that I'd left the short speech I'd prepared, folded and lying on the dressing table.

"I have to go back to the room," I mumbled, while searching my pockets.

"The taxi won't wait, Kress. You won't need your notes," said Ferry.

"We'll be cutting it pretty close, Sir."

"Go on ahead. I'll be five minutes behind you."

"I'll wait and go with Dr. Schumacher," said Carl.

"Ridiculous, I'd rather you both stay with the ladies."

The taxi driver honked his horn, followed by another parked anxiously behind him.

After convincing everyone that I needed my absentminded abettor, I urged them on; there was a line of taxi's waiting for the chance to bilk a few extra coins from another unwitting outlander.

It actually served two purposes – I did need my one paragraph speech of course, but it also gave me another five minutes alone to speak with Pitre.

Once inside the elevator…, alone…, "Pitre, I have something to say to you. It doesn't have to be face to face…, but I would like to know that you're listening."

"Of course, Kress."

His voice sounded as close as my own inside my head, the voice I hear when I'm speaking. I only had a few minutes so I didn't bother with explanations.

"Pitre..., when we first met..., I didn't care for you much. In fact I pretty much hated you..., the very idea of you. After Chaste was safe I didn't much care what became of our agreement."

"Kress..., wait."

"No..., let me say this. I need to get this out for my own conscience sake.... I want you to know that I appreciate how you've helped me..., but more importantly how you helped my daughter and Ferry. You've been a true friend."

It was one of those rare occasions where Pitre was silent.

"Whatever happens today..., and don't lie to me..., I want you to promise that you'll watch after my daughter and Ferry."

"Kress..., I'm the one that is indebted to you. If anything unexpected should happen, if I'm allowed, I promise to watch over your family."

I knew what he meant by the 'allowed' addendum from our previous talks. He had to answer to a Higher power now. That much was understandable and acceptable.

"Good."

Our business was concluded just as the elevator opened. I rushed to our room, found my crumpled speech and stuffed it in the lapel pocket of my nice blue suit.

Pitre was silent, close, unnerving. I could actually feel him peering through my eyes, sensing my thoughts, following my plans to the taxi and to the ceremony.

By the time I arrived at the event, the streets were stuffed with hundreds of shoulder to shoulder onlookers. The taxi driver tried but it was impossible for him to drive past the waving police blockade, so I had to disembark several blocks from the actual podium. At least it was within sight in the distance and no one was on stage as yet.

I skirted the crowded streets and followed close to the edges of the closed shops and makeshift storefronts. Four more city blocks, past tight little alleys, and I'd be in front of the crowd with my party, ready to complete my final mission. I felt almost giddy with excitement with my objective just in sight up ahead. This last day of Owasu Satiiri's open air reverie was the same day twenty years prior that Elizabeth and I had embarked on our journey to this continent together. Today I'd complete that commitment, two souls striving for the same goal. I felt my face radiate a smile I hadn't been able to force for two entire years, since Elizabeth's death.

Two hands grasped my arms firmly and steered me into the brightly lit alley, then gave a shove to thrust me forward.

Bloody hell.

I spun around angrily and couldn't believe my eyes. There before me was the man that I loathed more than any other human being, pointing a gun in my direction.

The world around me darkened as I felt my back slam into a brick wall; one hand braced against my chest, the other sporting an instrument of death.

How did he get here? How did he find me? I'd seen no tall grey spectres peering over the crowd, no telltale pointing apparitions ready to judge my death and see it executed.

It was then that I noticed something interesting; the signature black haze I'd seen hovering close to his outline like steam was gone. Had he been abandoned by his internal driver?

My dreams these last few days began to toy with my vision, their fears attempting to manifest before my eyes.

"Remember your gifts," my friend whispered inside me. *"It's only fear. Fight it."*

There were six marks on my body, six gifts, but only the seventh was barking at me with instructions.

His hand fell away as I pressed from the wall and felt myself facing yet another opponent in yet another arena.

"Hello and goodbye," he gritted.

My old nemesis Agent Lily aimed the weapon at me and pulled the trigger. It only clicked noisily, several times.

The gun dropped angrily, "Looks like I'm going to earn my money the old fashioned way."

Before another word was uttered, Agent Lily lurched at me and his clubbed fist flew at my face followed by the growl of his intentions. I dodged instinctively, but his fist grazed my chin nonetheless.

He'd been paid to see me ended?

Lily looked confused and disgruntled, as if the little tap on my chin should have lay me on my backside or that I should have fallen down and played dead.

"I've been waiting for this for a long time Schumacher. There's no skirt for you to hide behind now."

I supposed that if things didn't go his way, the next thing I'd feel or maybe the last would be a bullet to my head from some unknown accomplice. But by George, I wasn't going to let an opportunity pass to wail on him for fear of being shot. I raised both my fists and pulled my elbows close, I'd done this once or twice myself.

My first two jabs hit Lily on the cheek and he fell flat of his canister. He hurried back up and my right fist caught the other side of his face, splitting his lips, sending him back into the dirt.

Now he looked even more confused at me.

He shook his head and spat blood, spewing his usual vulgarities my direction. At least his signature stare was gone.

Pleased with myself and Lily's angered state, I let him get up and he lunged his huge bulk straight at me once again. I stepped to the side and fed him an elbow to send him on his way past. He crumpled to his knees as if I'd hit him with a billet club and grunted painfully.

Now, Lily's expression was one of pain as well as anger.

He spat more blood past his swelling bulbous lips and stood to face me once again. Lily feinted a punch, then spun and kicked the side of my thigh. It was barely a tap and I dropped my fists, beginning to wonder what his real game was. It was like fighting a child.

I glanced around quickly to see if there were others or if someone had a gun pointed my direction, but we were essentially alone in the alley. None of this made any sense in the least.

"Your marks," whispered from inside me once again.

A middle aged couple were the only ones taking notice of our strange altercation while waving frantically at someone in the throng of the crowd.

Lily used my moment of quandary to mount another odd attack; rushing forward he grabbed my jacket with both hands, then dropped and stuck a foot against my chest, pulling me forward in a flip. I landed in a roll on the dirt alleyway and stood up quickly as he ambled to rise.

Lily was sweating and heaving like a mud trapped water buffalo.

After further inspection, both lapels on my new jacket were torn.

Suddenly, all I could think of was that Ferry was going to be sorely upset with me.

I heard a loud whistle blare coupled with shouting at the far end of the alley and Lily snarled at me, wiping at his broken mouth with his sleeve.

"This isn't over Schumacher."

He fled quickly toward the crowd at the other end of the alley and I saw what I'd suspected. In an instant a black cloak descended upon Lily, engulfing him in possession, disappearing into the empty host, just as two men in uniform flew past me in pursuit.

The tall black was petrified at facing Pitre in a fair arena and had abandoned Lily, leaving his human host to finish with me.

I knew it wouldn't be more than a few moments before those same uniformed gents returned to question me and detain me for participating in a public row and so I disappeared back into the crowded street, on to where I was supposed to be ages ago.

Someone was tapping the microphone on stage and I hurried the last three blocks, completely baffled by the strange altercation with Lily. I had every reason to be angry, to want to destroy the man, or to see him captured and placed where he could never harm anyone else.

Instead, I felt free; my death sentence was abated. The 'tomorrow' threat from my dream was past. I'd somehow survived my altercation with the dark forces and Lily and I was still breathing.

This country's laws viewed personal assault through a different lens than where we were now living. It was only a matter of time before Lily was locked away in an extradition friendly South Africa.

Now my mind turned to a sudden joy of what was taking place only a few dozen yards just ahead of me at the gaily decorated pavilion.

CHAPTER SEVENTY-ONE

I had to force my way forward through the last wave of
spectators before I spotted Carl's tall stature in the crowd. Huddled
between he and Brent was Ferry and Chaste, shielded as promised.

Ferry smiled furiously at the sight of me, then her face fell in
shock.

"Kress?"

"Everything is fine. What have I missed?"

"You're bleeding! Your jacket..., it's ruined. What happened?"

Ferry dabbed carefully at my lip and I felt a little sting. I saw
Chaste clinging to Ferry's side, her eyes desperately wide.

I turned to the stern faces of Carl and Brent, "Lily is here."

Both men spun, scouring the crowded street, but it would be
literally impossible to spot him in this large a throng of faces.

"Do you want to leave? We can take Ferry and your daughter to a
safer place."

I shook my head, "He's a little worse for wear than I am at the
moment, I assure you. The last I saw of him, two policemen were
chasing after him. I think we can finish up here before we have to
file a formal complaint with the local authorities."

I heard a familiar voice behind me and felt myself smile
uncontrollably.

"My brother..., are you a ghost?" whispered the tall slender young
man.

Satiiri's heavy mixed accent sounded like music in my ears. He
looked positively terrified at first, then flung to me in an embrace.

He pushed away suddenly at arms length, "What has happened to you?"

I smiled and shook my head, "Trouble still follows me wherever I go. It is so good to see you my little brother."

Owasu smiled even brighter, but only for a moment, "It was told to us that you were dead, everyone heard that the little sister had been killed."

Then something vile slurred into my understanding. When Elizabeth was poisoned, she wasn't the intended victim; Chaste was. It had been all about our daughter from the very beginning.

He looked past me in recognition of Chaste and smiled again, hopeful.

"She is alive," he barely whispered, then his smile broke too soon. "We saw what happened to your home and everyone believed the stories."

I had to tell him, but wasn't sure how.

"Elizabeth is…," I started, but my face froze and my eyes betrayed me.

The young man looked at me and I saw a stream of water begin to wash his dark cheeks.

"No…," he whispered sadly. "Miss Elizabeth saved my life."

I nodded, "She's gone. Right after we left."

"Such an evil thing. What happened at your Clinic, it is the reason I joined this work. The group is called Unify South Africa."

I nodded my head, "I know, that's why I'm here today, to help."

"But you cannot. You have the little sister to watch over now."

"You're right, I can't stay, but there are other ways I can help. I have a gift for you on behalf of Elizabeth, in her honor, through the European Medical Association; the ones that opened the door and gave us our beginning here."

"Owasu…, Mr. Satiiri."

Someone on stage was about to start the speaking engagement.

"Come Doctor…, hurry. Stand beside me."

"Wait…," said a small voice behind me.

Ferry had me slip off my torn coat and wiped the blood and dirt off my face, then gingerly flipped my hair with her fingers. She pecked a kiss on my cheek and forced a smile.

"Here, take this," said Brent above the rising noise of the crowd.

Brent shrugged out of his blazer and quickly handed it to me,

"You look like you need this more than I do."

It was a good fit, a little tight, but felt like I'd put on something found in an attic it was so stuffy.

Ferry smiled her approval and suddenly I didn't care if it was a potato sack covering my chest.

The crowd was already alive listening to the announcements and Owasu's seasoned voice as I watched him hurry forward with a slight limp. It was a miracle that he could walk at all, but for the experienced hand of Elizabeth.

He waved me up the steps on the platform and quickly introduced me to the crowd.

There was no mass of tall greys, no zombie-like throng attacking the stage with swinging arms; only smiling faces waiting to hear what Owasu Satiiri had to say.

He ushered me closer and had me stand beside him and I looked down at the beaming faces of Ferry and Chaste.

Ferry motioned for me to button my top latch on the jacket and wiped the corner of her mouth to get me to mimic her.

I was probably still bleeding, not a very personable stage presence.

"Today is a very special day," Owasu began. "Today..., a brother that I believed dead..., is now alive.

"Many of you know of my beginning. I have told the story many times before you all. This brother..., Doctor Schumacher and his family..., were the inspiration and my reason for joining Unify South Africa."

I almost felt the heat of embarrassment as a roar of applause waved toward us from the crowd.

"Without his family's many years of sacrifice, our story would have never reached the outside world. Their photographs and articles were among many others that fuelled the face of Unify South Africa."

The crowd grew still and quiet fixated on his every word. It was then that I understood. This was Owasu's gift. People listened to him and were willing to follow his leadership.

"Without this brother and his family, I would not be alive standing here before you today. Doctor Schumacher and his wife Elizabeth not only saved my life..., with their own blood..., but set me on the path to unify our brothers and sisters across this region."

There wasn't a sound; only the wind whispering across the

microphone.

"And only moments ago..., I learned of the loss of my friend..., Doctor Elizabeth Schumacher. And even now, despite that loss, my brother Doctor Kress Schumacher comes to us today bringing a gift to help our cause."

The applause was back, replacing the fretful silence.

I saw Ferry's face turn gaunt and she ruffled through the remains of my blue jacket hurrying to pull out a piece of paper. My ridiculous little speech pinched tightly in her hand as she hurried up to the edge of the stage below and handed me my helper and the all important donation receipt.

"Would you please welcome, Doctor Schumacher?"

It was my all important cue; thankfully all my schoolboy jitters had scurried away.

"Thank you Owasu for your kind words and thank you for inviting me as a brother to stand with you here today.

Today marks the very day, the twentieth anniversary of when Elizabeth Ellen Schumacher and I first set foot on the soil of this continent. Much of our time spent here was documented by the European Medical Association through articles and photographs we authored. Because of them, I have been authorized to present a gift to you Owasu, toward the goals of Unify South Africa.

It is with great honor and humility that I am allowed to present this check to you in the amount of ten million U.S. dollars, dedicated to the work of my deceased wife Elizabeth Ellen Schumacher...."

All the air expelled from my lungs and I saw a spray of red fly from my nose and mouth.

There was a single crisp pop, far in the distance.

Then, everything was suddenly quiet, white, and very still.

CHAPTER SEVENTY-TWO

It was as if I had stepped aside and watched.

My body fell limp to the platform and there I rested. Ferry turned aside, holding Chaste; my daughter's face buried tight and silent against her body.

Carl covered both of them with outstretched arms, while Brent leapt to the stage and covered my body with his own.

People scattered and fled the stage as was to be expected, until it was only my body, Brent, and Owasu kneeling beside me.

Death was peaceful, I was ready to go, ready to end the dread, ready for the next phase of life.

This was Pitre's secret. My impending death had been his burden.

I was relieved it was over. Every pervading weight of dread began drifting away; I was truly free.

Immediately I was standing in a graveyard; bright cheerful rays of sunlight dancing across the ground. There before me was my daughter Chaste, standing with her back to me, looking down at a freshly covered grave.

A temporary plaque was anchored at the end with my name on it. Adjacent to the fresh earth was a headstone, with the name Elizabeth Ellen Schumacher chiseled deep into the face of the gray stone.

I was buried next to my wife.

The painful shock surged through me.

My field of vision suddenly changed and I was looking into the blue eyes of cold hard anger. My daughter was not weeping, not bearing flowers, there was no remorseful expression of loss.

She was there uttering bitter words at my grave, telling me that this was the last time she would ever visit this place again. That I'd made my plans to leave her alone, that I'd got my wish.

Now she was alone.

Another violent shock rippled into me.

Ferry came up behind her, tired expectant water filled eyes, and placed a caring arm around Chaste. She knocked Ferry away with a violent swing of an arm and stepped back, dragging a foot through the soft earth of the freshly covered grave.

My daughter kicked away the soil in anger and hurled words at Ferry that would scorch even the most jaded ear.

Ache soared through me.

Why was I being tormented by this vision? Hadn't I done everything that was asked of me?

This was all wrong…. I didn't want to leave Chaste. Not like this. There was no way that I could tell her how proud of her I was…, to be strong…, to live on; no way to beg Ferry to be patient with my daughter's pain.

My silent words were less than the breeze flicking the edges of Chaste's silken blond hair.

I began drifting away while grasping at nothingness around me with arms I couldn't feel or see.

"Is that what you want Kress?"

"Pitre? Is that you?"

I sensed his nod before he appeared before me in full display of splendor.

"No. This is everything I feared."

"Then you must decide."

I sensed urgency in those four little words.

"Tell me quickly, what can I do?"

"You can wallow in self pity and die…. Or you can choose to stay and live like you were intended."

"I didn't think I had a choice."

I felt that pain flow through me again; the loss of everything I'd hoped for, the loss of my daughter, of Elizabeth, and the newly blossoming feelings for Ferry.

"Choose now."

"I want to live of course."

In an instant I was back, standing beside my body on the stage with Pitre's huge hand across my back. Two men were hovering over me, working on my body, jolting it with electricity. Brent was spread like a brooding hen covering my prone lifeless body from some unseen evil. Pitre looked at me and pointed into the distance and I followed the trail of his arm.

He instantly disappeared from my side and lightning fell from the sky in the most massive brilliant blue white arc I'd ever seen. It hit the top of a building barely a quarter mile from where we were standing and the loud report of thunder shook me, knocked me down.

I wiggled my head and blinked, then coughed painfully.

It felt as if I'd been kicked in the chest by a mule.

"Kress?"

"He's breathing. I've got a pulse."

"Can we get him down from here? We're sitting ducks."

I tried to sit up and felt dizzy overtake me.

"Don't try to get up. You've been shot."

Whoever enlightened me of my situation left hurriedly to some unknown destination as I lay there trying to understand all that had just happened.

All I could sense was the cool breeze blowing across my bare chest and that incessant painful throb on the left side of my body. That was the result of my heartbeat, so…, painful or not it was a good thing. Now, if I'd been shot, where was all the blood; why wasn't someone applying pressure to the hole in my chest?

In the distance I could hear Ferry crying and trying fitfully to console Chaste.

"He's alive. Can you calm it down a bit?" yelled Brent.

What felt like two seconds later, soft brown hair was covering my face, followed by a barrage of kisses on my cheeks.

"Ferry please…, get back behind the stage. Whoever that was might still be able to get off another shot."

I shook my head, side to side groggily and hissed, "I doubt it very seriously."

Brent gave me his best scowl.

"Quit trying to talk. You're lung is damaged."

I'd seen what happened to the mysterious gunman. I'd seen the blinding flash of light fall from the sky and felt the thunderous report.

I smiled and felt my lip sting, then smiled all the more despite of it.

"What?" asked Brent.

I chuckled and that throb in my chest hurt like hell, but it felt good to be alive. I raised a few inches and kissed Ferry in a quick peck.

"Go let Chaste know I'm going to be alright," I whispered. "I love you Ferry."

Ferry nodded and slid away just as the other man returned with a crude body sling. Then we heard the sounds of a distant siren. Someone was coming to scrape up my remains, no doubt.

"Am I bleeding?" I whispered.

"Not that I can tell," answered Brent. "My ballistic vest you were wearing took most of the impact, but you've probably got a broken rib, some internal.... Why am I telling you this? You're the doctor."

I noticed that he was now wearing the uncomfortable suit jacket he'd loaned me. He stretched the lapel forward and stuck a finger into a round hole in the outer lining.

"You lead a charmed life Doc."

I was about to scourge him for the 'Doc' comment just as the two amateur paramedics lifted me onto the faux stretcher.

I let myself fade as soon as I felt an oxygen mask tighten over my face.

That was when I noticed the difference. Something was very, very wrong.

I think I passed out during the trip to the hospital; either that or the ambulance ride lulled me to sleep.

When I awakened next, sunshine was trying to peek through some heavy clouds and into my hospital room's window. Ferry and Chaste were slumped in two horrid little metal framed chairs against the wall nearest my bed.

I spoke, but it came out as a nasty hiss and my throat ached.

Evidently, during my absence, I was the victim of intubation leaving my throat feeling as if I'd been administered a drain cleaner.

The throb in my chest was negligible and I could breathe easily, so I guessed that I would probably live, just as Pitre had suggested.

I felt it then. As soon as I thought his name. I felt his complete absence. The one I'd so often referred to as my parasite was no longer attached inside me. I should have laughed for joy, or gurgled as it were, but all I could feel was extreme loss and deep sadness. I felt heavy tears pooling in the orbits of my eyes and tilted my head to let them drain away.

Then another thing made sense. I'd never seen Pitre emerge more than a few feet from where I was, yet the day I was shot I saw that amazing blaze of lightning execute final judgment on my would-be assassin on the roof of a building far away.

Proof that I'd died; proof that we were now separate.

Was that his last duty to perform as my protector?

Where was he now?

A tiny hand brought me back to the present. Chaste was daubing my face with a tissue, drying my eyes.

"Does it hurt much Daddy?"

"No sweetheart," I hissed awkwardly, then shaking my head no.

"Don't talk. The doctor said you'd be just fine," she whispered in my ear, hiding a sob in her voice.

She laid her head to my side hugging me, then looked over at Ferry still fast asleep.

"I don't hear him," she whispered, her expression seemed lost.

I shook my head no and she must have seen the sadness inside.

Chaste eased carefully up next to me, climbing up on the narrow bed and threw an arm across me.

"I won't leave you."

CHAPTER SEVENTY-THREE

Both of my expert helpers were milling about nervously in my private hospital room, probably anxious to be rid of me.

"As much fun as it's been, we've got to fly back to the states. We have another assignment almost as pressing as when we first met," said Brent.

I nodded, "Then I'm sure they'll be in capable hands."

"Are you sure you're going to be okay?" asked Carl.

I nodded and took another bite of the ridiculously spicy baked fish Carl had sneaked into my room.

"We'll be just fine. I'll call you the minute we get to London and give you an update."

Ferry and Chaste walked in the room together just as I covered my clandestine meal.

"I can smell your smoked fish halfway down the hall," she gritted. "Give me a bite or I'll tell the nurse what you're hiding."

Carl laughed and placed his linebacker shoulders against the closed door, daring anyone to try and press inside.

Caught with my mouth full and the threat of another lecture from the foul tempered head nurse, I offered up what was left of my meal.

"You couldn't wait two short hours before you were discharged?"

Ferry took a bite, "Oh, my goodness this is so good."

"We're going to be in southern California for a couple of weeks, near the border. If you can't reach us, leave voicemail. We'll probably be out of pocket most of the time we're there."

Brent stole a tiny pinch of fish, "I guarantee what we get to eat there won't be near as good as what we've been treated to this last week."

I could tell that neither of the men wanted to leave the cultural paradise of the Cape.

"If we ever fall on hard circumstances again, I'll make sure that I request you and Carl specifically. I have a couple of promises to keep...," I glanced at Chaste, making sure that our secret was still secure, "...before we leave. We should be back in Phoenix.... I suppose I'd better not promise an exact time or you'll send in the Marines to look for us."

There was a knock at the door and Ferry wadded up the remaining scraps of food and hurried with them into the restroom.

Carl laughed as he moved away from the door, knowing I was about to be in big trouble.

꒐

It felt strange, just the three of us..., small.

I made some needless excuses about wanting to see a few more places before we left Cape Town until I could get up the nerve to follow through with my plans.

Chaste was becoming a bother, prodding me to get on with it. I needed time to settle some personal waters before I moved forward and it felt good not to have ulterior motives involved, now that I was sure these were my exclusive desires and not the culmination of myself and Pitre.

I hadn't heard a peep out of my angelic companion since that fateful day at the pavilion. Pitre was what was missing.

Now to set the record straight, Pitre made good his promise. Those blasted 'marks' he left on my body were indeed gifts. I was still plagued with a foray of incriminating thoughts from those around me, whenever I pushed the limits of my curiosity. It was still just as much a bother to keep them all hidden. Brent never gave a hint that he'd opened up to Carl about the dark cabinet of secrets hidden inside, but I could tell that words had indeed passed between them the day we said our goodbyes at the airport.

It wasn't something specific that was said or anything I heard from their guarded thoughts, but Brent seemed more at ease and Carl less inquisitive as well as more forgiving about his partner's decisions.

Our final morning arrived and Chaste was beside herself.

"Dad, here..., take it. I can't stand it any longer."

She handed me the small red velvet box and I took it quickly as if Ferry could materialize out of thin air at any moment.

"Chaste, what are you thinking, carrying this around in the open? What if Ferry saw it?"

Chaste began to stare out the hotel window at the ocean again, with wheels turning like a locomotive in her head.

"Why don't you just leave Ferry a note and set it on the dressing table?" she mumbled. "Oh..., by the way Ferry...."

Her voice trailed off with her snide remark. She knew I wouldn't do something as insipid as leave an anonymous proposal of marriage. It was another jab at my backside to get me in motion.

"It's time. Get your things and we'll meet Ferry downstairs in the lobby."

Chaste snatched her windbreaker and stood at the door waiting before I pushed away my chair.

"Hurry up. You're obviously not getting any younger," she hissed.

"I'll have you know I'm still in my prime young lady."

I groaned as my bruised lung and fractured rib began reminding me to move slowly even if my heart was ushering me to hurry.

She grinned satisfactorily, not at my comment, but that she got me into motion. She stopped me at the hotel room door.

"Thank you Daddy."

She hugged me cautiously and finalized what little qualms I had about my motives. With every 'i' dotted and every 't' crossed in my mind, I could finally relax.

Ferry was still perusing the many gift shops in the hotel lobby, with two sacks looped across one arm, when we walked up behind her.

"What did you buy?" asked Chaste excitedly, digging into the sacks like a hungry raccoon.

"Memories..., lots of memories," sighed Ferry. "I wanted some reminders to go in my cabinet. I'll be able to pick them up and feel what it was like during my once in a lifetime trip to South Africa with you and your father."

"You sound as if you'll never take another holiday again."

The finality of her words distressed me greatly, as if this day was the end of the last adventure she'd ever have.

"Not like this one Kress. This holiday was definitely unique, one for the books."

I let her quip on my choice of words pass, "Well then, hurry up and come with us then. I have one last place I want you to see before we have to leave this evening."

I had to coerce a cabby with both money and food to drive us to a little rocky point far south of Cape Town. He agreed to eat his meal and wait on us while we did some sightseeing down on the oceanfront peninsula.

The road was rough, but thankfully the weather was holding steady, despite near gale force winds that had kicked up. From the ridge of the peninsula we could see the ice blue water on one hand and the murky wind-driven water on the other. Clouds were hovering off to the east as if waiting for someone to shoot a pistol at the starting gate of a great cosmic race. We stopped in a little visitor parking area and began our slow walk down a rocky path.

Ferry was already taking pictures of everything in sight and then seemed mesmerized at the weathered wooden sign that read, "Cape of Good Hope – The Most South – Western Point of the African Continent."

She handed me her digital camera and posed in front of the sign pulling her breaker tight to her body. Her hair whipped in the wind, her face staring longingly out at the ocean. I could see the lost child inside her peering out through those soft green eyes.

I took the snapshot just before Chaste nudged me.

"Go on," she hissed. "Don't take all day."

I walked over to where Ferry was still lost in thought and knelt down.

"Ferry, did you take a look at the colors of the stones the ocean washed up here?"

She looked down from her daze with a sigh.

"You should add a couple of these to your cabinet, they're quite unique…, see…, look at this one."

I lifted the open red velvet box and she reached without noticing… at first.

"Kress? What is this?"

She looked almost distressed, her business façade clouding her expression.

"It's the secret that I forced Chaste to keep from you until this moment. Ferry Dunavin, I…, we…, that is Chaste and I…, well…, not exactly Chaste...."

Oh blast it all.

"Would you please marry me?"

Ferry looked at the ring for another moment without taking it from my hand, then wilted down on one of the large rocks closest to where I knelt.

"Chaste?" Ferry motioned with her hand.

Chaste took another picture of us there together and hurried over. She was as worried as I was at Ferry's reaction.

"Chaste, you asked me once if I believed in angels. The answer is definitely..., yes."

It was our last day at my family's old estate at Cambridge, England. Tomorrow we'd take a morning flight back to the other part of our world, but this time we wouldn't be alone.

Ferry had explained to her partners that we needed a week to settle some private business and renew a caretaker account for the stone monstrosity my parents had called home while they were still alive. She also told them she needed one week with her new husband and her new daughter in their homeland.

That time had passed..., as quickly as a warm summer afternoon.

Now her office was pressing her. Ferry had to get back due to a sudden upsurge in clients, thrust upon their firm by the office of Arthur Jernigan. There were already a half-dozen cases on the docket – all to investigate and prosecute misconduct by senior government officials. Ferry made me promise that I'd be available as her personal lie detector and eavesdropper before she agreed to set a foot back in Phoenix.

And just as well. My days of being a doctor were over. I wanted only to be husband and father to my family.

I'd spent an entire day with the board of directors of the EMA while in London and signed a contract for a series of lectures on the lifestyle of field work for those about to make commitments to the Red Cross, Peace Corps, and a few other notable organizations.

Today, I was taking advantage of rehearsing boyhood memories before I had to leave once again. The lush green meadow at the foot of the property hadn't changed, not since I was very young. Surely the trees had grown, a few felled by storms, one of which I seated myself upon.

The steady chill breeze that had been blowing around a mist suddenly stilled itself and I felt a presence.

I turned expecting to see either Ferry or Chaste coming down the stony path from the back of the house but I was actually relieved to find a moment back alone with my thoughts.

"Kress."

I closed my eyes, listening to the voice I hadn't heard in several weeks; weeks that seemed like a dream.

"Hello my friend."

"I have good news Kress."

"Do tell."

"I've been assigned to you and your family."

"Chaste will be very glad to hear that, Pitre. We miss you."

"And I you."

I could sense he had more.

"Because of our history together, I was allowed this one meeting. You won't see me any longer, but I'll still be here, very close. Remember me...."

My head turned quickly as I spoke, hoping to catch one last glimpse of the winged wonder Pitre, but he was gone, with my parting words hanging in the quiet glen.

"How could I forget."

ABOUT THE AUTHOR

David Pyle is the author of several supernatural tales and short stories, most
of which are free for download at his website.
For more information please visit: www.pentwist.com

Other recent publications available at Amazon Books and Kindle:

Minutes

ISBN-13: 978-0-615-86051-0
ASIN: B00EHS79QY

www.ingramcontent.com/pod-product-compliance
Lightning Source LLC
Chambersburg PA
CBHW021839010726
47493CB00005B/1475